THE KILLING BOYS

LUKE DELANEY

I would like to dedicate this book to all the magnificent people I worked with during my time as a police officer in the Metropolitan Police and to all those currently serving as police up and down the country. Keep up the outstanding work.

PROLOGUE

Canada – Present Time

The man known as Peter Delph walked towards a small grocery store in a snow-hit rural town of Morecroft, near Montreal, Quebec. He looked like any other local, wrapped in warm clothing and wearing a Russian-style hat with ear flaps, but he was still recognisable. He entered the store, grabbed a basket and started browsing the aisles, selecting occasional items disinterestedly.

Outside, a nondescript pick-up truck rolled to a stop on the opposite side of the street, the exhaust fumes turning to clouds in the freezing air. The tinted windows made it impossible to see the driver.

Delph headed to the checkout and handed his basket to the middle-aged female attendant – avoiding returning her small talk, but smiling pleasantly. He thanked her and headed off carrying his loaded brown paper grocery bag.

The driver waited inside the truck, wearing sunglasses and

baseball cap pulled low – collar turned up. He held the prepared pistol across his lap as he looked across the snowy street at the small grocery store – waiting. After a few seconds Delph walked from the store and headed along the pavement. The driver climbed from his truck and crossed the street – following him along the pavement – closing all the time.

As Delph reached his car and fumbled in his pocket for the keys, the driver closed the distance until he was only a few feet away. 'Peter Delph?' he asked calmly.

Delph spun around, surprised to hear his name spoken in the street. A rare occurrence in his new life. Once turned, he saw the man standing with his hands by his side. 'Can I do something for you?' he asked in his English accent. The man raised his arm holding the pistol with silencer in his hand. Delph's mouth opened as two puffs came one after the other from the end of the silencer, blowing two holes in the shopping bag as the bullets passed through it before entering his torso. He collapsed to the floor – groceries spilling across the pavement as the man walked purposefully towards him and stood over him – steadily pointing the gun at his face as he struggled to breathe – trying desperately to speak – to plead for his life as the snow under him began to turn red. Two more puffs suddenly escaped from the pistol, one entering Delph's forehead and the other his right eye. He fell rigid into the snow before his body began to twitch as the body registered that his brain had been destroyed. His killer was already driving away in his truck before his body finally lay motionless.

1

Detective Sergeant Fraser Harvey drove along a bumpy service road approaching a modest-looking farmhouse in the near distance, scanning the area for signs of life, but could see none. As he pulled up outside the farmhouse a casually dressed man in his forties walked from inside and stood by the front door watching Harvey closely as he stepped from the car. They eyed each other, but it was clear they weren't strangers.

'Everything all right?' Harvey asked as he walked towards the man.

'Everything's fine,' DS Collins replied.

Harvey walked past him without speaking into the farmhouse, although once inside it was clear it was no ordinary farmhouse. It looked more like a cross between the inside of a police station and an inexpensive house. Two more detectives sat inside looking bored – the handguns clearly visible on their waist belts. They both nodded towards Harvey who nodded back before pulling up a chair and sitting down. 'What a fucking dump this place is,' Harvey complained. 'Stuck out in the middle of nowhere. I hate the bloody country – cow shit and tractors.'

'Suits our purpose,' Collins said with a smile. 'No prying eyes. This is the best safe house we have and one of the first. Built back in the days when some of the IRA boys first started turning on their brothers. After that it was used mainly for gangland types turning on their own. And now it's back to the terrorists – home-grown, easily led fools being enticed to the dark side and there's plenty of them, so the quicker you can do whatever it is you got to do with your two and free us up, the better. Know what I'm saying?'

'Yeah. I understand,' Harvey assured him. 'You'll have this shithole back as soon as I'm finished. Until then – everything that happens here is strictly confidential – even more so than usual. Under no circumstances are you to talk about the two men in detention to anyone other than me. Equally, neither you nor your people are to talk to the detainees other than for giving basic instructions and answering any questions they ask – providing those questions do not relate to why they're here or their historical case. I need to speak to them alone. No one else present. Clear?'

'Fine,' Collins agreed, happy not to be too involved. 'Whatever you say.'

'Good,' Harvey told him, nodding his head slowly. 'And no names, either. Not even if they tell you or your men who they are. They're Prisoner One and Prisoner Two until I say otherwise.'

'That's not a problem for people,' Collins assured him. 'So, when do you want to get started?'

'Straightaway,' he replied, getting back to his feet. 'I'll make a start with Prisoner One, then Two.'

4

'Okay,' Collins replied before changing the subject. 'You look knackered, Fraser. Everything all right?'

He sighed before answering. 'I've been trying to put this case behind me for more than eleven years,' he explained, 'but it keeps dragging me back in – like fucking quicksand. The sooner I get this done the sooner I can finally try to forget I ever met either of them.'

'If you wanted to just forget about them, why didn't you get someone else to relocate them?' Collins asked. 'Relocation's not your jurisdiction.'

'I volunteered,' he admitted.

'Volunteered?' Collins checked. 'Why would you do that?'

'I have my reasons,' Harvey answered. 'Maybe it's the only way I can ever really be free of them.'

'You really believe that?' Collins asked.

Harvey gave a resigned smile and shook his head slightly. 'No,' he admitted. 'Not really – but I can hope.'

'Hope?' Collins asked.

'Forget it,' Harvey told him. 'Time I moved on. That's all. Now, if you don't mind – I have a lot to get through.'

Harvey sat at the small table in a sparse interview room, next to the double-deck tape recorder – his briefcase next to him on the floor. The door swung open and after a few silent moments, Prisoner One was led in by one of the detectives Harvey had seen when he'd first arrived. Despite the passing of eleven years, the prisoner was still recognisable – as pale and unattractive as ever, only now his body was decorated with home-made prison tattoos and his teeth dyed yellow after years of heavy smoking and neglect. They both stared hard at each other for what seemed like a very long time before Harvey turned to the detective. 'You can leave us now,' he told him. The detective turned and left without saying a word. 'Take a seat,' Harvey ordered. The prisoner walked disinterestedly to the table and slouched on a chair. 'It's been a long time. Last time I saw you, you were little more than a boy. Now you're a man.'

The prisoner ignored the pleasantry and instead looked at the interview recorder with suspicion. 'You here to interview me?'

'No,' Harvey explained. 'The time for interviews has passed.'

'I remember you,' he replied after a few seconds, a smirk spreading across his face. 'You look old. You ill or something?'

Harvey fixed him with a cold stare. 'We're here to talk about you – not me.'

'Whatever,' he said with a shrug. 'Haven't seen you since you came to see me in Feltham – when you tried one last time to get me to confess to a murder I never committed.'

'Well,' he replied, sighing. 'Once you were convicted of the murder, there really wasn't any reason for me to come see you – was there?'

'Until now,' he said, the smirk falling from his face.

'Until now,' Harvey with a nod. 'I take it you know why you're here?'

'For my own protection,' he said, shrugging. 'Apparently.'

'That's right.'

'But I'm free – right?' he asked. 'I've served my time.'

'Technically,' Harvey answered. 'But you're on a lifetime licence. You breach your licence, you go back to prison.'

'Fine,' he replied impatiently. 'Then I promise not to breach my licence. Now give me my things and let me go. Can't stand being locked up in this shithole. Had enough of being locked up for a fucking lifetime.'

'Not that easy,' Harvey told him. 'One of the conditions of the licence is that you co-operate with the authorities. That you let us protect you.'

'I don't need anyone's protection,' the prisoner snarled. 'I just need to get out of here.'

'And how long d'you think it'll be before someone recognises you and sticks a knife in your belly or you're dragged out of your bed in the middle of the night by masked men – never to be seen alive again?' Harvey snapped at him, his voice raised for emphasis. 'There's still a lot of hate out there for you – especially since your release. Whole thing's blown up all over again. Lot of people out there would like to see you dead.' He sat silent and stony faced. 'Good,' Harvey told him as he reached down next to him and lifted his briefcase. He opened it and tossed him a packet of cigarettes and lighter. 'File says you took up smoking in prison.' The prisoner immediately opened the packet and took out a cigarette before lighting it, his eyes never leaving Harvey's, who pulled out a file marked *confidential* and opened it.

'What's that?' he asked.

Harvey flicked through the pages with his thumb. 'Your new life,' he explained. 'Your appearance has changed as you've aged, but not significantly enough to eliminate the risk of you being recognised or at least that would be the case if you were to remain in the country.'

'You're sending me abroad?' he asked, sounding alarmed.

'Yes,' Harvey told him, as if it was nothing. 'Canada to be exact. Rural Canada. You'll be watched and monitored, albeit not twenty-four hours a day. Your email and computer use eavesdropped on – your hard drive seized and examined from time to time, but you'll effectively be a free man.'

'Free?' The prisoner laughed. 'And what if I don't want to live in fucking Canada?'

'Then go back to the estate where you killed Abigail and see how long you last,' Harvey suggested.

'I didn't kill her,' he told him, just like he had years before, although there was no fight left in his eyes.

Harvey took a few seconds before replying. 'You need to understand the life you had before the murder doesn't exist anymore,' he explained. 'You can't just go back to it and pick up where you left off. You need to start again.' The prisoner just sat silent and brooding while Harvey looked down on the pages of the open file. 'As you chose to waste your time in prison and didn't acquire any qualifications or skills, we've found you a job working as a dogsbody in a wood mill close to where you'll be living. We were lucky to even find that. Fortunately, the local probation officer knew one of the bosses and swung the job. Story is you're a petty criminal looking for a new start in life.' He slid the file across the desk to the prisoner. 'Everything you need to know is in this file. Your new life – name, history, criminal records, family – everything. Study it like you've never studied anything before. You will be tested on it and will not be leaving this safe house until I'm satisfied you know it inside out. Understand?'

He pulled the file towards him and looked down at it. 'My new life?'

'Your new life,' Harvey repeated, getting to his feet. 'It's that or back to prison. Study it and study it well. Your life depends on it. I'll be back in a few days to see how you're doing.' He tapped his index finger on the file. 'Don't waste my time. I'm giving you a chance few believe you deserve.' The prisoner rested his hand on the file while looking up at Harvey without speaking. 'Until next time,' Harvey told him and headed for the door.

Harvey stood outside the safe house alone – looking out over the view of the countryside when Collins came from the house just as he popped a couple of pills from their packaging and tossed them into his mouth. He swallowed them with a drink from the mug he was holding – grimacing as he forced them down.

'Lunch?' Collins asked, having seen him take the pills.

'No,' he replied dryly. 'Breakfast.'

Collins smiled briefly before getting back to business. 'What you want to do now?'

'Want's got nothing to do with it,' he answered. 'Have Prisoner Two brought to the interview room. The sooner I get this over with the better.'

Harvey entered the same interview room and found the man now known only as Prisoner Two already sitting straight-backed at the table looking calm and composed. The same detective as before stood in the corner watching the prisoner intensely. He looked fit and lean – a half drunk bottle of water resting on the table in front of him. He watched Harvey's every move.

'You can leave us now,' Harvey told the guard.

The detective nodded and headed for the door. 'You need anything, just let me know,' he offered.

'Thanks,' Harvey told him, waiting for him to leave before taking a seat opposite the prisoner. The two men looked at each other in silence for a few seconds before the prisoner broke the peace.

'Detective Sergeant Harvey,' he greeted him with a slight smile. 'It's been a long time.'

'You remember me then?' Harvey asked.

'You expected me to forget?'

'Maybe,' he answered with a shrug. 'You were young – under a lot of stress. Sometimes that makes the person interviewing you little more than a faceless interrogator.'

'You were never just an interrogator though – were you?' he recalled. 'You were always very... purposeful.'

There was another silence while Harvey tried to get a feel for the man sitting in front of him. 'How d'you get on in prison? I know it can be tough.'

'Feltham was... difficult,' he admitted. 'Too many gang-bangers trying to make a name for themselves. Once we were old enough to be moved to Belmarsh things calmed down.'

'Rule 43,' Harvey reminded him. 'Kept away from the main prison population.'

'It was probably for the best,' he replied. 'I got used to the isolation.'

Harvey nodded slowly in agreement. 'Did you see much of your *friend* inside?'

'We saw each other, but rarely spoke,' he answered – knowing Harvey was referring to the man he was convicted with. 'He wanted to. I didn't.'

'How come?'

'He destroyed my life,' he said without anger or emotion. 'If I thought I could have got away with it, I would probably have killed him.' There was a long pause before he continued. 'Is he here – in this... place?'

'No,' Harvey lied. 'Only you. He's being held somewhere else – for his own protection.'

'I see,' the prisoner said, playing along. 'Only this place appears so large for just one prisoner and I'm only ever allowed outside at specific times – as if I'm sharing with someone they don't want me to see.'

'You're not,' Harvey told him.

'Not what?' he asked, sounding slightly confused.

'A prisoner,' he answered. 'You're not a prisoner anymore. This place is just a safe house – a secure facility. Somewhere you can be protected while we prepare you for your new life.'

'I see,' he said, his voice thick with suspicion. 'And vile creature – he's also no longer a prisoner?'

'That's correct,' Harvey confirmed. 'He's elsewhere being prepared for his new life.'

'Strange that we should be released at the same time,' he said changing tack. 'Given I was a model prisoner and he was not. He was a lazy troublemaker while I kept my head down and did whatever they wanted me to do.'

'I admit it's unusual as well as unfair,' Harvey explained. 'But after a lot of thought and talking it was decided if we were going to give you both new lives it would be best to do it simultaneously – given the unique nature of the crime and the media interest there still is in the case.'

'I understand,' the prisoner assured him. 'And to be honest, when and how you chose to release him has no interest to me. He's your problem now. Not mine.'

Harvey nodded silently before moving on. 'You did well in prison – used your time constructively. Got yourself some useful qualifications and even a vocation, although I never took you for a farmer.' The prisoner just stared at him in silence. 'I hear your behaviour was as good as it could have been. Never a moment's trouble.'

'I accepted my time in prison,' he told him. 'I deserved my punishment. You know why I feel that way, but it didn't mean that once I was caged with those animals, I wanted to become like them – trading in drugs and tobacco, always trying to fuck the system – demeaning themselves with other men just because there were no women. I needed to stay me.'

Harvey watched him for a long time before pulling a file from his briefcase and sliding it across the table to the prisoner.

'What's this?' he asked.

'Your new life,' Harvey explained. 'A new name. A new place to live.'

'Where?'

'Rural New Zealand,' Harvey told him. 'The further you're away from here the better – for you.'

'And if I refuse to go?'

'Your licence will be revoked and you'll be returned to prison to serve out the remainder of your sentence before being released into a community that wants you dead.' He leaned back in his chair, but said nothing. 'It could be worse. In light of your agricultural qualifications we were able to acquire a small farm for you. You'll soon be self-sufficient and even able to sell any extra produce you have and keep the profits.' He looked into his face for a reaction, but could see none. 'It's a good deal. Almost like starting over again. You'll be largely left alone, although there'll be discreet visits from the local police as well as from officers from the Met and your movements around New Zealand will be restricted – a few other things too, but it'll be a life.'

'On my own,' he replied. 'On a farm in the middle of nowhere – more isolation?'

'I thought you said you'd gotten used to isolation?' Harvey reminded him. He didn't answer. 'Besides – your options don't look very... appealing.' He tapped the file on the desk with his index finger. 'Study it well. Everything you need to know is in here. You need to memorise every detail. Once you're back in the world the slightest mistake could prove fatal. I'll be back in two days to see how you're getting on.' He stood to leave.

'Why should I trust you?' the prisoner suddenly asked. 'I know almost nothing about you, yet you know everything about me.'

'Because you have no choice,' he starkly reminded him.

'Tell me one thing about yourself and I'll do exactly what you say,' he promised. 'Just one thing.' Harvey stared at him for a while, but said nothing. 'Are you married?' he asked. 'Children?'

'Yes,' he found himself answering. 'I'm married.'

'I assumed so,' he told him before quickly reminding him of his other question. 'And children?'

'The file,' Harvey insisted, ignoring it as he turned towards the door. 'Read it.'

'Why New Zealand?' he asked, stopping him in his tracks. 'Why not South America or the US – somewhere the case wouldn't be so well known?'

'We needed it to be a Commonwealth country,' Harvey explained, 'where we could still apply a degree of legal jurisdiction.'

'Then I assume the same applies to *him*?' the prisoner said more than asked. 'Where's he being hidden away – Australia? No – too close – you'd want us as far apart as possible.' His eyes narrowed as he tried to work it out. 'Canada,' he suddenly declared. 'Yes – you're sending him to Canada – aren't you?'

Harvey didn't reply as he picked up his briefcase and headed for the door. 'Like you said – he's not your problem anymore. He's mine,' he reminded him. 'Two days. You don't leave here until I'm satisfied you won't compromise yourself. No matter how long it takes.'

'I'll study it,' the prisoner promised with a smile. 'You have my word.'

2

London – 2005

Abigail Riley hurriedly packed her school bag in the small family kitchen in their house in Kilburn, North London, as her mother Sarah, prepared breakfast for her and her younger brother.

'Come and eat now,' she told Abigail in her soft Irish accent as she placed a plate of food on the table. 'You'll be late for school.'

'I'm never late for school,' Abigail reminded her with a smile as she abandoned her packing and sat at the table.

'Remember you have to pick what GCSE's you want to do this week,' Sarah reminded her.

'Yes, Mum.' Abigail rolled her eyes like any other teenager would have before disinterestedly nibbling on a piece of toast.

'And come straight home after school,' Sarah insisted. 'I might need you to look after Jimmy while I go out.'

'Shouldn't I get paid for babysitting or something?' she asked cheekily.

'No. You should not,' Sarah answered. 'Board and lodgings are free. That's as good as it's going to get and no forgetting and going off with that boyfriend of yours.'

'Mum,' Abigail complained, blushing slightly. 'He's hardly even my boyfriend. We haven't even kissed yet.'

'Good,' Sarah said. 'Keep it that way and don't let your dad find out. He's not as understanding as me.'

'Yes, Mum.' She rolled her eyes again.

'Come on, Jimmy.' Sarah nudged the boy. 'Hurry up and finish your breakfast so I can get you to school.' Jimmy just shrugged.

Abigail quickly made a scruffy-looking bacon sandwich from some of the items on her plate and jumped to her feet. 'I'll eat this on my way to school,' she explained.

'That's not a proper way to eat your breakfast,' Sarah told her. 'Teenagers today – always doing everything on the run. I don't know how you're doing so well at school the way you carry on.'

'Grades don't lie, Mum,' she said with a satisfied smile.

'Well, just don't get too smug,' Sarah warned her. 'Good grades take hard work.'

'I know, Mum,' she assured her as she got to her feet and took her school blazer from the back of the chair and started pulling it on.

'You make your dad and me very proud,' Sarah suddenly told her. 'And remember – you can be...'

'I can be anything I want to be,' she finished for her. 'You tell me the same thing every day, Mum.'

'Because it's true,' Sarah told her. 'You're a special girl, Abigail. Don't ever forget it.'

'I won't,' she promised, warmed by the love of her mother

just the same way she was every day before she headed off to school.

Sarah kissed her on the forehead before issuing her final orders and advice. 'And be careful and don't be late.'

'Yes, Mum,' she agreed as she headed towards the door, nurtured and loved – her whole life ahead of her. She opened the front door and stepped out into the cold morning – just another ordinary day in the life of a bright, beautiful fourteen-year-old girl.

3

London 2016

Harvey knocked on the door of the Rileys' small, terraced house in North London, taking a step back while he waited for it to be answered. He heard footsteps approaching from inside before the door was opened by a young man in his early twenties, who despite the passing of time, he recognised as Jimmy Riley. He could tell by the burning look in his eyes that Jimmy knew who he was.

'You,' was all Jimmy said.

'Hello, Jimmy,' Harvey greeted him. 'Is your mother in? I need to speak with you both.'

Jimmy stepped aside and allowed him to enter before leading him into the kitchen where Sarah was busily cooking. She looked afraid and suspicious when she saw Harvey.

'Hello, Sarah,' he said. 'It's been a while. How've you been?'

'We've been keeping fine,' she told him cautiously. 'What is it that you want?'

Harvey took a seat without being asked. 'I have some information for you,' he answered. 'Not something you're going to want to hear, but you need to know.'

'So. The day has finally come,' she guessed, stiffening as she prepared for confirmation.

'I'm afraid so,' he told her straight. 'They're due for release. We can't hold them any longer. I'm sorry.'

She staggered to a seat and sat – giving herself time to regain her composure. 'How long?'

'Days,' he told her. 'A few weeks at most.'

'Good,' Jimmy jumped in, agitated and excited. 'Now we can finally get the justice Abigail deserves. Once they're out of prison you can't protect them anymore. The bastards can get what they deserve.'

'That's dangerous talk, Jimmy,' Harvey warned him. 'I wouldn't be going around saying stuff like that if I was you.'

'Yeah, but you're not me,' Jimmy snapped. 'And Abigail wasn't your sister.'

'Enough,' Sarah insisted.

'But Ma,' Jimmy complained. 'What we gonna do – just let them walk away – after what they did?'

'I said that's enough,' she insisted. 'Mind what you say, son.' She took a breath before turning to Harvey. 'Can you stop it? Is there anything you can do to stop it?'

'I'm sorry,' he answered. 'No. There's nothing I can do.'

'So that's it then?' she said, staring at the ceiling. 'They rape and murder my fourteen-year-old daughter – get locked up for eleven years then walk away free men. I lose my daughter and they lose little more than ten years of their worthless lives.'

'I'm sorry,' Harvey said again. 'It's because of their ages – at the time of the crime. So long as they behaved in prison, we were never going to be able to hold them for much longer.'

'It's not right,' she pleaded. 'How can it be right? I didn't just lose my daughter – I lost my husband too.'

'I heard of his passing,' he told her. 'I'm sorry.'

'You didn't come to the funeral,' she reminded him. 'I thought you'd come. Somehow expected it.'

'I didn't think you'd want to see police hanging around,' he explained. 'I knew what your husband thought of us.'

'Can you blame him?' she asked.

Harvey sighed before replying. 'We did everything we could. There was nothing I could do about the sentences. It's not a part of the criminal justice system we control. It hurts me too–'

'This is all fucking bullshit,' Jimmy interrupted. 'This isn't over. I'll find them. I swear I'll find them. They destroyed our family. They destroyed our lives.'

'There's no point, Jimmy,' Harvey warned him. 'You'll never find them. They'll be hidden away where no one will ever find them – given new identities and all the paperwork and background history they'll need – even cosmetic surgery if we think they need it. Trust me – we're good at this. You'll never find them.'

Jimmy looked back and forth from Harvey and his mother. 'You're fucking helping them – treating murderers like victims while you talk to us as if we were the criminals. How do you sleep at night, eh? You should be fucking ashamed of yourself.'

'I'm sorry, Jimmy,' Harvey told him. 'There's nothing I can do.'

'Fuck you and your excuses,' he cursed. 'I need some air. I can't breathe in this place.' He stormed past his mother and Harvey and out of the kitchen, heading for the front door.

'Jimmy. Jimmy,' Sarah called after him, but all they heard was the sound of the front door slamming shut. She turned to Harvey. 'Try not to think too badly of him,' she told him. 'He's been through a lot and still so young. Jesus – losing his sister when he was only ten and then his father. It hit him hard, you know. He still thinks of nothing but revenge – can't knuckle down to anything worth a damn – always just drifting and the papers and TV never far away – always reminding him what happened – sometimes asking if Abigail had somehow encouraged those animals – saying that at least one of them could be innocent. Innocent. Jesus.'

'I know,' he assured her. 'I see the same rubbish you do. Wish I could promise you it'll go away, but once they find out they've been released, and they will, it's only going to get worse.'

They sat in silence for a while before Sarah spoke. 'Well then, Sergeant Harvey – what now?'

He took a deep breath. 'As soon as they're released to start their new lives, I'll let you know. It won't be long. Once you hear from me, I recommend you go away for a while. There'll be a lot of media looking for you – trying to get your reaction – Jimmy's. Stay away as long as you can.'

'And then?' she asked.

'I don't know,' he admitted. 'Get a good lawyer and sue the shit out of anyone trying to exploit what happened to Abigail. Should put off all but the most determined. Other than that – try to move on with your lives. Somehow put it behind you.'

'Put it behind me?' she questioned him, pressing her hands together as if she was about to pray. 'Move on? And what would you have me do with the memories of a murdered daughter and a husband who chose to take his own life rather than suffer the pain of remembering?'

'I can't answer that,' he said, sighing. 'Memories aren't something I can help you with.'

'No,' she said solemnly. 'I don't suppose they are.'

'I'd better go,' he told her. 'As soon as they're released, I'll let you know.'

'Don't bother,' she replied, a bitterness in her voice. 'I never want to hear about them again, unless it's to tell me they're both dead.'

'All the same.' He shrugged. 'Take care, Sarah.'

'One thing.' She stopped him. 'Before you go.'

'Yes?' he asked.

'Are you helping to hide them?' she demanded. 'Do you know where they'll be?'

'Not this again.' He shook his head before lying. 'No. I won't know where they're relocated and even if I did, I've told you before, I wouldn't tell you.'

'Then there's no chance of justice for Abigail,' she insisted.

'Things happen to people like them,' he told her. 'People like that don't live long, happy lives.'

'Maybe,' she said without belief. 'I think you should leave now.'

'I understand,' he replied. 'Take care of yourself, Sarah.'

'You too,' she said without looking at him.

'I'll see myself out,' he told her and headed slowly for the front door, wondering if he'd ever see her again. When he reached it, he could hear her beginning to sob. For a moment he almost went back to her, but instead, he opened the door and headed for his car.

Harvey stood outside the front of the safe house looking pensive as Anderson was led from the building by Collins and one of the other detectives he'd seen before. Prisoner One stopped dead when he saw Harvey, despite his escort trying to move him on.

'Come to wave me off?' he asked aggressively.

'Something like that,' Harvey replied, looking him up and down. 'Just remember you're Peter Delph now. The person you used to be is dead.' The prisoner just grunted and smiled unpleasantly before the detectives ushered him forward and into the rear of a waiting unmarked car. Harvey stood silently watching as the car drove off towards the distance along the deserted country road.

'Piece of shit that one,' Collins told him. 'Glad to see the back of him. Gave me the fucking creeps.' Harvey ignored him, continuing to watch the car until it was almost out of sight. Collins shouted back over his shoulder into the house as another unmarked car pulled up where the first had been. 'We're clear. Bring him out.' Another detective Harvey recognised led Prisoner Two from the house who, just like his one-time friend, stopped in front of him when he saw him waiting.

The prisoner smiled pleasantly and spoke softly. 'Well – I suppose this is goodbye.'

'Probably,' Harvey answered, still struggling to get a sense of who the man really was, even after all these years as man and boy. 'The local police in New Zealand will be keeping tabs on you, but you'll also receive the occasional unannounced visit by detectives from the Met – to update your risk-threat.'

'Risk of what?' he asked. 'The public to me or me to the public?' Harvey didn't answer. 'You still don't believe me, do you? You still think I killed her.'

'Just remember – you're Alexander Knight now,' Harvey told him, not prepared to be drawn one last time. 'The person you were doesn't exist anymore.'

He nodded slowly. 'That person hasn't existed for a very long time, sergeant,' he replied. 'He died in that cellar with Abigail Riley.' He looked at the waiting car then back to Harvey. 'I assume that's for me?'

'It is,' Harvey confirmed.

The prisoner took a step forward before pausing and turning to Harvey. 'They asked me to do a blood test while I was in prison,' he stated. 'Long after I was convicted. They said you'd asked for it. I agreed to it. Perhaps now you can tell me what it was for?'

Harvey paused before answering, ever wary of the man he'd first met when he was little more than a boy. 'It was to test for a double Y chromosome,' he eventually answered.

'Ah.' He smiled and nodded, as if he knew exactly what Harvey was talking about.

'You're familiar with it?' Harvey asked.

'Enough,' he replied, giving little away. 'And did you find it – in me?'

'No,' he told him. 'No. We didn't.'

'And *him*?' the prisoner pried, refusing to use his old co-defendant's name.

'That's confidential,' he answered, knowing that he'd already worked it out.

'I see.' He smiled slightly. 'Goodbye, sergeant,' he added, sounding slightly sad. 'Take care.'

Harvey said nothing as he watched the prisoner walk casually to the waiting car and climb into the back. The doors slammed shut as it immediately pulled away and sped along the country road – watched all the way by Harvey as he thought about his own future and a life, or at least what was left of it, without the shadow of Abigail Riley's killers in it.

'Doesn't come across as your normal sexually motivated killer – does he?' Collins broke his thoughts.

'Whatever a *normal* killer is,' Harvey replied.

'You think he killed her?' Collins asked.

'Jury found him guilty, didn't they,' Harvey reminded him.

'Juries?' He gave a short laugh. 'Since when were they infallible?'

'Maybe,' he partly agreed. 'But he was there. He got no more than he deserved.'

'Whatever you say,' Collins said before walking back inside, leaving Harvey to stare at the car carrying Alexander Knight as it disappeared into the distance.

~

Night-time and Sarah was sitting in her dimly lit kitchen sipping a small whisky and poring over old photographs of Abigail and her dead husband. She looked up when she heard the front door open then slam shut. A few seconds later Jimmy walked into the kitchen looking a little drunk. He said nothing to his mother as he searched in the fridge for something to eat.

'Where have you been?' she demanded.

'Out,' he replied dismissively.

'I know how you feel about your sister and dad,' she told him. 'Her killers, but you need to let it go, Jimmy – before it destroys you too.'

He slammed the fridge shut and spun to face her. 'I can't,' he told her through gritted teeth. 'Look at you – staring at those bloody pictures again. Let it go yourself, have you?'

She self-consciously gathered up the photographs. 'That's different,' she insisted. 'They help... they help me remember them – how they were.'

'I remember how they were,' he told her. 'And I remember how they ended up. I'll never let it go. I can't. Not until they pay for what they did.'

'You're wasting your time,' she argued, raising her voice slightly. 'It's pointless. You'll never find them. No one will.'

'I'll find them,' he promised. 'I don't care how long it takes. I'll find them.'

'Jesus, you sound just like your dad, but what's the point, Jimmy?' she shouted at him. 'They've been gone for years. It's in the past. Leave it there.'

'The past,' he said before laughing cynically. 'Revenge is a dish best served cold. Isn't that what the Italians say.'

'Aye – they do,' she agreed. 'But you're Irish and we have a different saying.'

'Yeah?' he asked, sipping on a beer he'd taken from the fridge. 'Which is?'

'Before setting out for revenge,' she told him, 'first dig two graves.'

He gave a short, quiet laugh, but the smile slipped from his face as he stood in silence for a few seconds before walking slowly from the kitchen without speaking, watched all the way by his mother. Once he was gone, she went back to her whisky and photographs. Back to the life she once had before hell visited Sarah Riley and her family.

4

London – 2005

DS Harvey and DC Connie Matthews drove towards a small piece of waste ground in a built-up area of North London. The flashing blue light attached to the roof of their unmarked car swirled, warning of their approach, although the siren was silent. The area ahead of them was taped off and guarded by a few uniformed officers. A few locals were milling around trying to find out what's going on while hooded youths shouted the occasional insult – making it clear the police were not welcome in the area. It was growing dark and beginning to rain.

Through the windscreen they saw a stocky man in a raincoat hurriedly walking away from the small crowd towards them – waving them down. He looked serious and concerned. They guessed he was from the local CID.

'Someone's in a hurry,' Matthews said, nodding towards him.

Harvey sighed. 'In a hurry to make his problem ours.' They

pulled over and climbed out the car just as the man in the coat reached them.

'DS John McCoy,' he hurriedly introduced himself. 'You MIT?' he asked, sounding a little flustered.

'We are,' Harvey confirmed as they shook hands and kept walking towards the taped-off cordon. 'DS Fraser Harvey – DC Connie Matthews. You call us?'

'Yeah, I called you in,' he replied, sounding concerned.

'We were told a young female?' Harvey checked. 'You sure it's suspicious?'

McCoy looked back and forth between them – struggling to know what to say as they kept walking towards the tape. 'It's... it's probably easier if you just take a look for yourselves,' he explained. Harvey and Matthews looked at each other – both sharing the same expression of concern. McCoy noticed it. 'But you should know – it's bad. Like nothing I've ever seen before.'

There was a moment's silence before Matthews spoke. 'Anyone else been in the scene – apart from you?'

'No.' McCoy shook his head. 'Only the constable who went in there with me. He's back at the station now – not feeling too good.'

'Anything in the scene been disturbed?' Harvey asked, as they continued to walk. 'Has the body been moved?'

'No,' McCoy assured him. 'I checked for a pulse – for what it's worth. Other than that, there was no point disturbing anything. This was no accident and you can rule out suicide,' he added. 'She didn't do this to herself.'

'We need to take a look,' Harvey told him, trying to keep his mind clear and not be affected by McCoy's words.

'Be my guest,' McCoy agreed as they reached the tape. He lifted it for them as Harvey and Matthews ducked underneath while he remained behind.

'We were told the body was on waste ground,' Harvey said,

pointing with his head across the land in front of them. 'I don't see anything that looks like a scene.'

'Not on waste ground. Under it,' McCoy explained. 'In an old bomb shelter or something. The local kids mess around in there – when it's not being used by the resident crackheads looking for a bit of privacy. This isn't Chelsea, detectives.'

'Who found her?' Harvey asked, ignoring McCoy's remark.

'Some local kids,' McCoy answered. 'Sneaked into the shelter looking for somewhere to have a smoke. They'll all need counselling.'

Harvey and Matthews glanced at each other once more. 'Where are they now?' Harvey asked, remaining stoic, on the outside at least.

'At the hospital with their parents,' McCoy told him. 'I don't suppose they'll ever forget what they saw down there. I know I won't.'

'We'll need their clothes,' Harvey instructed, still not reacting to McCoy's foreboding words.

'No problem,' McCoy assured him. 'I'll have it taken care of.'

Harvey looked over his shoulder with some concern at the growing number of people behind the cordon. 'Crowd's getting bigger.'

'Word spreads fast around here,' McCoy warned them.

'You'd better get some more uniforms down here,' Harvey told him. 'And say nothing to anybody until we get back. I need to see what we're dealing with.'

'We already know what we're dealing with,' McCoy replied. Harvey looked at him, waiting for an explanation. 'A monster. What other explanation can there be?'

The two detectives locked eyes for a second before Harvey spoke. 'Do we know who she is yet?'

'No.' McCoy shook his head. 'We couldn't find any ID. Maybe the full forensic examination will find something.'

'Maybe.' Harvey shrugged. 'No one passes this point unless I've okayed it. Clear?'

'Whatever you say.' McCoy didn't argue. 'It's your show now.'

'Yes,' Harvey told him. 'Yes. It is.' He nodded at Matthews before both turned and headed towards the scene.

'He seems more than a little spooked,' Matthews said in little more than a whisper.

'Yeah.' Harvey sighed. 'That's what's worrying me.' They gave each other a knowing look as they picked their way across the rubbish-strewn wasteland.

Harvey descended the metal stepladder that was attached to the wall of the old bomb shelter – his small Maglite torch gripped between his teeth – his shoes already protected with forensic covers that looked a lot like shower-caps. A little light penetrated the interior and gave some visibility, but he needed his torch. After stepping off the ladder he turned and took a couple of steps forward as Matthews followed him down – also with a torch between her teeth.

The smell of damp was overpowering as he scanned the floor with the beam of light from his torch, passing over a carpet of rubbish that bore the evidence of hard drugs being used by the shelter's frequenters. He followed the stream of light until suddenly it fell on the naked, mutilated body of the victim – a white girl aged about fourteen years, lying on her back, her limbs twisted and her long brown hair a tangle of matted blood. He turned away in shock and put his hand up to stop Matthews. 'Stop,' he ordered. 'Just wait.' He took a couple of deep breaths to combat his rising nausea. 'Jesus Christ,' he pleaded. 'Jesus Christ.'

'What is it?' Matthews asked, her voice thick with anxiety.

Harvey recovered and shined his torch towards the body. 'Over there,' he told her.

Matthews looked to where the light was pointing. It took her a few seconds to process the scene of horror she was looking at before turning away and gagging dryly, the sound of her retching filling the underground shelter. Eventually she recovered enough to speak. 'Dear God. McCoy was right.'

'Don't assume anything,' Harvey warned her before walking slowly closer to the body, checking the area around it for anything obvious or dangerous, before crouching next to it – sweeping his torch slowly back and forth across the length of the dead girl. The victim had suffered dozens of deep stab wounds all over her body and her throat had been cut so deeply she was partly decapitated. Her breasts had been removed. There was a heavy pool of blood around where she lay.

'My God,' he whispered to himself more than to Matthews. 'Who could do this?'

Matthews didn't answer as she began to walk around the perimeter of the shelter, wiping her mouth with the back of her hand as she swept the floor with her torch beam – highlighting items of bloodied, discarded clothes. 'Looks like our victim's clothing,' she said quietly. 'Whoever we're looking for wasn't smart enough to take them with him. Place is a forensic treasure chest.'

'It'll help us convict him,' Harvey told her. 'But it'll only help us catch him if he's already on file.'

'He has to be,' Matthews argued. 'No one's going to jump straight in with this as their first offence. Must have been building up to this for years.'

Harvey continued to scan the body with his torch. 'Probably,' he partly agreed. 'But not always. There's always the occasional rare one – looking to make a grand entrance.'

'You think that's what we've got here?' Matthews asked.

'Don't know,' he answered with a shrug. 'Too early to say. Wish we had some damn light in here,' he complained. 'Can hardly see a thing.' He shone his torch on the girl's torso, examining the dozens of puncture wounds that appeared to have been made by a relatively small blade, although he couldn't tell its length. That would have to wait for the post-mortem. He took out his phone and began to take photographs of the body and area around it. There would be plenty of pictures and videos from the scene examination team later, but he liked to have his own to hand when he needed them. 'See anything that looks like it could be the weapon?' he asked Matthews as she continued to sweep the cellar.

'No,' she replied, shaking her head. 'Place is a crime-scene nightmare. There's crap all over the place. Forensic team are going to love it.'

'Doesn't look like they used any kind of *zombie knife*,' he said over his shoulder.

'Meaning?' she asked.

'That the knife wasn't for intimidation?' he questioned. 'That it was selected for purpose alone?'

'So he was always going to kill her,' Matthews concluded.

'I think so,' he agreed. 'If this was a rape gone wrong – if he panicked and killed her to keep her quiet or maybe because she knew him, I wouldn't expect to see this level of violence. This is rage.'

'You ever seen anything like this before?' she asked.

'Not this bad,' he admitted. 'Never this much anger.'

'Are any other teams investigating anything like this?' Matthews checked, more in hope than expectation.

'Not that I know,' he answered. 'And if they were, I reckon we would have heard about it.'

'Then this is his first,' she concluded.

'It would appear so,' he agreed. 'But one thing's for sure.'

'What?' Matthews asked.

He shined his torch directly on to the dead girl's face, the glow from its light making her pale, blood-stained skin look like a grotesque waxwork. 'It won't be his last.'

'Then this is just the start?' Matthews said what they were both thinking.

'Only if we don't find him first,' Harvey reminded her. 'Just pray his DNA is already on file.'

They took a few seconds to allow what they'd seen and thought to sink in.

'This may not have been a rape gone wrong,' she said, reminding him of his earlier statement, 'but do you think she was sexually assaulted?'

'Almost certainly,' he answered. 'It fits with everything else I'm seeing – type of victim, clothes removed, nature of her injuries. For him, sex and violence are one and the same thing. He probably can't have one without the other. I've no doubt she was raped, but whether it was before or after death, I can't say. Maybe it was both – if he stayed here for a while. If he wasn't disturbed.'

'You seem to know a lot about him already,' she said, although she'd worked with him long enough to know he was a *thinker* – someone who liked to try and get into the mind of the killer and not just see where the hard evidence led.

He again scanned the body with his torch, fighting against the revulsion he felt so he could do his job. 'He didn't want this to be over quickly,' he explained. 'Inflicting this many injuries took time. I just don't see him running away like a scared animal once she was dead. He would have wanted to stay with her – probably until he was able to have sex again – with her dead body.'

'Christ.' Matthews recoiled from what she was hearing, even though she knew he was probably right.

'This was probably the greatest moment in his life,' he added. 'He wasn't going to walk away from it until he had to.'

'You said this doesn't look like he killed her because she could have identified him,' Matthews reminded him, moving to his side, wincing as she looked at the girl's ravaged body. 'But could she have known her attacker?'

He looked around the room nodding his head. 'He knew about this place, didn't he?' he reminded her. 'He either brought her here or he followed her inside – either way he'd have to know about this place, which means he's probably local and if he's local he may have known her or at least he'd seen her around – watching her – coveting her – fantasising about her.'

'No chance he was just passing through and locked onto her?' Matthews asked. 'An opportunistic killer taking his chance?'

He shook his head. 'Not in this place. The more I think about it the surer I am he knew about this place.'

'Maybe she came here to meet someone,' she suggested, 'and he just got lucky and followed her inside.'

'I don't think so,' he disagreed. 'But we need to keep an open mind.'

'If he's local,' Matthews explained, 'it's going to make it a lot easier to flush him out.'

'Only if I'm right,' he cautioned her. 'I've seen enough. We need to scramble the forensic team and give the boss the good news.' He looked down at the victim one last time shaking his head. 'Christ. What did she do to deserve this – in this place?' he asked with a sense of foreboding.

'Nothing,' Matthews told him, shaking her head. 'Wrong place, wrong time. It happens sometimes. This one – he's a bolt of lightning. Isn't any reason to it.'

'No doubt,' Harvey agreed, his mind racing with thoughts about the man he now had to hunt down before he struck again.

'But we still have to find him and this'll have given him a real taste for it. Won't be long before he needs it again.' He let out a long sigh before continuing. 'Come on – let's get out of here.'

After escaping the horror of the cellar, they walked back towards the cordon where the crowd had swelled. Harvey's attention was drawn to a woman at the front of the crowd holding a young boy, no more than ten, close to her side. She was clearly very upset and was arguing with one of the uniformed officers, demanding to be let through while begging for information. Harvey made a line straight for her, his instinct telling him the white woman in her mid-forties could somehow be connected to the dead girl.

'Is there a problem?' he asked the uniformed cop.

'Lady here's worried about her daughter,' the officer told him.

'Oh?' he said, turning to the woman.

'My daughter,' the woman managed to say through her distress. 'She didn't come home. They say you found a body?'

'I need you to calm down a little,' he told her as gently as he could, giving her a few seconds to compose herself before he went on. 'Who said we found a body?'

'People on the estate,' she replied. 'They're all saying it.'

'They know nothing,' he tried to reassure her. 'But if your daughter's missing we need to find her. What's her name?'

'Abigail,' she answered, quickly wiping away tears of fear from her eyes. 'Abigail Riley.'

'And how old is Abigail?' he asked.

'Fourteen,' she told him. 'She's just turned fourteen.'

He felt an old, familiar sick feeling spreading through him, but managed to keep his expression emotionless. 'And what does she look like?'

'I don't know,' she said, sounding confused. 'A little shorter than me, slim – long brown hair.'

'Can you tell me what she was wearing the last time you saw her?'

'N-no,' she stuttered slightly. 'I... I can't remember.'

He and Matthews glanced at each other before he turned back to the woman – hoping what he felt in the pit of his stomach wasn't showing on his face.

'What's your name?' he asked her, trying to sound unconcerned.

'Sarah,' she answered with a shaking voice. 'Sarah Riley.'

'You'd better come with us, Sarah,' he told her as casually as he could.

'Why?' she demanded, sounding increasingly panicked. 'What do you know? Why do you want me to come with you?'

'If your daughter's missing you need to come to the station and report it,' he explained, although it was only partly the truth. 'We can take you there – that's all. Is there someone who can look after the boy?'

'No,' she snapped a little and pulled him closer. 'He stays with me.'

'Fine,' he agreed, lifting the cordon tape which he and Matthews ducked underneath before taking Sarah by the arm and leading her past the other onlookers towards their car. He could hear the muttering of the crowd mixed with the odd anti-police shout from further back.

'You know something,' she told him once they're away from the crowd. 'I know you know something.'

'Listen.' He tried not to panic her. 'Your daughter's probably just with her friends or boyfriend and has lost track of time. Reporting her missing is just a precaution.'

'No. No,' she insisted. 'She's a good girl. She's never been this late and not told me where she is – who she's with.'

'It's not that late,' Matthews joined in, trying to keep her as calm as possible.

'But she didn't come home after school,' Sarah explained. 'She would never do that.'

'Maybe she had an argument with her boyfriend or something,' Matthews suggested. 'She has a boyfriend, right?'

'Nothing serious,' said Sarah, dismissing the idea. 'Just a kid himself.'

'I'm sure she'll be fine.' Harvey kept up the pretence until finally they reached their car. He opened the rear door for her, but she stopped before getting inside.

'What's in that old shelter?' she demanded, her eyes red with tears and terror. 'What did you see?'

'Nothing,' he answered, but he looked as pale as he felt sick. 'Just...'

'Don't lie to me,' she warned him. 'I need to know.'

'Not here,' he told her. 'Not now. Please. You and the boy need to get in the car now.' She looked to the sky before reluctantly climbing into the back of the car with her boy. Harvey closed the door before getting into the front passenger seat. As the car pulled away, they all settled into an awkward silence – everybody alone with their thoughts and fears.

Harvey sat at a desk he'd borrowed in the CID office of Kilburn Police Station, the closest station to the scene. He sipped a coffee from a polystyrene cup while the other hand kept the phone pressed to the side of his face. He paid little attention to the young, casually dressed man who entered the office and headed towards him. 'Just keep me informed,' he told whoever was on the other end of the line before hanging up and looking at the same young man who now stood on the other side of the desk. 'Can I help you?' he asked impatiently.

'PC Ruben Jameson,' the young cop introduced himself. 'I'm from the crime squad here. My sergeant, DS Waite, said the MIT were looking for extra bodies to help with their investigation.'

'We are,' Harvey confirmed, looking him up and down. 'How long you been out of uniform?'

'A few months,' Jameson told him.

'Been on a murder investigation before?' he asked.

'No,' Jameson answered bluntly.

'I see.' Harvey toyed with him, leaning back in his chair. 'Well, you won't be in the thick of it – arresting or interviewing suspects. Nothing interesting like that.'

'I understand that,' Jameson said. 'I'd just be glad of the experience.'

'You'll be running uninteresting actions, filing and making tea when you're told to,' Harvey explained. 'Still interested?'

'Yes,' Jameson confirmed, sounding enthusiastic.

'Okay then,' Harvey agreed. 'Get yourself over to Colindale tomorrow – 8am – the MIT office. The real work starts then. And wear a suit – if you have one.'

'I'll be there,' Jameson assured him before turning on his heels and marching out the office just as Matthews barrelled through the door, almost bumping into him. She strode across the floor and slumped into a chair having just returned from visiting the forensic team at the crime scene.

'Where's Mrs Riley and the boy?' she asked without bothering with any pleasantries.

'I've got them tucked up in the victim suite,' he told her. 'I couldn't handle any more of her questions and looks. Jesus.'

'You think it's her daughter then?' Matthews told more than what was asked of him.

'It's not looking good,' he admitted, collapsing back into his chair. 'Did you get what I wanted?'

'Not exactly,' Matthews replied as she pulled some Polaroid pictures from her pocket and tossed them on the desk. 'They wouldn't let me have the actual items – forensics are very twitchy about that sort of thing, but they took these for me.'

Harvey picked up the photos and examined them closely. Pictures from the scene of personal items – jewellery, a cheap watch, some clothing.

'The real things would have been better,' he complained. 'People sometimes don't recognise things in photos they've had for years.'

'She's a mother,' Matthews reminded him. 'If they belong to her daughter, she'll recognise them.'

'I suppose so,' he said as he stood, looking tired and older than his thirty-eight years. 'Well – might as well get this over with. Waiting won't make it easier.'

'Okay,' she agreed. 'Let's get it over with.'

They walked silently and purposefully along a corridor in the depths of the police station, looking deadly serious as they passed uniformed officers who were chatting and smiling, until finally they arrived at the door of the victim/witness suite. Harvey rested his hand on the handle before looking at Matthews. 'You ready?' She just nodded. He twisted the handle and pushed the door open before they both entered the drab-looking room furnished with a cheap-looking desk and chairs, along with a shabby but comfortable sofa where Sarah Riley and her boy sat. She jumped from it as soon as she saw them, while the young boy remained seated and silent, eyeing everybody with suspicion.

'What's going on?' she demanded, sounding panicked and afraid. 'Why are we still here? Why won't anybody tell me anything?'

Matthews gently rested a hand on her shoulder. 'Please – we're here to try and give you some answers,' she told her. 'I can only imagine how difficult this must be for you, but we have some photographs of things we need you to look at – tell us if you recognise anything in the pictures.'

'I... I don't understand,' Sarah replied, the fear in her eyes growing ever more intense.

Harvey took a deep breath before explaining. 'They're photos of... certain items we found at the crime scene – personal items – from the crime scene you saw us at.'

Sarah clutched at her chest and tried to compose herself before being able to speak. 'What did you find? What did you find in the cellar?'

Harvey knew he couldn't stall telling her any longer. 'A young girl,' he admitted. 'I would say about fourteen or fifteen.'

Sarah clamped a hand over her mouth as the tears welled in her eyes before spilling over and running down her face.

'She was dead.' Harvey told her the brutal truth. 'We believe she was murdered.'

'What did she look like?' Sarah asked, suddenly sounding more stoic – as if bracing herself for the worst.

'Mrs Riley,' Harvey tried to explain. 'I think it's best...'

'What did she look like?' Sarah demanded, her voice raised. 'Tell me what she looked like.'

Harvey took another deep breath before answering. 'Slim. Long brown hair.'

'No,' Sarah pleaded as her legs buckled slightly. Harvey noticed it, stepping forward to support her. 'Dear God, please no.' All the while the boy sat silent and still, but his eyes wide with fear. After a few seconds she was able to talk again. 'Can I see her? I need to see her.'

'Not yet. I'm sorry,' Harvey explained. 'We need to be sure first. I need you to look at the photographs.' She took another few seconds before nodding her agreement. They all took a seat around the desk, the atmosphere thick with a stifling silence and fear of the inevitable. Harvey spread the photos across the desk. 'Take your time. Take as long as you want.'

Sarah picked up a photo of a necklace and examined it for a few seconds before again clamping a hand over her mouth and beginning to sob.

'Mrs Riley,' Harvey interrupted. 'I have to ask – do you recognise the item in the photograph?' She managed to nod through her tears. 'Does the item in the photograph belong to your daughter Abigail?' Her sobbing deepened. 'Mrs Riley – I'm really sorry, but I have to know.'

She nodded slowly before managing to speak. 'Yes. It's Abigail's,' she answered before randomly picking up other photographs – looking at each one for little more than a second before moving on to the next. 'They're all hers. They're all hers,' she ranted before dropping them on the table. 'Can I see her now? I want to see my daughter.'

'Sorry,' he told her. 'Not yet. There are important things we have to do before she can be moved.'

She recoiled from his words. 'You mean she's still down there? In that godforsaken place?'

'We have to take things slowly,' he tried to explain. 'If we're going to find who did this, we need to do things properly. I'm sorry. She'll be moved later today. Then there'll be a post-mortem examination tomorrow. After that we'll need you to formally identify her.'

She closed her eyes, squeezing out more tears. 'Is there a

chance – a chance it's not her – that her things got there some other way?'

'There's always a chance,' he said without conviction, moving uncomfortably in his chair. 'But I don't want to lie to you, Sarah. I'm so sorry, but...'

'Then there's not even hope,' she replied, opening her eyes which again danced over the pictures. 'You can't even give me hope.'

Harvey took a while to answer. 'We haven't been able to find your husband yet,' he moved on, speaking quietly. 'He needs to know what's happening. He's not at work and he hasn't gone home yet either. Do you have any idea where he might be?'

'Try the Red Cow,' she answered, with a little bitterness in her voice. 'It's on the estate.'

'Okay.' He nodded. 'Thank you. Perhaps it would be better if both of you were present at the formal identification.'

'We're a family,' she told him. 'We'll be there.'

Their private sadness was disturbed when the door opened, a young female detective entering before nodding at Harvey.

'Mrs Riley – this is DC Diane Sinclair from our family liaison team. She'll be staying with you now – looking after you – answering any questions you might have. It's important you follow her instructions.' Sarah just nodded. He stood slowly, Matthews following his lead. 'There's a lot of things I need to do. Anything you need – just ask DC Sinclair.'

'Find him,' she said angrily, tears flowing freely down her cheeks. 'Find whoever did this. I want you to find him.'

'We will,' he assured her. 'I promise you we will.'

'I want justice,' she demanded. 'An eye for an eye.'

'I'm really sorry,' he told her. 'I have to go now. As soon as we know something you'll be informed. In the meantime, if you think of anything we should know about, tell DC Sinclair straight away. I'll see you at the formal identification if not before. We'll do everything we can to catch whoever did this.'

'Just find him,' she said, choking as her throat tightened with grief. 'Find him and lock him up forever. I want to know he's rotting in some prison somewhere – that he'll never get out.'

'I will,' he promised. 'You have my word.'

5

Montreal – 2019

Harvey stood in the line for passport control at Montreal Airport feeling tired and sick after the long flight. Finally, he was waved forward by the bored-looking immigration officer. He stepped up to the cubicle and handed his passport over.

'Good morning,' the officer greeted him politely.

'Morning,' he replied tiredly, surprised at the unexpected friendly welcome. He reminded himself he was in Canada and not the United States.

'Can I ask you what brings you to Canada?' the officer asked cheerfully.

'Visiting my daughter,' he lied. 'She married a Canadian and moved over here a few years ago.'

'She live in Montreal?' the officer enquired.

'No.' He stuck to his cover story. 'She lives in a small town – a hundred miles from here. Morecroft. You know it?'

'No.' The officer shook his head slightly. 'Can't say I do.' He examined the passport for a few seconds before looking up at Harvey. 'What you do for a living back in England?'

'I'm a cop,' he admitted. 'Detective Sergeant with the Metropolitan Police.'

The officer looked at him for what appeared a long time before tapping the passport and handing it back to him. 'Have a nice stay,' he told him.

'Thanks,' Harvey replied, taking his passport back. 'I will.' He walked through the checkpoint and into Canada.

An hour later Harvey entered his nondescript hotel room and threw his small suitcase onto the bed before walking to the window and looking out over the view of Montreal. After a few minutes he returned to the suitcase, opened it and searched inside for a washbag. As soon as he found it he unzipped it and began to carefully empty and line up the contents on his bedside cabinet – coughing slightly as he did so. The bag contained multiple small plastic bottles and packets of drugs for the treatment of cancer. He opened three of the bottles – took a pill from each and tossed them into his mouth, swallowing them without water before returning his attention to the suitcase from which he pulled a plain brown cardboard file. He flicked it open to reveal a mugshot photograph of how Peter Delph looked today – three years since he saw him. 'Last time,' he whispered to himself. 'Last time.'

Harvey drove the plain-looking hire car through rural Quebec paying little attention to the beautiful scenery as he thought of what lay ahead. His mind wandered to his dead wife and how alone he was now. His life like an empty shell that used to be inhabited with life, but no longer. He suddenly began to cough and reached for one of the bottles of pills that were scattered across the passenger seat. He managed to undo the lid of the bottle with one hand before tipping several pills into his mouth and swallowing dryly. 'Fuck,' he swore, grimacing as he sped past a road sign saying *Welcome to Morecroft: Population 2,368*. 'Christ,' he moaned and eased down on the accelerator.

A short drive later he stood on the pavement of a quiet street and closed the car door behind him as he looked towards the small ramshackle house on the outskirts of the small town that had seemingly been forgotten by the rest of the world. He walked along the short, cluttered path and knocked on the front door just loud enough to alert the occupier he was there without attracting the attention of any neighbours. He heard someone inside the house approaching and saw the handle turn just before the door was opened wide by the man now known as Peter Delph, dressed in his dirty work clothes, who looked him up and down nodding his head slowly.

'Hello, Peter,' Harvey greeted him.

'You.' Delph acknowledged him after a few seconds.

'We need to talk,' Harvey told him, but he didn't reply. 'Aren't you going to ask me in?' It was more of an order than a question and Delph knew it as he stepped aside allowing him to enter before he sloped off to the kitchen followed by Harvey who took time to take in his surroundings. Once they reached the unkempt, old-fashioned kitchen, Delph took a seat at the small table. Harvey sat opposite.

'How've you been keeping?' he asked. 'I hear you still work at the mill.'

Delph took his time lighting a cigarette. 'Job sucks,' he finally answered. 'Just like everything else here.'

He ignored his complaining and pulled a file from his small briefcase before opening it and ceremonially laying it on the table in front of him. He took a pen from his jacket pocket and prepared to make notes. 'Questions,' he told Delph who took a long drag of his cigarette before tapping the ash from the end into a mug of cold coffee. 'Have you any reason to believe anyone you've come into contact with may suspect your true identity?' Harvey began.

'Yeah.' He smiled falsely. 'Next door's fucking dog.'

Harvey fixed him with a cold stare before continuing. 'We've got a lot to get through and I've got a flight to catch. This'll go a lot better if you just answer the questions.'

Delph gave a bored sigh before answering. 'No.' He shook his head. 'No one knows who I am. No one round here knows fuck all about fuck all. Too busy interbreeding to give a fuck what's going on in the world.'

'Have you been having trouble with anyone?' He pressed on. 'Anyone giving you a hard time for reasons you don't understand?'

'After where I've been?' Delph replied. 'Feltham. Belmarsh. You really think any of these pricks could scare me?'

'That's not what I asked,' Harvey told him.

Delph leaned back in his chair. 'No. No one's giving me a hard time.'

Harvey scribbled some quick notes in the file. 'Have you formed any relationships – close friends or a sexual partner or partners?'

Delph gave a short laugh. 'Do whores count?'

'No,' Harvey answered. 'No, they do not.'

'Then no,' he told him, the smile having disappeared from his face. 'No friends. No... partners. You lot saw to that.'

'You know the deal, Peter,' he reminded him. 'Long-term intimate relationships – marriage – are not possible. They would

46

be based on a lie. Legally we'd be obliged to inform them of your past.'

'That's what it comes down to, isn't it?' Delph asked. 'I have a past, but no future. This isn't a life.'

Harvey looked around the dingy room. 'You come home from work – nobody tells you what to do,' he argued. 'You can cook and eat what you like – have a beer or a glass of wine or watch your own TV. Nobody tells you what time to go to bed or when to get up. You can go into town – get drunk. It could be worse, Peter. It could be a lot worse.'

'Worse?' Delph disagreed. 'What could be worse than spending the rest of my life paying for a crime I didn't commit?'

Harvey leaned back in his chair and sighed. 'Nine months ago, during a routine check on your computer, we found hidden images of pornography.'

'So?' He tried to dismiss it. 'I'm a red-blooded male – what do you want from me?'

'Images of teenage girls being violently raped,' Harvey accused him.

'It wasn't real,' Delph argued. 'It was staged. They were actors.'

'And your latest psychological report,' Harvey continued, 'states you're resentful, anti-social and that you display considerable psychopathic traits.'

'So what?' He shrugged. 'Doesn't make me guilty of what happened to that girl?'

'Her name was Abigail,' Harvey reminded him bitterly. 'Abigail Riley.'

'What about *that* bastard?' Delph asked after a few seconds. 'Checked his computer as well, have you?'

'Clean,' Harvey told him.

'And his psych reports?' he pried.

'Basically normal,' Harvey shared with him. 'Although he was shown to be deeply regretful and slightly depressed.'

'Then he worked out how to fake it,' Delph sneered.

'We shouldn't discuss him anymore.' Harvey decided he'd revealed enough. 'We shouldn't discuss him ever again. It could lead to a compromise.'

'Going to see him, are you?' Delph wouldn't let it go. 'Pay him a little visit like the one you're paying me?'

'Maybe,' Harvey answered, his tone betraying nothing. 'Maybe not.'

'Tell that cunt I said hello,' he told him before taking a long drag on his cigarette.

'My advice,' Harvey replied, 'forget him. Accept your guilt – maybe even admit it and get on with the rest of your life.'

'I'll never give you bastards the satisfaction,' Delph swore.

Harvey took a deep breath through his nose before getting back to business. 'Have you received any unpleasant or threatening phone calls?'

Delph took another long drag on his cigarette as he shook his head. 'No,' he answered. 'Nothing.'

Harvey made a few more notes. 'Any text messages or emails we need to be concerned about?'

'Uh, uh,' he answered before changing the subject. 'You don't look too good. Sick. You dying or something?' he asked with an unpleasant smile.

'It would be unlucky for you if I was,' Harvey answered, wiping the smile from his face.

'What's that supposed to mean?' he asked, suspicious.

'Nothing.' Harvey replied before quickly moving on. 'Has anyone looked like they might be following you? Watching you?'

'No,' Delph assured him, looking bored again.

'Any concerns at all?' Harvey threw it open.

'You're joking right?' Delph laughed, looking around the small kitchen. 'Take a look around you.'

'I was talking about your safety,' Harvey clarified.

Delph sat silently for a while before ignoring the question. 'You came a hell of a long way to ask a few stupid questions.'

'I'm one of only a very few people who know your true identity and location,' he explained. 'The fewer who know the better.'

'Yeah,' Delph said, leaning forward. 'But you could have sent somebody else, so why you?'

Harvey stood and packed his briefcase, ignoring the question. 'We're done here,' he told him. 'Good luck, Peter. It's been a long journey. But it's come to an end now – for me at least. We won't be seeing each other again. Ever.

'Is that why you came this time?' Delph asked. 'To take one last look at your *prize* before quitting the police or something?'

'Something like that,' Harvey answered. 'Goodbye, Peter. You take care of yourself.'

Delph didn't reply as his eyes followed Harvey out the room and towards the exit. When he heard the front door slam, he took a nervous drag on his cigarette before dumping it into the mug he'd been using as an ashtray and immediately lit another. 'Fuck,' he cursed bitterly. 'Fucking cops. Fuck them all.'

6

London – 2020

Jimmy Riley was busy fitting a new tyre to a wheel in the Kwik Fit garage where he worked. He looked bored and frustrated when his boss appeared, looking down on him disapprovingly.

'Get a move on, Riley,' he ordered. 'You ain't getting paid by the hour.'

Jimmy increased his pace, but didn't try to hide his annoyance or dislike of the man. He rushed to finish the job and headed to the backroom where he was changing out of his overalls when his boss came in looking for him.

'Where the fuck d'you think you're going?' the overweight man in his late forties asked.

'My shift's over,' Jimmy told him. 'I've had enough of this place for one day.'

'Put your overalls back on, Riley,' his boss ordered. 'I need you to work overtime.'

Jimmy ignored him and continued to get changed. 'Like I said – my shift's over.'

'Do the overtime, Riley or don't bother coming back tomorrow,' his boss demanded.

Jimmy moved close to his boss showing no fear or respect. 'I said I've had enough,' he snarled.

'Fine,' his boss agreed, taking a few steps back. 'But you owe me one.'

Jimmy smiled unpleasantly and walked past him, brushing his shoulder across the man as he did so before walking out of the front of the garage and into the street where the rain was teeming down. His hands were deep in his pockets, his face tilted to one side to keep the freezing pellets of water from his eyes. He hurried along a street in Kilburn, North London before stopping outside a cheap-looking café. It had pictures of the food on the laminated menus and everything appeared to come with chips. He walked inside, closed the door and unzipped his jacket while he scanned the few customers there before heading to his usual seat – one of four around a small square table. The young waitress spoke to him from behind the counter.

'All right, Jimmy?' she asked. 'Your usual?'

'Yeah. Thanks,' he replied, taking his seat and pulling out his phone that he immediately began playing on – oblivious to the world and to the sound of the café's phone ringing that was soon answered by the waitress, her words loud enough to be heard by everyone.

'Hello,' she greeted the caller before suddenly looking confused. 'Er, yeah. He's here,' she continued before coming from behind the counter and heading to Jimmy's table, making him look up as she hovered close by. 'It's for you.'

'What?' he asked, sounding puzzled.

She held the phone out for him. 'They say they want to speak to you.'

He tentatively took the phone and held it to his face. 'Hello.'

'James Riley?' the distorted voice of a man he didn't recognise asked.

'Who wants to know?' he questioned cautiously.

'Just tell me,' the man asked, 'are you still interested in finding the men who killed your sister?'

He was in shock for a few seconds and couldn't talk until he answered in little more than a whisper. 'Why you asking me this? Who are you? If you're a journalist I swear I'll–'

'I'm not a journalist, Jimmy,' the voice cut him off. 'Just someone trying to do the right thing. Someone trying to help you.'

Jimmy looked all around the café to make sure no one was paying too much attention to him. 'Why do you want to help me?'

'I told you,' the man replied. 'I just want to do the right thing.'

'Why should I trust you?' Jimmy asked. 'How can I believe you when I don't even know who you are?'

'You don't need to know who I am,' the voice answered. 'Just that I'm your only hope of ever finding them.' There was a silence while Jimmy considered what to do next – his desire to want to believe the mystery caller battling with his natural inclination to be suspicious, as he'd trained himself to be ever since he lost his sister. 'Well?' the voice pressed him.

'How do I even know you can help me?' Jimmy asked.

'Look under the table,' the man instructed. 'On the chair next to you.'

Jimmy tensed. 'You're watching me?'

'Relax,' he assured him. 'I'm not watching you. Let's just say I know your habits.' Jimmy nervously pulled the seat next to him out and immediately saw a large brown paper envelope lying on it. He carefully lifted it. 'Do you have it?'

'What is it?' Jimmy asked, his mind racing with possibilities.

'The answers you've been looking for,' the anonymous caller told him. 'Be careful when you open it. Don't let anyone else see what's inside.'

He carefully opened the envelope and half pulled the contents out – peeking inside where he saw photographs of two separate men along with other documents. 'What's this?'

'They're the men you've been looking for,' he answered, 'as they are today. Everything you need is there. What they look like. Where they work. Where they live.'

'How did you get this?' Jimmy asked suspiciously.

'You don't need to know,' the man assured him. 'I have connections. A lot of people want to see them get what they deserve. Let's just say someone passed the information on to me and now I'm giving it to you. But take some advice – don't go after them yourself. You'll be the first person the police will look at. You need distance.'

'What do you mean?' he whispered.

'Find someone,' the man explained. 'Find someone who knows what they're doing. You'll need money. There's a piece of paper in the envelope. It has a number you can reach me on. When you need money call me and it can be arranged. Only ever use that number and show it to no one. It can't be traced. And don't use your own phone. Buy a pay-as-you-go phone with cash and use only that. Keep it secret from everybody and hidden somewhere safe. Same goes for the other things. Don't keep anything I've given you in your house or anywhere the police know you have access to. Hide them well. Understand?'

Jimmy nodded. 'I understand.'

'You have everything you need for now,' the man told him. 'Goodbye, Jimmy.'

'Wait,' Jimmy said, but the line went dead. He stared at the envelope for a few seconds before slipping it into his jacket. He jumped to his feet, crossed the café and headed through the door into the rainy street outside.

He arrived home shortly after and went to the kitchen where his mother was sitting at the table smoking and looking her usual sad self. She looked up when she saw him enter. 'Everything all right?' she asked.

He took his time before answering, making sure he would be calm and steady when he spoke. 'I know where they are, Ma,' he told her. 'Both of them.'

Her jaw dropped slightly open, instinctively knowing who he was talking about. 'How?' she demanded. 'How could you know that?'

'Someone gave me this,' he explained, pulling the envelope from his jacket and dropping it on the table in front of her. 'One's in Canada. One's in New Zealand. I even have their addresses. Everything.'

'Who?' she asked, her voice thick with suspicion. 'Who gave you this?'

'I don't know,' he admitted. 'I only spoke to them on the phone'

'You don't even know who they are?' she asked, increasingly afraid.

'No,' he confirmed – more excited than concerned.

'Then you can't possibly trust them,' she insisted. 'Or this information.'

Jimmy angrily picked up the envelope and tipped the contents on to the table – jabbing his finger into the photographs of the two men. 'Look at the photographs, Ma,' he ordered. 'It's them.'

There was a moment's silence before she lifted a photograph

of one of the men before throwing it back on to the table as if it had burnt her fingers. 'Dear Jesus.'

'The information's good, Ma,' he tried to persuade her. 'I just know it is.'

'But why would they give it to you, Jimmy?' she pleaded. 'Why?'

'A lot of people would like to see them get what they deserve,' he said with a shrug. 'The man who gave me the information said it had been leaked to him.'

She looked down at the photographs and documents. 'By someone in the government or the police maybe,' she suggested. 'Jesus, Jimmy – what if someone is trying to set you up?'

'Like who?' he asked. 'Who cares about me? I'm nothing to them. The police. The government. Why would they want to set me up? I haven't done anything wrong.'

'What if it's a journalist trying to use you to create a story?' she went on, her eyes darting from picture to picture. 'You know what those bastards can be like.'

'How would a journalist get this sort of information?' he asked. 'These photographs?'

'I don't know,' she admitted. 'By paying a bent copper – someone at the CPS. I don't know.'

He considered it for a few seconds before discounting it. 'No. I don't think so. Something about this feels real. At the very least I need to check it out.'

'What?' Sarah snapped at him. 'You're not actually thinking of going after them?'

'Don't start that again, Ma,' he told her, his frustration growing. 'If the information is genuine then you know I have to go after them. I've waited all these years. It's what I've lived for.'

'It'll be what you die for if you go after them,' she warned him.

'I need to do this,' he said with a sigh.

She pushed the photographs away from her and looked into his eyes. 'These animals took my little girl and my husband. Now they want to take you too.'

He sat slowly at the table. 'It'll be different this time,' he reassured her. 'This time they'll be the ones to suffer.'

'No,' she told him. 'I don't want them to suffer. We're not monsters like them.'

'So, you agree to it?' he asked, interpreting her words as consent.

'That's not what I said,' she insisted.

'Sounded that way,' he argued. 'Like you wanted them *put down* like the rabid dogs they are.'

'No,' she insisted, but her voice wavered as her eyes darted from side to side as she battled with her conscience. 'This isn't me.'

'Abigail,' he reminded her. 'Dad. They took them both from us and much more too. You and me left behind, treated like some sort of *freak show*.'

'But to take a life,' she argued with the voices in her head more than Jimmy. 'It's wrong. It can never be right.'

'They're not people,' he told her. 'We wouldn't be taking human lives. We'd be ridding the world of a couple of monsters.' She didn't reply, but he could see that she was deep in thought – an inner conflict raging inside her. 'It's the right thing to do, Ma,' he insisted as he stretched his hands across the table and wrapped them around hers. 'You must have thought about it?' he pressed her. 'Must have wanted it – the chance to find them and finish this.'

'But revenge,' she said, looking down at their entwined hands as she battled with herself. 'It's wrong.'

'Well, now is our chance,' he told her. 'We know where they are. What they look like.'

'I... I just can't.' She shook her head.

'Remember what that cop as good as told us?' he asked, changing tack. 'DS Harvey. He said they'd do it again if they ever got the chance. That they were serial killers in waiting. If not for Abigail then we owe it to other families to stop them tearing them apart like they did us. We owe it, Ma.'

'Harvey said they'd be watched,' she reminded him. 'That they wouldn't be able to...'

'You can't be sure of that,' he warned her. 'If they're the sort of killers Harvey thought then they'll find a way. When they see an opportunity, they'll take it. More victims. More families destroyed. Is that what you want?'

'How can you even ask me something like that?' she snapped before looking away. She took a few seconds before — continuing speaking slowly and forebodingly. 'If we do this, we do no more than put them out of their misery.'

'Fine,' he quickly agreed, sounding relieved. 'Fine,' he repeated more reluctantly.

There was a long silence before Sarah spoke again. 'Do you think it could have been him?' she suddenly asked.

'Who?' Jimmy shook his head, confused.

'DS Harvey,' she answered. 'Could it have been him?'

'Harvey?' Jimmy repeated as he considered it before shaking his head. 'No. Why would he tell us now? I practically begged him to help us find them before, but he never did. Always reminding us he's a cop. Telling me to move on with my life. No. It's not him.'

She considered telling him that she, too, had secretly begged him to help her, only to be refused, but decided not to. 'Then we don't know who we're dealing with,' she warned him.

'No,' he agreed. 'But I have to trust them. This could be the only chance I'll ever have of finding them.'

'You'll need money,' she said quietly.

'I can get the money,' he told her.

'Where from?' she asked. Jimmy just shrugged. 'This person who contacted you – did they offer to give you money?'

'Yeah,' he answered.

'You can't trust them, Jimmy,' she insisted. 'I'll give you the money.'

'You can't,' he explained. 'One of the first things the police will look for is any large withdrawals from your bank.'

'It's not in any bank,' she said, surprising him. 'The police will never know.' She took a deep breath. 'You'll need other things too.'

'Get me the money and I'll get what I need,' he told her.

'Aye and you'd know where to go for these things would you?' she asked. 'Who to see?'

'I'll find out,' he replied, irritably. 'I'll be fine.'

'No,' she insisted, lowering her voice as if they could be overheard. 'You need to go and see your uncle Eamon – in Belfast. He'll know what to do – get you the things you need.'

'Your brother?' he asked, sounding surprised.

'Yes,' she answered. 'There's things about Eamon you never knew. Things that are never discussed. He'll help you if I ask him to.'

'Fine,' he agreed before looking at her in silence.

'What is it?' she asked, sensing his hesitation.

'Why are you helping me?' he asked. 'You've always told me I was wrong to want justice for Abigail.'

'Maybe I changed my mind longer ago than you know,' she replied.

'Why?' he asked.

'Because I can't stand seeing it destroy you,' she explained. 'I don't want to lose you as well to those animals. We do this smart, then you come back to me. You forget any of it ever happened and start to live your life like Abigail would have wanted you to. Agreed?'

He nodded his head before answering. 'Agreed.'

She got to her feet, looking down on the photographs of her daughter's killers. 'Go get your things ready. I'll tell Eamon you're coming.'

7

London – 2005

Harvey walked through the modern corridors of Colindale Police Station with his boss, DCI Louise Richards, a tall, slim woman in her late forties dressed in a sleek suit with an expensive haircut. Her appearance contrasted sharply with his own. Harvey was almost ten years younger, average height and heavily built wearing his old suit – his brown hair a dishevelled mess. They discussed the new case as they walked.

'Has the briefing been organised?' Richards asked in her clipped accent that matched her look perfectly.

'Yes, boss,' he answered. 'I got hold of most of the team. Pretty much everyone should be there.'

'Good,' she replied without looking at him. 'We need to get a move on with this one. I visited the scene this morning. Looked like a bloody slaughterhouse. I've got a horrible feeling whoever did this will do it again – unless we stop him. Serial killers are bad for the reputation of the Met and bad news for careers. Know what I'm saying?'

'Yes, boss,' he told her, not that he really cared about either.

'Any early clues – anything to suggest we can get someone in custody within hours instead of days?' she asked with a sense of urgency. 'Any local nutters or sex offenders people are pointing the finger at? Family members?'

'No,' Harvey answered. 'Not yet.'

'Shame,' she told him with a disappointed frown as they swept into the main incident room where there were about fifteen detectives gathered. The room was full of cheap desks, chairs, computers with clothing and bits of kit scattered everywhere. Large whiteboards stood at the front of the room already adorned with photos of the victim and the crime scene. Richards called everyone to attention. 'All right everyone, drop what you're doing and listen in,' she ordered. 'As no doubt you all know by now, we've inherited a new investigation. The other MITs in North London are already busy with new cases, so we get this one – and it's a bad one. As bad as I've ever seen.' She paused for a few seconds to be sure her warning had been heeded.

'Young girl about fourteen,' she continued. 'Believed to be Abigail Riley, although not formally identified yet, found naked in an old bomb shelter on the Falmouth Estate in Kilburn. She has multiple stab wounds and her throat was cut so deeply her head was partly severed. There's evidence of sexual assault. Her breasts were also removed. As yet, they have not been found.' She looked around at the concerned faces of the assembled detectives.

'So far there are no leads, no obvious clues and no indication of an early arrest, but that could all change once we start knocking on doors – which is exactly what we're going to do. DS Kohli will sort out some door-to-door teams and assign them streets and blocks. Somebody somewhere knows something. Somebody saw something or heard something. Let's find them and find them quickly.

'Davey and Sam.' She addressed two of the team. 'You two take care of checking local intelligence records and the Sexual Offenders' Register. Our boy may have not killed before, but he's offended. You don't just jump in at this level – it's a progression. Early signs are he's left us plenty of material that should yield DNA, but it'll take time to process. I'd rather not wait around for the results, so let's find him the old-fashioned way and let's do it quickly. Media are all over this already – just the sort of unpleasantness they like – so be careful who you're talking to and let's beat them to the punchline. We have the family tucked away in a safe house with family liaison. It'll keep the press off their backs for now, but we can't keep them there forever.

'I can't stress enough the importance of catching this bastard fast. Chances are now he's crossed the line and killed someone he'll have a real taste for it. It's only a matter of time before he goes after someone else.'

'Is it possible he could just stop?' a female detective in her late twenties asked. 'That this was just a one-off attack? Maybe something just made him flip?'

'Personally – I don't think so,' Richards replied. 'But DS Harvey has more experience with these sorts of crimes than me.' She looked at Harvey who was already looking uncomfortable. 'Fraser?'

He nervously cleared his throat before beginning. 'We're keeping an open mind – it's early days. But I believe it'll only be a one-off attack if we make it that way and we only do that by finding him quickly. It's possible that the motivation for her murder was something we haven't uncovered yet – that the mutilation is designed to throw us off the scent... but personally I don't think so.'

'Then what do you think?' the female detective pushed.

The eyes of the office burnt into him. 'Well... I believe the motive

for the attack was sexual and that her killer probably knew her or at least had followed her...'

'What makes you say that?' the same detective interrupted.

'Because of where he attacked her,' he explained. 'Only a local could have known about something like that – or he watched her and followed her inside – knew her movements – and he did all this in broad daylight. A stranger would be spotted quickly in a place like the Falmouth Estate – so he either watched her from the safety of perhaps his own house or flat or he was able to move around the estate without looking out of place. Someone people there are used to seeing.'

'Seems like we're drawing a lot of conclusions from not much information,' an older male detective spoke up. 'How can we be so sure the killer wasn't just passing through – saw an opportunity and took it?'

'No,' Harvey insisted, sounding a little frustrated. 'Killers of this type aren't drawn to residential areas like this to commit their crimes. Too risky. Too frightening.'

'Frightening?' another detective asked.

'They like to operate in a comfort zone,' Harvey told them. 'Which means an area they know well and feel safe in. A travelling killer is a very rare animal. Whoever killed her will be close. We just have to find him.'

'All right.' Richards came to his rescue. 'One thing's for sure – we won't find him hanging around here, but when you're knocking on doors remember what DS Harvey's just told you: we're probably looking for a local man, so anyone comes across a bit strange – a bit evasive – don't fuck about – nick them and search their home. You never know your luck. Okay, people – let's get on with it. Check with DS Harvey and DS Kohli for your assignments and let's get this solved before anyone has a chance to accuse us of dragging our feet. You all know what you have to do.'

The meeting started to break up just as Harvey's phone started to ring. He answered it cautiously. 'Hello.'

'This is Sergeant Newton,' the voice on the other end of the line told him. 'Coroner's officer. Thought you'd want to know the girl's body has been moved from the scene.'

'Where to?' he asked.

'The Royal Free,' Newton told him. 'Any idea when you'd like the post-mortem done?'

'As soon as possible,' he replied.

'Okay,' Newton agreed. 'I'll tell the pathologist you're on your way.'

'I'll be there,' he assured him before turning to Richards.

'Trouble?' she asked

'No,' he explained. 'Coroner's officer. The body's been moved from the scene – taken to the Royal Free. They can do the post-mortem as soon as we can get there.'

'Good,' Richards said, although her expression betrayed her true feeling. 'I'll go myself. You can come with me – unless there's someplace else you need to be.'

'No,' he insisted. 'I want to go.'

She looked him up and down a little suspiciously. 'You want to go to the post-mortem of a fourteen-year-old girl?'

'Seems like the right thing to do.' Harvey shrugged.

'And?' She pressed him, knowing him well enough to suspect there was more to his motivation than sentiment.

'And I might see something,' he admitted. 'Might learn something about who we're looking for.'

'Very well,' she agreed. 'Well, it won't get any easier the longer we wait. Shall we?' she asked, turning on her heels and heading for the exit before he could answer.

A teenage boy, no older than sixteen, walked along the outside walkway of a block on the Falmouth Estate. He stopped at a front door and immediately knocked on it, shifting from foot to foot as he waited for an answer. After a few seconds the door was opened by his friend, Paul Anderson, an unattractive fifteen-year-old dressed in a dark-blue tracksuit that did nothing to flatter his skinny physique.

'Yeah?' Anderson asked bluntly.

The teenage boy looked him up and down before answering excitedly. 'What you doing hanging around at home, man? Ain't you heard?'

'Heard what?' Anderson asked, sounding disinterested.

'Abigail Riley, bro,' the boy explained. 'She's gone missing. People are saying the body the Old Bill found in the bomb shelter is Abigail's. People are saying she was murdered, bro.'

'Abigail?' Anderson repeated her name, looking even paler than usual.

'Yeah,' the boy confirmed. 'Abigail Riley. Fuck – what's the matter with you? You look like you've seen a ghost. Did you know her or something?'

'Yes,' he stuttered slightly.

'Oh,' the boy said, looking a little sheepish. 'Sorry, man. I didn't know.'

'I mean I saw her around a bit,' Anderson clarified. 'Talked to her a couple of times.'

'Listen – whatever, man,' the boy said, suddenly in a hurry again. 'Some of the parents are organising a search party. They're trying to get as many people as they can to join in. We're gonna search the whole estate – you know – like you see people on TV doing.'

'What's the point in searching for her if you know she's already dead?' Anderson asked, sounding confused.

'Not for Abigail,' the other boy explained. 'For clues and stuff, bro – you know. We might even find the killer – hiding on the estate somewhere. Listen.' He leaned in closer and lowered his voice. 'I've heard some people saying if they find him, they ain't gonna hand him over to the Old Bill. They're gonna take care of him themselves.'

'Take care of him?' Anderson asked, sounding concerned.

'You know,' the boy said. 'Do him, bro. They're gonna do him.'

'How?' Anderson naively enquired.

'I don't know.' The boy shrugged as if it wasn't important. 'Come on, bro – let's go. Everyone's meeting outside the Red Cow.' He started to walk away, but Anderson didn't follow. 'Come on. What you waiting for?'

'I'll... I'll meet you there in a minute,' Anderson nervously replied. 'I just have to do something first.'

'Don't be long,' the boy warned him, shaking his head. 'They won't wait for you.'

'Don't worry about me,' Anderson reassured him. 'I'll catch you up.'

'Whatever.' The boy shrugged before walking away.

As soon as he was sure he'd gone, he closed the door and stood with his back against it – closing his eyes for a few seconds. 'Fuck,' he swore. 'Fuck. Fuck.' He pulled his mobile from his trouser pocket and called a number. After a few seconds it was answered by a voice he knew well.

'Hello.'

8

Belfast – 2020

A nondescript taxi pulled up outside a typical small, terraced house in Belfast. Jimmy climbed from the back of the cab carrying a small travel bag and paid the driver through the window with cash before walking to the door of the house and knocking. He stood back and waited for an answer. A few seconds later the door was opened by his uncle, Eamon Rafferty, who smiled as he looked him up and down.

'Jimmy,' Rafferty greeted him as he stepped into the street and embraced him. 'It's been a long time. Last time I saw you, you were still knee high to a grasshopper.' Jimmy smiled with nervous embarrassment. Suddenly Rafferty sighed sadly. 'I think you'd better come in.' He ushered Jimmy inside, checking the street in both directions before closing the door and leading Jimmy through the house to the kitchen. 'Sit down, son,' Rafferty told him. 'I'll put the kettle on.' Jimmy sat at the table looking uncomfortable as Rafferty paced around the room preparing the tea – occasionally pulling aside the net curtains and looking into the street.

'Still have to be careful, you know,' Rafferty explained. 'They tell me the Troubles are over. Doesn't feel like it most of the time. Old scores to settle, you understand.'

'Were you involved?' Jimmy asked naively. 'In the Troubles?'

Rafferty moved away from the window and sat opposite him. 'Well now.' He smiled mischievously. 'That's not something I'd be wanting to discuss with my sister's kid.' There was a long silence, broken only by the sound of crockery being gathered and a kettle boiling as Rafferty studied the young man sitting in front of him. 'So,' he suddenly said. 'Why don't you tell me why you're here, Jimmy? Your mother couldn't say too much on the phone. Cursed things aren't to be trusted. You remember that, son.'

'Unfinished business,' Jimmy told him, trying to sound tough.

'Oh aye.' Rafferty smiled wryly. 'And what would that be?'

'Abigail's killers,' he told him. 'They're out.'

The smile fell from Rafferty's face. 'You mean released?'

'Yes,' he answered. 'But I know where they are.'

'London?' Rafferty asked.

'No,' Jimmy explained. 'They've moved them out the country. Given them new names.'

Rafferty suddenly looked suspicious. 'How do you know all this?'

'I was contacted by someone,' he explained. 'They gave me this.' He opened his travel bag and pulled away a false lining to reveal the envelope. 'Everything I need is in here.'

Rafferty, unfazed, poured boiling water into the teapot and set it down on the table before sitting opposite Jimmy and sliding the envelope across to himself. He half-pulled the contents out before pushing them back in and dropping the envelope onto the table as if it could poison him. 'And who is this person who contacted you?'

'I don't know,' he admitted. 'Contact is by telephone only.'

'Then how did he get this...' – he looked at the envelope – 'material to you?'

'He left it in a place he knew I'd be,' he replied.

'Then he'd been watching you?' Rafferty said, his eyes growing narrow.

'I suppose.' He shrugged.

Rafferty nodded as he thought about what he was being told. 'Do you think he knows you?'

'He at least knows of me,' Jimmy concluded.

Rafferty leaned back in his chair, not speaking.

'Ma's afraid someone could be trying to set me up,' Jimmy said, breaking the tension.

'I don't see it,' Rafferty dismissed it. 'What are you to them? The brother of a victim. No reason to set you up.'

'To get to you?' he suggested. 'Because of your... past?'

'They couldn't have known you'd come to me and even if they did this would be blatant entrapment,' Rafferty explained. 'They'd never get away with it. Back in the day maybe Special Branch would have tried it, but not now.'

'What about the military?' Jimmy asked.

Rafferty laughed slightly. 'They don't give a flying fuck about us anymore. Too busy with ISIS and the far right to worry about us. More likely to ask for our help these days than try and fuck us.'

Jimmy sipped his tea as he tried to think of something else. 'Ma thought maybe a journalist trying to use me to create a story,' he remembered.

'Clever woman, your Ma.' Rafferty smiled warmly. 'If anyone is trying to play you then I reckon that'd be it.'

'You think that's what's happening?' he asked.

'Best to be wary of everything,' Rafferty warned him. 'Always assume the worst. It's kept me alive a lot longer than I should have been.'

'Could I have been followed here?' he asked, sounding concerned. 'Led them here?'

'Relax.' Rafferty smiled. 'The cab driver who brought you here's an old friend. He knows what he's doing. Trust me – you weren't followed.' Jimmy looked confused. 'Did you really think that was a random cab you were getting into? You've got a lot to learn, son.' Rafferty leaned forward. 'So – assuming this information is true – what d'you intend to do about it?'

'Find them,' he answered. 'And kill them. Ma said you could get me things I'd need.'

'Really,' Rafferty said, leaning away again, studying Jimmy hard. 'Ever been in trouble, Jimmy – with the police?'

'I suppose,' he answered. 'Couple of times.'

'What for?'

'Drunk and disorderly,' he admitted. 'Fighting.'

'Convicted?'

'Yeah,' he replied with a shrug.

'And where are these men you intend to find and kill?' Rafferty asked, condescendingly.

'Canada,' he told him. 'And New Zealand.'

Rafferty gave a short ironic laugh. 'Good luck getting into either of those countries with a criminal record.'

'I thought maybe you could get me something,' Jimmy explained. 'A false passport or something.'

Rafferty ran his hand through his thick brown hair. 'Jesus, Jimmy,' he argued. 'Even if I could get you a passport – get you close to these bastards – what you going to do? Walk up to them and stick a knife into their chests? Kill them with your bare hands?'

'I thought you might know someone who could get me a gun,' he replied.

'And what the fuck would you do with a gun, son?' Rafferty asked, sounding frustrated and a little annoyed – the reality of his past a stark contrast to Jimmy's ignorance of the situation and how things *really* happened. 'Have you ever even fired one?'

'No,' he admitted, looking crestfallen.

'No,' Rafferty rubbed it in. 'I fucking thought not.' He took a deep breath before continuing. 'Hell of a thing to kill a man, Jimmy,' he warned him. 'Haunts you forever – even with a couple of animals like these bastards.'

'I don't care,' he argued. 'With or without your help I'm going to find them and I'm going to kill them.'

The room fell into a deep silence before Rafferty spoke again. 'Aye,' he said sadly. 'I suppose you are. But it's not the way things get done. Not in the real world. Not in my world.'

'I don't understand,' Jimmy told him, shaking his head.

Rafferty lowered his voice to a whisper, looking and sounding deadly serious. 'When – if they go down, you need to be back home in London – with plenty of witnesses,' he explained. 'You're too close to this. You'll be the first person the police think of. Best you have an alibi.'

'How then?' he asked.

Rafferty took a second to answer. 'You need to go see a man. A friend of mine – not that anyone knows it.'

'Who?' Jimmy pressed.

'The best I've ever known,' Rafferty told him before letting out a long sigh. 'Someone who the authorities never connected to the *organisation*. Totally unknown to the police. A ghost. He received his orders from me and me alone. No one else ever even met him. He would never allow it. Now things have changed he no longer works for anyone but himself. For the right money and so long as there's no *innocents* involved – he may consider taking the job on.'

'Where do I find him?' Jimmy rushed him.

'I can arrange it.' Rafferty nodded slowly. 'If you're absolutely sure it's what you want?'

'I'm sure,' he insisted.

Rafferty sighed deeply again. 'Really? Then on your head be it, son,' he told him leaning in closer. 'On your head be it.'

Jimmy entered a smart pub-cum-restaurant in the countryside outside Belfast, scanning the customers as he headed towards the bar, behind which a white man in his late thirties, slim but muscular with short fair hair, stood polishing wine glasses. The man immediately looked up when he saw Jimmy approaching before quickly glancing at an older man who was sitting in the corner of the pub, close to the door, subtly shaking his head, as if to let the man know there was no need for him to be concerned. The man nodded back at him once just as Jimmy reached the bar.

'I'm looking for someone called Liam,' Jimmy told the man behind the counter. 'Liam O'Doherty.'

'And who are you?' the man asked casually.

'Jimmy,' he answered, looking all around him. 'Jimmy Riley.'

The barman studied him hard for a few seconds, his piercing blue eyes cutting through him. 'Who sent you?'

Jimmy looked a little confused. 'Are you O'Doherty?' he asked.

'Just answer the question,' the man told him, matter-of-factly as he continued to polish a glass.

He hesitated before answering, feeling very much out of his depth – for the first time since leaving London wondering if he hadn't made a serious mistake walking into a world he knew nothing about. 'My uncle,' he managed to say. 'Eamon Rafferty. He said you... he said Liam O'Doherty could help me.'

'Is that what he said?' the barman asked, nodding knowingly as he studied Jimmy. 'Come on,' he said after what seemed an age. 'We'll talk in the back.' He lifted up the bar hatch and allowed Jimmy through before leading him silently to a private office and closing the door. 'Sit,' the man ordered while he poured them both a whisky – his back to Jimmy who he'd sat at the table. 'So, what is it you want my help with?' he asked without looking at him. 'Your uncle Eamon didn't tell me much over the phone. He's wise not to trust them – phones that is.'

'So you are Liam O'Doherty?' Jimmy asked, excitedly.

'I am,' O'Doherty answered simply.

'My uncle said you're the best he's ever known.' He flattered him without meaning to.

'Your problem?' O'Doherty immediately moved on – not interested in being complimented at being good at what he did.

'There's two men,' Jimmy clumsily rushed to explain. 'I want them... dead.'

O'Doherty half-turned towards him – holding the two drinks, but still not looking directly at him. 'And why would a young fella like you want these two men dead? Are they criminals?'

'Yes,' he told him through gritted teeth.

'Are you a criminal?' O'Doherty asked calmly. 'Are they your... former associates in any way?'

'No.' He shook his head. 'No. It's not like that.'

'Then they've wronged you in a way that's enough for you to want them dead?'

'They killed my sister,' he answered bluntly.

'Oh,' O'Doherty said, moving to the table and handing him a drink before sitting opposite. 'So, it's personal.'

'They raped and murdered her when she was only fourteen,' Jimmy told him.

O'Doherty frowned slightly. 'Difficult to get to them while they're in prison.'

'They're not,' Jimmy told him.

'Oh?' he asked, looking perplexed. 'So somehow you know who killed your sister, but the police don't. I find that hard to believe.'

'They know,' Jimmy replied.

'Yet they're not in prison?' O'Doherty questioned.

'I was ten when they killed her,' he explained. 'Fifteen years ago. The men who killed her were teenagers too, at the time, but older than Abigail.'

'But now they're not.' O'Doherty began to work it out.

'No,' he answered before taking a sip of his drink.

'Then I assume they're not in prison because they've served their time and have been released,' O'Doherty surmised.

'Yeah, but it's not that simple,' Jimmy told him. 'They've been given new identities. Moved out the country.'

'Where to?' O'Doherty asked.

'Canada and New Zealand,' he answered.

'Uhm,' O'Doherty mused, staring into his glass. 'Not easy countries to get into.'

'But can you do it?' Jimmy immediately asked, concerned he was about to hit a brick wall.

'What about protection?' O'Doherty checked, ignoring the question. 'They getting any close protection?'

'No,' he explained. 'Random visits and monitoring, that's all. Old Bill are relying on their background stories and locations to keep them safe.'

'How d'you know all this?' O'Doherty asked. 'Where you getting your information?'

'I don't know,' he admitted, looking a little sheepish. 'An anonymous source.'

O'Doherty shifted uncomfortably in his chair. 'And why would this... anonymous source want to help you find them?'

'Plenty people want to see them dead,' he argued. 'I remember them arriving at court. The people outside wanted to lynch them.'

'I see.' O'Doherty nodded. 'Still a little vague though – don't you think?'

'There was a letter too,' he hurriedly added. 'In the envelope he left me with the information.'

'And?'

'It said people were trying to help me because they thought they would do it again,' he explained. 'That they wouldn't be able to stop themselves killing again. That it was in their... in their nature. It said certain people just wanted to stop them doing it again.'

'And you believed that?' O'Doherty asked.

'Can't think of any reason to lie to me,' he answered. 'Unless it's a journalist trying to set me up – create a story.'

'And how would a journalist get this information?' O'Doherty examined the possibility.

'A contact in the police maybe,' Jimmy suggested.

'I suppose. It's happened before,' he agreed before taking a few seconds to consider it. 'No matter. If it is a journalist, the trail stops with you. They'll never know you contacted me. It won't be my problem.'

'So, you'll take the job then?' he asked, his eyes wide with hope.

O'Doherty studied him for a few seconds before answering. 'Well, if I was to take the job – how you going to pay for it?'

'I have some money from my dad's will,' he explained. 'It's

not much. Would have been more, but he took his own life. Couldn't live with the pain.'

'How much?' O'Doherty asked casually.

'Fifteen thousand,' he said, without sounding confident it would be enough. 'Pounds.'

'You think I'd kill two men for fifteen thousand pounds?' O'Doherty asked.

'I don't know,' he admitted. 'But I can probably get more if you need it. The man I spoke to – the man who told me where the envelope was, said he could get money if I needed it.'

'I thought you said the information came from an anonymous source?' O'Doherty reminded him.

'It did,' he clarified. 'We only spoke on the phone. He wouldn't say who he was.'

'I see.' O'Doherty nodded.

There was a long silence before either man spoke again.

'How many other men have you killed?' Jimmy finally asked the question that had been on his mind since O'Doherty first revealed himself.

O'Doherty took his time before answering. 'Maybe none at all.'

Jimmy understood – O'Doherty wasn't about to discuss the past with him. He got back to business. 'When you find them,' he asked, 'how will you do it?'

'Asking questions can be very dangerous, Jimmy,' O'Doherty warned him. 'Best not to want to know too much.'

'Fine,' he agreed, a little frustrated. 'But will you do it? I need to know.'

'Your sister.' O'Doherty ignored his question and instead asked one of his own. 'Where was she killed?'

'Murdered,' Jimmy bitterly corrected him. 'She was murdered.'

'Sorry,' O'Doherty told him. 'Where was she murdered?'

'London,' Jimmy answered, looking into his drink as he remembered the older sister he'd idolised. 'Kilburn – on the Falmouth Estate.'

'I remember it.' O'Doherty surprised him. 'If it had happened a few years before that perhaps I wouldn't – we were all so obsessed with what was going on over here. But things had begun to calm down by the time your sister was *murdered*.'

'My uncle must have mentioned it?' Jimmy asked.

'No,' O'Doherty replied. 'He never said she was related to him. Never talked about it. I'm not surprised. Eamon would have never wanted anyone to know his personal business. He couldn't risk attracting attention to himself – journalists knocking on his front door asking questions. Still, must have been hard keeping all that to yourself – never being able to talk about it.'

'I suppose,' he agreed, without looking convinced. 'He never even came to the funeral,' he added.

'He couldn't have,' O'Doherty explained. 'Too many journalists and photographers – not to mention Special Branch would have been all over him if he'd tried to travel to the mainland.'

'Still.' Jimmy just shrugged, as if it wasn't reason enough. O'Doherty saw it.

'Tell me, Jimmy,' he said. 'Months after your sister was buried, did you ever visit her grave and see flowers or anything else left there with no name?'

Jimmy cast his mind back through the years until he remembered a time when he'd gone to the churchyard with his mother, long after people who'd never even met Abigail made her grave a shrine – when only his mother tended to it. A freezing morning, he couldn't remember the day or the time, but he could remember a bouquet of flowers – a beautiful bouquet with no card, that made his mother cry even more than usual. He'd asked her who they were from. His mother had simply told him they were from someone who loved Abigail very much. He'd never thought any more about it until now.

'Yes,' he told O'Doherty. 'There were flowers. I remember flowers, but no card.'

'Eamon,' O'Doherty simply said with a slight smile. 'He found a way.'

'Will you do it?' Jimmy suddenly returned to the real business of why he was there.

'My advice,' O'Doherty said. 'Forget about them. Move on with your life. Leave them to God's justice.'

'I can't do that,' Jimmy argued. 'I've wanted this for too long. Everybody tells me I'm no killer and they're right. I'm not. But this is something I have to do. For myself as much as Abigail, I suppose. I'm no psychopath, but the thought of them living their lives as if nothing happened is killing me. It's been killing me since I was ten-years-old.'

O'Doherty sipped his drink. 'Go home now, Jimmy,' he told him. 'You'll have my answer soon enough. One way or the other.' He raised his glass. 'To your sister.'

Jimmy followed suit. 'To Abigail.'

9

London – 2005

Harvey and Richards entered the mortuary through a set of large, soft-plastic swing doors, designed to allow the dead to be wheeled inside with the minimum of disturbance. The room was large and pristine white. There were a number of trolley tables neatly lined up – some of which had bodies on them covered in green sheets.

The pathologist – Doctor Becky Cantrell – was preparing her instruments as she stood next to a covered body that was already on the main operating table that looked like a huge, very shallow, stainless steel sink. Her ash-blonde hair was pulled back into a ponytail for practicality, but it also revealed more of her attractive face. They already knew each other from previous cases. Cantrell looked up through her spectacles as they entered.

'DCI Richards. DS Harvey,' she greeted them. 'I was told this one had fallen into your lap.'

They closed the distance to her and stood by the operating table.

'Good morning,' Richards acknowledged her.

'Doctor,' Harvey simply replied.

'It's an ill wind indeed that brings you here today,' Cantrell told them.

'As always,' Richards reminded her. 'Only this one's worse than most.'

'Yes... Yes it is,' Cantrell agreed, taking a moment before moving on. 'I've carried out a superficial examination of the body. I'll complete the full examination later, but I can give you my observations, if you like?' She took hold of the top of the green sheet. 'Shall we?' Richards nodded once at which the pathologist folded the sheet down the body until all but the lower legs were revealed. Harvey and Richards both took a deep breath.

'Good God.' Richards said what they were all thinking.

'I'm sorry,' Cantrell apologised. 'Is it the first time you've seen her?'

'No,' Richards answered. 'I saw her at the scene, but somehow

she looks even worse now she's here.' There was a long silence as they all looked at the body.

'You said you have some observations,' Harvey reminded her, ending the quiet memorial.

'Yes,' Cantrell began, jolting herself back to the task at hand. 'She has a deep laceration to her throat which has actually severed her trachea and exposed the upper vertebrae of her neck – but she may well have already been dead before the wound was inflicted. There are fifty-eight separate stab wounds to the upper torso, abdomen and thighs. From the wounds I've examined more closely, they all appear to have been made by a four-inch bladed instrument – bladed on one side only and about one inch wide. I expect the other wounds will have been made by the same weapon, but I can't be sure until I finish my examination. The cuts to her arms and hands appear to be more superficial and are probably defensive injuries. Of course, the most obvious injury is the removal of her breasts.' She paused for a second to allow them to consider what she'd just said. 'I'm afraid to say there is evidence that she was still alive when they were removed.'

'Jesus Christ,' Richards said, looking away from the body for a second. 'The person we're looking for must be completely insane.'

'Were her breasts recovered at the scene?' Cantrell asked.

'No,' Harvey answered. 'We haven't found them.'

'Then he took them with him?' Cantrell suggested.

'I believe so,' Harvey agreed. 'He's a trophy taker.'

'But her breasts?' Richards argued. 'What the hell's he going to do with them?'

Harvey considered the possibilities for a second. 'Dispose of them after a time or maybe freeze them. There's a chance he may eat them.'

'Eat them?' Richards questioned.

'That way, in his mind, he gets to keep her forever,' Harvey explained. 'She becomes a part of him.'

No one spoke for a while until Cantrell broke the silence. 'In my opinion,' she said as she pointed to the left side of the victim's chest, 'these are the injuries that most likely killed her. Eight stab wounds to her heart. I expect to find massive internal injuries once I examine it. I dare say any one of these injuries would have killed her.'

'So why stab her there eight times and another fifty times elsewhere?' Richards asked. 'And why the injury to her throat if she was already dead?'

'Because he's in a rage,' Harvey told her. 'His motivation

wasn't just sexual. I believe he was always going to kill her. For him the sex and the violence are strongly linked. The violence no doubt heightens the sex.'

'So, we're looking for another madman who can't get it up unless he's raping someone?' Richards asked.

'I think this one's more complicated than that,' Harvey replied. 'His strong sexual drive may well mean he has no physical problems of a sexual nature, but sex alone isn't enough. He needs the violence and the greater the violence the greater the pleasure. If he's wired wrong, then the need to feel pleasure can be difficult to satisfy.'

'You sure he didn't just panic and kill her after he raped her?' Richards suggested. 'Killed her to get rid of the only witness? Maybe she knew him? You said we're looking for a local man.'

'I can't be sure of anything until I find him.' Harvey shrugged. 'But the knife sounds relatively small – chosen for the purpose of killing, not intimidation, which indicates he always intended to kill her.'

'Any knife in the hands of a grown man would be intimidating to a fourteen-year-old girl,' Richards argued.

'True,' Harvey admitted, 'but combine that with the level of violence and it doesn't look like a murder simply to get rid of the main witness.' He looked over Abigail's mutilated body. 'This level of injuries suggests more. If he'd killed her to protect himself, I'd expect only several stab wounds or possibly even strangulation. Not this. This suggests a combination of rage and a need to satisfy whatever desire he was feeling. He's a pleasure hunter, only no matter what he does, his need to do it again will only intensify–'

'You seem to know a lot about the psychiatry of the subject,' Cantrell interrupted.

'He reads a lot,' Richards answered for him. 'My money's still on a paranoid-schizophrenic running around off their meds,' she added. 'But say you are right and he is this *pleasure hunter*, what would that mean we're dealing with?'

Harvey took a moment before answering. 'Somebody who… who kills because they want to – because it's in their nature – because they like it – because they need it.'

'Well,' Richards said through a sigh, 'no doubt they'll turn out to be another lunatic with the usual story of being abused and rejected as a child. Poor bastards are practically victims themselves.'

'They are,' Harvey agreed a little too quickly. 'They are victims. The world betrayed them when they were children and now they want their revenge. They are made into monsters, not born that way. But if it's someone who has no reason to be like that, but is anyway – how would we explain that?' Neither Richards nor Cantrell answered. 'Can you confirm she was raped?' Harvey suddenly returned to the post-mortem examination.

'I can confirm she recently had sex,' Cantrell answered. 'There's a definite presence of semen. Your man didn't use a prophylactic – and there's bruising and tearing to her labia and lower vagina – so yes, it would appear she was raped or was at very least subjected to very rough sex. Whether she consented or not I cannot say for sure, but the defensive injuries imply it wasn't consensual.'

'How long before she can be cleaned up and released for formal identification?' Richards asked.

'Certainly not any time today,' the pathologist answered. 'Probably tomorrow. We'll make sure her body is fully covered. My assistant's good with faces. We'll do what we can, but…'

'I'm sure the family will appreciate anything you can do,' Richards told her.

'Of course,' Cantrell agreed, looking down at the girl's broken body. 'And may God be with them.'

A large group of local people; men, women and children of all ages, searched some waste ground on the edges of the estate – looking in the long grass as well as amongst the rubble and rubbish. Paul Anderson was with them. He looked uncomfortable and unhappy as he used his hands to sift through the vegetation. One of the older men in the group looked across before quietly calling to him.

'Hey,' the man asked. 'You okay?' But Anderson didn't answer. 'You don't look too good. Why don't you take a break?'

'No,' Anderson replied. 'No, I'm fine.'

'Everybody's upset by what happened,' the man tried to reassure him. 'Everybody's feeling sick, you know. Nobody's going to say anything if you don't want to do this anymore.'

'No, really,' he insisted. 'I'm fine. Just a bit tired.'

'Okay, son.' The man smiled. 'Take a break whenever you need to.'

Anderson just nodded as the man went back to searching. Once he was sure the man was no longer watching, he slowly turned to look at another teenage boy helping with the search. The boy returned his gaze. They stared at each other for a few seconds before the other boy returned to pushing his way through the long grass. But Anderson's eyes never left him as he continued to stare at the other boy, until he, too, finally returned to searching through the grass.

10

Canada – Present Time

O'Doherty approached an immigration checkpoint at Montreal airport, wearing a suit and carrying a small travel case as well as a computer bag. He looked like any other travelling businessman and handed the immigration officer a French passport.

The officer spoke in French as he checked the passport. 'Can I ask what's the purpose of your visit?'

'Business,' O'Doherty replied in the same language.

'Any idea how long you'll be staying for?' the officer asked.

'Shouldn't be more than three days,' he answered, still speaking perfect French, sounding casual and relaxed. 'No time for sightseeing. Just boardrooms and hotels.'

The officer stamped his passport and handed it back to him. 'Enjoy your stay.'

Two hours later O'Doherty walked along the pathway to an

unkept house in a rundown part of town. It was bitterly cold and snowing slightly. He'd changed his clothes and now dressed like a local. The suit was gone and everything he wore was designed to protect him from the freezing conditions. He knocked on the door and waited a long time before knocking again. A few seconds later the door was finally opened by a scruffy-looking man in his fifties.

'Jesus Christ,' the man said in genuine shock, speaking with a local accent. 'I heard you were dead.'

'Sorry to disappoint you,' O'Doherty replied before pushing past him, entering without being invited, walking along the corridor casually checking every room until he reached the kitchen and took a seat.

'So,' the man asked nervously having trailed after him. 'What is it you want?'

'Relax,' he told him, looking all around the outdated kitchen. 'I'm not here to kill you. If I was, you'd be dead by now.' He pulled his gloves off and dropped them on the table. 'I need a semi-automatic – nothing too big. A Sig Sauer P226 Nitron if you have one and a silencer for the same model. One clip of ammunition will be enough.'

'As efficient as ever, eh?' The man laughed nervously. 'Straight down to business, eh?'

O'Doherty fixed him with a hard look. 'I haven't got much time – so if you don't mind.'

The man nodded anxiously before walking from the room, leaving O'Doherty alone in the kitchen. He sat almost motionless looking out of the dirty window at the deserted street outside for several minutes until the man returned carrying a wooden gun box which he placed on the table in front of him.

'It's no good to me if you use it on a job,' the man told him. 'I'll not be able to use it again if you fire it.'

'You'll be well compensated if that's the case,' he explained as he examined the box. 'I need to be alone.'

The man nodded and left again without speaking. O'Doherty popped open the case to reveal the pistol, silencer and ammunition. He removed each item from the case and examined them thoroughly before expertly assembling the firearm and making sure it appeared to work properly. He stood and walked to the back door before opening it slightly. He peeked outside through the gap to make sure there were no neighbours about and stepped outside – his breath forming large clouds of mist in the cold as he slid the top of the pistol back to chamber a round before raising the weapon and taking aim at an old metal bucket full of half-frozen water. He squeezed the trigger smoothly and quickly twice in close sequence, sending two silent bullets smashing into the bucket. The only sound was that of the metal being punctured and the water inside splashing slightly.

Satisfied, he recovered the ejected cases from the ground and placed them in his pocket. He'd toss them from the car window on his way back to Montreal where they'd never be found. He went back inside and began to dismantle the weapon before packing it into its box as the other man re-entered the kitchen looking nervous.

'Everything all right?' he asked.

'Everything's fine,' O'Doherty told him as he lifted the box and tucked it under his arm.

The man's frightened, but greedy eyes fell on the box. 'And payment?' he asked as he winced – his eyes growing wide with fear as O'Doherty's right hand reached inside his thick jacket. Fear was replaced with relief as he pulled an envelope that bulged in the shape of cash and dropped it on the table.

'This will be enough,' O'Doherty told him. The man didn't argue, but just nodded. 'There's two bullets in the bucket outside,' he added. 'Get rid of them.' The man nodded again as O'Doherty lifted his gloves from the table and headed for the front door, brushing past him before walking from the house without saying another word.

11

London – 2005

Harvey sat alone in the canteen in Colindale Police Station, oblivious to his surroundings with his head down as he read through the latest reports from the investigation. The canteen was practically his second office and he was well practised at working there without being bothered by the comings and goings of other police officers chattering and laughing as they ignored the familiar figure hunched over a table as much as he ignored them. Matthews dumped a coffee cup and saucer opposite him and sat without being invited.

'You all right, Fraser?' she asked, sounding concerned. 'You don't look so good.'

He glanced up at her before immediately returning to his reports. 'I'm fine,' he assured her.

'You don't look fine,' she argued.

'Just tired,' he insisted without looking up. 'And sick of reading these door-to-door forms.'

'Anything?' Matthews pried.

'Nothing,' he answered wearily. 'Apparently nobody heard or saw a damn thing.'

'Early days,' she encouraged him. 'Give it time, Fraser. Something will turn up.'

'Time is what we don't have,' he snapped at her a little, looking up from the reports. 'Pressure's already building.'

Matthews sighed and leaned back in her chair. 'What were you hoping for?' she asked. 'A lucky break? A name already?'

'I don't know,' he admitted. 'Something. Whoever did it must have been covered in blood. I'd hoped someone had seen him in a mess or maybe trying to clean himself up. Something.' He picked up his coffee, but the cup slipped, splashing hot liquid onto his hand. 'Shit,' he cursed with increasing irritation.

'You should run it under cold water,' Matthews advised him.

'No,' he insisted. 'I'm fine.' He shook his head while dabbing the coffee off his hand with a paper tissue – annoyed at the distraction. 'Maybe someone came home to a wife, or a girlfriend or parents, in a state.'

'Maybe they did.' Matthews shrugged. 'They just haven't reported it yet.'

'Maybe,' he agreed, 'but in the meantime we've got nothing.'

'Don't get too frustrated, Fraser,' she warned him. 'We'll find the bastard.'

'I've got a dead fourteen-year-old – raped and murdered by someone who's still out there, so forgive me if I sound a little *frustrated*,' he told her bitterly.

Matthews gave it a couple of seconds before replying. 'Sorry,' she said.

'We need to find him, Connie,' he explained – calmer now but deadly serious. 'Before this investigation turns into a circus – with us as the clowns.'

Paul Anderson anxiously, restlessly paced around his small bedroom in the council flat he shared with his doting mother. His father had long since abandoned them. He had no brothers or sisters and as a consequence his troublesome, often anti-social behaviour, was usually left unpunished by his mother who always found a way to blame someone else for her son's problems. He pulled his mobile phone from his trouser pocket and sat heavily on his unmade bed before calling a much-used number, muttering under his breath as he waited for an answer.

'Come on. Come on,' he repeated impatiently until it was finally answered by the voice of a young man.

'What do you want, Paul?' the voice asked, sounding irritated at being disturbed.

'This is fucking bad, man,' Anderson immediately told him.

'You need to calm down,' the voice warned him.

'That man on the search – he knows something,' he insisted – his voice tight and high-pitched with tension.

'You're being paranoid,' the voice told him.

'No,' Anderson argued. 'He knows something.'

'You'd probably be dead now if he did,' the voice reminded him. 'We both would. People around here wouldn't just hand us over to the police, Paul. We're in this thing together. Remember?'

Anderson nodded his head as he tried to calm down and gather his thoughts. 'But what if people find out?' he asked, sounding a little less panicked. 'We're dead. They'll fucking kill us.'

'Paul,' the voice said, trying to calm him down. 'Don't panic. They won't find out. Not if we stick together.' Anderson listened intently as he chewed his fingernails. 'We were both there. Means we're both guilty. They call it joint enterprise. Doesn't matter who did what. We were both there.'

'That fucking bitch Abigail is going to get us both locked up for life,' he exploded. 'Or worse. Fucking whore.'

'Not if we stick to the plan,' he was calmly but firmly told – an edge to the voice. 'We need to stick to the plan.'

Anderson just shook his head – his levels of anxiety rising uncontrollably once more, until he suddenly remembered something important. 'Did you get rid of it?' he asked, his voice lowered as if they could be overheard 'The bag?'

There was a silence before he received an answer. 'Not yet,' the voice told him. 'Too many people around. Safer to keep it until things quieten down.'

'I told you to get rid of it,' Anderson almost shouted down the phone at him as he leapt off his bed, barely able to control his anger. 'You said you'd get rid of it.'

'I will,' the voice reassured him. 'When it's safe. Calm down.'

'Stop fucking tell me to calm down,' Anderson warned him as he paced the room, running his hand through his hair – a stress-relieving mechanism he'd used ever since he was a young child. 'You've got to get rid of it. Now.'

'I have to go,' the voice said, ignoring him. 'It's better we don't talk for a while or call – until things cool off.'

'No,' Anderson disagreed. 'We need to stay in touch. I need to know what you're doing.'

'Just... just trust me,' the voice told him, irritably. 'I have to go now.' A second later the line went dead.

'Hello,' Anderson forlornly spoke into the empty phone. 'Hello. Shit,' he cursed and threw the mobile onto the bed before burying his head in his hands – his entire body shaking with fear as he felt the noose tightening around his neck.

12

New Zealand – Present Time

DS Ruben Jameson sat in an unmarked police car with DC Kate Mills hidden away as they kept watch on a bookmakers in Glen Innes, South Auckland, New Zealand.

'You sure about this, Ruben?' Mills asked in her Kiwi accent as she fidgeted nervously with her ponytail. 'Pulling an armed arrest without proper authority. Something goes wrong we're both screwed.'

'There's not enough time to get it authorised,' Jameson answered, speaking with an English accent with a London slant. 'This thing's happening soon.' He glanced at his partner and could tell she wasn't convinced. 'Look – by the time the paperwork and risk assessments are done this crew would have pulled the robbery, probably shot some poor bastard and be home counting their cash. Trust me – this way's better.'

'I don't know, Ruben.' She shook her head. 'Word is Professional Standards are keeping a close eye on you.' She gave a little sigh. 'You got history, Ruben. You know what this job's like. Doesn't matter if you travel halfway round the world – doesn't take long for your past to catch you up.'

He rolled his head to look at her. 'Don't worry about my past. I can look after myself.' He went back to looking straight ahead.

'I hope so,' she told him, 'and I hope you've got why we're here waiting for an armed robbery to go down without telling anyone or getting backup covered too.'

'It's covered,' he reassured her. 'Informant only just found out the information and passed it straight to me. We didn't have time to put it into the system – right? And anyway, we do have backup.'

'What?' she said, more than asked. 'One patrol car?'

'Frank's a good cop,' he argued. 'He knows the score.'

'I didn't think you hard-boiled ex-London detective types trusted the uniform cops?' she teased him.

'You've been watching too much TV, Millsie,' he told her, using her nickname. 'A good cop is good cop.'

'Whatever the hell that's supposed to mean,' she said, rolling her eyes. But before he could reply a battered old car pulled up too quickly outside the bookmakers with three young Polynesian men inside. Two immediately climbed out wearing long coats, despite the summer heat, while the third stayed in the car – engine still running.

Both Jameson and Mills became animated and excited. 'That's them,' he shouted into his hand-held radio. 'Now, now, now,' he ordered before dropping the radio and driving hard and straight at the suspects' car – engine screaming – making them look in his direction as he swerved at the last minute and stopped directly in front of it – blocking their escape, just as their backup screeched up in a marked police car – sirens and lights full on – and blocked the suspects' car from the rear.

Jameson and the others were out of the cars fast and

pointing their guns at the suspects, shouting out commands. 'Freeze. Freeze. Armed police. Don't fucking move. Show us your hands. Show us your hands.' The driver and one of the men on the pavement froze and raised their hands, but the third pulled a sawn-off shotgun from under his coat and started to raise it towards Jameson.

'Fucking freeze,' he warned him, but the would-be armed robber ignored him and continued to raise the shotgun until Jameson fired once – hitting the suspect in the shoulder, making him drop the shotgun and fall to the ground. The cops rushed in and handcuffed all three on the ground – including the injured man who was bloody and dazed, but conscious and screaming in pain.

They all looked at each other, smiling and laughing softly with relief more than elation. Jameson lifted one of the uninjured suspects from the ground making him moan with the pain of the tightening handcuffs. 'You're fucked, my friend,' he told him with some glee. 'You're going away for a long, long time.'

'Get me my lawyer,' the man demanded.

'It'll take more than a lawyer to save you, son,' Jameson told him. 'It'll take a fucking miracle.'

'Fuck you,' the man replied, fighting against the handcuffs.

'Whatever,' Jameson said as he looked over to one of the uniformed cops. 'Nice work, Jack,' he told him. 'I owe you one.'

'Yeah,' Sergeant Neil replied with a slight smile. 'And not for the first time, eh?'

He nodded in agreement as he turned towards Mills. 'Okay Millsie. Let's get some transport for these jokers and you'd better get an ambulance for Ned Kelly over there,' he told her, looking down at the injured would-be robber. 'I'll let Scenes of Crime know we need them.'

'No worries,' she assured him as she surveyed the scene in

front of her. 'But you'd better get your story straight, Ruben. If Professional Standards weren't all over you before, they sure will be now.'

'You worry too much, Millsie,' he told her. 'The shooting was justified. Professional Standards can't touch me. Even if they wanted to.'

~

Jameson and Mills sat in their large open-plan office in Central Auckland Police HQ – working away on their computers, getting the last of the paperwork for the armed robbery completed. Jameson suddenly stretched and yawned, making sure Mills saw him. 'Millsie,' he called to her. 'I'm about done in. Can you take care of the rest of the paperwork for me? I need to get home. I've hardly seen Jenny all week.'

'Sure,' she agreed with a knowing smile. 'No problem.'

'Thanks, Millsie,' he told her, standing and pulling his jacket on. 'I owe you one.'

'You owe me more than one,' she reminded him as he began to walk away. 'Hey,' she called after him, making him stop and look back. 'That was a good result today, but others may not see it that way. Better make sure all the i's are dotted and the t's crossed. Know what I'm saying?'

'Relax, Millsie.' He smiled mischievously. 'They will be. See you tomorrow.'

'Yeah. Sure,' she said. 'See you tomorrow.'

~

Ten minutes later Jameson entered a smart-looking modern bar somewhere in the Auckland Viaduct. It was busy with well-dressed city business types, but he managed to make his way to the bar and grab a seat. He got the barman's attention with a wave of his finger.

'What can I get you?' the barman asked.

'Bourbon,' Jameson told him. 'With ice. Jack Daniels if you have it.'

'Large or small?' the barman checked.

Jameson raised his eyebrows. 'What d'you think?'

'Large JD coming straight up,' the barman replied and spun away, leaving Jameson sitting self-consciously waiting for his drink – looking all around him and checking the clientele until his bourbon arrived.

'That'll be twelve dollars,' the barman told him.

'Start a tab,' he instructed.

'Sure thing,' the barman agreed before leaving him alone with his drink. After a few sips he started to relax a little more when suddenly a tall, slim, well-dressed, attractive woman with long, wavy, dark-brown hair sat on the stool next to him. He looked at her out of the corner of his eye but said nothing. She nodded to the barman who made his way quickly to her.

'What can I do you for?' he asked, flirting with his eyes.

'Vodka and tonic,' she told him, oblivious to his charms. 'Large.'

'Sure thing,' he replied, looking disappointed as he turned away.

Jameson smiled to himself but kept looking straight ahead. After a few seconds she broke the ice.

'I've been waiting for you to walk in here all night,' she told him.

He looked all round to make sure she was speaking to him. 'Excuse me.'

'I said I've been waiting for you to walk in here all night,' she repeated.

'Me?' He checked he wasn't imagining it.

'Yes.' She laughed a little. 'You.'

'Oh yeah? Why me?' he asked, still looking around the bar. 'Place is full of men.'

'They're not really my type,' she replied.

'Oh?' he said. 'How so?'

'Businessmen,' she complained. 'Bankers. Financers. All very dull.'

'And how do you know I'm not a... man of business?' he asked.

'Oh, you're a man of business,' she answered. 'Just not the business of making money.'

'You seem pretty sure.' He allowed himself to smile slightly.

The barman interrupted as he placed her drink on the bar. 'Large vodka and tonic for the lady.'

'On my tab, yeah,' Jameson told him.

'Of course,' he agreed before once more leaving them alone.

'How can I tell?' She picked up where they'd left off. 'Oh, I don't know – the way you walked in here. The way you've been checking everybody out. The fact you're sitting alone for that matter.'

His smile grew a little wider. 'So, what is it that you think I do?'

'Now, let me see,' she began. 'You're confident enough to be alone. Possibly you are a bit of a loner. You're naturally a bit suspicious of people and you like to know what's going on around you and you have an intense look about you – like you're seeing the world through different eyes to the rest of us.'

'So...?' he asked, knowing she was probably about to guess right.

'So...' she repeated, 'you must be a... cop? I'm thinking a detective who investigates very serious things.'

He nodded with a wry smile. 'That obvious, eh?'

'I guess so,' she answered. 'But you're not a Kiwi. You're a Brit, right?'

'I am,' he admitted.

'Were you a cop back there before here?' she asked.

'Yeah,' he answered guardedly.

'So,' she replied in a tone that emphasised he was being hard work. 'How does a cop from England end up being a cop in Auckland?'

'Ah,' he reluctantly answered. 'I was in the Met. You know – in London?'

'I know who the Met are.' She smiled.

'Something happened.' He shrugged. 'Something went wrong – you know.'

'Something that meant it was better for you to move here?' she persisted.

'Basically.' He shrugged, nursing his glass.

'Don't want to talk about it?'

'Not really,' he told her. 'And you? What do you do?'

'I'm the marketing manager for Travel-Globe,' she told him, making it sound like the world's most boring job. 'The travel agents. All very uninteresting. You know them?'

'Not really,' he admitted, wishing he'd lied instead. 'I don't go on many holidays.'

'Got to stay on the edge, eh?' she said, gently making fun of him. 'Don't want to lose your sharpness by going on holiday?'

'Something like that.' He smiled, taking a sip of his drink.

They took a long look at each other before either spoke again.

'So,' she broke the silence, 'what brought you here tonight? Another tough case?'

'Not entirely sure,' he answered honestly. 'I wasn't planning to.'

'And what were you planning?'

'To go home,' he told her. 'See my daughter.'

'Oh,' she said, suddenly, looking a little disappointed. 'I don't see a ring on your finger. Most men these days give a girl a clue.'

'No.' He shook his head, a little confused until he realised what she meant. 'No, I'm not married. Not anymore.'

'A little unusual isn't it?' she asked. 'The man being given custody of the child?'

'No,' he explained. 'No, I'm not divorced. She died – couple of years ago. Breast cancer. An aggressive strain. It spread fast.'

'Oh.' She tensed. 'I'm sorry.'

'It happens, you know.' He shrugged. 'Not your fault.'

'I'm not doing very well, am I?' She laughed nervously.

'You're doing fine.' He smiled. 'In fact, you're doing better than fine.' He raised his glass. She did the same before they chinked them together, both taking a sip. 'Want to get a little drunk with me?' he asked.

'Yeah,' she replied, her eyes glistening with mischief. 'Sure. Why not?'

'What's your name?' he suddenly remembered to ask.

'Lisa,' she told him.

'Ruben,' he replied. 'Ruben Jameson.'

Thirty-one-year-old Alexander Knight sat on the porch of his small farmhouse in the Pukekohe countryside, west of Auckland, sipping from a mug of coffee as he looked into the night sky watching the stars falling and satellites burning up as they re-entered the atmosphere. The only sound was that of the breeze and cicadas singing. Suddenly in the distance the black sky changed to one of flashing blue and red as the sound of an engine grew louder and louder although there was no sound of sirens. He threw his coffee away and stood – looking tensely in the direction of the approaching lights until he saw the marked police car driving along the service road towards him. He watched the car pull up close to the house. The engine and lights died as two uniformed police officers climbed from the vehicle looking serious.

'You Alexander Knight?' the older, male cop asked.

'Yes.' He nodded. 'What's this about?'

'Sir,' the same cop told him, 'I need you to come inside.'

'Can you tell me why?' Dolby asked, intrigued but not alarmed.

'Right now we just need you to come inside,' the younger female cop insisted as she and her partner stepped onto his porch.

Dolby said nothing as he scanned the horizon, as if he could see or sense something in the thick bush that surrounded the perimeter of his small farm, afraid that his past was finally coming back to haunt him. He nodded once and headed inside followed by the cops.

13

London – 2005

DC Hannah Green headed along the walkway that led to yet another floor of flats in an old tenement block on the Falmouth Estate. She looked purposeful in her dark raincoat, carrying a clipboard, but she was tired and a little frustrated after knocking on doors all day. Many times she received no answer and even when she had the occupants had little or no information of use. She took a breath and knocked on the door in front of her. After a few seconds she knocked again, but again there was no answer. She gave a little sigh and moved on to the next door, knocking once more and waiting in hope more than expectation, only this time there were definite signs of life from inside. Before long the door was opened by a curvy woman in her early thirties with dead straight shoulder-length blonde hair. The sound of a TV and children playing came from behind her. She eyed Green with some suspicion.

'Yeah?' she asked Green before she could speak. 'You police?'

Green pulled her warrant card from her coat pocket and held it open for the woman to see. She hadn't been greeted warmly by the occupants of the estate and it appeared this would be no different. 'DC Green,' she introduced herself. 'We're investigating the suspicious death of a young girl not far from here. I'm checking with everyone in the area. Did you see or hear anything?'

'You mean Abigail Riley?' the woman asked bluntly.

'We don't know the name of the victim yet,' Green half-lied.

'Everyone's saying it's Abigail,' the woman told her.

'If you could just tell me if you know anything,' Green repeated.

'No,' the woman answered, folding her arms across her chest. 'I didn't see nothing.'

Green was about to move on, convinced the woman was of little help, when a young, wispy girl, no more than twelve, peered from behind her mother. Green sensed her shyness and gave her an encouraging smile. 'And who's this?' she asked.

'My daughter,' the woman answered for the girl, keeping her behind her. 'Kaitlyn.'

Green was about to thank them and move on to the next door when Kaitlyn surprised them both. 'I seen her,' she declared, causing Green and her mother to look at each other – neither quite believing what they were hearing.

'Saw who, Kaitlyn?' Green asked.

'Abigail,' she replied – looking back and forth between her mum and Green, not understanding the importance of what she'd said. 'I saw her with them,' she explained. 'She was with them.'

Harvey was working away at the computer on his desk back in the Murder Investigation Team's office in Colindale Police Station when he was approached by DC Jonnie Alston. Harvey looked up at the handsome black detective standing in front of him without speaking, but he could tell Alston had important news.

'I think I've got something,' Alston told him a little breathlessly.

A minute later they were walking and talking fast as they made their way through the corridors of Colindale.

'A DC on one of the door-to-door teams was canvassing a block on the estate that overlooks the scene,' Alston explained. 'They were speaking to a woman who said she heard and saw nothing when her twelve-year-old daughter apparently appeared behind her saying she may have seen something.'

'Which was?' Harvey hurried him.

'She says she saw two boys,' Alston continued. 'Teenagers – from the estate, leading the victim across the waste ground towards the bomb shelter.'

'Teenagers?' Harvey asked, sounding concerned.

'Apparently that's what she said,' Alston answered.

'Does she know them?' Harvey asked.

'I don't know,' Alston told him. 'The door-to-door team who found her aren't child interview-trained, so they just scooped them up and brought them back here.'

'Did she say if Abigail looked distressed at all?' Harvey dug for details.

'She was too far away to tell,' Alston explained. 'But she thinks one of the boys was holding her, although she can't remember which one.'

'Holding her?' Alston just shrugged, unable to elaborate. 'Anything else?'

'Only that she saw them go into the shelter together,' he replied. 'Less than two hours before the body was found.'

'Christ,' Harvey exclaimed as he suddenly stopped walking.

'D'you think this could be a joint enterprise?' Alston asked. 'Two killers working together?'

'Maybe,' Harvey admitted, as he started walking again. 'Teenagers. Killer children. Fuck. Bloody media are going to have a field day.'

'That's why we got them off the estate,' Alston explained. 'Before she started telling all the wrong people what she'd seen.'

'They did the right thing,' he told him as they came to a stop outside the victim/witness suite. 'You'd better tell me their names.'

'The girl is Kaitlyn Macey,' Alston replied. 'And the mum's first name is Rachel. Both a bit shaken, but they're okay.'

'Good,' Harvey said as he rested his hand on the door handle. 'Because I don't have time to tread softly. None of us do.'

Harvey and Alston entered the room where Rachel and Kaitlyn were sitting nervously with a uniformed constable keeping them company. Harvey wasted no time. 'Mrs Macey – I'm DS Fraser Harvey from the Murder Investigation Team. I believe you've already met my colleague DC Alston?' She just nodded once at him. 'Mrs Macey – I need to speak to your daughter about what she says she saw on the estate. If what she's saying is correct – then it could be very important to the investigation.'

Rachel looked nervously from one detective to the other before speaking. 'Shouldn't I have a solicitor or something?'

'Mrs Macey,' he tried to reassure her, 'your daughter's not in any trouble. She's here as a witness – to help us. At this stage I'm not looking to make this a formal interview. I just want to speak with Kaitlyn with you here.'

'I'm not sure about this.' She shook her head.

'Mrs Macey,' he told her. 'I'm trained to interview child witnesses. I'll be as gentle as I can, but I have questions I need to ask.'

'But what if she has to go to court?' she fretted. 'What if she has to give evidence against these boys she's talking about?'

'We're a long way from that,' he explained, 'but if need be, she can give evidence anonymously via a video link. No one will ever see her or know who she is – that's even if she's required to give evidence. Right know I just want to talk.'

Rachel looked pensive as she held Kaitlyn's hand. 'People on the estate are saying you found the body of a young girl in that bomb shelter. Is it true?'

'I can't discuss that,' he answered. 'The victim hasn't been formally identified yet, but yes, we've found someone who died in suspicious circumstances.'

'And you think it's Abigail?'

'I can't discuss that,' Harvey repeated.

She pulled Kaitlyn closer. 'I saw her around the estate – said hello to her a few times, you know. She was a nice kid. Beautiful.'

'I can't speculate on whether the person we found is Abigail,' he told her. 'But I know we need your help. I can't speak with your daughter without your permission.'

'It's just...' She hesitated. 'It's just I can't help thinking that if they did that to Abigail, then it could have been Kaitlyn – couldn't it?'

Harvey and Alston looked at each other before turning back to Rachel. 'That's why we need your daughter's help,' Harvey encouraged her.

She took a long while before eventually agreeing. 'Okay. Okay.'

'Thank you,' Harvey told her as he and Alston pulled up a couple of chairs close to the frightened-looking Kaitlyn. Rachel took hold of her small hand and squeezed it between her own.

'Hello Kaitlyn,' Harvey began as gently as he could. 'My name is Fraser and this is my friend Jonnie. We're both detectives from the police. I need to ask you some questions.'

'I know who you are,' the slight twelve-year-old answered, sounding surprisingly strong and streetwise. 'You're from the Murder Squad, ain't you? You're trying to catch who killed her.'

Harvey and Alston looked at each other in surprise. 'That's right, Kaitlyn,' Harvey told her. 'We're from the Murder Squad and yes – we're trying to find who did this and I've been told you might know something that'll help us do that.'

Kaitlyn looked at her mum before answering. Rachel nodded once to let her know it was all right. 'I seen something – something on the estate. I ain't making it up.'

'I believe you,' Harvey assured her. 'I believe you saw something – so why don't you tell me what it was? You've nothing to be afraid of.'

'I ain't afraid,' she told them, sounding insulted at the suggestion she could be. 'I know what I saw.'

'What was it, Kaitlyn?' Harvey coached her, fighting his own frustration and excitement. 'What did you see?'

Again, she glanced at her mum before answering. 'I seen Abigail – with them older boys. They were walking across the waste ground – heading towards the old bomb shelter. We all use it – sometimes. We just mess around in it – we ain't doing nothing wrong.'

'Did she seem worried or frightened at all?' Harvey tried to get her back on track.

'I don't know.' She shrugged. 'Maybe.'

'Were they arguing at all – did you hear raised voices or anything like that?' he asked.

'I couldn't really hear,' she replied. 'They were too far away.'

'I see.' Harvey nodded. 'Was anybody holding her – touching her?'

'I think so,' she told them. 'One of the boys, I think, was holding onto her... sort of, by her arm, I think.'

'Can you remember which one?' he gently coaxed her.

'No.' She shook her head. 'I didn't think anything about it, so I don't remember. I just thought they were messing about.'

'And where did they take her, Kaitlyn? Can you tell me where they took her?'

'Into the bomb shelter,' she answered, her eyes suddenly growing wide and frightened. 'They took her into the old bomb shelter.'

'Who, Kaitlyn?' Harvey asked, trying to conceal his sense of anticipation. 'Who took her into that old bomb shelter?'

Again, Kaitlyn looked at her mum before answering. 'Paul and Michael,' she finally answered. 'It was Paul and Michael took her inside.'

'That's good, Kaitlyn,' Harvey told her, leaning in closer. 'That's really good. Now, can you tell me the boys' surnames? Do you know their second names?'

'I'm not sure.' She shrugged. 'But they always hang around the estate together.'

'I know these boys,' Rachel interrupted excitedly. 'Everyone does. That's Michael Dolby and Paul Anderson. Michael always seems like a nice kid, but Paul's been a little so-and-so since he was no more than ten. Always in trouble. It has to be them.' She paused to shake her head. 'I could never see why Michael started hanging around with him. Maybe he was afraid of him.'

Harvey and Alston shared a knowing look before Harvey spoke. 'Is that them, Kaitlyn? Is that their names?'

Kaitlyn nodded her head slowly. 'Yeah. I think so.'

'And they both live on the estate?' he checked.

'No,' Rachel answered for her. 'Only Paul. He lives in one of the flats in Moland Mead with his mum. Dad took off years ago – in and out of prison before that.' She glanced at Kaitlyn then back to Harvey. 'Michael doesn't live on the estate. Can't be far away though – the amount of time he spends here. His parents do all right for themselves. Like I said – him and Paul make a strange couple.'

Harvey nodded knowingly before turning to Kaitlyn. 'Did you see them again, Kaitlyn? Did you see either Paul or Michael again – after they went into the shelter?'

'Yeah,' she revealed. 'About half an hour later. I saw them running across the waste ground, but they were already far away.'

'And Abigail?' he asked with mounting trepidation. 'Did you see Abigail again?'

Kaitlyn took a long time to answer. 'No,' she finally revealed. 'But I remember there was something different about them – when I saw them again, they didn't look the same.'

Harvey leaned forward – intrigued. 'What d'you mean, Kaitlyn? What d'you mean they didn't look the same?'

'Their clothes,' she explained. 'They were wearing different clothes.'

'Are you sure?' Harvey checked, aware of its potential importance. 'Are you absolutely sure they were wearing different clothes?'

'I'm sure, because the first time I saw them their hoodies were really plain,' she explained.

'What do you mean – *really plain*, Kaitlyn?' Harvey asked.

She glanced at her mum again before answering. 'No colour,' she described. 'Like white or grey, but when I seen them again, they were wearing really dark ones. Red and black, I think.'

'Were they wearing the hoods up?' Harvey asked.

'No,' she answered. 'I could see their faces. It was them.'

Harvey took a deep breath before continuing. 'Kaitlyn – were they carrying anything? Were either of them carrying anything?'

She squinted in concentration. 'Yeah. Yeah. Paul – I think it was Paul. He was carrying a backpack – over his shoulder.'

'Paul?' Harvey checked. 'You sure it was Paul?'

'Yeah,' she confirmed. 'I'm sure. Pretty sure.'

'And the first time you saw them,' Harvey asked, talking deliberately slowly to give Kaitlyn time to think, 'did he have the bag with him then – when they were with Abigail?'

'Yeah,' she answered after a few seconds. 'Yeah. I remember now. Paul had the bag with him. When I first saw him, he had the bag with him.'

'Then it was planned.' Harvey accidentally said what he was thinking. 'They planned it.'

'What?' Rachel interrupted his thoughts. 'What do you mean?'

'Nothing.' He quickly recovered, getting to his feet. 'Thank you, Kaitlyn. You did very well. We'll arrange for someone to take Kaitlyn's statement sometime in the next couple of days,' he told Rachel. 'Jonnie will make sure you get home.' He hurried for the door before stopping and turning back to the others. 'Your information could be extremely important, but when you get back to the estate it's important you say nothing to anybody. We'll have an officer stay with you until things calm down.'

'I don't want any of this coming back to Kaitlyn,' Rachel told him.

'It won't,' he assured her. 'I promise.' With that he left the room and walked quickly through the corridors of the police station as he pulled out his mobile and dialled a contact.

~

Richards chatted to a group of detectives in the function room at New Scotland Yard, staying as far away as she could from the several high-ranking uniformed officers and dignitaries who circled the room, chatting with officers who'd just been presented with commendations for everything from bravery to professionalism. The walls were adorned with paintings of previous commissioners, all looking down on the strange function below. Most people were holding cups and saucers of tea or coffee, but not Richards. She wanted away as she constantly checked her wristwatch. She was just about to make her escape when a tall thin man in a uniform ambushed her from behind.

'A word please, Louise,' Assistant Commissioner George Lewis smiled his reptilian smile.

'Sir,' she agreed as soon as she realised who'd crept up on her.

Lewis moved away from the group, giving her no choice but to follow. 'I'm aware you have a new case,' he told her.

'Sir,' she said again in answer.

'A very unfortunate incident,' Lewis continued. 'The media are all over it, as expected. And not just the local sources. It's gone national.'

'Nothing we can do about that,' she replied, looking around uncomfortably.

'No,' he agreed. 'But you can get this thing resolved quickly. A bit of positive PR for the Met wouldn't go amiss,' he added before taking a sip of tea.

'We're doing everything we can,' she insisted, trying to quell her rising irritation. 'No one's dragging their feet here, sir. Believe me, my team wants this bastard caught more than anyone.'

'Good.' Lewis smiled, showing his small white teeth. 'Because the commissioner has taken a personal interest in this case. She doesn't want it to become a seeping sore in the side of the service. Understand?'

'I understand,' she answered through gritted teeth.

'Excellent,' Lewis replied, his smile fading to little more than a scowl. 'It would be unfortunate if I had to put someone else in charge.' He suddenly pretended to see someone he wanted to speak with. 'Superintendent Helliwell. How nice to see you.' With that, he walked away leaving Richards standing on her own feeling like a volcano about to explode.

'Shit,' she snarled under her breath before her phone vibrated in her jacket pocket and distracted her. She checked the caller ID and saw it was Harvey, quickly swiping the screen to answer.

'Fraser,' she said with a sense of urgency. 'Please tell me this is good news.'

'I think we just made a major breakthrough,' he told her.

'Go on,' she encouraged him with rising excitement.

'Local girl's come forward to say she saw Abigail with two known faces heading into the shelter shortly before she was found,' he explained. 'She saw the same two a little while later without Abigail, wearing different clothes.'

'Christ,' Richards exclaimed. 'You're saying we're looking for two suspects? Do we have names?'

'The girl gave us their first names,' Harvey explained, 'and the mum came up with a couple of surnames. The girl should be able to identify them.'

'Thank fuck,' she told him, the relief clear in her voice. 'Your timing's impeccable. I've just had the assistant commissioner breathing down my neck.'

'The girl's mum virtually gave us one of the suspect's home address,' he continued. 'A local shit living on the estate.'

'One bad seed at least then,' she said, swapping her phone to the other side of her face.

'Sounds that way,' he confirmed. 'The other lives in a private house with his parents. Intelligence checks gave us a name for him, but you need to know something else.' He took a moment before continuing. 'They're young, boss.'

'How young?' she asked, moving further away from prying ears. 'How young?'

'Fifteen – sixteen,' he broke the news.

'Christ,' she replied, momentarily closing her eyes. 'You sure about this?'

'The witness is only twelve,' he answered, 'but seems solid. She's sure about the change of clothing and says they had a rucksack with them...'

'Are you saying they planned this?' she asked. Harvey's silence told her everything. 'All right. All right. If you're happy with the witness, then we need to bring them in – get their homes turned over – see what we can find. Hit them hard with the Tactical Support Group. Scare the hell out the bastards and get them talking.'

'There's still a lot of media floating around, boss,' he warned her. 'Best keep it low-key. I'll use some people from the MIT and borrow some local uniforms who know the estate. We'll go in quick and quiet and snatch the suspects away before anyone has a chance to stir up a lynch mob. We should keep them apart – one to Colindale and one to Barnet – secure their homes and turn them inside out.'

'Fine,' she agreed. 'Get it done. Get it done now.'

'Consider it so,' he assured her before she heard the line go dead, leaving her staring into the room full of people, but her mind was elsewhere. After a couple of seconds, she noticed Lewis, busy chatting to a group of people. She seized her chance and left through the nearest exit.

14

Jameson and his partner from the Metropolitan Police Anti-Terrorist Unit, DC Jim Clark, known to everyone as 'Clarkie', were parked hidden amongst other cars on a London housing estate as they kept watch on the address of a suspected Islamic terrorist. They'd been there for hours and were growing bored and frustrated as most cops did on surveillance operations when nothing ever happened.

'How did we end up being left to watch this address?' Jameson complained. 'Suspect isn't gonna show up here.'

'You know why,' Clark, a big man in his mid-thirties, reminded him. 'Because everyone else has fucked off to check out the latest tip-off. Someone had to stay behind. Just in case.'

'Should have just left a couple of the surveillance team here,' Jameson moaned. 'This isn't our job.'

'They're all needed at the new target address,' Clark told him. 'So that leaves you and me to nursemaid this waste of time.'

'Who propped up this address anyhow?' Jameson asked. 'Suspect ain't gonna show here. Probably already back in Pakistan or Birmingham.'

'Don't know,' Clark replied disinterestedly. 'Some informant Special Branch are running, I think.'

'Fucking Special Branch,' Jameson protested. 'Why don't they get their arses down here and sit on the address if their information's so good?'

'Fuck,' Clark suddenly said, tensing as he sat bolt upright.

'What?' Jameson stared out of the windscreen trying to see what Clark had spotted.

'Four o'clock,' Clark answered. 'Coming round the side of that block. Is that our fucking target?'

Jameson saw an Asian man in his early twenties dressed in casual Western clothes walking through the estate. He lifted a small pair of binoculars to his eyes and focused them on the man. 'Shit,' he declared. 'I don't believe it. It's him. It's Sarwar. You'd better make a call.'

Clark immediately called up a number on his smart phone. 'Keep watch,' he told Jameson until the phone was answered. 'Boss. It's me – Clarkie. We have target one at our address – repeat – we have target one at our address.' There was a silence as Clark listened. 'Yeah I'm sure. We have eyes on him.' He paused to listen again. 'Yeah – I still got Ruben with me. Target's just entered a stairwell and appears to be heading for the target address.' There was a long pause as he took instructions. 'Okay. Target's reached the address.'

Jameson watched Sarwar looking all around before pulling some keys from his trouser pocket. 'Target's produced a set of keys,' he told Clark. 'Stand by. Target's now opening the door. Stand by. Target is now entering the address.'

'Target has now entered the address and closed the door.' Clark relayed into the phone before falling silent again as he listened. 'Okay. Will do. Will do,' he assured his boss before hanging up.

'Well?' Jameson asked impatiently.

'Boss wants us to wait until the team get back here,' Clark explained. 'Then we take him out.'

'Yeah and what if he leaves the flat?' Jameson questioned. 'What if he makes it to a Tube station? How are we supposed to follow him – just the two of us?'

'Boss's orders.' Clark shrugged.

'Come on,' Jameson suggested. 'Let's take him out.'

'That's not a good idea, Ruben.' Clark shook his head.

'He's walking around an East London housing estate,' Jameson argued. 'He must be confident he's not being watched. Let's catch him with his pants down.'

'Fucking bad idea.' Clark continued to shake his head. 'Bad idea.'

'Come on,' Jameson encouraged him. 'Let's do it. You've got your body armour on. Let's take him out.'

'Even if I agree,' Clark softened, 'how you going to get him to open the door – ring the bell and tell him it's the Old Bill?'

'No.' He paused for a while to think. 'We'll use the postie scam on him. I've got the jacket and parcel in the boot. Postie with a parcel never fails.'

Clark shook his head again. 'Yeah but this guy's supposed to be fucking serious,' he argued. 'Intel says he's planning to strap about fifty kilos of Semtex to himself and walk into a West End cinema. I'm not sure, Ruben. Maybe we should just wait.'

'Once he's out that flat we lose control of him,' Jameson countered. 'We can't let that happen.'

Clark let out a long sigh before replying. 'What you want to be – postie or gunman?'

'You be the postie.' Jameson smiled. 'As soon as he opens the door, he'll have my Glock in his face. It'll be over before he has a chance to do anything about it.'

'It'd better be,' Clark said before both men climbed out of the car and moved to the boot that Jameson opened. Clark swapped his jacket for the postman's uniform and gathered the large fake parcel while Jameson discreetly drew his pistol and checked it was loaded. He quietly closed the boot and turned to Clark.

'Shall we?' he asked. Clark headed off first across the car park, while Jameson waited a few seconds before also heading off, making sure he kept his distance. A few seconds later they met up at the bottom of the stairwell.

'We good?' Jameson asked.

'Yeah,' Clark answered, sounding a little unsure. 'We're good.'

'Then let's do it,' Jameson told him in his usual, confident, gung-ho way. Clark nodded once before heading up the stairwell shaking his head, followed by Jameson. When they reached the front door, Jameson stood with his back pressed flat against the wall with his pistol drawn, held in both hands, pointing upwards. Clark stood directly in front of the door to ensure he could be seen through the spyhole dressed in his postal uniform. He glanced at Jameson who nodded once and braced himself as Clark knocked three times on the door. They waited anxiously for a few seconds, listening to the silence before Clark tried again. Almost immediately a voice came from the other side of the door.

'What do you want?' a voice they believed to be Sarwar's answered with a Midlands accent.

'I've got a parcel for a Mr Saheed Sarwar,' Clark replied casually.

There was more silence before the voice spoke again. 'Just leave it on the ground outside.'

'I can't do that, mate,' Clark bluffed. 'I need someone to sign for it.'

For a few seconds the world seemed to stand still when suddenly the door opened without warning to reveal Sarwar standing pointing a pistol directly at Clark. Without saying a word, he shot him with a single bullet through the head. Clark immediately collapsed – folding in on himself as if the bones in his legs had been removed.

For a second Jameson was paralysed with shock until his survival instincts took over, spinning through ninety degrees into shooting position as he started firing repeatedly into Sarwar's chest, pushing him back and pinning him to the wall with constant fire, all the time screaming the name of his dead partner.

The next thing he knew he was sitting bolt upright in bed, covered in sweat and trying to remember where he was. 'Shit,' he cursed into the twilight. He felt a hand softly touch his shoulder which initially made him flinch until he heard Lisa's voice.

'You all right?' she asked.

'Yeah,' he told her. 'Just a bad dream.'

'Bad dream or a bad memory?' she gently pried.

He ignored the question as he rubbed the back of his neck and looked at his watch. 'I have to go,' he told her.

'Duty calls?' she asked, lying back on her pillow.

'Something like that,' he answered.

'Will I see you again?' She shrugged.

'I'll call you,' he told her, swinging his legs over the side of the bed.

'Promise?' She smiled seductively.

'Yeah,' he assured her, reaching out and touching her face. 'I promise.'

15

London – 2005

It was night-time on the estate as Harvey, a couple of other detectives and two uniformed officers walked quickly along the communal balcony until they reached the front door of flat number 15 Moland Mead. It was eerily quiet. A barking dog and the sound of their footsteps the only noise. Harvey knocked gently on the door. There were signs of life inside – light and a TV playing. After a few seconds he knocked again. Through the opaque glass window in the door someone could be seen approaching. A few seconds later the door was opened by slim woman in her late thirties, although the strain of her life made her look older. She looked them up and down suspiciously. She knew who they were.

'Yeah?' she asked unpleasantly. 'What do you want?'

'Mrs Anderson?' Harvey asked quietly, showing her his warrant card.

'Yeah,' she replied. 'So what?'

'I'm Detective Sergeant Fraser Harvey,' he told her. 'Murder Investigation Team. These other officers are with me. Is your son Paul at home?'

'Why?' she asked them guardedly. 'Why do you want to know?'

He looked beyond her into the flat. 'Is Paul at home, Mrs Anderson?'

'I...' She struggled to know what to say.

Harvey nodded to the others and gently pushed past her, walking deeper into the simple, but well-ordered flat. He followed the sound of the TV towards the living room, pursued by Mrs Anderson.

'You can't just barge in here,' she protested. 'Paul ain't done nothing.'

'It'll be easier if you just co-operate,' he told her as he entered the living room where he found Paul sitting on the sofa eating his dinner off a tray while he watched coverage of the murder on the television. Harvey flashed his warrant card at him, talking as he did so. 'Paul Anderson – I'm arresting you on suspicion of the abduction and murder of Abigail Riley.'

'What?' Anderson asked, sounding shocked.

'You don't have to say anything,' Harvey continued, 'but it may harm your defence if you fail to mention something when questioned that you later rely on in court. Anything you do say can be used as evidence against you. Do you understand?'

Anderson's eyes grew wide as he started to shake with fear. He suddenly tossed the tray into the air, springing from the sofa before trying to run past Harvey, but it was futile. He was easily wrestled to the ground as his horrible high-pitched screaming filled the room.

'No. No,' he begged. 'Get off me. Leave me alone.'

'Get cuffs on him,' Harvey ordered as they fought with the struggling boy. 'Get the fucking cuffs on him.'

'Leave him alone,' Mrs Anderson joined in, screaming at them, as she tried to pull her son free. 'Leave him a-fucking-lone.' A uniformed officer pulled her away from the melee as Harvey and the other detectives managed to handcuff the still-screaming-and-crying Anderson.

'Mum. Mum,' he begged as Harvey and the others lifted him into a standing position.

'Get him the fuck out of here,' Harvey breathlessly ordered the others. The two DCs immediately started pulling and pushing him towards the front door as he continued to scream.

'No. No. Let me go,' he pleaded. 'Mum. It wasn't me. It was Michael. It was Michael's idea. He made me do it. It was Michael.'

'Leave him alone,' she continued to demand as she struggled with the constable holding on to her. 'Leave him alone, you bastards.'

Harvey took hold of her by the shoulders and shook her just enough to silence her. 'Stop,' he told her. 'Just stop. You keep screaming and we'll never get him out of here in one piece. People are angry – they want revenge. D'you understand? I need you to understand.'

She dropped to her knees crying – clutching hold of Harvey's trouser legs. 'Please,' she begged. 'Don't take my boy. Please.'

'I have to. I'm sorry. I'll arrange for someone to take you to Colindale Police Station,' he told her. 'We'll need you there for the interview.' He peeled her from his legs and stepped away as she fell to the floor sobbing. He looked at the uniformed officers. 'Secure the flat. No one in or out without my permission until forensics take over. Start a crime-scene log of visitors.' The uniform officers nodded their understanding.

'Please,' Mrs Anderson tried desperately. 'I'm begging you, please. He's all I got.'

Harvey helped her struggle back to her feet. 'Your son is in a lot of trouble, Mrs Anderson. Best thing he can do now is tell us the truth. Things will be easier for him if he co-operates.'

She seemed to recover some composure as she pointed an accusing finger at him. 'Who was he with – when he did this thing he's supposed to have done? Who was he with?'

'I didn't say he was with anyone,' he reminded her.

'No,' she agreed, 'but Paul did. He said Michael made him do it. You heard him. He was with Michael, wasn't he?' Harvey said nothing. 'He was with that evil bastard Dolby. If my Paul's done anything wrong – it's because Michael made him do it.'

'Mrs Anderson,' Harvey explained. 'You need to know, if anyone made anyone do anything they didn't want to do, it was your son.' He turned and headed for the door, her words following to him as he tried to escape.

'You'll see,' she warned him. 'He'll fool you all. He'll blame my Paul – just like he always does. He'll fool you all.'

Harvey kept walking and never looked back.

Harvey stood next to his unmarked police car while Anderson was already in the back with a uniformed constable – handcuffed and sobbing. He pulled his mobile from his pocket as he looked out across the estate, noticing more and more locals drifting out from their flats and talking to each other – pointing at him and the other cops. The lynch mob was gathering and he knew they needed to get Anderson away quickly. He called a number on the phone that was almost immediately answered by Matthews.

'Fraser,' she greeted him.

'Did you get him?' he asked.

'Yeah,' she confirmed. 'We got him.'

'He said anything?'

'No,' she told him, sounding a little confused. 'It's almost as if he was expecting us – just sitting – waiting for the inevitable. Hardly said a word – even when I arrested him for murder. Could be in shock or something.'

'How does he look?' Harvey checked, his eyes narrowed with interest.

'Like nothing's happening,' she answered. 'I can't read him.'

'Has he said anything about Anderson yet?' he asked as he watched the dark figures of the locals growing ever closer.

'No,' she replied. 'Like I said – he's hardly said a word.' It wasn't what he was expecting to hear and for a moment it silenced him. 'Fraser? You still there?'

'Yeah. Yeah.' He snapped out of it. 'I'm still here. Listen – I need to get Anderson off the estate on the hurry up. Looks like the locals are beginning to stir. I want Dolby's clothes and samples.' A bottle thrown from the crowd smashed at his feet, but he remained composed. 'Intimate and non-intimate and listen – no one speaks to him until I get there. No one. Understood?'

'No problem,' Matthews told him. 'He'll be waiting for you.'

'And get him a solicitor,' he added. 'Even if he or his mum say they don't want one. I'm not interviewing a fifteen-year-old boy for murder without a brief.'

'Will do,' Matthews agreed.

More and more people began to emerge from the shadows, coming ever closer to the car – fingers pointing and fists waving as angry voices called for Anderson to be handed over to the crowd. Harvey knew his defiant presence wouldn't hold them back for much longer. It was time to go. 'Give them minimum disclosure only,' he told her, talking faster now. 'What he's been arrested for and little background. No details.'

'It'll be done,' she assured him.

'Good,' he told her. 'I'll be in touch.' He slipped the phone back in his pocket as he watched the growing number of vengeful residents spilling from the walkways into the car park – heading towards him – egging each other on. He quickly climbed into the front passenger seat and slammed the door as a bottle smashed onto the bonnet. 'All right, Jonnie. Let's get the fuck out of here.' As they pulled away more and more bottles smashed around them as the mob began to circle their car. 'Jesus Christ,' Harvey called out in alarm.

'They're going to kill me,' Anderson shouted from the back in panic and fear. 'Don't let them kill me.'

Alston floored the accelerator and the car sped out of the estate and into the safety of the streets, leaving the angry mob swarming behind. Harvey looked over his shoulder at Anderson. 'No one's going to kill you, Paul,' he told him. 'You're safe.' He looked straight ahead again before whispering under his breath, 'For now.'

16

New Zealand – Present Time

Jameson walked through the corridors and open-plan offices of Auckland Central Police Headquarters, yet despite taking out the robbery crew the previous day, he wasn't exactly being treated like a hero and was mostly blanked by the other cops he passed with the occasional dirty look thrown his way. They knew about his past in London and the death of his partner. It may have happened on the other side of the world, but cops were cops and someone who many people blamed for the death of one of their own was always going to be treated with suspicion and dislike until they proved they deserved better. Eventually he reached the office of Detective Inspector Harry Finch and knocked on the door frame. The door was already open and he could see that Finch was on the phone, summoning him in to sit with a wave of his hand and a point of his finger. He did as he was told and waited for Finch to finish his call while he sat silently looking a bit sheepish. A few seconds later his boss hung up and looked at him, apparently not happy.

'Do you know who that was?' Finch immediately asked. He just shrugged. 'That was Inspector Mark Warren from Professional Standards,' Finch explained. 'I'll tell you now, Ruben, he's after your blood.' Jameson sat looking disinterested.

'Listen, Ruben,' Finch warned him. 'I know coming from the Met you probably think you know it all, but let me explain something – Warren is bad news. He goes after anyone he believes is a cowboy cop like I would go after a rapist. He just won't quit. Know what his nickname is?'

'No,' he replied with another dismissive shrug.

'The Pit Bull,' Finch told him. 'They call him the fucking Pit Bull. Now why d'you think that might be?'

'Because he's got bad breath?' he replied with a smile.

Finch leaned back in his chair in frustration. 'You'd better just make sure you've got the paperwork around the informant on your latest little stunt watertight,' he warned him again. 'It'll be the first thing Warren goes after.'

'It's covered,' Jameson assured him. 'Informant's solid. He knows the score.'

Finch took a few seconds before continuing, eying Jameson as he considered his next words. 'A lot of people know what happened to your partner back in London,' he reminded him.

'So I've been told,' he replied.

'And a lot of them don't understand why you were given a second chance here in New Zealand,' Finch finished.

'I wasn't given a second chance,' Jameson reminded him. 'I was cleared – by a Central Board. I was entitled to apply to join the police here.'

'Save the party line for everyone else, Ruben,' Finch replied.

'I know that the assistant commissioner here used to be your boss when he was still in the Met.'

'So?' he asked.

'So, he *arranged* for you to be cleared on your Central Board,' Finch explained. 'Just so long as you agreed to move halfway round the world. The best result for everybody. Out of sight, out of mind.'

Jameson sat stony-faced saying nothing.

'Speaking of which,' Finch continued, 'I have a little job for you. Something that should keep you nicely out the way while hopefully, Mr Warren loses a bit of interest in you.'

'Which is?' he asked, his eyes narrowing with suspicion.

Finch took his time taking a file from his desk drawer and dropping it in front of him. 'Do you remember the case of a teenage girl called Abigail Riley?' he asked. 'She was raped and murdered by two teenage boys – Paul Anderson and Michael Dolby. A particularly nasty case. It got a fair bit of coverage over here, but nowhere near as much as it got back in the UK.' Jameson seemed to freeze for a moment. Finch noticed it. 'You all right?'

'Yeah,' Jameson told him – a sudden paleness washing over his face. 'I remember it. Most people do. I was on the original investigation team.'

'You were on the investigation?' Finch checked.

'I was already in the Met when it happened,' Jameson confirmed. 'I'd just joined the CID. I was just a young buck on the crime squad looking for something more interesting than nicking local drug dealers. Well I certainly got that for my troubles. I was little more than a gofer, but I learned enough about the case to know we were looking for some sort of rabid dog, or dogs as it turned out. Dolby and Anderson. Two names I hoped never to hear again.' He took a breath before continuing. 'They were released a few years ago and the whole story blew up again. But what's this got to do with me? This is all history. It's all in the past.'

'Not anymore,' Finch told him before opening the file on his desk and taking out a crime-scene photograph of the dead Paul Anderson before sliding it across to him. 'Paul Anderson. Shot in the head and chest while living his new life under a different identity in some hick town in Canada, a couple of days ago.'

'A professional hit,' he more stated than asked. 'So, someone connected with Abigail Riley finally caught up with him. The immediate family most likely. Shouldn't be too hard to find out who. Bigger question is where did they get their information from? Only someone connected with the investigation or their relocation could have such accurate intelligence.'

'That's people enough,' Finch argued. 'You'd also have to consider CPS and Home Office employees or maybe someone just got sloppy and left a file where they shouldn't have. The Brits are looking into it, but don't hold your breath.'

'I bet they are,' he agreed, 'but none of this explains why you're telling me. You say I'm part of the investigation, but what's a hit in Canada got to do with me?'

Finch stood with his hands on his hips for a while before pulling another photograph from the file – of Michael Dolby as he looked now. He slid it across to Jameson who looked at it with confusion. 'Michael Dolby,' Finch explained. 'Anderson's partner in crime, as he appears today.'

He nodded his head as he began to understand. 'So Anderson went to Canada, but Dolby came here?' Finch pulled a face that let him know he was right. 'So, what was the deal – New Zealand takes a problem off the UK's hands and they take one off yours. Who did they get in exchange? A blown informant? Protected witness?'

'You don't need to know and apparently neither do I,' Finch answered. 'This is all way above our pay grade.'

'Which brings me back to why are you telling me any of this?' he reminded him.

'Because you're going to babysit our unwanted guest,' Finch told him with apparent glee. 'Keep him safe from whoever may be out there looking to put two in his chest and two more in his head. As of now you're officially assigned to Michael Dolby's bodyguard team. To start with you'll be working with Millsie, on the day shift.'

'You're joking, right?' he argued. 'You want me to waste my time keeping this bastard safe. I remember the case, Harry. Don't put me next to this filth.'

'Sorry,' Finch told him. 'No choice. He served his time and now we have a duty of care, regardless of his past.'

'Well, then have someone pick him up,' he suggested. 'Put him in prison under protective custody.'

'It was considered,' Finch explained, 'but you know what prisons are like. He'd be asked a hundred questions a day by the other inmates: why you here? What you in for? Only a matter of time before they get suspicious or he makes a mistake. Eventually he may even be recognised. Prisoners have long memories.'

'Then put him in a safe house,' he tried. 'Keep him in isolation until the threat passes.'

'And when would that be?' Finch threw his hands up. 'Months? Years?'

'Who cares?' Jameson argued.

Finch took a breath before answering. 'Well apparently *he* does.'

'Excuse me?' he asked.

'He refuses to move to a safe house,' Finch told him.

'He what?' Jameson shook his head.

'It was... offered,' Finch explained. 'He won't go. Won't leave his farm.'

'Then don't give him a choice,' he replied, as if it was straightforward.

'Technically he's a free man,' Finch elaborated. 'On licence, yes, but there's nothing to say he has to surrender to a safe house or help us keep him safe. Without his co-operation a safe house isn't going to work.'

'What?' Jameson asked. 'He's got some sort of death wish?'

Finch shrugged before chucking the file across the desk to him. 'Everything you need to know is in there, including the fact that Michael Dolby is no longer Michael Dolby. He's now Alexander Knight.'

He shook his head and laughed ironically. 'Alexander Knight. He gets to make up his own name or something?'

'This all just came in overnight, Ruben,' Finch said, ignoring the question. 'You need to grab Millsie and get over to Knight's farm in Pukekohe as a matter of urgency. There's no way Anderson's killer could have got to New Zealand already, so you've got a head start securing his farm, but it's the only advantage we seem to have so let's not lose it.'

'Pukekohe?' he questioned.

'A good place to hide someone like Knight,' Finch answered. 'Apparently he keeps himself to himself. Sticks to the rules of his release. Never causes anyone any trouble. Farms his smallholding and tries to live a normal life. Maybe you could learn something from him.'

'You want me to learn from a rapist and a murderer?' he asked sarcastically.

'That's not what I meant,' Finch told him, drumming his fingers on his desk. 'Just certain things need to be left in the past. What happened back in the UK needs to be left there.'

He took a deep breath through his nose. 'It is.'

'Good.' Finch nodded. 'Now get yourself over to Pukekohe. The sooner I know you're babysitting Knight, the better I'll feel.'

Jameson stood to leave. 'Don't forget this,' Finch reminded him, tapping the file on his desk. Jameson reluctantly picked it up. 'Make sure you read it. The more you know about Knight the better you'll be able to protect him.'

Jameson shook his head and walked from the office without saying another word as he seethed inside.

17

London – 2005

Alston was in the medical examiner's room at Colindale Police Station with Anderson and his mother. DC Tony Cooke was assisting him. The room was quite small and plain, with an examination bed up against a wall while cabinets and drawers adorned the others. Anderson was still upset and crying, but his mum had calmed down.

'Why are we in here?' she asked, looking around. 'Why are we in... this room?'

'We need to take Paul's clothes,' Alston explained. 'All of them. We also have authority to take both intimate and non-intimate samples from him. I can take the non-intimate ones in your presence, but we'll have to wait for the medical examiner to take the intimates.'

'I don't understand,' Anderson sobbed. 'What d'you mean take samples from me? I don't know what you're talking about. I don't know what this means.'

'Non-intimate samples, Paul,' Alston told him. 'Things like saliva, hand swabs, hair. Intimate samples are things like blood, semen, swabs from your private parts, pubic hair. Only the examiner can take them.'

'But I didn't do anything,' he pleaded.

'That's why we're taking the samples and your clothing,' Alston explained, lifting a large, brown paper evidence bag from the examination table. 'To help us find out.'

'It wasn't me,' Anderson tried to convince them.

'I need you to start getting undressed.' Alston persisted. 'Place each item of clothing in a separate bag, please.'

Anderson began to undress as the tears flowed down his face.

A mirror image of the scene taking place at Colindale was happening at Barnet Police Station where Matthews and DC Simon Reger were in the medical examination room with Michael Dolby and his mother, Fiona, an attractive woman in her mid-forties, who was pacing around the small room looking agitated while Dolby sat impassively on the examination bed.

'Why are we here?' Mrs Dolby asked in her accentless voice. 'In this place – this room?'

'We need to take some samples from Michael,' Matthews explained. 'Some only the police doctor can take. And we need his clothes. If you want to arrange replacements, that's fine.'

'Samples?' she questioned, sounding alarmed.

'Blood, semen, swabs from Michael's skin,' Matthews told her. 'Each will be explained before it's taken.'

'Jesus Christ.' She laughed nervously. 'You're joking, right?'

'No, Mrs Dolby,' she replied. 'I'm afraid I'm not.'

'But this is all clearly a mistake,' she argued. 'I mean, do you really think Michael could be involved in something like this. Frankly... frankly it's ridiculous.'

'We have information to suggest otherwise,' Matthews explained.

'Information from who?' she asked. 'Paul Anderson? Is he blaming this on Michael?'

'No,' Matthews answered. 'Not Anderson.'

'Then who?' she demanded. 'I have a right to know.'

'No. You don't,' Matthews told her. 'But I can tell you the source of the information has no reason to lie to us.'

'Then whoever's saying these things is lying,' she insisted, still pacing the room.

'Mum,' Dolby suddenly spoke, sounding calm, but a bit frustrated. 'Just let it go.'

'Let it go?' she said, throwing her hands in the air. 'Do you have any idea of how much trouble you're in? What you're accused off?'

'I know,' he told her, sounding assured. 'But I didn't do anything. It'll be fine. It's just a mistake.'

She spun to face Matthews. 'Has anyone else been arrested? Has Paul Anderson also been arrested? Is he blaming Michael to try and save his own skin?' The two detectives glanced at each other. Mrs Dolby saw it. 'He has, hasn't he? And now he's lying to try and save himself. I should have known. I should have known,' she repeated, shaking her head before rounding on Matthews. 'You... you don't actually believe him, do you? You know he's been in trouble with the police before – more times than I can remember?'

'Mum,' Dolby interrupted. 'Just drop it. You're not helping.'

'I don't know why you want to spend time with him,' she questioned. 'I told you he'd get you into trouble sooner or later. Paul is bad news. There's something wrong with him. You can see it in his eyes – like he's...'

'You don't know what you're talking about,' he argued. 'Paul's okay. You just don't know him.'

'That's typical,' she said before forcing an ironic laugh. 'He blames you for something he's probably done and yet you still stick up for him. He says jump and you say how high.'

'It's not like that,' he insisted. 'We're friends.'

'Mrs Dolby,' Matthews intervened. 'I need to remind you that Michael is still under caution and that any unsolicited comments he makes could be used as evidence against him. Perhaps it's best if you don't say anything else until you've had a chance to speak with your solicitor.'

'Fine,' she agreed with a frustrated shrug.

'Michael,' Matthews told Dolby, picking up a brown paper evidence bag and handing it to Reger. 'I need you to hand all your clothes to DC Reger. As a female officer, I can't be present.' She nodded to Reger before turning towards the door.

'How long is this going to take?' Mrs Dolby stopped her. 'How long will we be here for?'

'We'll interview Michael as soon as we can,' she answered. 'After you've had a chance to speak with your solicitor.'

'And then?' Mrs Dolby pressed.

'We'll be as quick as we can,' Matthews told her. 'I promise.'

'You're not really taking this seriously are you,' she asked, sounding nervous. 'I mean I know you have to take Michael's clothes and these samples, but you don't actually think he killed that girl, do you? This is all just procedure, right – to eliminate him from your enquiries – isn't that what you police say?'

'This is a murder investigation, Mrs Dolby,' Matthews reminded her. 'We take everything very seriously.'

'Then you do think he was involved,' she said, speaking slowly and intently. 'You really believe he could have killed her.'

'Best just to do as DC Reger says,' Matthews replied. 'I'll be back as soon as I can.'

'I don't want her here,' Dolby suddenly spoke up. 'I don't want my mum here when I'm undressing.'

'If that's okay with your mum,' Matthews agreed. 'Mrs Dolby?'

'Fine,' she agreed, sounding annoyed. 'Whatever.'

'Mrs Dolby,' Matthews said as she headed for the door. 'If you could follow me.'

'This is a nightmare,' she complained before doing as she was told. 'A living bloody nightmare.'

Harvey, Alston, Anderson and his mother were all crammed into the interview room at Colindale Police Station along with their solicitor – Neena Barnwell. They sat on uncomfortable wooden-and-cloth chairs around a cheap table upon which the recording equipment stood. Harvey leaned forward and pressed the record button – filling the room with the shrill sound of the warning buzzer for about five seconds. When it stopped, he began.

'This interview is being recorded for both audio and video,' he explained. 'The date is 10th February and the time is 9.40pm and we are in the interview room at Colindale Police Station. I am Detective Sergeant Fraser Harvey and the other officer present is...'

'Detective Constable John Alston,' he introduced himself.

'I'm interviewing – could you please state your name clearly for the tape please.'

'Paul Anderson,' he replied quietly.

'Also present is Paul's mother, acting as his appropriate adult.'

She knew the drill and leaned forward to say her name. 'Donna Anderson. Paul's mother.'

'Thank you. Also present is...'

'Neena Barnwell,' she introduced herself, recognising her cue. 'Solicitor for Barnwell, Compton and Howell. I'm here to advise both Paul and Mrs Anderson on their legal rights and to challenge any inappropriate questioning or conduct towards my client.'

'Paul,' Harvey continued. 'I need to remind you that you are still under caution, which means you do not have to say anything unless you wish to do so, but it may harm your defence if you fail to mention when questioned something that you later rely on in court. Anything you do say may be given as evidence.'

'I've discussed the implications of the caution with my client,' Barnwell answered for him. 'And he fully understands them.'

'Okay.' Harvey nodded. 'Thank you. You have the right to free and independent legal advice any time, night or day and as it happens you've chosen to have your solicitor, Miss Barnwell present during the interview. If at any time you want to consult privately with her or any other legal representative, just say so and I'll stop the interview while you have that consultation. Do you understand?' Anderson just nodded sheepishly. 'You need to speak, Paul, so the tape can record your answers.'

'Sorry,' he replied in little more than a whisper. 'Yeah. I understand.'

Harvey took a deep breath through his nose before continuing. 'Paul – do you know why you've been arrested? Do you know why you're being interviewed?'

He looked to his mother and then to Barnwell who subtly shook her head. He looked down at the table. 'No comment.'

'You've been arrested for the suspected murder of Abigail Riley,' Harvey explained. 'A fourteen-year-old girl we found in a disused bomb shelter. She was all but naked when we found her.' He paused to allow his words to sink in. 'She'd been stabbed over fifty times – had her throat cut so severely that she'd been partly decapitated. We believe she was also raped. Her breasts had been cut off and seemingly removed from the scene.'

Donna looked pale and sick. 'Oh my God.'

'No comment,' he answered, still looking down at the table.

'Officer,' Barnwell interrupted. 'I should remind you that my client is only fifteen.'

'And the victim was only fourteen,' he countered. 'A fourteen-year-old girl who we believe is Abigail Riley. Do you know her?'

'No comment,' he replied, shaking his head.

'What was your relationship with her?'

'No comment,' he answered, sounding meek and worried.

'Was she your girlfriend?'

'No,' Anderson slipped. 'No comment.'

'No or no comment?'

'No comment,' he recovered.

'Did you have sex with her on the day she was killed?'

'No comment.'

'Did you have sex with her any time before that?'

'No comment.'

'I'm talking about consensual sex,' Harvey explained. 'Did you ever have consensual sex with Abigail?'

'No comment,' he answered, but he sounded unsure and confused.

'Then did you rape her?' Harvey pushed him.

He closed his eyes and shook his head. 'No comment.'

'It's a simple question.' Harvey tried to further rattle him. 'Yes or no – did you rape her?'

'No comment.'

'Do you actually know she was raped?' Barnwell came to Anderson's momentary rescue.

'Early medical evidence suggests it,' Harvey told her.

'But you don't know it?' she guessed.

'Once the full post-mortem's been completed it'll be confirmed,' Harvey assured her.

'But at this moment you don't have the evidence to prove it,' she argued.

'I'm not here to play games, Miss Barnwell,' Harvey told her, the irritation clear in his voice. 'We all know she was raped.'

'Not until it's confirmed we don't,' she insisted. 'Which means your questions about whether my client did or not are hypothetical and therefore inadmissible and inappropriate.'

'Inappropriate?' Harvey asked, leaning back in his chair. 'I wonder if the victim's family would consider them inappropriate.'

'Well,' she coldly reminded him. 'Right here and now their opinions are irrelevant. And while we're on the subject of hypothetical – has the victim been formerly identified yet?'

'Not as yet,' Harvey admitted. 'But there's little doubt it's Abigail Riley.'

'But again, you don't know,' Barnwell insisted. 'Not for sure?'

'Unfortunately for her family,' Harvey told her, 'I'm sure they'll make a positive identification.'

'But until they do,' she argued, 'my client can't possibly be expected to answer questions about a person who you don't even know for sure is the victim. He has the right not to incriminate himself. Perhaps you'd be better off asking these questions when you're more sure of the relevant facts, instead of asking questions based on your assumptions.'

He took a deep breath through his nose before replying. 'Very well. Let's check some facts – like what is your relationship with a boy called Michael Dolby?'

Anderson's head snapped up as he glared at Harvey – his eyes wide and wild before his gaze returned to the table. 'No comment.'

'Something you want to tell me?' Harvey asked. 'You look angry with him, or scared.'

'I'm not scared of him,' he answered a little too quickly.

'Paul.' Barnwell reminded him to stick to the plan.

'No comment.' He returned to the script with a shake of his head.

'What's your relationship with him?' Harvey kept with the same line of questioning. 'What's he to you? A friend?'

Anderson squirmed in his seat. 'No comment.'

'Does he ever make you do things you don't want to do?'

'No comment.'

'Do you ever make him do things he doesn't want to do?'

'No comment,' he replied, looking increasingly uncomfortable.

'Was this all his idea?' Harvey kept the pressure on. 'Did he make you abduct, rape and murder Abigail Riley?'

Anderson looked at the ceiling and closed his eyes. 'No comment.'

'Then was it your idea?' Harvey asked. 'Did you make Dolby abduct, rape and murder her?'

'No comment,' he answered, his fists repeatedly clenching and unclenching.

Harvey changed his approach. 'Would you like to take this opportunity to deny it was your idea?

Anderson looked at Barnwell who shook her head. 'No comment.'

'Or take this opportunity to deny your involvement in her rape and murder?' Harvey tried again.

'No comment.'

'I'm sorry,' Barnwell interrupted, 'but what exactly is the evidence against my client?'

'You were seen, Paul,' Harvey told him, directing his answer at Anderson. 'You were seen with Dolby leading Abigail Riley into the underground shelter. The same shelter we later found her body in.'

'A body,' Barnwell pointed out. 'But not necessarily hers.'

'Abigail has been missing for hours now and no other girls that match the description of the dead girl have been reported missing,' Harvey explained. 'I'll risk an assumption we've found Abigail. Sometime later you were seen leaving the shelter, again with Dolby, only this time you were wearing different hoodies – dark-coloured – not light. You'd changed your clothes, Paul. Why did you change your clothes? Why would you do that?'

Anderson cleared his throat. 'No comment.'

'You were carrying a rucksack?' he continued. 'Were the clothes the rucksack?'

'No comment,' Anderson struggled to reply.

'Were they covered in blood?' Harvey asked. 'Was that why you had to change – because your clothes were covered in blood?'

'No comment,' he answered, looking frightened.

'Soaked in Abigail's blood?'

'No comment,' he answered more loudly.

'And the knife?' Harvey pressed unrelentingly forward. 'Was the knife you used to cut her throat also in the bag?'

'No. No comment,' Anderson replied, his voice even louder.

'Was it your idea to bring a change of clothes?'

'No comment,' he angrily spat.

'Because you knew you'd be covered in her blood?'

'No comment.'

'You'd never make it home covered in her blood,' Harvey told him. 'So, you had to take a change of clothing, didn't you?'

'No comment,' he answered.

'Which means you planned it,' Harvey explained. 'You planned to abduct her and take her to that godforsaken place and stab her to death.'

'No,' Anderson shouted. 'No.'

'You planned to take her there,' Harvey continued, speaking faster now. 'Take her there, rape her and then kill her, otherwise why would you have the clothes with you, Paul? Why?'

'No,' Anderson screamed, jumping to his feet. 'No. It wasn't like that.'

'Sit down, Paul,' Harvey told him calmly. He did as he was told and slumped back into his chair, putting his head in his hands as he started to cry. 'Wasn't like what, Paul? If that isn't what happened, then tell me.'

'I think...' Barnwell intervened. 'I think I'm going to have to call a stop to this interview. My client is very young and needs a break. It's also getting late – especially to be interviewing a young person. I suggest we speak again when you actually have some hard evidence instead of just... theories.'

Harvey leaned back in his chair. 'Fine.' He stretched a hand towards the tape machine. 'This interview is concluded.' He pressed the stop button.

Anderson stopped crying and looked up from his shaking hands. 'Can I go home now?' he asked. 'I want to go home.'

'No, Paul,' Harvey told him, sounding suddenly tired and sad. 'Not yet. Maybe not for a very long time.'

Harvey and Alston stood in the custody area checking some paperwork.

'So, what d'you think?' Alston suddenly asked.

'Of Anderson?' Harvey replied without looking up.

'Yeah,' Alston confirmed. 'D'you like him for it?'

Harvey took a couple of seconds before looking up. 'Yeah. I like him for it, but is he the leader or the follower?'

'Maybe they were equals,' Alston suggested.

'No,' Harvey said, shaking his head. 'No. I don't think so. Two killers coming together is rare enough, but two that are equals is pretty much unheard of. One of them is the main instigator. Question is – which one?'

'Anderson looked weak,' Alston reminded him. 'Which points the finger at Dolby.'

'Or Anderson's playing us,' Harvey warned him. 'His tears crocodile tears. Wouldn't be the first time. Whoever killed Abigail is clearly psychopathic and one thing about psychopaths is their ability to act and lie – and act and lie convincingly.'

'What now?' Alston shrugged.

Harvey looked at his watch. 'Think I'll go over to Barnet and have a crack at Dolby before he has a chance to sleep on it.'

'It's late,' Alston pointed out. 'Think the custody officer will allow it?'

'We're investigating the rape and murder of a fourteen-year-old girl,' Harvey reminded him. 'The custody officer will do the right thing. They don't really have a choice. Get Anderson bedded down for the night and see to it his mum gets a lift home or better still, goes to stay with family or friends somewhere other than the estate. Then try and get some sleep yourself. Tomorrow's going to be another very long day.'

18

New Zealand – Present Time

O'Doherty strode through Auckland Airport wearing an expensive suit, sharp shades, looking well-groomed and fit. Just another successful businessman in his late thirties. He joined the mercifully short queue for immigration control and stood in line checking the stocks and shares markets as if he was really interested, aware the airport CCTV cameras could focus in close on his phone's screen if they wanted. He reached the front of the queue and headed to the first desk that became free and handed his Australian passport bearing a false name with immigration stamps from countries all over the world to make it look even more genuine, to the bored-looking immigration officer.

The officer looked inside the passport then looked up at him. 'Can I ask what the purpose of your visit to New Zealand is, Mr Howard?'

'Just some business with my Kiwi colleagues,' he answered

in a perfect West Coast Australian accent. 'I shouldn't be here more than a few days.'

The officer pulled a disinterested face and shrugged before stamping the passport and handing it back to him. 'Have a nice stay.'

An unmarked police car bumped its way along a dirt road of the small farm in Pukekohe, throwing up plenty of dust in its wake. The surrounding area was completely rural – rolling green fields rising and falling in the hilly countryside. It was a far cry from urban, cosmopolitan Auckland. Jameson and Mills looked out of place inside the car wearing their big-city suits and shades as they drove towards the small farmhouse in the distance.

Michael Dolby sensed them coming and stopped cutting wood with his chainsaw before removing his safety goggles to better see the approaching car. He stood unblinking and rigid until the car stopped close to him in a cloud of dust that didn't seem to bother him. Jameson and Mills climbed out of the car and walked slowly towards him, glancing at one another as they approached. Jameson caught sight of a uniformed cop he knew standing on the porch. He acknowledged him by raising one hand. The cop nodded in recognition and went inside. They kept walking until they were close to Dolby and stopped. He looked from one to the other but said nothing.

'Alexander Knight?' Jameson asked.

'Yes,' he answered, laying his chainsaw on the ground.

'I'm Detective Sergeant Ruben Jameson,' he told him before nodding towards Mills. 'This is my colleague, Detective Constable Kate Mills.'

'I know what you are,' Dolby said without a hint of emotion.

The detectives glanced at each other. 'We're from the Serious

Crimes Unit,' Jameson explained. 'We have reason to believe your life could be in danger.'

Dolby jutted his chin towards the farmhouse where two uniformed cops were waiting. 'I know what you believe,' he told them. 'Everything's already been explained to me.'

'Then you know someone killed your friend Paul Anderson?' Jameson tried to provoke a reaction from him.

'He wasn't my friend,' Dolby answered quickly, but calmly.

Jameson looked around the farmland for a few seconds before continuing. 'Well, whatever he was – he's dead now,' he explained. 'Shot twice in the chest and twice in the head. Whoever did it was a professional.'

'I spent eleven years in prison, Detective Jameson,' Dolby replied as he bent over and stacked some of the chopped wood. 'I know the difference between a professional hit and a random attack.'

'Yeah,' he answered, barely able to hide his contempt. 'I suppose you do.' The two men locked eyes.

'Perhaps we'd better go inside,' Mills suggested. 'You need to know what's going to happen next.'

Dolby thought for a couple of seconds before answering. 'Very well... Kate,' he agreed politely. 'Please. After you.'

She turned and headed to the house followed by Dolby and then Jameson, a look of disgust on his face.

They reached the farmhouse and entered to find a neat and tidy kitchen – everything very ordered, the opposite of what Jameson had expected. He'd dealt with men who'd committed terrible crimes before and almost invariably found their personal lives to be a confused mess – something which was usually reflected in their inability to keep themselves or their homes clean or organised. But not Dolby, whose appearance had also wrong-footed him – a good-looking man with a pleasant disposition and disarming smile – although there was a sense of sadness about him. Dolby wasn't like any killer he'd encountered before.

'Our... assignment, Mr Knight,' Mills explained as she looked around the orderly kitchen, 'is to keep you safe.'

'Make sure you don't end up like Paul Anderson.' Jameson couldn't resist a little dig at him.

Mills gave him a cold stare. 'This is a serious situation, Mr Knight,' she continued. 'We need you to understand that.'

'I understand the situation, Kate,' Dolby assured her.

'DC Mills,' she told him. 'It's better you call me DC Mills.'

'Of course,' he agreed with a pleasant smile.

'You need to understand we're here to keep you safe,' she repeated.

'I understand that some amongst you would rather see someone put a bullet through my brain,' Dolby replied as he glanced at Jameson. 'It's all right. I get used to a certain look in people's eyes. Usually cops – prison guards. I understand.'

'Whoever killed Paul Anderson went to a lot of trouble to find him,' Jameson moved on. 'If they can track him down to some nowhere town in Canada, then they can probably track you down to here.'

'Canada?' Dolby smiled wryly. 'Paul was in Canada?'

'Something amusing you?' Jameson asked confrontationally.

'No.' Dolby shook his head. 'Just something from the past. Something I asked DS Harvey – last time I saw him.'

'I understand you've refused to go into protective custody?' Jameson continued, not interested in Dolby's past.

'Isn't that what you are?' Dolby asked. 'Protective custody?'

'You know what I mean,' he told him. 'Your refusal to go to a safe house. Would have been easier all round.'

'For who?' Dolby questioned. 'For you? For me? And how long would I be there? Until you catch whoever killed Paul? And how long would that be? Weeks? Months? If he's as professional as I believe you think he is, maybe never? Then what?' He looked around the house and out the window. 'This farm is all I have, Sergeant Jameson. I'll take my chances here, if it's all the same. Whatever's going to happen is going to happen anyway. Besides, I have every confidence in you and DC Mills.'

The detectives glanced at each other. 'It's likely that Anderson did something to compromise himself,' Mills warned him. 'Which is how he was found. If he hadn't, he may well still be alive.'

'Paul got no less than he deserved,' Dolby said coldly.

Again, Jameson and Mills looked at each other.

'Then you have no... feelings about his death?' Mills asked.

'Only that it was long overdue,' Dolby answered with what sounded like a sigh of relief.

'That's a little cold,' Jameson accused him. 'Don't you think?'

'The world's a better place without him in it,' Dolby replied.

Jameson was silenced for a while before he returned to business. 'You want to stay alive you do exactly as we tell you. Understand?'

'Very well,' Dolby agreed.

'Good,' Jameson told him. 'You can start by showing us around. We need to see everything.'

'Of course,' he politely consented. 'It's only a smallholding. It shouldn't take long to show you the whole place.'

'Good,' Jameson said, sounding anything but grateful. 'Then let's get on with it.'

19

London – 2005

Awhile later Harvey sat in a near identical interview room to the last, but this one was in Barnet Police Station. Matthews sat next to him while Michael Dolby sat on the opposite side of the cheap desk, flanked by his mother and his solicitor, Dominic Powell. Harvey pressed the record button on the machine and filled the room with a five-second shrill buzz. When it stopped, he began.

'This interview is being recorded both for audio and video. It is taking place at Barnet Police Station on 10th February and the time now is about 12.30am. I am Detective Sergeant Fraser Harvey and the other officer present is...'

'DC Connie Matthews,' she introduced herself.

'I'm interviewing,' Harvey continued, 'could you state your name for the tape please?'

'The interview is being recorded on video as well?' Dolby asked.

'Yes,' Harvey answered. 'That's correct. Is that a problem?'

'Just I've never been interviewed before,' he told them. 'But I've seen some on the TV. I thought only the really serious cases were videoed – serial killers and stuff.'

'This is a very serious matter, Michael,' Harvey explained. 'You need to understand that.'

Dolby continued to look calm and together. 'So, you really do think I was involved,' he stated more than asked. 'I'm not just here to be eliminated from your enquiries?'

'We'll get into that once the interview starts properly,' Harvey answered. 'I have a few things to get out the way first. Your name?'

'Sorry,' he said. 'Michael. Michael Dolby. It's just this is all new to me. I'm a little nervous. A bit afraid I suppose.'

'That's understandable,' Harvey reassured him. 'Anyway, as I was saying, also present and acting as your appropriate adult is your mother. Could you say your name clearly please?'

'Fiona Dolby,' she replied, sounding frustrated and annoyed. 'Michael's mother.'

'Fiona,' Harvey explained. 'As Michael's mother you're entitled to be involved in the interview and offer him any advice you care to and to challenge or question anything you don't understand or think Michael doesn't understand. All right?'

'I understand,' she replied, looking at Dolby from the corner of her eyes.

'Also present is...' He looked at Powell who knew the routine.

'Dominic Powell,' he stated. 'Solicitor from Hopkins, Powell and Lumen.'

'Thank you,' Harvey said, concealing his inherent dislike of solicitors. 'Michael – I need to remind you that you are still under caution, which means you do not have to say anything unless you wish to do so, but it may harm your defence if you fail to mention when questioned something you later rely on in court. Anything you do say can be used as evidence. Do you understand the caution?'

'Yes.' Dolby shrugged. 'I think so.'

'I've fully explained the caution to Michael and I'm happy he understands it,' Powell added.

'Fine,' Harvey acknowledged, keen to move on. 'Michael – you have the right to free and independent legal advice anytime night or day and as it is you've chosen to have your solicitor, Mr Powell here, present throughout the interview. If at any time you wish to consult in private with Mr Powell or any other legal representative, just say so and I'll stop the interview while that consultation is organised. Do you understand?'

'I understand,' he replied, looking nervous but composed.

'Okay.' Harvey nodded. 'Michael, it's getting quite late, gone midnight and I appreciate you're only fifteen, so if you feel you're too tired to be interviewed, you need to say so.'

'No.' He shook his head. 'I'm fine. I'd rather get it over with.'

'Mrs Dolby?' he asked.

'If Michael's happy to continue them so am I,' she replied. 'He's an intelligent boy. He knows his own mind.'

'Very well,' Harvey continued. 'Michael – do you know why you've been arrested?'

'I was told it was for the suspected rape and murder of a girl,' he answered without hesitation.

Powell jumped in as quickly as he could. 'My advice to answer all questions *no comment* remains the same.'

'Sorry.' Dolby shrugged. 'No comment.'

'That's right, Michael,' Harvey confirmed. 'You've been arrested for the suspected rape of a young girl. A fourteen-year-old girl who we believe to be Abigail Riley. Can you tell me anything about that?'

Dolby appeared to be struggling to speak, sighing before answering. 'No comment.'

'Brutally murdered after no doubt being brutally raped.' Harvey tried to provoke some emotion. 'Stabbed over fifty times and her throat cut so severely she was almost decapitated. Anything you want to say about that?'

'No comment,' Dolby replied before sighing once more, as if he was frustrated at not being able to talk freely.

'We found her nearly naked, lying on the floor of an old bomb shelter on the Falmouth Estate,' Harvey persisted. 'Discarded like she was nothing. One of the worst crime scenes I've ever been to.' He waited a few seconds for effect before speaking again. 'Her breasts had been cut off.'

'For God's sake,' Mrs Dolby said, looking away from her son.

'No comment,' Dolby insisted, shaking his head.

Harvey picked up on the boy's frustration. 'You look like you want to talk to me, Michael. Like you want to say something. Get something off your chest.'

Dolby shook his head again and breathed deeply through his nose, as if battling an inner turmoil. 'No. No comment.'

'Did you know her?' Harvey asked, backing off somewhat. 'Did you know Abigail Riley?'

Dolby looked at the ceiling and closed his eyes. 'No comment.'

'Were you in any sort of relationship with her?' Harvey continued to probe him – building the pressure that could eventually make him crack.

'No comment,' Dolby resisted.

'Perhaps she was your girlfriend?'

Dolby shook his head. 'No comment.'

'You're shaking your head,' Fraser said. 'Does that mean you weren't having a relationship with her?'

'No comment,' he answered, deliberately holding his head still.

'Then she was a stranger to you?'

'No comment.'

'Then what made you select her as your victim?' he asked. 'Was it because she was so pretty? Did you want her – sexually?'

'No comment,' he answered with closed eyes.

'Sergeant,' Powell interrupted. 'I think your questions are getting a little off-line. You haven't even explained the evidence against my client yet.'

'Fair enough,' he replied after a pause. 'Tell me about your relationship with Paul Anderson.'

'What d'you mean?' Dolby asked, sounding different now – suspicious but also intrigued.

'I mean what is he to you?' Harvey clarified.

'A friend, I suppose,' Dolby answered with a shrug.

'Michael,' Powell interjected. 'I would remind you of my advice.'

'Sorry,' Dolby told him. 'No comment.'

'Strange friends,' Harvey kept going. 'You and he.'

'They should never have been friends,' Mrs Dolby spoke up. 'It was only ever going to lead Michael to trouble, but even Paul couldn't have been involved in something like this. It has to be some sort of case of mistaken identity.'

'Well, if it is, we'll know soon enough,' Harvey told her before continuing. 'How long have you known Paul for?'

'A couple of years,' Dolby answered.

'Michael,' Powell reminded him, sounding slightly irritated.

'Sorry,' Dolby apologised. 'I forgot. I'm not used to this sort of thing. I've never been arrested before. It's not easy.'

'Unlike Paul — who's been arrested and interviewed several times,' Harvey reminded him. Dolby answered with silence. 'So how did you two end up being friends?'

'Paul's all right... I mean, no, no comment. Sorry,' he said, sounding frustrated. 'I just want to go home, you know.'

'I understand.' Harvey tried to sound sympathetic. 'But this is as serious as it could possibly be and we have evidence to suggest you were responsible or at least involved. You need to start accepting the situation you're in. You can't run away from it and it's not going to suddenly disappear. So, if you know something or there's something you want to tell me, then here and now is the time and the place.'

Dolby sighed deeply. 'No comment.'

Harvey deliberately allowed a long, oppressive silence to hang in the room before continuing. He'd seen as many suspects cave in to silence as they had to questioning in his time. 'You were seen by a witness, Michael,' he finally explained. 'You and Paul. They told us everything – you and Paul leading Abigail into the shelter – some time later coming out without her – wearing different clothes. The rucksack you were carrying. You need to talk to me, Michael.'

Tears formed in Dolby's eyes. 'No comment.'

'The bag, Michael,' Harvey told him, calm but deadly serious. 'The bag and the clothes mean it was planned. Makes the whole matter look even worse, if that's possible. Question is who planned it? You or Paul?'

'No comment.'

'Paul's no stranger to trouble,' Harvey reminded him. 'Although I have to admit this is far more serious than anything he's done before. Whereas this is all new for you, Michael. Everything points to Paul as being the ringleader, but we can't prove that unless you talk to me. Paul can say whatever he likes about you unless you talk about him first. He can blame it all on you – lay it all at your doorstep.'

Dolby wiped away tears – although he wasn't sobbing and stayed composed enough to answer. 'No comment.'

'You know, Michael,' Harvey explained, 'hidden in here behind these walls – in this small room – it's easy to trick yourself into believing that everything is... contained – that this is just between the five of us. That we can talk about it and discuss it – argue about it and that somehow you'll find a way out of this... situation. But that's a lie, Michael. Out there, in the real world the wheels of the media will be in full spin. They'll certainly know we have two people in custody by now and if they don't already have your name they will by morning. Probably already trying to think of what they'll call you in their newspapers – teenage terrors, kid killers – that sort of thing. It's real, Michael. This is really happening and it's not something you can contain. You are in the middle of a nightmare. If you can save yourself – if you can possibly save yourself, now is the time to do it.'

Dolby battled with his tears while looking at the ceiling. 'I... I can't. I'm sorry.'

'What d'you mean you can't?' Harvey asked.

Dolby suddenly stiffened, as if he was steeling himself against the questioning – determined not to crack. 'No comment.'

'You said you can't – you can't tell us,' Harvey pressed him. 'What did you mean?'

'No comment,' Dolby answered, stony-faced now. Emotionless.

'Did Paul say something to you about not talking?' Harvey asked. 'Did he threaten you?'

'No comment.' Dolby shook his head.

'I can't help you unless you help yourself, Michael,' Harvey warned him.

'No comment.' Dolby refused to move.

'For God's sake, Michael,' his mother spoke up. 'If Paul made you do something, if he made you do it with him, then you have to tell us.'

'No,' he snapped at her angrily, before recovering his composure. 'No comment.'

'I think maybe we've all had enough for tonight,' Powell intervened. 'It's getting very late and Michael is legally still only a young person. I feel he's coming under undue pressure to waver his right not to answer your questions. He needs his eight hours' statutory rest now – as is his right under the Police and Criminal Evidence Act.'

'Fine,' Harvey agreed after a lengthy pause. 'Fine. I'm concluding this interview so Michael can get some sleep. No doubt he will be further interviewed at some stage tomorrow.' He leaned forward and turned the tape off.

It was deep into the hours that existed somewhere between night and day as Harvey walked the short distance along a corridor back at Colindale before arriving at the open door of Richards' office. He knocked on the door frame and made her look up from the reports spread across her desk.

'You're working late, boss,' he told her.

'You and me both,' she replied. 'Come in and pull up a chair.' He accepted her offer, sitting heavily – yawning and rubbing his temples. Richards opened a desk drawer and pulled out two glass tumblers and a bottle of Scotch. 'Here,' she told him, pouring them both a glass, sliding one across the desk. 'I don't make a habit of it, but I think we both could use it.' She raised her glass. Harvey followed suit. 'Cheers.' She saluted him.

'Good health.' He returned the gesture before they both took a long drink.

Richards nodded towards the TV that was on in the corner – the volume turned low, but audible. It was tuned in to a twenty-four hour news channel showing coverage of the investigation. A correspondent was reporting live from the estate.

'The media are all over this already,' she complained.

'Guessing what's happening with the investigation – guessing what happened to the victim – who she is. They already know we have two in custody and are inching closer to finding out who they are. As soon as that's imminent, I'll slap a restraining order on them to stop them revealing their identities, but that'll only hold them for so long. Once they find out we have kid murderers in the frame they're going to go fucking crazy. Could be the biggest domestic story of the year. I'll keep them off you and the team for as long as I can, but...' She spread her arms wide.

'Appreciated.' He nodded, holding his glass up to her before taking a sip, enjoying the brief moment of pleasure in an otherwise nightmarish day.

'So – what now?' Richards ended his respite. 'Do you like these two kids for it?'

'Yeah, I like them for it,' he confirmed. 'Both answered no comment in interview, although I got the feeling they would have liked to have talked. Briefs got into them and made sure that didn't happen. My guess is Anderson's keen to blame the whole thing on Dolby.'

'And Dolby?'

'Not sure,' he admitted. 'Seems to have some sense of... loyalty to Anderson. Something. I don't know. Can't be sure.'

'Could he be afraid of him?' she asked.

'I suppose,' he replied, sounding unconvinced. 'Maybe if we can get some physical evidence their briefs will encourage them to get their blame in first.'

'But what do you think?' she pressed him, sure that he would already have his own ideas. 'Think we've only got one player here and one watcher? Or could we have genuine joint enterprise? Two bad seeds attracted to each other? It's rare, but it wouldn't be the first time.'

'Don't know and I don't want to guess,' he told her. 'Not with this one. When we get some more evidence, I'll show them and see what happens – even if it's just the formal identification of the victim. One thing's for sure – we're gonna need more than just the eyewitness evidence of a twelve-year-old girl. That's not even enough to get it to trial.'

'Um...' Richards considered for a moment. 'And the victim's identification – any news on when that'll take place?'

'Should be tomorrow,' he told her. 'Morning if we're lucky.'

'Lucky?' she said with an ironic laugh. 'Doesn't feel like being lucky.'

'No,' he agreed, sipping his drink. 'I suppose not.'

'It's a bad one this, Fraser,' she continued after a long pause. 'Really fucking bad.'

'I can't disagree,' he replied with a heavy sigh.

'The sort of case that stays with you forever,' she explained. 'Follows you round your whole career – your entire life. Can drag you down, a case like this – can destroy you if you let it – burn you up from the inside out. It's not like we can go home and chat about it with your wife or my husband and kids. Cases like this we just have to let live inside of us – take them to your grave.'

Harvey didn't know what to say, so he said nothing. The landline phone suddenly rang loudly on the desk, shattering the silence. Richards snatched it up.

'DCI Richards.' Harvey watched her intently, trying to guess what she was hearing. 'I'm listening.' He leaned in closer, his instinct telling him it was something important. 'What exactly?' More silence. 'Anything at the other address?' She waited for the answer. 'Okay. I understand. You find anything else, let me know immediately.' She slowly replaced the handset before turning to him, expressionless. 'That was the search team – they found the rucksack hidden behind the bath panel in Dolby's house. It's full of blood-soaked clothes.'

'Thank God,' he replied, sounding both relieved and excited.

'There's more,' she told him. 'The knife was in the bag too.'

He shook his head in disbelief. 'Anything from Anderson's address?'

'No,' she answered. 'I guess Dolby didn't trust him to get rid of it.' Harvey just frowned. 'You don't look exactly overjoyed. Problem?'

'It's just... if he didn't trust Anderson to get rid of it, why didn't he get rid of it himself?' he asked. 'Why take it home?'

'Because he's still young,' she suggested. 'A fledgling killer still learning his trade? Young criminals, even killers, make stupid mistakes. Best not to overthink it. Important thing is we have the evidence we need.'

'I suppose,' he agreed with a sigh.

Richards raised her glass. 'To a quick result and the chance to move on.'

Harvey returned the gesture, but he couldn't hide the look of concern on his face. 'To a quick result,' he repeated, but his instincts told him things would be anything but quick and that moving on would be all but impossible.

20

The morning light struggled to pierce the thick, reinforced windows into the bland-looking kitchen of the police safe house where Sarah Riley sat at the breakfast table with a cup of tea while Jimmy toyed with a bowl of cereal. Abigail's father, Daniel, paced around the room impatiently, occasionally mumbling to himself inaudibly. DC Diane Sinclair, the family liaison officer, also sat at the table, her attention mainly focused on Jimmy.

'Why are we still here?' Daniel suddenly asked her, his Irish accent betraying his roots. 'Why are we stuck in this God-cursed place? We should be out there looking for Abigail. We don't know the girl they found is her. I want to go home. I want us all to go home.'

'I understand, Mr Riley,' Sinclair said placatingly. 'I really do, but right now it's just not possible. There's a lot of media on the estate digging for information. At this point we can't be sure what they know. The last thing any of us want is them taking pictures and asking questions. You're safe here. Right now, this is the best place to be.'

'But I should be looking for her,' Daniel argued.

'We are looking for her,' Sinclair assured him. 'Search teams, dog units – even the helicopter's up, searching for heat sources. If she's out there, we'll find her.'

'You mean if she's still alive,' he resentfully accused her. 'If she isn't the girl you found in the shelter.'

She tried to think of what to say when her mobile rang – breaking the awkward silence. She checked the caller ID before quickly answering.

'Fraser,' she greeted him.

'The victim's body's been moved from the scene,' Harvey told her. 'I need one of the parents to identify her.'

'Any particular time?' she asked.

'As soon as possible,' he insisted. 'I don't have time to wait.'

'Okay,' she agreed. 'I'll let them know.' She hung up before looking back and forth between Daniel and Sarah. 'The body of the girl we found in the shelter has been released by the pathologist,' she told them. 'I'm afraid I need one of you to see her and tell us if it's Abigail.'

Sarah just closed her eyes and silently started praying – her lips moving but no words coming out. Eventually Daniel nodded slowly.

'I'll do it,' he agreed. 'I'll do it.'

'No,' Sarah insisted. 'We go together. We'll do it together.'

'Okay,' Sinclair replied. 'I'll make some arrangements for Jimmy to be looked after while you're–'

'No,' Sarah interrupted. 'He's family. She's his sister. He comes too.'

'Are you sure?' Sinclair checked. 'This is not the sort of thing I recommend for a child. It can be very–'

'I'm sure. We do this together.' She put an arm around Jimmy's shoulders and pulled him close. 'We do this together.'

'Okay,' Sinclair agreed with a nod. 'I'll make the arrangements.'

❧

Harvey was waiting anxiously outside the small chapel area of the mortuary used for showing the dead to relatives for identifying their loved ones. But it was very different from the scenes often depicted on TV – where the victims were pulled from metal fridges on stretchers and the sheet covering them quickly pulled back for identification before being slammed back into cold storage. It was a separate area specifically set aside so relatives could see their loved ones with as much dignity and as little shock as possible – away from any other bodies or signs of death. He saw the Riley family approaching with Sinclair and braced himself. As they drew closer, he gave a knowing nod to Sinclair before offering his hand to Daniel. 'You must be Mr Riley?'

'I am,' Daniel replied, eyeing him suspiciously, but accepting his hand.

'DS Fraser Harvey,' he told him. 'I'm sorry for what you must be going through.' Daniel just nodded as Harvey looked towards Sarah and her son who clung to her. 'Mrs Riley. Jimmy. It's probably better if Jimmy waits outside with DC Sinclair.'

'No,' she insisted once more. 'He stays with me.'

'Sarah, for God's sake,' Daniel tried to persuade her. 'He's just a boy.'

'He stays with me,' she reiterated, speaking slowly and deliberately.

Harvey looked backwards and forwards between them. 'If you insist.'

'I insist,' Sarah ended it.

'Okay,' Harvey agreed before explaining what was about to happen. 'We've tried to make this as easy as possible for you. She'll be fully covered except for her face. There are some facial... injuries, but her wounds have been cleaned and dressed.

We've done everything we can for her.' He took a breath before continuing. 'Are you ready to see her?' Daniel and Sarah held each other's hands, looking pale and frightened as they nodded together. 'Once we're inside the chapel I'll give you as long as you need, but at some point I'm going to have to ask you if it's Abigail.' Sarah's legs suddenly buckled a little, but Daniel managed to hold her up.

'We understand,' he assured Harvey. 'We need to see her now.'

Harvey opened the door to the chapel and led the others inside the small room mocked up to represent a chapel of rest. The walls were painted purple and there were even purple curtains hanging from them. There was a large wooden crucifix attached to one wall with Christ still nailed in torture to it. In the centre of the room there was a large oblong table with velvet material hanging from its sides to the floor. Flowers surrounded the edge while lights shone down on whatever lay in the middle.

'This way,' Harvey told them softly as he led them towards the table with its sunken centre section in which someone lay beneath a pristine white sheet. Harvey hung back as the family walked tentatively towards the table until they were close enough to look down on the face of the girl who lay inside – her hair clean and brushed and the worst of her facial injuries covered with clean dressings. Her eyes were closed and only her paleness betrayed that she was dead and not just asleep. Her parents simultaneously burst into tears, before Sarah gently rested her head on Abigail's chest – one hand on her face and the other resting on her abdomen. Daniel dropped to his knees sobbing, while Jimmy silently stared at his dead sister wide-eyed, but there was no other reaction from the boy.

Harvey watched the scene for several minutes before speaking. 'I'm sorry. Mrs Riley, I'm so sorry, but I have to ask – is this your daughter? Is this Abigail?'

She lifted her head from her daughter's body and nodded before speaking very quietly – wiping the tears from her face. 'Yes,' she simply confirmed before laying her head back down on Abigail's chest. 'It's Abigail.'

Harvey stepped forward and rested a hand on Sarah's shoulder. 'I'm sorry. I'm really very sorry.'

'Why?' she asked, so quietly he could barely hear her. 'Why would anyone want to do this to her? She never did anything to deserve this. Who would want to hurt my baby? Who did this to my baby?'

Daniel hauled himself back to his feet and looked at his dead daughter – the tears still rolling down his face. 'I'll find him,' he threatened. 'Whoever did it, I'll find him and I'll make him pay.'

'Mr and Mrs Riley,' Harvey explained. 'You should know we already have someone in custody on suspicion of committing this crime.'

'What?' Daniel asked, turning slowly to face him. 'Why didn't you tell us? You should have told us.'

'I'm sorry,' he replied. 'But we needed to wait until after Abigail had been identified.'

'Who?' Daniel demanded. 'Who've you arrested?'

Harvey cleared his throat before answering. 'Two teenage boys. We have two teenage boys in custody.'

'Two boys?' Daniel repeated, his face twisted with hate. 'Two boys did this to my Abigail?' He turned back to look at his daughter. 'Who? I want to know their names.'

'Paul Anderson and Michael Dolby,' Harvey told him after a few seconds. 'Do you know them?'

'No,' Daniel answered, shaking his head. 'No, I don't.'

'I do,' Sarah said, quietly raising her head. 'I know them.'

'How do you know them?' Harvey asked.

'I've seen them,' she explained. 'Hanging about on the estate with the other kids. They looked so... so normal.'

'Is that all?' he checked. 'You've just seen them hanging around?'

'Abigail mentioned them once or twice,' she said through her tears. 'I think she liked Michael, but said Paul was trouble. She stayed away from him. That's all I know.'

'Bastards deserve to die,' Daniel insisted, his voice raised in fury. 'For what they've done, they deserve to die.'

'They won't get away with what they've done,' Harvey tried to reassure them. 'I promise.'

'Is it them?' Sarah asked calmly. 'Are you sure it's them?'

'I can't say too much,' Harvey replied with a sigh. 'Not yet. But the evidence is mounting up against them.'

'But do you believe it's them?' she pressed.

He took a moment before answering. 'Yes,' he told her. 'I believe it's them.'

21

New Zealand – Present Time

Finch was in his office when DCI Rebecca Bishop, a tall, thin, serious-looking woman in her late forties and the boss of the Serious Crimes Unit – entered and closed the door. Finch sank into his chair knowing trouble was coming. Bishop started to pace around the office like a caged tiger. 'Have you seen this?' she demanded, waving a report file in the air. 'That bloody Pom Jameson's more trouble than he's worth. An unauthorised armed operation to arrest an armed robbery crew, with no proper backup, in the middle of the afternoon in Glen Innes. Lucky no one was killed.'

Finch cleared his throat before replying. 'I'm aware of the operation.'

'Operation?' she protested. 'I would hardly call this an operation. More like cowboy-cops thinking they're back in the seventies.'

'From what I understand Jameson received very reliable

information from a registered and highly regarded source only minutes before the robbery was due to take place,' he tried to explain. 'He felt he had to act immediately. He scrambled Sergeant Barnes to provide cover. It was apparently all he had time for.' He took a breath. 'Look – Jameson's a good cop – better than good. Just a little reckless.'

'Too reckless,' she insisted, before seeming to calm down. 'Listen – if Jameson wants to throw his career away that's his problem. He's been given a second chance, but if he doesn't want to take it... But I won't have him drag a good detective like Millsie down with him.'

'I understand,' he assured her. 'I'll speak to him.'

'Make sure you do,' she told him.

'I will,' he promised. 'In the meantime, I've got them both tucked away in Pukekohe providing close protection for Alexander Knight.'

'So I heard.' She nodded. 'Well, they'd better not fuck that up or they'll really be in the shit.' She glanced at her watch as if she needed to be somewhere. 'Just make sure Jameson's got the paperwork around the source for the robbery one hundred per cent. Some people in Professional Standards are very unhappy a man with his background was ever allowed to join the New Zealand Police. Even if they don't nail him for this one – they won't quit.'

'I understand,' he replied.

'I hope you do,' she warned him. 'For Jameson's sake – if not your own.' She spun on her heels and strode from the office leaving him to sink further into his chair.

'For fuck's sake, Ruben.' He cursed him in his absence. 'What the hell did I do to deserve you?'

O'Doherty sat outside a café in Auckland Viaduct sipping a coffee and looking out to sea – just another office worker on a break, when he was approached by a smartly-dressed man in his early sixties who stopped and stood in front of him. O'Doherty continued to sip his coffee.

'Mr Latham?' the man asked, using another of O'Doherty's aliases.

'Yes,' O'Doherty replied casually – unconcerned by the stranger's approach.

'I believe you've been expecting me,' the man said.

'You must be Mr Tucker,' O'Doherty used the prearranged code.

'I am,' the man confirmed, discreetly placing a briefcase on the floor next to him. 'The equipment you requested. Everything's there. Goodbye, Mr Latham.' Without saying another word he turned and walked away without looking back. O'Doherty slid the case casually under the table and continued to stare out across Waitemata Harbour at the glistening dark-blue sea.

Jameson and Dolby walked around the farm together – Dolby occasionally stopping to tidy or fix something minor while Jameson looked out over the surrounding countryside and bush – considering the possibility of a hitman using a high-powered rifle to take Dolby out – thoughts he didn't share with the man he'd been sent to protect.

'I assume looking after me constitutes something of a punishment posting,' Dolby said, trying to break the ice. 'Isn't that what you call it – you cops?' Jameson ignored him. 'So, detective,' he tried again, 'what did you do to deserve a *punishment* posting?'

Jameson continued to ignore him. He didn't want someone like Dolby getting inside his head. 'Why don't you tell me the real reason you wouldn't go to a safe house?' he asked instead.

'I thought I'd already explained,' Dolby answered unconvincingly.

'The others may have believed you,' he said, looking over his shoulder towards the house, 'back there. But I don't.'

Dolby stopped and turned to face him. 'I see,' he replied, before continuing to walk. 'I learnt a lot in prison, Detective Jameson.'

'Meaning?' he asked, struggling to keep up with Dolby's pace.

'Meaning I know how things sometimes work,' he told him. 'In the police – especially back where we both come from I think – judging by your accent.'

'I was in the Met.' He shrugged. 'So what?'

'So, we both know that there's only one way whoever killed Paul got the information,' Dolby explained. 'Only someone in the police could have provided such... detailed information.'

'That's a very serious allegation – for a convicted murderer and rapist,' Jameson warned him. 'And you're forgetting other people would have been involved. The CPS. The Home Office.'

'All the same,' Dolby argued, 'If they provided information about Paul's whereabouts, the chances are they did the same about me. If I moved into a safe house, how long before that was leaked too – and I'd be trapped – like a rat in a barrel.' He took a breath. 'I'd rather take my chances here. Besides – it's possible Paul's death was something else. It was in Paul's nature to be a criminal. A leopard can't change its spots, detective. There's always a chance he upset the wrong people. Paul had a weakness for most things. It made him... vulnerable.'

'And if someone has put a price on your head?' Jameson asked. 'If they find you and somehow get past me? What then?'

'I'm not afraid of dying, detective,' Dolby told him casually. 'Maybe it's what I deserve.'

'Because of what you did?' Jameson jumped on it, half-expecting some kind of confession.

'No.' Dolby disappointed him. 'Because of what I didn't do?'

'I don't understand,' he admitted, looking confused. 'You're saying Anderson died because of what he did, but someone wants to kill you because of something you didn't do? What's that supposed to mean?'

'It doesn't matter.' Dolby shrugged. 'Not anymore.'

'And Anderson,' he asked a little breathlessly. 'You really as pleased to see him dead as I think you are?'

Dolby stopped suddenly and spun to face him, looking cold and serious. 'Like I said – the world's a better place without him in it, detective. Safer.' He turned away and started walking again.

'What do you mean safer?' Jameson demanded, chasing after him.

'Paul could no more change his nature than a scorpion,' Dolby answered without looking back.

'A leopard can't change its spots?' Jameson set his trap, repeating Dolby's own words.

'I guess not,' Dolby agreed.

'Then I'd better keep a close eye on you then,' Jameson told him with an air of satisfaction. 'Hadn't I?'

Dolby stopped and slowly turned his head to face him before nodding once, as if acknowledging Jameson's right to be suspicious, before turning and walking away. Jameson looked back at the farmhouse and considered heading back to join the others – leaving Dolby to take his chances with the hitman who may or may not be watching their every move. After a few seconds, he followed after him, wondering whether if it came to it, he'd be willing to risk his own life to save the life of someone he wouldn't mind seeing dead himself.

22

London – 2005

Harvey and Alston were back in the interview room at Colindale Police Station with Anderson, his mother Donna and their solicitor. The interview was already underway, after all procedural matters had been dealt with as quickly as Harvey could, such was his keenness to ask the questions that burned in his mind.

'Do you remember our previous interview, Paul?' he asked.

'No comment.' Anderson continued in the same manner as he had during his first interrogation.

'There was still some... questions about the identity of the victim,' Harvey reminded him.

'No comment,' he replied with a dismissive shrug, looking tired and drawn.

'You need to know that earlier today the mother and father identified the victim as their missing daughter – Abigail Riley,' Harvey told him, hoping to knock Anderson out of his comfortable routine. 'Makes things look very bad for you, Paul. The witness saw you and Michael Dolby leading Abigail towards the bomb shelter.'

'No comment,' Anderson replied, suddenly looking agitated and upset. Frightened.

'The witness says you led Abigail into the shelter.'

'No comment,' he answered, shaking his head.

'Carrying a rucksack,' Harvey continued, unrelenting.

'No comment.'

'And then they saw you again,' Harvey explained. 'Later – only now you were wearing different clothes, but you were still with Michael. Why did you change your clothes, Paul? In the middle of the day – why did you change your clothes?'

'I just want to go home,' he pleaded as tears began to stream from his eyes. 'I don't want to stay here anymore.'

'Home's a long way away for you, Paul,' Harvey warned him. 'You need to start realising... you need to start dealing with the reality of your situation. You're accused of the murder and rape of a fourteen-year-old girl and the evidence is beginning to stack up against you, Paul. You won't be going anywhere for a very long time.'

'No,' he cried, holding his face in his hands as his head slumped to the table.

'Okay,' Harvey relented, sure that he'd broken Anderson's will to defy him. 'Okay, Paul – take a few minutes.'

His solicitor cleared her throat before speaking. 'The word of one witness isn't enough to convict Paul of rape and murder,' she argued. 'Do you actually have any physical evidence?'

Harvey sighed as if her challenge was nothing more than a minor irritation, before slowly opening his clipboard folder and taking some Polaroid photographs from inside. He spread them neatly across the table like a pack of cards. They were pictures of a heavily bloodstained hoody, trousers, socks, underwear, training shoes and the rucksack. The clothing had been shaped as if someone was wearing them for the purposes of display.

'What are these?' Barnwell asked, sounding concerned.

'Photographs of clothing found in this rucksack,' he explained, tapping the picture of the bag. 'The rucksack we found hidden in Michael Dolby's home address – behind the panel of the bath.' He paused, waiting for Anderson to raise his head and look at the photographs. 'Do you know why I'm showing you photographs instead of showing you the clothes themselves, Paul?' Anderson shook his head. 'Because they're still soaked in blood – the blood of Abigail Riley. We have to dry them in a special room before they can be bagged as evidence. Too soaked in blood to be bagged, Paul.'

'I never touched her,' Anderson ranted. 'Maybe I was there, but I swear I never touched her. It was Michael. Michael did it. It was all Michael's idea.'

'Paul,' Barnwell intervened. 'I would remind you of my advice to say nothing. These clothes were found at Michael Dolby's home – not yours.' She turned to Harvey. 'That is correct isn't it?'

'It is,' Harvey confirmed.

'And therefore, they are not connected to my client,' she argued.

'They will be,' Harvey assured her. 'It's only a matter of time before DNA evidence links the clothes to Paul – the smallest drop of his blood, a fleck of skin, a trace of semen or saliva. And then there's the evidence to be processed from the victim herself. You can't argue with DNA, Paul.'

'It was Michael,' Anderson insisted once more. 'He made me do it to her. I... I thought he'd kill me if I didn't.'

'Made you do what to her?' Harvey seized on it.

'Have...' Anderson began before stalling for a few seconds. 'Have sex with her.'

Harvey let the magnitude of what Anderson had said sink in for a few seconds before continuing. 'Did he force you to kill her too?'

'No,' Anderson angrily insisted. 'No. I didn't kill her. I swear. It was Michael.'

Harvey gave him a few moments to compose himself before tapping the photographs on the table. 'Which of these clothes are yours?'

'I advise you not to answer that,' Barnwell intervened.

'We're beyond playing games,' Harvey warned her. 'Now, which of these clothes are yours?' Anderson leaned forward before slowly selecting several photographs and pushing them towards Harvey who looked at them for a second before speaking. 'They're covered in blood – as much blood as is on the other clothes – Dolby's clothes. If you didn't help kill her then how did you get as much blood on you as Dolby?'

Anderson closed his eyes and shook his head before answering – struggling to force himself to say the words. 'Because... because he'd already stabbed her before I had sex with her. She was already bleeding.'

'Jesus Christ,' Donna said before covering her mouth with her hand, looking pale and sick.

'She was already dead?' Harvey asked.

'No,' Anderson replied, staring down at the table. 'He hadn't... he hadn't stabbed her in the chest yet.'

'Or cut her throat?' Harvey reminded him.

'No.' Anderson shook his head.

'Or cut off her breasts,' he continued relentlessly.

'No,' Anderson confirmed. 'No... I don't feel very well.'

'Her breasts that we couldn't find at the scene,' Harvey told him. 'So someone must have taken them from the bunker. Was that you?'

'No,' he pleaded. 'Michael must have taken them.'

'Why would he do that?' Harvey asked.

'I don't know,' Anderson insisted, shaking his head. 'Why don't you ask him?'

'But she was probably already dying.' Harvey continued. 'You had sex with a fourteen-year-old girl who was already dying?'

'Oh my God,' Donna spoke again, shaking her head in disbelief and horror – looking like she wanted to run from the room and never come back.

'He made me,' Anderson almost shouted, tears flowing freely down his face as he looked around the room for someone to believe him. 'He made me do it all. You don't understand what he's like. He planned it all. He... he enjoyed it. He was laughing. When he was raping her – when he was stabbing her, he was laughing.' He paused, trying to compose himself. 'You don't know what you're dealing with. I'm telling you he's sick. There's something wrong with him. He talked about Abigail for weeks. Every time we saw her on the estate, he'd be going on about her – about how pure she was and... and how loved she was.'

'Loved?' Harvey jumped on it. 'What did he mean how loved she was?'

'I don't know,' Anderson answered, sounding desperate. 'He didn't explain and I didn't ask. You don't ask Michael to explain himself.'

'Why?' Harvey asked, intrigued.

Anderson gave a little laugh, as if surprised that they didn't already know. 'You just don't.'

'So,' Harvey continued, 'you want us to believe that a sixteen-year-old boy, who's never been in trouble in his life is some sort of dangerous psychopath who threatened you, forced you to help him abduct, murder and rape a fourteen-year-old girl?'

'Yes,' he pleaded. 'Yes. He used me. He set me up. That's the only reason he hasn't done this before – because... because he needed someone to blame it on.'

'And that someone is you?' Harvey asked, sounding sceptical.

'That's what he's doing, isn't it,' Anderson argued. 'Saying it was me?'

'Not yet he's not,' Harvey told him. 'But when he finds out what you've been saying I dare say he'll turn on you. Just like you have on him.'

'What?' Anderson asked, confused. 'You mean... he hasn't said it was me? He... he didn't try to blame me?'

'Not yet,' Harvey explained, studying every move and expression Anderson made – looking for some sign of who he really was. 'But we're still to reinterview him about the new evidence that's come to light.'

'You can't,' Anderson pleaded in a panic. 'You can't tell him what I've said. He'll kill me. He'll find me... he'll find me and he'll kill me.'

'He's a co-defendant,' Harvey reminded him. 'He has the right to know what you've accused him of.'

'Please,' Anderson begged. 'I'll tell you everything I know about him – everything about what happened. I'll go to court and give evidence about him, but you have to give me immunity. You have to give me a new identity and stuff – hide me like I've seen in films.'

'That's make-believe, Paul,' Harvey told him truthfully. 'Maybe in America, I don't know, but there is no such thing as immunity in British law. You have to admit your crimes and do time for them. In your case a lot of time. You've committed a terrible crime and now you have to pay for it. Best I can do is promise you Rule 43. At least you'll be kept away from the rest of the prison population where you'll be safer. Prison can be a dangerous place for sex offenders. Even young ones.'

'No,' Anderson shouted and banged his fists on the table. 'I didn't do anything. You can't do this to me. You have to help me.'

'You've admitted to rape and assisting in a murder, and that's if I believe everything you've said, which I don't,' Harvey explained in a raised voice. 'I don't have to help you with anything. What I have to do is get justice for Abigail and her family, which means putting you before the court with enough evidence to lock you away for the rest of your life. That's what I have to do.'

'But it wasn't me,' Anderson pleaded again before burying his head in his hands. 'It wasn't me.'

'I need to speak with my client in private,' Barnwell demanded, her voice sounding croaky and unsure. 'As a consequence of what's been said I need to give him further advice.'

'Yes,' Harvey agreed, leaning back in his chair. 'I'm sure you do.' He looked at the cowering Anderson for a few seconds, feeling both loathing and pity for the boy, before reaching out towards the tape recorder. 'This interview is concluded.'

Harvey and Alston stood next to a vending machine in a corridor at Colindale Police Station. Harvey was hitting the machine with the palm of his fist in frustration as it swallowed his coins, but wouldn't provide the drink he'd paid for.

'Damn these thieving things,' he complained. 'Should have gone to the canteen.'

'So, what you think?' Alston asked, ignoring Harvey's moaning.

'Anderson?' Harvey shrugged. 'The only chance he's got is to make a jury believe Dolby made him do it – that he genuinely feared for his life if he didn't do as he was told. If that's his defence then it's down to him to prove it. Not for us to prove it's a lie.'

'No jury's going to believe him,' Alston insisted. 'He's fucked.'

'Yes. Yes he is,' Harvey agreed. 'But the question remains – was he the leader or the follower?'

'Who gives a shit?' Alston waved it away. 'Doesn't matter – so long as they both go down?'

'I just like to know what I'm dealing with,' Harvey told him, trying to conceal his irritation at Alston's lack of desire to know the absolute truth.

'Seemed scared enough of Dolby in the interview,' Alston replied.

'Or he's putting it on,' Harvey explained. 'Working towards his defence. Don't forget he lied to us about raping her – said he'd never touched her, until he realised DNA would say otherwise – then he switches his story to Dolby made him do it. We've seen it all before – a suspect building their lies around the evidence.'

Alston looked around to make sure no one was listening. 'So, he's lying to save his own skin,' he said quietly. 'He was there – in some way involved – that's good enough for me. Let them turn on each other and send each other down for life. This is a bad one, Fraser. Everyone just wants a result. If they never tell us exactly who did what, who cares? So long as they go down for a very long time everyone'll be happy.' He looked around to make sure they weren't being eavesdropped on. 'We push too hard to find out who was the leader and we might just hand the other some sort of defence. Nobody wants that – least of all the powers that be. Let's just put this one to bed and move on.'

'And the truth?' Harvey asked, keeping his voice low. 'I mean the absolute truth of what happened in that godforsaken place. Don't you want to know?'

'Not if it plays into Anderson's hands,' Alston replied. 'Or

Dolby's or whichever one of them is trying to play us.' He took a moment to breathe. 'A murder like this is like... like a black fucking cloud – hangs over the whole country. The closer you are to it the darker things get. It's not a good place to be for long. With what they're saying about each other and the forensics to come we can bury the both of them. I don't give a damn who did what. They were both there – both had a hand in raping and killing a fourteen-year-old girl. Let's just bury the evil bastards and move on.'

'And if one of them was under duress to do what they did?' Harvey questioned. 'We send an innocent kid to prison for a very long time?'

'They're not the victims,' Alston reminded him. 'Abigail Riley's the victim. Maybe one of them is... less guilty than the other, but they're both damned by what they did. If they spend the rest of their lives in prison, it'll be no more than they deserve.'

'Yeah, well, that won't happen,' Harvey explained. 'Too young. Judge couldn't do it even if he wanted to. Maybe they'll get fifteen years – do maybe eight or nine then out.'

'Jesus.' Alston shook his head. 'For what they did? How we supposed to tell her family that's justice – that Abigail at least has justice. We're giving them nothing.'

'We're giving them everything we can,' Harvey told him before letting out a long sigh. 'The rest's got nothing to do with us. Remember that or you won't last long in this job.'

'Not entirely sure I want to anymore,' Alston confessed, before quickly moving on. 'So, what now?'

'I need to get over to Barnet and interview Dolby,' Harvey answered. 'Give him the good news about what Anderson's saying.'

'Want me to come with you?' Alston offered.

'No,' Harvey said. 'Take a break. I'll pick up Connie when I get there. You watch things here. I want to hear what Dolby has to say about what we found in his house. Anything changes here – you let me know. You let me know immediately.'

'No problem,' Alston assured him, but Harvey was already walking away, his mind turning to Dolby and how best to use Anderson's treachery to make him talk.

23

New Zealand – Present Time

O'Doherty was in his Auckland hotel room stripped to his boxer shorts, covered in a sheen of sweat as he finished his workout routine with a long series of perfect push-ups before springing to his feet and heading for the bathroom. He splashed his face with cold water and stared at himself in the mirror before patting his face dry with a towel, turning the lights off and heading back into the bedroom. He sat on the bed next to the briefcase he was handed earlier before unlocking and opening it to reveal a semi-automatic pistol inside, plus a silencer, spare magazine and ammunition. He took his time to assemble the pistol, making sure it all appeared to be working before breaking it back down, packing it away and locking it in the safe. He stretched the stiffness out of his lithe body and headed to the shower.

~

Jameson arrived late back at his home in Grey Lynn and made his way to the kitchen where he found his nanny-cum-housekeeper-cum-general-lifesaver, Rose Leofa, cooking away with an energy that belied her sixty years and large frame as she sang to herself in her native Samoan tongue. She looked up from the stove when she heard him enter. 'You're late,' she accused him in a friendly, motherly tone.

'Not that late,' he argued.

'At least you came home this time,' she said with a mischievous grin.

He cleared his throat, slightly embarrassed. 'You er... you were okay covering for me?' he asked.

'You're a young man, Ruben,' she told him, looking him up and down, not disapprovingly. 'Don't be afraid to live a little.' She turned back to the stove. 'I hope she was worth it.'

'I...' he struggled to know what to say.

'Dinner won't be long,' she chuckled, saving him any more blushes.

'Okay,' he nodded. 'I'm just going to look in on Jenny.'

'Remember to knock first,' Rose reminded him. 'She's thirteen now.'

'Yeah, yeah,' he waved it away and headed off out of the kitchen. Moments later he was standing outside his daughter's bedroom, knocking and waiting to be invited before entering.

'Who is it?' he heard her say on the other side of the door.

'It's me,' he replied. 'Can I come in?'

'If you want,' she told him.

He turned the handle and entered the typical bedroom of a thirteen-year-old daughter – a mixture of young girl and young woman – posters of pop stars on the walls, but she still had her teddies and dolls on the bed.

'You not getting a little too old for dolls?' he asked.

'They're just there,' she said, glancing at the bed before looking at him. 'Can't be bothered to tidy them away.'

'Uh-huh.' He shrugged, a little uncomfortable. 'How was your day?'

'Same as any other,' she answered disinterestedly.

'Make any new friends?' he pried.

'I don't need any new friends,' she insisted. 'I already have lots of friends.'

'Back in London?' he asked, a little frustrated, not wanting to get drawn into the same conversation they'd been having for weeks. Jenny just shrugged. 'I meant here – in Auckland.'

'You didn't come home last night,' she said, changing the subject.

'I... I picked up a new assignment,' he half-lied. 'Had to work through the night.'

'What's the assignment?'

'Ah, nothing important,' he said, trying to convince her, not wanting to tell her its true nature. 'Just long hours is all.'

'So you won't be around much then?' she accused him.

'I'll do my best,' he assured her. 'At least I'm on the day shift now.' She slowly turned her back on him and returned to her studies. He tried to rub the tension out the back of his neck, knowing this was her way of letting him know she wasn't happy with him. 'Don't stay up too long studying. You need your sleep.' He couldn't see her rolling her eyes. He didn't know what else to say so, instead, he backed out the room and closed the door – pausing on the other side before heading towards the kitchen where Rose was still cooking.

'How's work?' she asked.

He unclipped the holster containing his pistol and emptied his pockets onto the kitchen table. 'Fine,' he lied. 'Busy.'

Rose looked over her shoulder at the gun on the table. 'I wish you wouldn't bring that thing into this home,' she told him.

'I'll lock it away later,' he assured her, sounding disinterested as he thought about Jenny.

'Thought you were all supposed to leave them at work.' Rose wouldn't let it go.

'Yeah, well,' he casually explained, 'I've been put on a special assignment. I'm allowed.'

'Special assignment?' she asked excitedly.

'Close protection,' he elaborated without wanting to say more.

'Oh?' she said. 'And who needs your close protection?'

'You don't want to know,' he told her.

'Sure I do.' She smiled, her eyes wide with interest.

'I can't tell you much.' He sighed. 'It's... confidential.'

'Dangerous?'

'No,' he reassured her. 'Well, no more than a lot of the stuff I deal with.'

'And Jenny?' she asked as she turned to face him. 'If something happens to you?'

'Nothing's going to happen to me,' he said, dismissing it. 'I know what I'm doing. I'm careful. I just got to babysit some ex-con for a while. Somebody may be trying to find him – that's all.'

'Someone who wants to harm him?' she pressed. He just shrugged. 'Someone who wants to kill him?' He shrugged again. 'And what did this man do to make someone want to find and kill him?'

He gave a long, resigned sigh before answering. 'A long time ago he raped and killed a teenage girl – when he was still in London.'

'How long is a long time?' she asked.

'About fifteen years,' he told her.

'Only fifteen years?' she checked. 'For what he did? Why was he released so soon and how did he end up living here? I didn't think people like that were allowed to come here.'

'Because he was only fifteen or sixteen when he did it... and he's here because if he'd stayed in the UK he'd have almost certainly been recognised and God knows what would have happened to him. Would have probably been lynched,' he explained. 'New Zealand government did some sort of swap deal.'

'He committed those terrible crimes when he was only sixteen?' she asked, barely able to believe it. He just nodded. 'I've seen programmes on the TV about people like that. They say people like that can't be changed. Can't be... cured. Most are turned into these monsters when they're only children themselves, but some, a tiny few, are just born that way. They say they're the really bad ones. That they can't stop what they're doing once they start. They have to be stopped.'

'You've been watching too much TV,' he told her, although he knew she wasn't wrong. But was that Dolby? If he was a killer, he was like no other killer he'd ever met before. Had the leopard somehow learnt to change his spots or had he never killed in the first place? He decided he needed to know a lot more about the man he was supposed to keep alive. 'Real life is more complicated. There are many different types of murderers – all motivated by different things – from the mentally ill to sexual deviants. Don't get the feeling this one is either of them. Besides, I'm supposed to be keeping him safe, not investigating him.'

'Maybe you shouldn't try too hard to do that,' she replied. 'Doesn't sound like he's worth you risking your neck for.'

'He's not,' he agreed. 'It gets too close for comfort – he's on his own.'

24

London – 2005

Harvey was back in the same interview room at Barnet Police Station he'd used the previous day. Matthews was again present as was Dolby's mother and his solicitor. The tapes were already recording – the legal procedures and introductions completed. Dolby sat opposite him looking calm and collected, if a little tired, though clean-cut and respectable in the change of clothes his mother had brought for him – a marked contrast to Anderson who had still been dressed in his white paper-like forensic suit. He looked anything other than a killer.

'When we interviewed you yesterday, Michael,' Harvey began, 'there was still some small doubt over the victim's identity. I can now confirm that the victim is indeed Abigail Riley. Is there anything you'd like to say about that?'

Dolby moved a little uncomfortably in his chair but maintained eye contact. 'No comment.'

'You and Paul Anderson were the last people to be seen with

her before her body was discovered in the bomb shelter,' Harvey explained, concealing his slight disappointment that the revelation hadn't produced more of a reaction from Dolby, or even a spontaneous confession.

'No comment.' Dolby remained unmoved.

'And then later you were seen in different clothes,' Harvey continued.

'No comment.' Dolby stood firm.

'But still carrying the same rucksack you'd been seen with earlier,' he told him.

'No comment,' Dolby answered, momentarily closing his eyes. Harvey noticed it, but so apparently did his solicitor.

'We've already discussed this in the previous interview.' Powell had stepped in to try and lessen the pressure on his client. 'Is there any point in going over it again?'

Harvey pulled out the same Polaroids of the blood-stained clothes he'd shown Anderson and spread them across the table like playing cards. 'Photographs, Michael,' he explained. 'Photographs of the clothes we found still in the rucksack – hidden behind the panel of the bath in *your* home.'

'Oh my God, Michael,' Fiona said, lifting her hands to the sides of her face. 'My God, what have you done? What have you done?'

'Nothing,' he snapped at her. 'I haven't done anything. You don't know anything. None of you know anything.'

'Then talk to us,' Harvey encouraged him. 'Help us understand.'

He looked to the ceiling shaking his head as a single tear leaked from each eye. 'No comment.'

Harvey took his time before continuing. 'Do you know why I'm only showing you Polaroids of your clothes instead of the clothes themselves?' he asked, trying the same tactic he'd used on Anderson. 'D'you know why I'm doing that, Michael?'

Dolby shook his head and wiped away the tears. 'No.'

'Because the clothes were so heavily soaked in blood that they're still drying,' Harvey explained. 'We can't bag them as evidence until the blood is dry. Until Abigail's blood is dry on your clothes, Michael–'

'I don't feel very well,' Fiona interrupted. 'I need to take a break.'

'Michael?' Harvey ignored her, desperate not to lose momentum.

'No comment.' Dolby said, returning to his stock answer.

Harvey studied him for a while before remembering Fiona's plea. 'You all right?' he asked her. 'Want some water?'

'Yes,' she replied, looking white with shock. 'Yes please. That would be good. Thank you.'

He gave a nod to Matthews, who understood as she got to her feet and headed for the door. 'DC Matthews is just leaving the interview room to get Mrs Dolby some water,' Harvey explained for the benefit of the recording before turning his attention back towards Dolby. 'The clothes in the photographs, Michael – do you recognise any of the clothes?'

'No comment,' he answered, but looked stressed and agitated.

'The clothing will be a minefield of forensic evidence,' Harvey told him. 'Do you understand that?'

'I suppose,' Dolby slipped.

'Could end up telling us who really did what to Abigail,' he explained. 'You need to tell me what clothing is yours and which is Paul's. You don't want to take the blame for something he may have done? Or do you? Is this what this is? Are you protecting him?' Dolby's eyes narrowed, but he said nothing. 'Maybe when I tell you what he said when I reinterviewed him this morning, you won't feel like protecting him so much?'

'If my client's co-accused has made any allegations against him then we have the right to know,' Powell argued.

Harvey waited a few seconds before replying. 'He said it was all Michael's idea,' he revealed. 'That it was all your idea, Michael. Everything. He admitted to raping the girl, but said he only did it because he was afraid of what you would do to him if he didn't.'

Dolby stared wide-eyed in disbelief. 'You're lying. He wouldn't say that.'

'Said you and only you were responsible for her death.' Harvey twisted the knife. 'That he stood and watched as you firstly raped her and then killed her – but not before you'd forced him to rape her too.'

'No,' he said, his voice trembling with anger as he shook his head continuously. 'No. No. Paul is my friend. He wouldn't do this to me.'

'He just did, Michael.' Harvey pushed the blade in deeper. 'I can't lie to you about what Paul said in the interview, as Mr Powell will no doubt confirm.' Dolby quickly looked at his solicitor who just nodded slowly. 'He's blaming it all on you, Michael. Everything.'

Dolby covered his face with his hands. Harvey gave him the time he needed to recover before he was able to speak. 'He told me... he told me that if we said nothing everything would be all right,' Dolby eventually explained.

'When did he tell you that?' Harvey asked. 'When did he say that?'

'After... after he'd killed her,' Dolby answered, his face still hiding behind his hands.

'After he killed her?' Harvey checked.

'I didn't touch her,' Dolby suddenly declared. 'I swear I didn't touch her.'

'Be careful what you say, Michael,' Harvey told him. 'If the forensic evidence contradicts you, you'll just look like you're lying to save your own skin. No one will believe anything else you say.'

'It won't contradict me,' Dolby assured them, sounding confident. 'I never touched her. I didn't hurt her.'

'But both sets of clothes we found in your house are covered in blood,' Harvey reminded him. 'You must have been wearing at least one of those sets – so if you never touched her, how come you ended up covered in blood?'

'Because...' he began before faltering. 'Because I tried to help her – before... before he made sure she was dead, when I thought there was still a chance to save her – I tried to stop the bleeding, but he dragged me off her and then he... he used the knife... on her throat.'

Harvey paused for a second as the image of Anderson drawing the knife across Abigail's throat flashed in his mind. 'For the record, which of the clothes in these photographs were you wearing?' he asked when his mind cleared.

Dolby leaned forward and examined the pictures on the table for a few seconds before pointing to several of them. 'These,' he admitted.

Harvey carefully collected them together. 'For the benefit of the tape Michael has identified exhibits NM/1, 2, 5, 6 and 8. The notes made on the back of the Polaroid photographs describe those items of clothing as a light-grey Fred Perry polo hoody – blue Armani jeans – white Calvin Klein underwear – white socks and a pair of white Nike trainers. Can you confirm these were the clothes you were wearing at the time of Abigail's murder?'

Dolby nodded his head mournfully. 'Yes.'

'And the other clothing?' Harvey continued. 'Who does it belong to?'

Dolby looked all around the room, searching for a way out before closing his eyes and answering the question. 'Paul.'

'Paul Anderson?' Harvey asked, wanting absolute clarity.

'Yes,' Dolby confirmed. 'Paul Anderson.'

'Yet all the clothing was found hidden in your house,' Harvey questioned. 'Behind the bath panel?'

'Paul made me take them and hide it,' he insisted. 'He said they'd be too easy to find in his flat. There was more room in my house. More places to hide it.'

Harvey tapped the picture of the weapon. 'And the knife?' he asked. 'It was found in the same bag as the clothing.'

'Paul's,' Dolby answered. 'He made me take it.'

Matthews re-entered the room carrying a plastic cup of water before he could ask the question on his lips.

'DC Connie Matthews re-entering the interview room,' she told the tape before handing the water to Fiona.

'Thank you,' she said, taking the drink as Matthews settled back into her chair. When she was done, Harvey continued.

'And the clothing you changed into?' he asked. 'Where's that now?'

'At home,' he replied. 'Washed. Hanging up drying.'

'Describe them for me,' Harvey ordered.

'A dark-red hoody.' Dolby shrugged. 'Underneath that I had a white T-shirt.'

'Trousers? Shoes?' Harvey pressed.

'Grey Lonsdale tracksuit trousers,' Dolby recalled. 'My red Puma trainers.'

'Underwear? Socks?' Harvey pushed for everything.

'I... I don't remember.' Dolby shook his head. 'No socks.'

'Have you showered since the murder?' Harvey checked.

'Yes.' He nodded his head. 'As soon as I got home. I had to. I couldn't stand...'

'Couldn't stand what?' Harvey encouraged him.

'Her blood on me,' he admitted, looking like he was close to throwing up. 'It was all over me.'

'Dear God, Michael.' Fiona shook her head in disgust. 'Dear God, what have you done?'

'But your hands must have been covered in blood,' Harvey pointed out. 'Your faces. Weren't you worried about someone seeing you before you got home?'

'We had water,' he explained. 'A bottle of water. We used it to wash the blood off our hands and faces – as best we could.'

'Whose is the rucksack, Michael?' Harvey deliberately changed the immediate subject – the information he'd already gained logged in his mind to be used later – when it would cause most damage.

'Mine,' Dolby admitted. 'Why?'

'So you had water and a change of clothes,' Harvey recapped. 'You were very well prepared.' He let his words sink in to Dolby for a few seconds. 'Who brought the change of clothes?'

'I brought mine and Paul brought his own,' he answered.

'But they were all in your rucksack,' Harvey reminded him.

'Paul gave me his when we met up,' he tried to explain.

'And the water?' Harvey delved deeper into the details.

'Paul's,' he answered without hesitating. 'He gave it to me – with his clothes.'

'Whose idea was it to bring all these things?' Harvey closed in.

'Paul's,' he insisted. 'Paul told me what to bring.'

'So, you arranged to meet Paul?' Harvey lined up his pins.

'Yes.' He nodded, looking slightly confused and wary.

'With spare clothes?' Harvey clarified.

'Yes,' Dolby replied. 'I've already told you all of this.'

'And water and a rucksack?'

'Yes,' Dolby answered – confusion turning to irritation. 'Yes.'

'So together you planned what you were going to do after you raped and killed her?' Harvey ambushed him, his voice slightly raised for effect.

'No,' he argued in a panic. 'It wasn't like that.'

'Not like that,' Harvey continued to speak in a raised voice. 'Come on. Then what the hell did you think you were going to do with a change of clothes and water? You tell me, Michael. What did you think you were going to do?'

'I... I don't know,' he replied unconvincingly. 'Paul didn't say. He just said he had an idea – that we were going to mess around and have some... some fun.'

'Have some fun?' Harvey asked, sounding incredulous. 'Is that what you thought you were going to do when you were leading Abigail to the shelter? When you were leading her to her death? When you both raped her?'

'No,' Dolby insisted, animated and upset. 'No. I never touched her except... except to try, to try and stop it – to try to stop him, but it was too late. It all happened too fast and then it was over. Nothing seemed real anymore.'

'What about when you cut her breasts off?' Harvey demanded. 'Did that feel real?'

'Oh Jesus Christ,' Fiona exclaimed, covering her mouth and gagging slightly.

'I didn't do that,' Dolby pleaded. 'I didn't even know that had happened to her.'

'How could you not?' Harvey asked.

'He must have done it when I wasn't looking,' he offered in explanation. 'Or went back later when he was alone. I don't know.'

'I don't believe you,' Harvey calmly told him. 'Michael. I don't believe a word either of you have said. I think you planned this together – that you took Abigail to that shelter with both the intention of raping her and killing her and that you thought you were clever enough to get away with it, but you're not. You made mistake after mistake and those mistakes are going to bury the both of you.'

'Then do it,' Dolby told him, suddenly very calm, as if resigned to his seemingly hopeless position. 'Do it. I want you to do it. My life is over anyway. I don't care. I don't care what you do to me.'

'Why?' Harvey asked, slightly caught off guard by Dolby's surrender. 'Why don't you care?'

Dolby took a few seconds to compose himself before answering. 'Because... because I should have stopped him,' he told them. 'But I didn't. I just stood and watched. I should have dragged him off her – I should have... I should have taken the knife off him, but I didn't... because I was afraid of him and now she's dead and I'm here.' He took a deep breath. 'Paul... Paul should have killed me as well. My life's over anyway. I deserve whatever happens to me. Maybe I could have stopped him – maybe I couldn't, but I should have tried. But I did nothing.'

Harvey gave it a few seconds before continuing. 'But you knew he was going to do something to her – when you were leading her towards the shelter – you knew he was going to do something to her.'

'No,' he insisted, shaking his head. 'No. I didn't.'

'Then what did you think he was going to do to her?'

'Nothing,' he tried to persuade them. 'He said... he said he'd heard from some other boys on the estate that Abigail was... that she liked boys. That she'd let you kiss her and stuff.'

'Stuff?' Harvey asked.

'Maybe other things – if she liked you.'

'Like what?' Harvey pressed.

'I don't know,' he replied, squirming in his chair. 'Touch her, I suppose.'

'And did she give you or Paul permission to touch her at all?' Harvey checked.

'No,' he answered, sounding frustrated. 'Like I said – it was only what Paul told me he'd heard.'

Harvey paused while he considered what direction to go in next. 'You and Paul were seen pulling her or at least encouraging her to go to the shelter with you. You had hold of her, but I'll admit it doesn't appear as if you were exactly dragging her. She doesn't appear to have been struggling. So how did you get her to go with you?'

'She knew Paul, a bit,' he explained. 'He told her he wanted to show her something. Something really cool.'

'And?' Harvey encouraged.

'She wasn't that keen, so we... we pulled her along a bit,' he admitted. 'She wasn't fighting or anything.'

'And you're saying you went along with it in the hope of some sort of sexual encounter with Abigail?' Harvey asked.

'I suppose so.' He sighed.

'And when that wasn't forthcoming you and Paul raped her?' Harvey accused him.

'No,' Dolby snapped back. 'No – I never touched her.'

'Except when you were trying to save her.'

'Yes,' he insisted, sounding shocked that Harvey didn't appear to believe him. 'I didn't rape her – Paul did. Do your forensic tests – you'll see. You'll see.'

'I don't believe you,' Harvey told him straight. 'I don't believe either of you. The rucksack, the change of clothes, leading the victim together – your victim selection. You planned it – you planned it together and you raped and killed her together – a fourteen-year-old girl who never hurt anyone and now she's dead.'

'No,' Dolby insisted, banging both fists on the table. 'No. Do your tests and you'll see. You'll see.'

'Yes, Michael – we will see,' Harvey told him before taking a long pause to let things settle. 'This could be your last chance, Michael. Your last chance to tell me what really happened. The truth.'

'I am telling you the truth,' he refused to waiver. 'I swear I'm telling you the truth.'

'Then we're just going around in circles,' he said. 'I've got nothing more I want to ask.' He stretched a hand to the tape recorder. 'This interview is concluded.'

25

New Zealand – Present Time

Jameson entered the small police station in Pukekohe, flashed his badge to the constable on the front desk and was allowed into the building where he went looking for the man he'd come to see. He found the office he wanted and knocked on the frame of the open door, making the heavily built man in his fifties with greying hair wearing a sergeant's uniform look up from the files spread across his desk.

Jameson flashed his badge again. 'I'm looking for Sergeant Hodges,' he told the man.

'Well then I'd say you found him,' Hodges cheerily announced, getting to his feet and offering his hand.

He entered the office and accepted the outstretched hand. 'Detective Sergeant Ruben Jameson, Serious Crimes Unit.'

'Serious Crimes?' Hodges smiled. 'Well, if you're looking for serious crime, you're in the wrong place. Plenty drunk and disorderly at the weekends – a few assaults. That's about it.'

'I'm here to ask about Alexander Knight,' he told him straight.

'I see,' Hodges replied, suddenly looking very serious – as he walked to the door and closed it, before returning to his desk and sitting. 'And what do you want to know about Alexander Knight?'

'I understand you know his true identity?' he asked. 'Michael Dolby?'

'Yes,' Hodges confirmed. 'I know who he really is and what he is. The only other person who knows is the inspector here. We have a small group of officers here who, amongst their normal duties, help us keep an eye on Knight, but as far as they're concerned, he's an ex-informant for the police in London now living here under protection. They don't know the truth. If there's any personal visits to be carried out they're done by myself or the inspector. The routine patrols generally just drive by the farm or keep a watch from a distance. The fewer who know the better. And now I'm told he may be in serious danger. Possibly even a contract on his head.'

'Possibly,' he told him quickly, eager to get back to questioning him about Dolby. 'How do you find him? How's his behaviour been? Any concerns?'

'He's a model citizen.' Hodges shrugged. 'Keeps himself to himself. Christ – probably the best character in town.'

'As far as you know, has he ever had any visitors to his farm?' he asked.

'Visitors?' Hodges repeated.

'Specifically – women?' he elaborated. 'Young women?'

'I've never seen it myself,' Hodges answered. 'Never been mentioned in any of the visitation reports. It was my understanding that he's been strongly discouraged from forming any... relationships.'

'He has?' Jameson checked.

'Part of his deal,' Hodges confirmed. 'But why all the questions about Knight? I assumed you were part of his protection team.'

'I am,' he quickly answered before returning to the same line of questioning. 'Have there been any missing persons reported in the last few years? Since Dolby arrived?'

'Of course.' Hodges shrugged. 'Where doesn't. Kids run away. Wives run away. Probably happens a little more round here than most places, truth be told. Not many people dream of living a life in Pukekohe.'

'I'm not interested in the everyday rubbish,' he told him.

Hodges leaned back in his chair looking serious. 'No,' he said. 'Of course you're not.' He took a couple of seconds before continuing. 'About two years ago a young female backpacker apparently went missing on the outskirts of town. I remember she was from Lithuania or Latvia. Some place like that. She was last seen by a local resident trying to hitch a ride to Auckland. It's possible she made it to Auckland before disappearing, I don't know. Exactly where she went missing was never established. It was investigated, but nothing ever turned up, so it was assumed she deliberately dropped off the radar and became an illegal immigrant. It's not uncommon now with people from Eastern Europe.'

'But you know Dolby's history,' he argued. 'You must have feared the worst?'

'Well, I'd already had several interactions with Dolby before then,' Hodges explained. 'So, I can't say I was overly concerned.'

'But?' he pressed.

'But I checked him out anyway,' Hodges told him.

'You were concerned enough to check?'

'Regardless of how... normal he may appear,' Hodges replied, 'I was aware of the nature of his conviction. Seemed sensible to look into it. So yes. I visited him. He was very accommodating and understanding. Even let us search the farm. No fuss. No problems.'

'And?' he encouraged him.

'And nothing,' Hodges said, spreading his hands apart. 'We found nothing. Searched the place bloody hard too – but nothing.'

'You searched the whole farm?' he asked impatiently. 'The fields?'

'Of course,' Hodges assured him. 'This may not be the big city, but we know what we're doing.'

'Sorry. I'm sure you do,' he quickly replied, eager to continue. 'What about any reports of hitchhikers, particularly young women, being harassed or followed at all? Anything like that?'

'Sure.' Hodges nodded. 'But it's always just young local men trying to get lucky. Nothing too sinister and nothing to do with Dolby – which is why I assume you're asking.'

'The Eastern European girl who went missing,' he ignored the question. 'I need her missing person's report.'

'If you insist,' Hodges agreed with a sigh. 'Should be filed somewhere.'

'And all other missing person reports since Dolby moved here,' he demanded. 'Just the ones involving young people – under thirty years old to start. Both sexes.'

'That'll be a fair few reports,' Hodges warned him.

'I'm not asking you to read them,' he told him. 'Just to get them for me.'

'Very well.' Hodges sighed loudly. 'I'll have someone from admin find them, but I'm telling you now – you're wasting your time. You won't find anything. The Eastern European girl is the only one that could be classed as even slightly suspicious.' He took a breath before continuing. 'You know, I looked into the case against him. Not just the file they gave me, but on the internet – some TV documentaries too. Seems some people think there could be some doubt about his conviction. That he was dragged down by Anderson – someone who'd already had his fair share of trouble.'

'I wouldn't be listening to that shit,' Jameson warned him. 'It's not a good idea to get confused about someone like Dolby.'

'No harm in keeping an open mind,' Hodges argued.

'All the same,' Jameson told him, not wanting to discuss it further. 'Call me when you find the missing person reports.' He pulled a business card from his wallet and dropped it on the table before turning and heading to the closed door – opening it and leaving – watched all the way by Hodges who shook his head slightly before picking up the business card, pulling open a drawer and tossing it in.

26

London – 2005

Harvey walked through the corridors of Colindale Police Station until he reached the open door of DCI Richards' office. She looked up while talking on the phone and beckoned him inside and to take a seat. He accepted the invitation and sat waiting a few seconds while Richards quickly finished her call and hung up.

'Well?' she asked. 'What did they have to say for themselves?'

He took a deep breath before answering. 'Both blaming each other – surprise, surprise.'

'At least they're talking,' she said, trying to cheer him.

'The evidence we have against them – almost better if they weren't,' he argued.

'Do you think it's going to cause us a problem?' she checked.

'No,' he told her with a sigh. 'They're fucked. There's enough there for joint enterprise to bury the pair of them. Anderson even admitted raping her, although he says he was forced to by Dolby. Dolby's defence is basically the same, although he swears he never raped her – says the forensic evidence will prove he's telling the truth, although no doubt it'll prove the opposite. His lies are more elaborate and well considered than Anderson's, but they're lies all the same. Isn't a jury in the country won't convict the pair of them.'

'But if they're both blaming each other,' she argued, 'then one of them could be telling the truth, right?'

'No, they're both lying – I'm sure of it now. They planned it together and they carried it out together. Probably convinced each other they could get away with it too. Now they're resorting to plan B – blame the other guy.'

'What now?' she asked after a short pause. 'We're about out of holding time. I can't keep them in custody while we wait for the forensic results.'

'We have enough without it,' he assured her. 'Put it up to the CPS with a recommendation to charge them both with abduction, rape and murder. They'll be remanded in court in the morning. Then we wait for forensics to come back and put the final nails in their coffins. And may God help them once they're banged up in Feltham. They'll be prized scalps for every vicious little bastard with a home-made blade.'

'Fine,' she agreed. 'I'll speak with the CPS – get them charged. Might as well charge them with false imprisonment too. They'll want to do a media release – as will the assistant commissioner. They like to get good news out there fast.'

'Good news?' he questioned. 'This is good news?'

'We caught them quickly and with enough evidence to charge them,' Richards reminded him. 'Most would consider that good news.'

Harvey nodded towards the TV playing the news in the

corner of the office. 'Think they'll give a shit about our...
efficiency?'

Richards just shrugged.

'We'll barely be mentioned,' he complained. 'It'll be all
about the suspects – who they are – their backgrounds, families.
Were there any early signs that they'd grow up to be *monsters*?
Then there'll be the inevitable discussion about what should
happen to them – how long they should serve – the public
outrage when they find out they're unlikely to do much more
than ten years because of their age. Probably already assigning
people to track them through to their release date, so they can
start the whole story again in a few years' time.'

'Christ.' Richards laughed slightly. 'Since when did you get
so cynical? It's a good result – try and enjoy it for a while.'

'What about the family?' Harvey continued with his
downcast outlook. 'What about the victim? Not much for them
to enjoy.'

'It'll be a lot better for them knowing the people responsible
have been caught,' she reminded him.

'Maybe.' He shrugged. 'So long as they don't turn on a TV,
radio or open a newspaper for about the next year. Every half-
baked journalist will be out there searching the internet and
social media for photos of the victim they can splash over
screens and papers. She was pretty too. Beautiful.'

'Meaning?' Richards asked, sensing it could be important.

'Media like their victims to be beautiful,' he explained.
'Keeps the public interested for longer. The loss of something
beautiful hurts people more than losing something they see
every day.'

Richards cleared her throat before replying. 'So long as we
have the family tucked away somewhere the media won't be able
to get to them.'

'We can buy them a few weeks, maybe,' he told her. 'But

eventually they're going to have to survive in the world on their own. They have a lifetime ahead of them trying to protect her... reputation – and the memory of her from exploitation. No one will ever let them move on. For the rest of their lives there'll always be some prick knocking on their door wanting to ask their questions about Abigail's murder. They get a life sentence, while Anderson and Dolby get a few years.'

'Way of the world, Fraser. Fuck all we can do about it. Catching them is our business. After that...' She gave a little shrug of her shoulders.

'I'll be sure to pass that on to the Rileys,' he replied, showing his irritation.

'Jesus,' Richards said. 'Don't take it out on me. I'm on your side. Remember?'

'Sorry,' he said with a sigh. 'It's been a long few days.'

'Yes. Yes it has,' she agreed, leaning back into her chair. 'You've done all you can here, Fraser. You've done a bloody good job. Go home. Get some sleep. Come back tomorrow fresh and start getting this whole thing courtworthy. Nothing more you can do tonight.'

'I'm fine,' he insisted. 'I'd rather stay here and keep on it. Wouldn't be able to sleep anyway.' He pushed himself up from his chair. 'Thought I'd check in with the door-to-door teams – see if they've managed to turn up any more witnesses.'

Richards gave another shrug of her shoulders. 'If that's what you want to do.'

'I find anything – I'll let you know,' he assured her before heading wearily towards the door.

Richards shook her head slightly as she watched Harvey leave, before looking towards the TV and turning the volume up. A pretty, young female reporter was speaking live from the Falmouth Estate. Richards listened to what she was saying.

'While details of this tragic case remain unclear,' the

reporter explained, 'it is now believed that the victim is a fourteen-year-old local girl, Abigail Riley. The news of her murder has clearly shocked the local community in this usually...'

Richards immediately hit the mute switch, a look of disgust on her face. 'Shit,' she said. 'Shit.'

27

London – Present Time

After work, Jimmy Riley had gone straight home to have dinner with his mum before heading to his favourite pub in Kilburn. He had a couple of drinks and then headed to the underground station and disappeared into the system of tunnels while all the time checking he wasn't being followed. He'd wandered around the West End for over an hour, still always making sure he wasn't being tailed before once more diving into the underground and making the short trip to London St Pancras. Once there he made his way to the left-luggage area where he kept a small locker. Once he was satisfied that he couldn't possibly have been followed, he opened the locker and took the envelope he'd found in the café from inside. He removed the pay-as-you-go mobile phone from the package and slid it quickly into his jacket pocket before locking the envelope back inside and heading to the main concourse. After circling the station a couple of times to ensure he still wasn't being followed, he bought a coffee in an anonymous café and settled at a table as far back as he could find. He pulled the mobile from his pocket, looking more suspicious the harder he tried to appear casual and called the only number in the phone's memory – a number he'd called before but never got an answer. He listened to the dial tone for what seemed an age and was about to swallow a mouthful of hot coffee when a man's voice suddenly answered.

'Yes?' he asked in a thick Belfast accent.

'I need to speak to Graham,' Jimmy explained, using the code name Rafferty had told him to use, knowing that he was probably speaking to one of his uncle's neighbours. Rafferty was too smart to speak about anything *sensitive* on his own phone and had a long-established system of complicit *sympathisers* living within walking distance of his home.

'What about?' the man asked bluntly.

Jimmy hesitated before answering. 'About a plumbing job,' he replied, sticking to the codes he'd memorised.

Whoever he was speaking to knew better than to ask any more questions. 'Wait on the line,' he instructed. 'Don't hang up. I'll be a few minutes.'

'Okay,' Jimmy said, sounding tentative before finding himself listening to nothing but silence. A few tense minutes later the sound of his uncle's voice made him jump.

'Hello, Frank,' Rafferty greeted him, using Jimmy's prearranged false name. 'Everything all right?'

'Yeah,' he answered unconvincingly. 'I was just wondering if... anything had happened?' he explained. 'I haven't seen anything in the news.'

'You haven't been using the internet from a source anyone could connect to you to search, have you?' Rafferty asked tentatively.

'No,' Jimmy assured him. 'I know that could be checked.'

'Good,' he told him. 'Don't.'

'I won't,' he promised. 'But has *anything* happened?'

There was a long pause before Rafferty answered. 'Yes,' he said. 'Paul Anderson's gone.'

For a moment he couldn't breathe as the magnitude of what he was involved in swept over him. He swallowed the bile that had jumped into his mouth and waited a few seconds for the dizziness to pass. 'Gone?' he asked, although he knew what it meant.

'Yes,' Rafferty answered calmly. 'He's gone.'

Again, he was unable to speak for a few seconds as body and mind recovered from the overwhelming emotions that swept through him. 'But there was nothing on the news,' he repeated.

'There was hardly likely to be,' Rafferty explained. 'A nobody gets killed a long way from here. Hardly likely to make the news.'

'But he wasn't a nobody,' Jimmy argued. 'He murdered my sister.'

'As far as the rest of the world's concerned, he was a nobody,' Rafferty reminded him. 'Check the internet if you feel you need confirmation – but remember not to use your own devices or servers. Use an internet café or some place.'

'Can I use this phone?' Jimmy asked. 'Connect to the internet in a café or station – some place like that?'

'Is this a *clean phone*?' Rafferty checked. 'Have you used the phone for anything other than calling me?'

'No,' Jimmy cringed as he lied, not wanting to explain who the only other person he ever called on the phone was – sure it didn't put his uncle at risk. 'It's a pay-as-you-go.'

'Then yes,' Rafferty agreed. 'Search under his new name – Morecroft, Canada. You'll find it.'

'Okay.' He nodded, trying hard to remember what he was being told as his head continued to spin.

'Listen,' Rafferty suddenly said, sounding even more serious than he had before. 'Are you sure you want to go ahead with this – to go after the other one? I need to know it's still what you want now you know what's happened to Anderson.'

He took a deep breath – his heart racing and his head pounding – the taste of bile still in his mouth and the nauseous feeling still in his stomach. For a second, he almost said no, before the memory of Abigail and his father crushed his doubts. 'Yes,' he answered. 'I still want it done.'

'Fine,' Rafferty agreed. 'I'll leave things to proceed as planned. There's no point in calling for a few days. Wait until Friday – then call me at 5pm exactly. Understand?'

'I understand,' Jimmy answered.

'Be careful,' Rafferty told him before the line went dead.

Jimmy kept the phone pressed to his ear for a long while as he considered everything he'd been told. He was now responsible, if not solely, for the taking of a man's life. The dizziness and sickness immediately returned as he tried to tell himself that Anderson was – had been, a monster, not a man, but still his head spun and his stomach churned as the blood all but drained from his face. He waited a few minutes before he felt recovered enough and called the only other number in the phone's memory. After a few rings the phone was answered.

'Yes?' the man asked in a voice that was very different from that of the man who'd called him in the café in Kilburn just a few short weeks ago and changed everything. It no longer sounded altered or mechanical. He thought he recognised something about it but couldn't pin it down to anyone he knew.

'It's me,' Jimmy whispered before realising it was more likely to attract unwanted attention than if he just spoke normally.

'I know,' the voice told him. 'What do you want?'

'I've called before,' Jimmy said, ignoring the question. 'But no one ever answers.'

'I don't have it with me much,' he explained. 'You shouldn't have yours with you either.'

'I don't,' Jimmy answered. 'I keep it...'

'Don't tell me,' the man urgently ordered. 'Never say where you keep it on the phone, even to me and never tell anyone about it.'

'I haven't,' Jimmy nervously reassured him. 'I wouldn't.'

'If I don't answer leave a text message,' he instructed. 'I'll get back to you.'

'I understand,' Jimmy agreed.

'Good,' the voice told him before coughing violently for several seconds.

'You all right?' Jimmy asked. 'You don't sound too good.'

'Just a cold,' the man assured him. 'Flu maybe. Now, why don't you tell me what you want?'

'I... I have some news,' he tentatively told him.

'Oh?' the voice enquired.

'About one of our mutual friends.' He cautiously began to explain before the man he'd called interrupted.

'Be careful about using names on a phone,' he warned him.

'The phone's safe,' Jimmy reassured him.

'Did you get a new pay-as-you-go like I told you to?' the man asked.

'Yes,' Jimmy answered.

'Used cash?' he checked.

'Just like you told me to,' he assured him.

'Have you used it to call anyone but me?'

'No,' he lied to him for the same reason he'd lied to his uncle when he'd asked the same question.

'Ever connected it to the internet through a server you can be tied to?'

'No,' Jimmy insisted. 'I only use places with free wifi. Cafés and stuff.'

'Good,' he said before once more coughing violently.

'You sure you're all right?' Jimmy asked, unconvinced it was just a cold.

'I'm fine,' came the answer. 'And if you're about to tell me about our friend in Canada, I already know.'

'How?' Jimmy asked, a little suspicious. 'There's been nothing on the news.'

'I wasn't checking the news,' the man told him. 'I have my ways. Peter Delph was apparently gunned down for no reason. The local police have put it down to mistaken identity.'

'I just thought it would be on the news,' Jimmy explained. 'Thought once he was dead his real identity and what he did would be revealed.'

'That'll never happen,' the man insisted. 'His past will be buried with him. His mother will be informed what's happened and where he is, as will his lawyer, but no one else. I don't suppose either will be making a fuss.'

'People have a right to know,' he argued.

'No. They don't,' the man told him. 'No good would come of bringing Paul Anderson back to life. It's better this way.' The end of his sentence was punctuated by another coughing fit. It was several seconds before he'd recovered enough to speak. 'So, if you didn't find out from the news, how did you find out?'

'My...' He managed to stop himself from saying *uncle*. 'My contact told me.'

'And did he tell you anything about our other person of interest?'

'He's still...' He looked around at the few other customers sitting some distance away, paying him no attention, but still making him wary. 'He's still... you know.'

'And do *you* still want that to change?' he asked.

Again, he was flooded with doubt. 'I don't know,' he admitted.

'He's dangerous,' the man warned him. 'Possibly even more dangerous than the other one.'

Jimmy closed his eyes as he remembered Abigail and the things he'd heard they'd done to her. He told himself it was as much about stopping it happening to anyone else as much as it was revenge for his sister and father. 'Things are still going ahead,' he finally answered.

'I understand,' the man replied. 'Remember to follow the rules I've given you,' he reminded him. 'They'll keep you safe. Call me if you hear anything. Leave a text message if I don't answer. Be careful.' The line went dead before he could reply.

Jimmy stared at the phone in his hand for a while, unsure of what to do next as he tried to come to terms with the fact he was now guilty of murder on the grounds of joint enterprise – just like Anderson and Dolby had been. He took a sip of coffee to steady himself before lowering the phone, connecting it to the café's internet and entering *Morecroft, Canada* into the search bar and pressing *go*.

28

New Zealand – Present Time

Jameson arrived at Dolby's farm and entered the kitchen where he found Mills sipping a coffee while looking out the window. As soon as she saw him she turned and snapped at him. 'Where the hell have you been?' she demanded. 'We're supposed to be doing this together.'

'Sorry,' he said. 'I needed to call by the local station.'

'What the hell for?' she asked, incredulous.

'Just some information I needed,' he told her casually. 'Nothing important.'

'Well, if it wasn't important why were you there instead of here?' she argued.

'Where's our man?' he asked, looking around the room, ignoring her question.

'Outside,' she replied, looking back through the window. 'Fixing stuff.'

He stood next to her and peered outside where he could see

Dolby mending a fence, as if he didn't have a care in the world. 'Look at him.' Jameson spat the words out. 'Playing at being a farmer. A murderer and rapist. This posting sucks. I can barely stand to be in the same room as him. Makes my skin crawl.'

'Get over it, Ruben,' she told him. 'Our job's to keep him alive.'

'You really think he's kept clean?' he asked after a few seconds. 'All these years?'

'What?' she snapped at him again.

'Dolby,' he explained. 'A sexually motivated killer is a sexually motivated killer. You really think he could just stop?'

'I don't know,' she answered, a little frustrated. 'Maybe. I know that everything he does is watched. Even if he had motive, he has no opportunity. Sort of predator you're talking about needs motive and opportunity.'

'Maybe,' he partly agreed before pausing for thought. 'His original crime was committed underground. In an old bomb shelter or something.'

'So?' she asked, not following him.

'So offenders like Dolby like to find a method and stick to it,' he reminded her. 'Makes them comfortable.'

'What the fuck are you talking about, Ruben?' She laughed.

'The farm been checked for any underground shelters?' he asked. 'Underground storage rooms?'

'As far as I know.' She shrugged.

'And?' he hurried her.

'Clean,' she told him. 'Satisfied?'

'All the same,' he continued after a few seconds. 'Think I'll take a look for myself.' He started to walk away before she stopped him.

'Where you going?' she asked.

He nodded towards the kitchen window. 'Think it's time I had a little chat with our friend Dolby.'

'Be careful, Ruben,' she warned him, sounding concerned. 'Don't do anything stupid.'

'Just going to talk,' he assured her unconvincingly. 'That's all.'

He left Mills shaking her head as he went outside and walked towards Dolby who was still working away on the wire fence before he suddenly stopped and looked over his shoulder as Jameson approached. He watched him all the way until Jameson was standing right in front of him.

'Can you fix it?' Jameson asked, pointing his chin at the broken fence.

Dolby straightened, looking from Jameson to the fence and back again. 'Shouldn't be too difficult.'

Jameson took his time looking all around the surrounding farm. 'Pretty big place for one man to take care of,' he told him. 'Anyone ever come over to give you a hand?'

Dolby looked him up and down suspiciously. 'Such as?'

'I don't know.' He shrugged. 'A farmhand? A friend?'

Dolby turned his back on him as he answered. 'I don't have any friends, detective.'

'Really?' Jameson said in a doubtful, unsympathetic tone. 'Must get very lonely, stuck out here on your own?'

Dolby returned to fixing the fence. 'Relationships – even friendships aren't... encouraged,' he replied. 'Although you probably already know all this.'

'All the same,' he continued, 'living in isolation can't be easy.'

'I see people,' Dolby told him. 'When I go into town. Everybody's always very... friendly.'

'Pukekohe?' He smiled condescendingly. 'Not exactly London is it?'

Dolby turned to face him. 'It's been a very long time since London was a part of my life,' he reminded him. 'I have no more desire to be back there than I do to be back in prison. Being here suits me fine.'

'So, you've never had a visitor?' he asked. 'Never had a visitor to this farm?'

'Of course,' Dolby replied, sounding somewhat irritated. 'People I've met in the town. Other farmers – suppliers. Always during the day. Never at night and I've always reported the visits to Sergeant Hodges. You can check if you want.'

'Any women?' Jameson provoked him.

'Look,' Dolby bit. 'Why don't you just say what you're thinking?'

'And what am I thinking?' he asked.

'That I'm a murderer and a rapist,' Dolby said, his anger seeping to the surface. 'That I won't be able to stop myself from murdering and raping again.'

'Can you?' Jameson kept it up. 'Can you stop yourself?'

Dolby sighed as he composed himself. 'I'm aware of the psychological profile of someone convicted of the types of crimes I was convicted of,' he answered. 'But I can assure you – they don't apply to me.'

'But you were, weren't you?' he used Dolby's words against him. 'Convicted.'

Dolby went back to fixing the broken fence. 'The public wanted their pound of flesh.'

'Christ,' Jameson said. 'You see yourself as the victim here?'

Dolby spun around to face him – his lips thin with anger. 'You think you know everything about me,' he said through gritted teeth. 'Truth is you know nothing.'

'I know you raped and murdered a fourteen-year-old girl,' Jameson told him, ready to defend himself should Dolby snap and launch at him.

'Then do it. Do what you really want to do, detective.' Dolby surprised him. 'If we're being truthful, then why don't you at least be truthful to yourself and march me into the bush and use that gun of yours to put a bullet through my head. No one will blame you. Probably be lining up to shake your hand.'

There was a long silence as both men stared at each other – sizing each other up before Jameson broke the tension. 'But then I'd be as bad as you – wouldn't I?' There was another long moment of silence as they eyed each other, before Jameson turned his back on Dolby and walked back to the farmhouse as Dolby stood motionless. A minute or so later he entered the kitchen and found Mills was still keeping watch over Dolby from the window.

'I hate the fucking countryside,' he complained. 'We should drag his arse back to Auckland and lock him in a safe house.'

'Think we should stop him walking around outside?' she asked, ignoring his grumbling. 'Country like this it wouldn't be too hard for a sniper to get close enough to take a shot.'

'Snipers are for the films,' he told her. 'Real professional killers like to get close. A handgun – a knife if they can get up close and personal enough. Back in London the most common weapon used was a car. You get a lot less jail time for a hit-and-run than you do for murder.'

'Why would they get so close?' she wondered. 'Why take the risk?'

'So they can confirm their kills,' he explained, matter-of-factly. 'The sort of people who use a contract killer don't pay until they have evidence the job's been done.'

'I never knew that,' she admitted. 'I've never dealt with a contract killing case before.'

'They're rare enough in London, let alone here, ' he casually said as he walked back to the window and looked out with Mills at Dolby who'd resumed working on the fence. 'I take it you read the background file on him?' he asked.

'Of course,' she told him, never taking her eyes away from the window.

'Those sorts of crimes are rarely... one-offs,' he said, repeating his thought from earlier.

'Even if he wanted to, he couldn't,' she argued. 'Not with so many people watching him. This isn't London, Ruben. It's a small community. People go missing – people notice.'

'Maybe he found a way?' he said as he looked out at the man he was supposed to be protecting.

'Jesus, Ruben,' she told him, finally turning away from the window. 'Just let it go. We're here to protect him. Not investigate him. Besides – I've talked to him a couple of times – just about his life – since he was convicted. Doesn't seem the type to do something like that. The file said he's always maintained his innocence. Maybe he was. The other guy – Anderson – sounded like bad seed from birth.'

'They were both tried and convicted by a jury,' he reminded her. 'There are no doubts.'

'Like a jury's never been wrong before,' she said quietly.

He turned to look directly at her. 'I don't know what he's been saying to you, Millsie,' he warned her, 'but trust me – you don't want someone like Dolby playing with your head. Remember what he is and don't let your guard down. I don't like him and I don't trust him. And neither should you.' He returned his gaze to Dolby – his contempt for him leaving a bitter taste in his mouth.

'Don't worry about me,' she assured him. 'I know what I'm doing. No one's "playing with my head". I'm a cop – remember?'

'Killers like Dolby are experts at manipulating people,' he warned her. 'Especially women. It's part of their twisted psychology. You've got self-confessed murderers locked up for life or sitting on death row, all getting piles of fan mail from women wanting to marry them – because they *believe in them* or *think they can change them*. Truth is, if they were ever alone with them, these madmen would rape and kill them in a blink of the eye. They wouldn't be able to stop themselves. You'd do well to remember that, Millsie.'

'I'll remember it,' she told him, sounding annoyed. 'And you need to remember why we're here.'

'If it comes to it,' he assured her, 'if I have to take someone down to keep him alive, I'll do it. I won't like it, but I'll do it. Who knows – with a bit of luck, we might get to take down two killers for the price of one.'

29

London – 2005

Harvey arrived home at his flat in Crouch End, North London, even later than Matthews had. He and his wife had never been able to have children, as a consequence of which they had chosen to live in an enviable area for a cop – the reasonably spacious flat being enough for their needs. He'd left the disappointment of not being able to have children behind many years ago, but he could see the sadness in his wife's eyes whenever she saw couples with children, although she always denied it. The investigation into Abigail's death left him almost relieved he didn't have children to worry about, although he'd never tell his wife such a thing. He unlocked the door to his flat and stepped into the small hallway. As he was hanging up his coat, he heard his wife, Jemma, calling to him from the sitting room.

'Is that you, Fraser?' she asked, even though only he and she had keys to the flat.

'Just me,' he called back, dumping his warrant card and other detritus from his pockets on the small side table so he wouldn't forget it in the morning before taking the few steps into the sitting room where Jemma, a pretty, petite woman in her early forties, sat watching the news on the television.

'You all right?' she asked, sounding concerned. 'You're back very late again. It's usually something bad when you're late, isn't it?'

'You shouldn't have waited up,' he told her, secretly wishing she hadn't. 'You've got work in the morning.'

'It's fine.' She disappointed him. 'I can go in a bit later. It's only a part-time job at the end of the day. Can I get you anything to eat or drink?'

'No,' he answered, slumping on the sofa next to her. 'I'm fine. I was thinking,' he said, changing the subject, 'maybe you should get a full-time job. Get back into recruitment or something.'

'Why?' she asked suspiciously. 'Do we need the money?'

'No,' he reassured her. 'Just don't want you getting bored.'

'I don't sit around here all day, you know,' she explained. 'When I'm not at work I still have plenty to do. You shouldn't be at work worrying about me. Your job's difficult enough.'

'I don't,' he struggled to know what to say. 'I just...'

'You don't think I sit here feeling sorry for myself because I... we can't have children, do you?' She asked the very question he was hoping to avoid. His head was too crammed with ugly thoughts of Abigail and her killers.

'No,' he tried to shrug it away.

'Because I came to terms with that years ago,' she said, sounding forced and unconvincing. 'I have a good life. You don't need to have kids to have a good life.'

'No,' he agreed, wondering how he'd got trapped in another conversation about children.

'Even from the few things you've told me, I'm not sure I'd have even wanted kids,' she added.

'I guess,' he said, hoping the subject would burn itself out.

'Speaking of which,' she said, fortuitously changing the subject, 'this new one sounds bad. Want to talk about it?'

'Not really,' he told her. 'You know I don't like bringing my work home. Won't do you any good having that stuff in your head. How do you know anything about it anyway?'

'It was on the news,' she answered. 'Last night, you mentioned something about a teenage girl. Now they're talking about a teenage girl being murdered. I guessed it was probably the same girl.'

'You shouldn't upset yourself watching that stuff,' he said, unwittingly patronising her. 'It's not good for you. It's not good for anyone.'

'But it's all right for you?' she asked, sounding fed up.

'That's different,' he insisted. 'It's my job.'

'Stop trying to protect me from the big bad world, Fraser,' she told him. 'I'm not a child. I can handle it.'

'But it's my job to protect you,' he argued, losing patience. 'You and everybody else – so you can live in your safe little worlds and never have to deal with or even know about the shit people I have to deal with. Thank God the media doesn't know all the details.'

'They said she was repeatedly stabbed,' she said, ignoring his short speech she'd heard many times before. 'That she was probably raped.'

'They're guessing,' he said, trying to convince her. 'They only know what we've told them and we've told them very little.'

'All the same,' she added sadly, 'it sounds like a terrible thing to have happened to a young girl. And they said she was killed by two teenage boys. How could boys that age do such a terrible thing?'

'Boys younger than them have done things just as bad,' he told her. 'Worse even.'

'But why?' she asked, shaking her head. 'No right-minded person would do such a thing.'

'They're not right-minded people,' he wearily explained. 'It's believed that men... or boys who commit this sort of crime often have a double Y chromosome. It can make them *awkward* kids – loners. Combine that with a troubled family background, bullying or God forbid, abuse, and you've got the perfect storm. Then at some point, owing to the increased aggressiveness of the person due to the double Y chromosome, the worm turns and the bullied becomes the bully. The abused becomes the abuser. It can make for a very dangerous individual.'

'You've never told me this before,' she complained.

'Because I've never come across one this bad before,' he explained. 'This is an exceptional crime, which makes me think I'm dealing with an exceptional killer or worse – killers. But you don't need to know any of this.'

'I want to know,' she insisted. 'It's better to know there's a reason behind it rather than just assuming they must be evil.'

'Well it's not always a double Y chromosome issue,' he continued, finding talking to her was somehow helping him deal with the last few days. 'Mental illness is often to blame. If it's a really bad one then more often than not we know we could be looking for a paranoid schizophrenic off their meds, if they were ever on them. I'm pretty sure Jack the Ripper was one. The amount of damage he caused to his victims' bodies he has to have been, although double Y chromosomes have been known to mutilate too.'

'Why mutilate their victims?' Jemma asked, pulling a face of disgust at the thought.

'Different reasons.' He shrugged. 'Schizophrenics are seriously ill people. Sometimes they hear voices in their heads telling them to do things – that they're attacking demons or monsters. You have to feel sorry for the poor bastards. They neither know what they're doing nor can they stop themselves. With the right drugs they can go from a rampaging killer to being as sane as you or me.'

'And the other ones?' she persisted. 'These men with the double Y chromosomes.'

'Ah,' he nodded knowingly. 'That's a very different animal altogether,' he explained. 'Technically, they're not mentally ill, but they are generally highly aggressive, disruptive and often sexually pumped up one hundred per cent of the time. I don't think there's been any proper research into it, but I know many scientists believe our prisons are full of double Y inmates, although only a tiny amount will graduate into becoming serial rapists or killers. You would not want to meet one. Remember the killer I put away a couple of years ago – John Perry.'

'I'm not likely to forget about him,' she answered.

'I'll always remember what he said to me. That once he'd selected someone to be a victim, there wasn't a thing in the world that could have saved them. They were already as good as dead.'

'But why do they mutilate the bodies of their victims,' she asked again, her eyes wide with fascination.

'Sexual gratification,' he answered bluntly. 'It's not uncommon for them to return to the bodies multiple times to cause further mutilation while they masturbate over or next to the corpse – which is something a paranoid schizophrenic would not be expected to do.'

'My God.' She pulled another face to show her repulsion. 'And you have to deal with these people?'

'It's my job,' he reminded her. 'At least it's not boring.'

'I'll stick with boring,' she joked.

'You wanted to know about them,' he said. 'Now you do.'

'And these boys?' she asked. 'What are they?'

'Well,' he began, suddenly looking anxious. 'They're not paranoid schizophrenics, that's for sure. I've interviewed them both and they're as sane as you or I. Neither will be able to go with an insanity defence. They may both be sociopaths, but that doesn't make them insane – despite what they did to the victim.'

'That bad?' she winced.

'You don't want to know,' he assured her before adding his observation. 'It looks like the work of a madman, but it isn't.' He shook the images of Abigail's body from his mind. 'You know,' he moved on, 'once you catch the murderer you're looking for, more often than not you can... visualise them committing the crime – see them at the scene, but with these two – it's hard to imagine them doing this.'

'Maybe it wasn't them,' she suggested.

'Oh, it was them,' he assured her. 'Both admitted being there but are blaming each other. Still – it's difficult to accept those boys committed this crime. I almost wish they were insane.'

'If they're not insane,' she asked, 'what are they?'

'I don't know,' he admitted. 'I guess time will tell. Sometime in the future, maybe we'll know exactly what they are. Or...' He stopped before finishing his thought.

'Or what?' she encouraged him.

'Or perhaps we'll never know,' he told her. 'We accept it was just in their nature and try to live with it. Accept that two teenage boys could kill someone in this way and move on. At the end of the day, what else can we really do?'

'Will they ever get out?' she asked, sounding concerned.

'They're young,' he reminded her. 'I don't see how any judge can give them much more than twelve years. Maybe fifteen.'

'My God,' she said. 'How can they let monsters like that back out into the streets?'

'Law's the law,' he shrugged.

'Can they be rehabilitated?' she asked. 'Changed?'

'I don't think so,' he shook his head. 'Not from what I've seen. Despite what they've done, their behaviour appears normal. They're not aggressive. They appear remorseful. If you don't know what's broke – how can you fix it?'

'Then they'll kill again?' she asked. 'When they get out?'

He took a few seconds before answering. 'Given the opportunity,' he answered. 'Yes. I believe so. I think it's in their nature.'

'Then someone should do something about it,' she complained. 'They can't be allowed to do it again.'

'The law's the law,' he said again.

'Then the law's not enough,' she insisted. 'Not for something like this.'

'Well,' he sighed. 'Maybe on this one – I agree with you.'

30

New Zealand – Present Time

The big off-road motorbike sped along a dirt road through the bush, the rider handling it skilfully before pulling over and switching the engine off. O'Doherty removed his helmet and surveyed his surroundings. Once he was happy, he dismounted and pushed the bike deeper into the bush before hiding it under a heavy canopy of ferns. He swapped his motorbike boots and jacket for hiking gear and headed into the bush. A good walk later he emerged from the bush on the edge of a treeline. He crouched down and took a large camera from his backpack to which he attached a big zoom lens before raising it to one eye.

The telescopic lens gave him an excellent view of the farm below which he scanned for signs of life until he found Dolby working in one of the fields. He zoomed in closer on Dolby's face and immediately knew he'd found his second target. The camera clicked repeatedly as he took multiple pictures before he zoomed out again and continued to scan the farm until he spotted Jameson's car and instinctively knew it was a cop's car. He moved the view to the house and waited a few seconds until he saw Jameson coming out onto the porch – having a look around. He refocused the lens on his face and knew he was looking at a cop. Once more the camera's motor clicked away as he took more pictures. He watched him for a long time before lowering the camera, deep in thought as he considered the situation and how best to progress his *mission*. After several minutes he efficiently dismantled and packed the camera before slipping back into the bush and disappearing, as if he'd never been there.

31

London – 2005

An unmarked police car pulled up outside the front gate at Feltham Young Offenders Institution, with Harvey and Matthews inside. Harvey leaned out of the window and pressed the intercom. A voice eventually answered. 'Hello.'

Harvey held his warrant card up for the security camera to see. 'DS Harvey and DC Matthews,' he said. 'Murder Investigation Team – here to interview Michael Dolby.'

There was a long pause before the voice in the intercom spoke again. 'Okay. Wait for the barrier to be completely up and then drive forward. Stay in your car and follow my colleague's instructions.'

Harvey put his warrant card away without replying. A second later the gate began to slowly and noisily roll upwards. Once it was up a prison guard waved them forward before stopping them. They were faced with another roll-up barrier in front of them that remained closed as the one behind them began to come down.

'Bloody hate these places,' Harvey complained. 'Give me the fucking creeps.' The barrier behind them eventually closed at which point the one in front of them immediately started to rise. Once it was open the same guard waved them forward as if he was directing off a car ferry, but they weren't going on holiday or thinking about enjoying themselves. They were here on unfinished business – to pull an irritating thorn from the side of the investigation.

Dolby was led along a corridor in the young offenders institution by two guards. He wasn't restrained in any way and looked calm but tired. When they reached an interview room, the door was opened by one of the guards who gestured for Dolby to enter. When he did, he saw Harvey, Matthews, his mother and solicitor already waiting inside the room that looked remarkably similar to the one he'd been interviewed in back at the police station. His mother stood and gave him a short, forced embrace – her mother's bond all but broken by the revelations of the investigation.

'Here's your man,' the guard said. 'Michael Dolby, yes?'

'Thank you,' Harvey confirmed.

'We're all in the right place then,' the guard said cheerfully. 'You can use the phone on the wall over there to call when you're finished. Someone will come and collect him. With that both guards spun on their heels and left the room, closing the door behind them.

'Take a seat, Michael,' Harvey said. Dolby did as he was told – looking tired and emotionally dead – life inside already taking a heavy toll. 'How you getting on in Feltham? I hear it can be pretty tough.'

'Fine,' he lied.

'And Rule 43?' Harvey asked. Dolby just shrugged. 'At least it keeps you away from the general population – away from inmates who might want to... harm you.' Dolby stared coldly at him. 'Just you and the other Rule 43 prisoners – the rapists and child molesters and Paul, of course.' Harvey paused for a couple of seconds – his eyes never leaving Dolby's as he tried to read him. 'Speak to each other much? Paul?'

'I see him,' Dolby answered. 'But we don't talk.'

'How come?' Harvey enquired.

'Excuse me,' Powell intervened. 'Excuse me. Is this relevant to why we're all here? If it is, shouldn't my client be cautioned first and the interview recorded?'

'Just checking on Michael's welfare.' Harvey smiled.

'I think we should move on with the interview,' Powell argued.

'Of course,' Harvey agreed, still smiling a little as he unwrapped two tapes from their cellophane and put them in the double-deck tape recorder before looking at Dolby. 'You ready?' Dolby nodded once, prompting Harvey to press the record button, filling the room with the shrill warning sound. When it stopped he began. 'This interview is being tape-recorded. It's 21st February and the time is 2.45pm. I'm Detective Sergeant Fraser Harvey and the other officer present is...'

'Detective Constable Connie Matthews,' she answered.

'We are in an interview room at Feltham Young Offenders Institution,' Harvey explained, 'conducting an after-charge interview with – could you state your name for the tape, please.'

'Michael Dolby,' he answered, looking and sounding sullen.

'Thank you,' Harvey said. 'Also present is Michael's mother and appropriate adult – could you introduce yourself please?'

'Fiona Dolby,' she replied, shifting uncomfortably in her chair.

'And your legal representative...' Harvey continued.

'Dominic Powell,' the solicitor said, taking his cue. 'From Hopkins, Powell and Lumen. I would just like to remind everyone that my client has already been charged with offences he's accused of and therefore has no real obligation to co-operate with this interview. The fact you have already charged him means you believe you have sufficient evidence to convict him, therefore no further interview should be necessary.'

'Well, much of what you say is true,' Harvey admitted. 'However, some significant evidence has come to light since Michael was charged – evidence I'm sure he and you will want to be aware of and comment on.'

'Which is?' Powell asked, sounding suspicious.

'First things first.' Harvey smiled. 'Michael – before you answer any questions, I should tell you that you're under caution, albeit a slightly different caution to before. As you have already been charged no inferences can be drawn if you chose to answer no comment, but later answer the questions in court. However, you do not have to say anything unless you wish to do so, but anything you do say may be used as evidence against you. Do you understand the new caution?'

'I understand,' he replied, emotionless.

'You're still entitled to free and independent legal advice and you have Mr Powell here anyway,' Harvey explained. 'Michael – you're currently on remand in Feltham Young Offenders Institution awaiting trial for the abduction, rape and murder of Abigail Riley–'

'I didn't do anything,' Dolby interrupted, sounding defeated.

'So you've already said,' Harvey reminded him. 'When you were originally interviewed the full forensic evidence hadn't yet been prepared. It has now.' Everyone in the room seemed to suck in a deep breath – everyone except for Dolby who just sat impassively. 'The clothes that you identified as those you were wearing throughout the attack on Abigail were covered in blood. We also found traces of blood from the swabs we took from your hands, face and behind your fingernails. There were still traces in your hair – even after you'd washed it. I can now confirm that blood came from Abigail Riley.'

'I told you before,' Dolby replied, looking and sounding a little frustrated. 'I tried to help her. There was a lot of blood. I... I couldn't stop it getting on me.'

Harvey leaned back in his chair considering Dolby's answer before proceeding. 'The clothes were largely covered with heavy stains of blood – consistent with close contact between you and the victim. But on other areas, less heavily stained, we found marks that could only have been caused by finer sprays of blood. The sort of marks you'd expect to find on the clothes of someone who'd stabbed someone a number of times.' He paused to observe Dolby's reaction, but could see little or none. 'You see, as the attacker pulls the knife from the victim, thousands of tiny blood droplets travel through the air, leaving a particular type of pattern on whatever they land on. In this case they landed on you. How did you get these types of blood-spray patterns on your clothing, Michael?'

'Must have... must have happened while Paul was attacking her with the knife,' he suggested with a shrug. 'I was trying to pull him off. I remember blood flicking off the knife every time he... I... I felt it landing on me. My clothes. My... my face.'

The image of Abigail's blood spraying across Dolby's face momentarily silenced Harvey before he recovered his train of thought. 'Did you manage to take the knife off him?' he asked. 'At any point did you get the knife off Paul?'

'Michael,' Powell intervened. 'I want to remind you that you do not have to answer any of these questions. You've already been charged, so no inference can be drawn from you answering no comment.'

'No,' Dolby insisted. 'No, I want to answer. No. I never managed to get the knife off him.'

'The knife we found in your house,' Harvey went on, 'we now know it's the knife that was used to kill Abigail.'

'I already told you.' Dolby seemed to understand the implication. 'He gave it to me and told me to hide it.'

'And when we found it,' Harvey continued, 'it was still wrapped in the clothes that we know Paul wore during the attack on Abigail.'

'So?' Dolby asked, looking confused.

'So,' Harvey said, speaking slowly, 'how come your fingerprints were on the knife?'

Dolby hesitated before answering. 'Because he gave it to me to get rid...'

'Hold on,' Harvey said. 'Hold on. But when he gave you the knife to get rid of, it was already wrapped in his clothes. So how did your fingerprints get on the knife handle?'

'No,' Dolby argued. 'No. He handed me the knife. It wasn't wrapped in anything when he handed it to me. I wrapped it in the clothes.'

'Why did you do that?' Harvey quickly asked.

'I... I don't know,' Dolby stumbled. 'I... I suppose I just didn't want to look at it.'

Again, Harvey gave it a few seconds before continuing. 'So now you're saying he handed you the knife separately and you wrapped it in the clothes?'

'Yes,' Dolby confirmed.

'So that's why your fingerprints are on the knife?' Harvey tried to tie Dolby down.

'Yes,' Dolby answered cautiously.

'You never said any of this earlier,' Harvey told him. 'You never mentioned handling the knife before.'

'No one asked,' he shrugged.

Harvey and Matthews looked at each other and then back to Dolby. 'And what were you going to do with them – the knife and the clothes?' Harvey asked.

'I... I don't know,' Dolby answered. 'Paul said he would take care of everything.'

'Well that's a little strange,' Harvey told him. 'Because Paul said you'd told him to meet you that night, on the estate – that you were going to hide the knife where it would never be found and burn the clothing.'

'He's a liar,' Dolby insisted.

'This all sounds a bit too convenient to me,' Harvey argued. 'Anderson told you to do this – Anderson told you to do that. The blood-spray marks are because you were trying to stop him – your fingerprints are on the knife because he handed it to you and you took it without arguing or thinking. You're trying to build a defence around the evidence as it's revealed to you. I've seen a hundred suspects try to do the same thing, Michael. You really think you're the first?'

'I didn't do anything,' Dolby repeated. 'I swear to you. It was Paul. He's trying to set me up. He thinks he can get away with murder. Don't you see? He made me touch the knife – he made me take the clothes. He knew you'd find them. He's trying to make it look like I killed her – like it was my idea. He's... he's probably been planning it this way all along – for weeks.'

'Or you he, Michael,' Harvey accused him. 'Or you he.'

'No,' Dolby shouted before burying his head in his hands. 'No.' Harvey watched without saying anything until Dolby slowly looked up. 'What about Paul's clothes?' he asked. 'The blood-spray patterns you said were on my clothes. Were they on Paul's as well?'

Harvey took a deep breath before answering. 'Yes,' he admitted. 'We found similar patterns on his clothes.'

'You see,' Dolby said, sounding animated for the first time. 'I told you it was him.'

'Or it was Paul who was trying to stop you from stabbing Abigail,' Harvey pointed out, 'and that's how he got the blood spray on him.'

'Did he say that?' Dolby quickly asked.

'No,' Harvey admitted after taking a couple of seconds to recall the interview with Anderson.

'That proves it then,' Dolby insisted. 'If he'd been trying to protect her, he would have said so. But he didn't.'

'Michael makes a good point,' Powell interjected.

'All it proves is that you were both involved in the rape and murder of Abigail,' Harvey said, waving it away, although he knew it would become another irritating uncertainty in the investigation. An itch that could never be properly scratched unless Anderson and Dolby sat in front of him and told the same truthful story – admitting to all their sins instead of blaming each other. 'It's your word against his, but none of it really matters. The evidence of joint enterprise is overwhelming. The jury won't be interested in the details of who did what – just that you were both there willingly.'

Dolby's eyes closed for a second before firing wide open, as if he'd just remembered a crucial fact. 'What about the other thing?' he asked – speaking slow and deliberately.

'Other thing?' Harvey repeated.

'Evidence,' Dolby told him. 'Forensic evidence of who had sex with her. Did you check it?'

'Yes,' Harvey declared. 'We checked it.'

'And?' Dolby hurried him, barely able to contain his excitement.

Harvey delayed before answering. 'No semen or DNA belonging to you were found inside Abigail,' he finally revealed.

Dolby closed his eyes with relief. 'I told you,' he reminded them, looking at each and every one sitting around him. 'I told you.'

'Thank God,' Fiona joined in, as she also closed her eyes and looked as if the weight of the world had been lifted from her shoulders.

'Instead, we found traces of a lubricant commonly found on prophylactics,' Harvey told them, speaking deliberately quickly to kill their relief.

'What?' Dolby asked, looking confused again.

'Condoms, Michael,' Harvey explained. 'Prophylactics are condoms. We also found traces of a spermicide often used by condom manufacturers.'

'I don't understand,' Fiona intervened, the joy wiped from her face. 'What are you saying?'

Harvey took his time before answering. 'We found DNA and semen matching Paul Anderson.'

Dolby and his mother both simultaneously sighed loudly. 'I told you,' Dolby said triumphantly. 'I told you it was Paul. Now do you believe me?'

Harvey ignored the question. 'Which means Paul didn't have the sense to use a condom,' he explained before pausing. 'But someone did – someone who had sex with her at or close to the time she was raped. Someone cold enough and calculating enough to make sure they had a condom with them and to use it and take it with them from the scene. Someone who was thinking about evidence and not leaving any. Someone who didn't want to be caught.'

'She had a boyfriend,' Dolby blurted out. 'They must have had sex and used a condom.'

'We've already spoken to him,' Harvey said, shaking his head. 'Not only does he say they hadn't recently had sex – he said they never had. He believes Abigail had never had sex with anyone.'

'Then he's lying,' Dolby argued. 'Probably thinks he'll get in trouble.'

'I don't think so, Michael,' Harvey told him.

'Then what are you saying?' Dolby demanded.

'I'm saying that whoever used the condom planned to abduct, rape and murder Abigail,' Harvey spelt it out. 'That everything was premeditated – at least by one of you.'

'No,' he said loudly, his face twisted with anger. 'No. It was Paul. I'm telling you it was Paul. I didn't preplan anything and I didn't use a condom because I didn't touch her.'

Harvey let him calm down for a few seconds before continuing. 'I think you've got to the stage where you're beginning to convince yourself you never touched her...'

'Because I didn't,' Dolby insisted.

Harvey took another breath before trying something else. 'You might actually feel better if you just told us the truth.'

'I am,' Dolby snarled. 'I always have been.'

'You're carrying a heavy burden around with you, Michael,' Harvey persisted. 'D'you really want to carry it for the rest of your life?'

Dolby banged the table with his fists. 'They're lying to you. They're all lying.'

'Last chance to tell the truth, Michael,' Harvey warned him. 'Last chance.'

'Fuck,' he shouted. 'Why won't you believe me? I'm telling you the truth.'

Harvey took a long pause. 'I don't think you know what the truth is anymore,' he told him. 'No jury's going to believe you weren't involved. If you're not prepared to give me the truth, then I'd rather have nothing. This interview is over.' He reached for the off button.

'No wait,' Dolby pleaded, reaching forward and grabbing Harvey's wrist. 'Wait, please. Listen. Please listen to me.'

Harvey pulled his wrist free, but also moved his hand away from the recorder. 'I'm listening,' he told Dolby.

Dolby took a few seconds to compose himself before pleading his case. 'I don't care what happens to me,' he began. 'If... if they send me away forever, I don't care. I know I deserve it. I should have stopped him,' he chastised himself, looking down into the table before regaining eye contact with Harvey. 'I should have saved her.'

'Then why do you care if I believe you?' Harvey asked. 'If you believe you deserve to be locked away forever why not just say you did it? Why try so hard to persuade me you're telling the truth.'

'Because...' he began before faltering. 'Because, I need to know there's someone who believes me – no matter what happens.'

'Why?' Harvey asked, needing to understand.

'So that...' Dolby tried to explain. 'So that someone knows I'm not the person they're going to say I am.'

'Who's they?' Harvey asked.

'The TV,' Dolby answered. 'The papers. Everybody.'

'Why's that so important?'

'I don't want to die like this.'

'You'll be out of here a long time before you're dead,' Harvey assured him.

'But I'll be as good as dead, won't I?' Dolby mournfully stated. 'I'll never be able to have a life.'

'You should have thought about that before you led Abigail into that shelter,' Harvey replied without sympathy. 'Maybe if you had, none of this would have happened or maybe you just couldn't stop yourself. She was just so beautiful – so untouched – you had to have her, didn't you? Didn't you, Michael?'

'So loved,' Dolby suddenly said, ignoring the question.

'What?' Harvey asked, his eyes narrowing with suspicion and intrigue.

'What Paul said,' Dolby explained. 'About her being loved. He picked her because he knew she was loved.'

'You mean you picked her because she was loved, Michael,' Harvey accused him. 'You picked her.'

'No,' Dolby replied, calmly and quietly. 'You're wrong. You'll see. In time you'll all see.'

Harvey and Matthews were stuck in heavy traffic as they travelled back from Feltham. Matthews drove while Harvey seemed lost in thought. 'Penny for your thoughts,' she said, breaking the silence.

'What?' Harvey asked, before realising what she meant. 'Dolby? Anderson?'

'Who else?' Matthews replied.

'I think they're both murdering little bastards,' he said with a sigh. 'That's what I think.'

She looked at him for a couple of seconds before turning back to look at the back of the same car she'd been staring at for what seemed like forever. Finally, she decided to say what was on her mind. 'Plausible though, wasn't he? Dolby.'

'They're both convincing liars,' he answered without looking at her. 'If that's what you mean.'

'Dolby more so,' she added. 'He was very... believable.'

'He's not the first killer I've interviewed who was believable,' he told her. 'Lying's his only hope. I'd expect nothing less than his best shot. If you'd interviewed Anderson with me, you'd have thought him convincing too – just in a different way.'

'I don't know,' she continued.

Harvey turned to look at her. 'Know what I think?' She gave a little shrug. 'I think they're both wrong-uns. Whether they were born bad or made bad – who knows, but they're wired all wrong now. Some people will call them evil – I'm not sure about that, but what I am sure is that somehow they found each other – recognised the... bad intent in each other. Someone with those thoughts going around inside their head doesn't just walk up to anyone and ask them to help abduct and murder a young girl. No, these two found each other – were attracted to each other somehow – nurtured each other – encouraged each other until finally they turned one of their fantasies into reality. Maybe one was more dominant than the other, but they're the same animal.'

'Who do you think was the leader?' Matthews asked.

'Difficult to say,' Harvey shrugged. 'Dolby showed a greater degree of premeditation.'

'You mean the condom?' she checked. 'The fact he used a condom, but Anderson didn't?'

'It shows that he at least was planning to rape Abigail and wasn't planning on getting caught,' Harvey explained.

'Unless, of course, Dolby's right,' Matthews theorised. 'And her boyfriend's lying and did actually have sex with her and used a condom. If he'd admitted that he had he would have been guilty of unlawful sexual intercourse with an underage girl. She was only fourteen. Maybe he was too scared to admit to it?'

'I interviewed the kid myself,' Harvey reminded her. 'I got no sense he wasn't telling the truth.'

'Yeah, but he could have been,' she persisted. 'Even if he wanted to admit having sex with Abigail his parents probably wouldn't let him. They wouldn't want their fifteen-year-old son to have a conviction for sex with an underage girl. Families are funny like that.'

'Well, he says he didn't and I can't prove he did, so that's the end of it. We have DNA from the only semen we found and it's Anderson's. Other than that, all we have is spermicide. Even if her boyfriend volunteered his DNA, it wouldn't help us,' Harvey reminded her, trying to finish it. 'Up to a jury to decide now. Nothing more we can do.'

'But what if one of them really is innocent?' she persisted. 'Set up by the other, somehow? You know what juries are like – once they hear the sordid details they'll stop listening to the evidence and convict them anyway. Sexually motivated murders scare them – better to just convict than risk setting a monster free. Neither Dolby or Anderson stand a chance. Doesn't that bother you?'

He turned slowly to look at her. 'No,' he told her bluntly. 'No it does not. Don't get confused here, Connie. The only innocent person in this is Abigail and she's dead. Any chance of ever knowing what really happened died with her, so fuck them – the both of them. They knew what they were doing. They deserve everything that's coming to them. Perhaps even more.'

Matthews thought silently for a while before starting again. 'If they knew what they were doing,' she argued, 'how come we caught them so easy? And the clothes and the weapon still in Dolby's house? Not too smart.'

'They messed up because they were young,' he said, dismissing it. 'Learning as they went along – probably still young enough to think they could get away with anything. If they were older, they'd have planned more meticulously – taken less risks – been harder to catch. Believe me – they've learnt from their mistakes.'

'You sure that's all it was?' she questioned. 'Why do I get the feeling you're not telling me everything you're really thinking?'

He sighed and shrugged at the same time before replying. 'Cases like this,' he began, 'a murder of this nature – sexually motivated, extremely violent, is usually committed by a particular type of predator – one that would most likely want to return to the scene – to the victim's body ideally – to relive the murder. Probably for sexual gratification.'

'You mean to masturbate at the scene?' She reminded him she was an experienced detective as well.

'Exactly,' he replied. 'Only they didn't have a body anymore and we'd discovered the scene – something they would have probably guessed was going to happen quickly. So the next best thing they would have had would've been the bloodied clothing and weapon. If they were using it to relive the crime, then it would have been hard for them to let that go – to dispose of the items. They would have been emotionally attached to them.'

They drove in silence for a while before Matthews spoke. 'But do you really think both of them would be using the clothes to relive the crime?' she asked. 'Maybe one of them, sure, but both?'

'I'm not sure,' he shrugged before remembering something. 'I was talking to my wife a couple of weeks back – about killers with what's called a double Y chromosome condition. You know it?'

'Think I heard about it in some lecture in my detective training course,' she told him. 'Can't say I paid too much attention. Where do you learn all this stuff anyway?'

'I read,' he told her. 'The occasional lecture.'

'Yeah, well,' she said, giving a little shrug, 'the science should stop at forensics and leave the rest to us.'

'It's pretty interesting stuff,' he argued.

'Fine,' she casually agreed to hear more.

'Theory is these guys with the double Y chromosome are

something like two hundred times more likely to kill than people who aren't,' he explained. 'And this would certainly be the type of crime they would commit. But the point is teenage boys with the double chromosome are often physically awkward as well as socially. They become withdrawn and semi-nocturnal – often so their movements can't be observed and they tend to have a bad diet which leads to pale, poor skin. Remind you of anyone?'

'Certainly not Dolby,' she shrugged. 'He's a nice-looking boy. Well-spoken. Articulate. His social interaction, even under these stressful conditions is excellent. Doesn't sound like what you're describing.'

'And Anderson?' he asked.

'Well,' she answered, 'if your double Y chromosome theory is right, then yes, I suppose he fits the type. But what does it matter? They're both going to be found guilty anyway.'

'I guess,' he replied unconvincingly.

'What you thinking, Fraser?' she said, pushing him.

'That it would be good to know who the leader was,' he told her. 'And who just followed.'

'Maybe they were equal partners,' she suggested.

'I don't think so,' he admitted. 'There's always a leader. An instigator.'

'Anderson has the double Y chromosome,' she explained, 'and Dolby has the intelligence. Difficult to pick. But if it was Dolby, and he's neither mentally ill nor inflicted with a chromosome problem, then what type of person is he?'

'A dangerous one,' he told her. 'Very dangerous. At least as dangerous as Anderson and when they get out of prison, they'll be even more dangerous than they are now.'

'How come?' she asked.

'Because they'll have nothing but time,' he answered. 'Time to learn.'

'Not that they'll get the chance to put it into practice,' she argued.

'Won't they?' he warned her. 'They're only kids. Can't keep them locked up for long. They'll still be young men when they get out – with the same sick needs they have today.'

'But they'll be watched,' Matthews reminded him. 'For the rest of their lives, they'll be watched.'

'Where there's a will there's a way,' he told her. 'And now they've both got about ten years to plan it – to think through every detail. Ten years of learning from other older, smarter, more experienced predators. You really think they'll be less dangerous when they come out than they are now?'

'Great,' she rolled her eyes. 'Sounds like we'd be doing everyone a favour if we just put them down.'

'We wouldn't be short of volunteers to pull the switch if it came to that,' he joked darkly. 'Half the country wants to see these two dead.'

'If they knew the full details it'd be the whole country wanting them dead,' Matthews replied. 'Kids turned rapists and murderers – Jesus Christ.'

'Do you no good to dwell on it too much, Connie,' Harvey told her. 'Go to trial, get them convicted and move on. It's what we do.'

'As simple as that?'

'As simple as that,' he said with a shrug, not sure if he even believed his own words as he had the same feeling as he'd had before – that the case would haunt him for years to come. That it would never let them go.

32

New Zealand – Present Time

Jameson entered the small, local town council offices in Pukekohe and approached the receptionist who looked up and smiled.

'Can I help you with something?' she asked.

'Yeah,' he told her, showing her his police ID. 'I'm interested in local survey maps. Know where I could find them?'

'Sure,' she said, pointing to her right. 'Take that corridor and keep going. It's the third door on your left.'

'Thanks,' he nodded and headed off in the direction she'd indicated until he reached the third office and looked inside to see the only person there – a slim, tall man in his fifties typing away on a computer keyboard. 'Excuse me,' he said as he entered the room.

'Can I help you?' the man asked, looking up.

'I hope so,' he smiled without giving any idea of who he was. 'I'm researching the local area and need to get a look at some of the local farmland.' He strolled over to a large map of Pukekohe attached to a wall and traced his finger across it until he found the place he was looking for. 'I'm currently looking at the old farm right here,' he explained as he tapped the map.

'Can you tell me what the research is for?' the worker asked. 'It might help.'

'Government land valuations,' he lied. 'Nothing too exciting. Just need to see the size of the land and any structures it may have – including anything underground.'

'Underground?' the man asked, looking interested. 'Some farms used to have underground silos for storage, but most are above ground these days,' he explained as he stood and stepped towards a large wall-mounted cabinet full of pigeonholes. He searched quickly with his finger wandering around the cabinet until he pulled a long paper tube from its compartment. 'A more detailed plan of the farm you're interested in will be on this map,' he told him as he unrolled it, arranging objects close by to weigh it down. 'This is the area you're interested in,' he said, pointing it out to Jameson. 'It's pretty small for around here, but other than that there's nothing too interesting – nothing unusual.'

'And this is exactly as the farm is today?' Jameson checked.

'Yep,' the worker assured him. 'This is our most current survey map. Here you can see the farmhouse, the storage areas, barn. It's surrounded by some pretty thick bush, but that's about it.'

'Anything underground?' he asked.

The man looked at the layout of the farm again. 'No. Can't see anything underground,' he answered, sounding a bit confused. 'Is that important?'

'How old is this map?' Jameson asked as he stared down at the diagram of Dolby's farm.

'Four – five years old,' he shrugged.

He thought for a moment before speaking. 'D'you have anything older?'

'Older?' the man asked.

'Yeah, older,' he confirmed. 'Ten – fifteen years. Maybe more. Something that would show anything that's since been concealed – overgrown or covered with something?'

'Underground – you mean?' the man checked.

'Possibly,' he told him, trying to sound casual.

The man looked at him suspiciously. 'What government department did you say you were from again?'

'I didn't,' he replied, looking him hard in the eye. 'Can you show me the maps?'

The man nervously cleared his throat. 'We don't keep the old ones here. We don't have the storage. They're archived back in Auckland.'

'But you can get them?' he insisted more than asked.

'Yes.' The man nodded. 'Of course, but it'll take time. A few days. Maybe longer.'

'Get them,' he told him as he pulled a business card from his pocket and handed it to the man. 'Call me as soon as you have it.' The man looked down at the card and began to read Jameson's police credentials. By the time he looked back up, poised to ask a question, he was gone.

33

London – 2005

Abigail Riley's funeral was being held in the churchyard of her local Catholic church. The priest read the prayer *As I walk through the valley of the shadow of death* as the small coffin was lifted from its stand before being slowly lowered into the waiting grave using pulleys and straps. A small crowd of family and friends stood silently, tears seeping from many eyes. Daniel and Sarah Riley clung to each other crying painfully while Jimmy stood in front of them still looking like he was in shock – neither crying nor showing any emotion. Harvey, Matthews and Richards stood amongst the crowd looking uncomfortable. Two gravediggers began to cover the coffin with soil as the priest finished his prayer, signalling the breaking-up of the gathering, although her parents and brother stood firm. As the mourners began to drift away, Harvey headed for the family, looking over at the crowd being kept away by uniformed officers on the other side of the church gates, at the front of which journalists snapped away with their cameras, jostling each other for the best position from which to film the tragic scene.

Harvey managed to put his loathing of the media to one side as he reached Abigail's family. 'I can't tell you how sorry I am about Abigail,' he told them. 'I can only hope that in some way it helps to know we have the people responsible already locked up.'

Sarah steadied herself before replying. 'That won't bring her back though – will it?'

Harvey shook his head. 'No. No, it won't.'

'We don't even know if they'll get convicted and even if they do – they're not adults,' Daniel argued, angry and resentful through his tears. 'How long will they get – a few years then free to live the rest of their lives. What about my Abigail's life? What about her life?'

'I can promise you they'll get more than a few years,' Harvey said, trying to reassure them.

'Won't be life, though, will it?' Daniel said. 'They won't get life, but we have – a life sentence of thinking about what those evil bastards did to our Abigail. Are we just supposed to forgive and forget – is that it? You tell me – how are we supposed to do that? How are we supposed to do that?'

Harvey had no answer as he looked down at Jimmy and was sure he could see revenge already burning in his young eyes before he reminded himself the boy was probably still in shock. Without saying another word, the family moved away from him and drifted towards the exit of the churchyard. He stood alone for a few seconds before walking slowly back to Matthews and Richards, again scanning the crowd on the other side of the church gates as the journalists took yet more pictures.

'Fucking vultures,' he told his colleagues. 'Make me sick.'

'CPS are working on restraining orders,' Richards assured him. 'We might be able to keep them at bay – for a while, but with the court case to come and then sentencing – it'll be difficult, especially once they only get ten to fifteen years, maybe out in seven – the media will be all over it. The red-tops love a good campaign.'

'Justice for Abigail,' Harvey said, predicting the newspapers' campaign slogan. 'Maybe this time they're right.'

'Maybe,' Richards shrugged. 'Not our concern. Our job is to get them convicted. After that...'

'Something tells me this one's not going away, even after they get convicted,' Harvey voiced his fears. 'Media and the public got a real taste for it now. Dolby and Anderson are going to be with us for years.'

'Let's just concentrate on what we need to do next,' Richards told him. 'We can worry about the rest later. I want these two convicted – minimum fuss. Understand.'

'Yeah. I understand,' Harvey agreed. 'But maybe you should tell them,' he added, jutting his chin towards the pack of journalists. 'You think they're going to let us get this done with minimum fuss?'

'No,' Richards admitted. 'No, I do not. But I know we can't afford any mistakes under this amount of scrutiny. It's Dolby and Anderson they're really interested in, not us. So long as they're running around digging up dirt on the defendants they won't be getting in our way. Let's not do anything to distract them from that. No fuck-ups.'

'Fair enough,' Matthews shrugged.

'Yeah,' Harvey agreed, but sounded sceptical. 'Fair enough.'

34

New Zealand – Present Time

O'Doherty sipped his drink at the bar of a smart hotel in central Auckland, thinking about Dolby and the cops who were protecting him, when an attractive woman in her mid-thirties with long ash-blonde hair approached him and stood next to him.

'Do you mind if I join you?' she asked.

He looked around nervously, instantly attracted to her but suspicious of why she was talking to him. 'Why?' he said bluntly.

She gave a short laugh. 'Well...' she began, 'because I was waiting for a friend, but she hasn't shown up and I saw you sitting alone and I thought you looked very nice so... I thought I'd come and talk to you.' She sat next to him at the bar without waiting to be invited. He looked her up and down unwelcomingly. 'So – you live round here?' she persisted.

He gave a quick nervous glance around the bar. 'No. Australian.'

'Well,' she smiled. 'I wouldn't say that too loudly around here.'

'No,' he replied after a couple of seconds.

'So,' she persevered. 'What brings you to Auckland?'

'Business,' he replied curtly.

'What sort of business?' she continued.

'Business business,' he answered rudely.

She took a deep breath through her nose. 'You're not much of a talker, are you?'

'Lady,' he snapped at her slightly. 'Why you so interested in my business?'

'I'm sorry,' she told him after recovering from the surprise of his reaction. 'Looked like you maybe wanted some company. My mistake.' She stood to leave when suddenly he gently took hold of her forearm and stopped her.

'I'm sorry,' he quickly told her. 'Please. I was rude.' He took a breath. 'Can I get you a drink? By way of an apology.'

It was a while before she eventually smiled again. 'Sure,' she agreed as she sat back down. 'Why not? Dry vodka martini would be good.'

He nodded and looked slightly surprised by her choice. 'Okay. Vodka martini it is.'

'Not going to tell me it's a man's drink?' she teased him.

'Okay,' he smiled. 'It's a man's drink.'

'Would you rather I had something pink and bubbly?' she smiled back.

'No,' he told her. 'No. I would not.'

Neither of them spoke as they looked directly at each other, before he turned to the bar and put his finger in the air to attract the attention of the bartender who came straight over.

'What can I get you?' she asked.

He nodded towards his new companion. 'Vodka martini and I'll take another beer.'

'No worries,' she assured him before turning to the woman. 'You want that dry?'

'Three parts vodka to one part vermouth,' she told her, 'and three stuffed green olives. Thanks.'

The bartender raised her eyebrows before walking away to fix the drink.

'You seem to know what you want,' O'Doherty commented.

'Does that bother you?' she asked, flicking her hair behind her back.

'No,' he laughed slightly. 'It doesn't bother me. I like it.'

There was a knowing moment of silence between them before she spoke again. 'So, you were telling me what it is you do.'

'No, I wasn't,' he smiled.

'You said you were a businessman,' she reminded him.

'Of a sort,' he told her. 'It's very boring.'

'Well you're dressed like a businessman,' she said as her eyes moved over him. 'Got the hair – the manicure, but something about you tells me that whatever you do – it isn't boring.'

'Looks can be deceiving,' he tried to persuade her.

'I don't think so,' she replied. 'Not with you.'

'Never mind me,' he said, changing the subject from himself. 'What do you do? You got the suit – got the hair – got the manicure.'

'Okay,' she said, laughing. 'I probably asked for that. I'm a corporate lawyer – for an insurance company.'

'Protect the big guy from the little guy, eh?' he teased her.

'It's not that heartless,' she argued. 'If people have a half-decent claim, I usually just bargain it out. Nobody loses. Everyone wins.'

'A lawyer with a conscience?'

'I like to think so,' she told him before the bartender approached and placed the drinks on the bar.

'Vodka martini and a fresh beer,' she announced.

'Put them on my tab,' O'Doherty told her.

'No worries,' she nodded and left them alone.

They both lifted their drinks and raised them towards each other.

'To what the night may bring,' he toasted as they looked into each other's faces and chinked their glasses together.

'To what the night may bring,' she repeated. 'May we both remember it forever – no matter what might happen.'

35

London – 2005

A huge media scrum mixed with a baying mob of people gathered in the streets outside the Central Criminal Court, better known as the Old Bailey. Police and security guards tried to keep order, but as a prison truck arrived at the secure vehicle entrance, the mob went wild and a number of people, all hungry for retribution, broke through the thin blue line. They attacked all sides of the prison van, kicking and punching it as the crowd all chanted the same slogan together. 'Sex case, sex case, hang 'em, hang 'em, hang 'em.' People still behind the police line started throwing bottles and cans at the truck before a small force of police in riot gear managed to restore some order, chasing those who'd broken free back behind the police line just as the wooden security gate began to rise.

In the back of the van Paul Anderson sat in his tiny individual cell looking terrified, cowering and crying. Dolby sat in the cell opposite – eyes closed, muttering something inaudible, drowned out by the din outside – as if he was praying. The prison van lurched forward into the secure compound as the gate immediately began to fall, closing out the hatred that raged outside. As relative silence fell, Dolby opened his eyes and looked up at the ceiling above him as he practised controlling his breathing, but a familiar voice soon broke through his relative peace.

'Michael.' Anderson's petrified and panicked voice filled the van. 'Michael. Don't say anything, Michael. Don't believe them, Michael. Don't believe anything they say about me. I didn't tell them anything, Michael. You've got to believe me, Michael. I would never turn on you. You'd better not turn on me, Michael. Don't betray me, Michael. Don't fucking betray me, Michael.'

Dolby closed his eyes against Anderson's pleas and threats while covering his ears with the palms of his hands, pressing hard to form a tight seal. He needed darkness and quiet. He needed to think. He needed to prepare himself for what he knew was coming.

Harvey and Matthews sat outside Court 1 with the Riley family listening to the shouts and screams of the mob outside, everyone tensing as they understood what it must mean.

'I guess they must be here then.' Harvey said what they were all thinking.

'Listen to them,' Sarah said, sounding disgusted. 'Like animals – worse. Just as bad as...' No one said anything for a while as they thought about what she'd said.

'You shouldn't compare them to those bastards,' said Daniel breaking the silence.

'We should go into the court now,' Harvey intervened before

things got worse. 'Jury's been thinking on their decision all night. Won't be long before they're ready to give their verdict. You ready?'

Sarah stood first, followed by Jimmy and lastly, her husband. She took hold of Jimmy's hand before she closed her eyes and nodded once. 'We're ready,' she solemnly declared.

'All right,' Harvey said to them. 'Let's get it over with.' With that he turned and walked through the doors to the court. The hunched, shrunken figures of the Riley family followed him inside where Harvey led them to the seats reserved for the family. He and Matthews sat on the bench behind the barrister for the Crown Prosecution looking nervous. The case was overwhelmingly strong, but he'd seen enough juries deliver unfathomable decisions in his time to keep him on tenterhooks now. He heard a shuffling sound coming from the dock and turned around to see Dolby and Anderson being led into court, both looking very nervous. The noise of the jury filing into the courtroom and taking their seats made him look away from the teenage boys accused of a murder that united the country in revulsion and rage.

'The court rise,' the clerk of the court suddenly bellowed from his pulpit in front of the judge's bench, indicating that His Lord was about to enter. Harvey and everyone else got to their feet. A few seconds later there was a loud double-knock before the judge entered as if appearing from the wings of a stage. Once he was settled in his chair the clerk bellowed again. 'The court may be seated.' Harvey slumped tiredly into his chair. It had been a long trial and now he was more exhausted than he was excited about it reaching its conclusion. 'Could the foreman of the jury please stand?' the clerk ordered, prompting a man in his mid-fifties with grey hair and spectacles.

'Have you, the members of the jury, reached a unanimous decision?' the judge asked in his dour tone.

'Yes, my Lord,' the foreman answered.

'Very well,' the judge said before nodding to the clerk. 'Will the defendants please rise.'

Anderson and Dolby rose slowly to their feet to hear their fate.

'Ladies and gentlemen of the jury,' the clerk asked. 'On the count of murder, how do you find the defendant Paul Anderson?'

The foreman stiffened before answering. 'Guilty, my Lord.'

Harvey glanced over at the defendants in time to see Anderson try to say something before he was stopped by the guard resting a hand on his shoulder.

'And on the same count of murder,' the clerk continued, 'how do you find the defendant Michael Dolby?'

'Guilty, my Lord,' the foreman replied, clear and loud.

Harvey watched Dolby close his eyes and slump back onto his seat before looking across at Sarah and Daniel who held each other as they wept.

'On the count of rape,' the clerk proceeded, 'how do you find the defendant Paul Anderson?'

'Guilty, my Lord,' the foreman said, repeating the same damning words. Harvey found himself slowly nodding his head in agreement.

'And on the same count,' the clerk asked, 'how do you find the defendant Michael Dolby?'

'Guilty, my Lord,' the foreman answered as Dolby buried his head in his hands.

'And on the final count of false imprisonment,' the clerk said slowly as he reached the conclusion of the findings, 'how do you find the defendant Paul Anderson?'

'Guilty, my Lord,' the foreman said to no one's surprise.

Anderson just stared straight ahead, but with tears rolling down his face.

'And on the same count,' the clerk asked for the final time, 'how do you find the defendant Michael Dolby?'

The foreman took a deep breath before hammering the final nail in their coffin. 'Guilty, my Lord.'

Dolby closed his eyes and shook his head.

Again, Harvey looked over his shoulder at the defendants as Dolby's eyes suddenly fired wide open, staring straight back at him. He held his gaze for a few seconds before searching the courtroom for the family and found them still clinging on to each other and crying. The sound of the judge's forbidding voice made him look straight ahead.

'Paul Anderson and Michael Dolby,' he began. The jury have found you both guilty of a truly horrific crime. You have both committed possibly the most depraved and cruel act I have ever presided over in my court – a vile and merciless act that has shocked the entire country. The fact you were capable of committing such a terrible crime at such a young age is deeply troubling. I must now wait for pre-sentence reports from both social services and the probation service before I can pass sentence, but rest assured, you can both expect as lengthier prison sentence as the law allows. This court will reconvene in a month's time for sentencing. Until then, bail is denied and you shall both remain in custody. Take them down,' he ordered before standing without warning.

'The court will rise,' the clerk immediately ordered. The sound of people quickly getting to their feet reverberated around the court. Seconds later the judge left the court through the door concealed in the wings behind his bench as Anderson and Dolby were led from the dock by their guards – heads bowed until Anderson suddenly pulled away and turned back to the court.

'I didn't do anything,' he shouted across the court. 'You can't do this, please – I didn't do anything.' He was immediately grabbed by the guards and manhandled from the court.

Harvey watched the defendants being marched and dragged from the dock until they'd completely disappeared from sight, although he could still hear Anderson's mournful protests for several more seconds before they faded to nothing. He again scanned the court until he found the family still sitting huddled together – although Sarah looked to have regained some composure and looked more relieved now, whereas Daniel looked even more distraught than ever. The young boy still just sat impassively – staring straight at him as if he was the only person he could see in the court. The boy seemingly never spoke nor showed any emotion, but Harvey was sure he could sense a burning anger and hatred within his small frame. Where it would lead to, only the boy himself would know.

Harvey approached the Rileys outside the courtroom and sat down next to Sarah who had one arm around Jimmy while the other held a tissue she used to dab away some tears although she was largely composed.

'You all right?' he asked.

'I suppose so,' she answered, stiffening a little. 'Whatever all right is.'

'It was the best result we could have hoped for,' he assured her.

'Result?' she shook her head. 'You people speak in such strange ways. I've lost my daughter, Sergeant Harvey. She's never coming back to me. I don't want a result – I want my daughter back.'

'Sorry,' he said just before a man in a suit walked quickly up to them and pulled a small camera from his pocket and started to take photographs of them. Harvey jumped to his feet and snatched the camera from the man before pushing him away.

'Hey,' the man complained. 'Give me back my camera. You can't take my camera. I have journalistic privilege. That camera's memory is journalistic material.'

'Get the fuck away from them and stay way,' Harvey warned him, tucking the camera in his pocket. 'You want to make a complaint about your fucking journalistic material – be my guest. Now fuck off before I lose my temper.' The journalist scuttled away looking back over his shoulder. Harvey sat back down next to Sarah. 'How the hell did that scum get a camera into court?'

'How long is it going to be like this for?' she asked. 'How long till they leave us alone?'

'I won't lie to you,' he admitted. 'It's going to be a while. Sentencing next month will be... difficult.'

'We won't be here for that,' she said after a long pause. 'We've had enough of this place. If I never see the inside of another court again it'll be too soon. Me and my family are finished with this – all of it.'

'I understand,' he told her. 'I'll let you know what happens as soon as they're sentenced. You have my word.'

'Thank you,' she said as she looked down at Jimmy, straightening his hair with the palm of her hand. 'Whatever they get, it'll never be enough – not for what they did. Not for what they did to my Abigail. I hope they rot in hell.' As she got to her feet Daniel and Jimmy did the same. 'Come on now,' she told them. 'It's time to go home.' With that they walked off along the corridor watched all the way by Harvey.

～

Dolby and Anderson were being led through the bowels of the Old Bailey towards the underground holding cells, both flanked by guards – Dolby a few steps ahead of Anderson.

'We need to stick to the plan, Michael. Right?' Anderson called after him. 'Just stick to the plan.' Dolby didn't respond. 'Just like we discussed, Michael. We have to stick together – right? Stick together and everything will be all right.' Still Dolby didn't respond. 'Michael,' Anderson persisted. 'Michael.' But Dolby said nothing as the guards guided Anderson into a cell and closed the door, his voice echoing around the subterranean tunnels. 'Michael. Michael.'

The guards marched Dolby a little further along before he, too, was guided into a cell. He walked to the middle of the room, standing bolt upright, with his back to the door – unmoving – Anderson still calling his name as the cell door slammed shut behind him.

'Michael. Michael.'

36

New Zealand – Present Time

J ameson arrived home carrying a bunch of files and entered the kitchen where Rose was cooking as usual while Jenny was doing some homework at the table.

'Was wondering when you were going to get home,' Rose said over her shoulder while Jenny ignored him.

'Work's going to be long hours until I can get off this assignment,' he warned her as he looked down at his daughter. 'You okay, Jenny?'

'Yeah,' she answered unenthusiastically without looking at him. 'I'm fine.'

'Everything all right at school?' he risked asking.

'I said everything was fine,' she told him irritably before quickly gathering up her books, jumping to her feet and heading off towards her bedroom. 'I'm going to my room,' she called back without looking at them.

He watched her until she disappeared into her room and closed the door before turning towards Rose. 'Something I said?'

'She's a thirteen-year-old girl,' she reminded him. 'It'll get a lot worse before it gets better.'

'Great,' he said, raising his eyebrows.

Rose looked over her shoulder again at the files he was still holding as she continued to stir whatever was in her favourite cooking pot. 'What you got there?' she asked.

'Just a little homework,' he answered, trying to sound casual. 'I'll be in my office. Give me a shout when dinner's ready.'

'I will,' she agreed. 'Won't be long.'

'Okay,' he replied as he walked along the hallway and into his office before ensuring the door was closed. He turned the desk lamp on, illuminating an otherwise dark room and dropped the files on the desktop before sitting heavily in his old chair. He took a deep breath before lifting the missing persons file of the Latvian backpacker – Anna Sarfas. As soon as he opened the cover he was confronted by a photograph of a smiling, attractive young woman, full of life.

He talked quietly to himself as he read the information in the report. 'Anna Sarfas. Twenty-three-years-old.' He studied the photograph for a second. 'Looks younger. More like a teenager.' He continued to read. 'Last seen heading out of Pukekohe trying to hitch a ride to Auckland. What the hell happened to you, Anna?' he asked himself before tossing the file to one side and looking at the other files on his desk. He randomly started checking the others, but as quickly as he opened them he closed them again, putting aside if they didn't contain photographs of young white women. 'Ran away from home. Ran off with another man. Ran off with underage girlfriend,' he said, dismissing them until he came across one containing photographs of a young Columbian woman – Sofia Martinez, twenty-one-years-old, but again she looked younger.

'Sofia Martinez,' he read with increasing interest. 'On holiday from Columbia travelling around New Zealand when she suddenly disappeared.' He was lost in thought for a few seconds. 'Last seen trying to hitch a ride in a town called Tuakau. Where the fuck is Tuakau?' He quickly grabbed his phone and searched Google Maps for the town. 'About ten miles from Pukekohe,' he discovered. 'Never been heard of since.' He studied the map for a second and realised that if she'd been heading for Auckland she would have probably passed straight through Pukekohe. He suddenly tossed the file on the desk and shook his head. 'I must be going out of my mind,' he complained, rubbing his temples before leaning forward again and picking up the file. He touched the photograph of Anna Sarfas. 'Where are you?' he asked. 'What happened to you?'

He ran his finger across the file until it rested on the section titled – Informant. 'Evelina Gulbis,' he whispered. 'Also in New Zealand when her friend went missing. Was due to meet Anna in Auckland, but she never showed.' He swapped the file for the Martinez one and again looked up the informant. 'Daniella Perez,' he said, finding her. 'Interviewed by police but was unable to assist in the whereabouts of Martinez.'

A sudden knock at the door made him jump before he heard Rose's voice. 'Dinner's ready.'

'Okay,' he answered a little breathlessly. 'I'll be there in a minute.'

He stared at the file for a few seconds before tossing it on top of the Sarfas file as he leaned forward and turned the light off.

37

London – 2005

Harvey climbed from his unmarked car and walked the few steps to the door of the small terrace house in North London that was the Rileys' home – pulling his coat tight against the cold. He knocked on the door and waited – looking up and down the street nervously as he did so. Within a few seconds the door was opened by Sarah. She looked him straight in the eye. 'Well?'

'Can I come in?' he asked. 'We should speak indoors.' She moved aside without saying anything and let him enter before closing the door behind him. She led him to the kitchen where Daniel was pacing around, occasionally sipping a cup of tea. He nodded at Harvey, but didn't say anything.

'Go ahead,' Sarah told Harvey. 'You can tell us. Whatever it is – you can tell us.'

He took a deep breath before breaking the news. 'Fifteen years – with a minimum to serve of ten.'

Sarah staggered a little until she found a chair to sit on. 'Ten years?' she asked in disbelief. 'Ten years?'

'A minimum of ten years,' he reminded her. 'With a bit of luck, they'll do closer to fifteen.'

'Ten years – fifteen years,' Daniel said through clenched teeth, his eyes wild with anger. 'What the fuck's the difference? You call this justice? Fifteen years for what they did to Abigail. This isn't justice.'

'Because of their ages,' he tried to explain. 'It was all the judge could give them.'

'But you can appeal, yes?' Sarah pleaded. 'You can appeal against the sentences?'

'I'm sorry,' he told her. 'We'd be wasting our time. The judge has already given them the maximum he's allowed.'

'Then I'll get justice myself,' Daniel threatened. 'I don't care how long I have to wait – when they get out, I'll be waiting for them. They're dead, d'you hear me –they're dead.'

'Mr Riley,' Harvey appealed to him. 'This sort of talk isn't going to help anyone. I know you're angry right now. I understand that, but don't waste the rest of your life hating them. I've seen it before with the families of other victims. At first they can't believe they'll ever be able to move on, but they do – in time. They don't forget, but they do get back to living their lives.'

'I'm not moving on anywhere,' Daniel warned him. 'Not until I've put those two bastards in their graves.'

'You're wasting your time, Daniel,' Harvey explained. 'Because of their age and the public interest in the case, the state has a duty to protect them when they're eventually released.'

'What the hell are you talking about?' Daniel demanded. 'Protect them? Who was there to protect my Abigail when she needed it? When those bastards raped and...' He spun away from Harvey, unable to finish his sentence.

Harvey waited a while, until things seemed to have calmed slightly. 'They'll probably be given new identities,' he eventually continued. 'Hidden away somewhere and closely monitored – for their own protection as well as for the safety of others. I don't like it any more than you do, but I'm sure that's the way it's going to be.'

Daniel turned slowly towards him, his eyes squinted with suspicion. 'For the safety of others,' he repeated. 'For the safety of others. My God. You think they'll do the same thing again, don't you? If the bastards got the chance – they'd do the same thing all over again? Jesus Christ. What sort of animals do you think they are? Fucking serial killers or something?'

He stalled before answering. 'I've... considered it.'

'Then when they get out you tell me where they are,' Daniel whispered conspiratorially. 'You tell me their new names. If not for Abigail, then to stop them doing the same thing to someone else. You have to, man. It's your duty to protect people from these murdering bastards.'

'I can't do that,' he sighed.

'For the love of God, man.' Daniel raised his voice. 'Can you not hear yourself? If someone doesn't stop them, they'll do it again – to someone else's daughter and you're going to let them.'

'They'll be watched.' Harvey tried to reassure them, but his voice lacked commitment. 'Their computers and phones monitored.'

'And years from now?' Daniel demanded. 'When everyone except us has forgotten about Abigail. Who'll be watching them then?'

'We will,' Harvey answered. 'I can assure you–'

'You've betrayed us,' Daniel interrupted. 'You're more interested in protecting them than you ever were in Abigail. What was she to you – just the slut Irish daughter to a couple of bog-trotters?'

'Daniel.' Sarah reprimanded him just as Jimmy walked into the room – staring at them all.

'It's all right, son,' Daniel told him. 'Away about your business.'

'I'm sorry,' Harvey said. 'I think it's best if I leave.'

'Aye,' Daniel agreed without looking at him. 'Best you do that.'

'Sarah.' He nodded, but she just looked away. He headed towards the door before looking back. 'I'll keep you informed of any changes. I'm sorry we couldn't have done more.' He turned away and walked silently to the front door, desperate to be free of their accusing stares that he could feel burning into him. He eased the front door open and stepped out onto the pavement before closing it behind him. He pulled his coat tight against the cold, just as he had the night they found Abigail and headed to his car.

38

New Zealand – Present Time

O'Doherty woke with a fright and immediately froze as he realised he wasn't in his own hotel bed. It took him a few seconds to recall where he was, a slight sense of panic gripping him when he remembered before checking the other side of the bed for the woman he met in the bar, only to find she wasn't there. He'd broken one of his own rules: he never fell asleep with someone he didn't know very well.

He sprang out of bed, pulled on his undershorts and went looking for her through the house – peeping into each room as he passed until he found her sitting nearly naked in the darkness of the living room smoking a cigarette and looking out over the view of Auckland from her. He crossed the room and stood next to her.

'Nice view,' he told her.

She jumped a little. 'You scared me. I didn't hear you coming.'

'Sorry,' he said.

She took a puff of her cigarette. 'You like cities?' she asked.

'I suppose so,' he shrugged.

'You know you talk in your sleep?' she smiled.

'I do?' he asked, sitting next to her.

'You said some things,' she told him. 'About being sorry for the things you've done. You were saying people's names. What are you sorry for?'

'It was just a bad dream,' he assured her.

'Didn't sound like you were dreaming,' she persisted. 'It sounded like you were remembering. Things you didn't want to remember.'

'I said names?' he asked, sounding casual.

'Yes,' she replied before taking another drag on her cigarette. 'Names of men and women.'

'Uh.' He shrugged as if it was nothing.

'I don't believe you're a businessman,' she said, suddenly looking serious.

'No?' he asked, his eyes narrowing slightly.

'No,' she answered. 'I think you probably do something a lot darker.'

'And what is it you think I do?' he asked, his heart beating hard and fast as he prayed she hadn't heard too much.'

'I don't know,' she admitted, taking a second before continuing. 'Your Australian accent is very good,' she told him, 'but it's not quite perfect. I have a very keen ear. Do I detect a little Irish in there?'

'Maybe,' he replied, still clinging to his false accent.

'The north?' she pressed.

'You got me,' he admitted, speaking in his real voice.

'So,' she said, before taking a drag on her cigarette, 'what's a man from the north of Ireland who talks in his nightmares and uses a fake Australian accent doing in Auckland?'

'Holiday,' he answered unconvincingly.

'Were you... *involved*?' she asked, ignoring his flippant answer. 'You can tell me. My family on my mother's side are Irish. What you tell me goes no further.'

He sighed deeply before answering – his path and her destiny already decided. He couldn't be sure what he'd said in his sleep and he couldn't take the chance she wouldn't go to the police. Telling her about himself couldn't make things any worse now. 'Not until I was into my twenties,' he told her. 'I was what the security services and my commanders called a *cleanskin* – someone who'd never been in or associated with any political or military organisation. Someone who wasn't on anyone's radar.'

'How did you become involved?' she asked.

'I grew up in an area where every kid wanted to be involved,' he explained. 'To go into the streets and chuck stones and petrol bombs at the police and the Brits, but the people around me would never let me.'

'People?' she queried before drawing on her cigarette.

'My own father for one,' he told her. 'My uncles, *known* men from the neighbourhood – all telling me I was being saved for something better. Something more important. They were keeping me *clean* – so I could move about without being watched – even travel abroad. I never went to a demonstration, a republican funeral, a speech. Nothing. I wasn't the only one. There were others like me too.'

'And when you got older, what did you do?' she asked tentatively.

'I was a soldier,' he answered. 'Or at least that's what I believed.' He took a deep breath before continuing. 'I killed people for the cause,' he admitted. 'British soldiers, police officers, informants – anyone connected to the security services. Anyone who was deemed to be an enemy.'

'How many people have you killed?' She surprised him with

the bluntness of her question, making him lean away from her before answering.

'I don't know,' he told her. 'I never kept count. Enough.'

'Do you still work for them?' she asked. 'This *organisation*?'

'No,' he shook his head. 'Not for years. They don't need a man like me anymore. As far as they're concerned, I'm just an embarrassing relic from the past.'

'So why you here?' she said, confronting the obvious.

'A job,' he answered without hesitating.

'To kill someone?' she asked, the hand holding her shrinking cigarette shaking slightly.

'Yes,' he confessed.

'But you said you weren't with any organisations anymore,' she reminded him.

'I work for myself now,' he explained.

'You're an assassin?' she calmly asked him.

'I only take certain jobs,' he said, trying to excuse himself. 'Criminals. People who've done very bad things. No innocents.'

'Are you going to kill me?' she asked bluntly, her eyes glassy with moisture.

'No,' he said after too long a beat. 'I'm going back to bed,' he told her as if nothing had happened, before walking away, leaving her smoking as she looked out at the view when suddenly he burst from the darkness and grabbed her around the neck in an arm lock. His grip was so tight she couldn't speak as he dragged her backwards over the chair and into the centre of the room away from anything she could grab. He kept her pinned to the floor, his forearm crushing her throat as her struggling grew weaker and weaker until she fell still, before slumping in death. He released her, gently lowering her head to the floor. In the semi-darkness a slight shimmer of perspiration shone on his skin, but nothing more. 'Sorry,' was the last thing he said to her.

39

Jameson walked the short distance along a corridor in Auckland Central Police HQ before entering Finch's office just as he was gathering his things and preparing to leave.

'What the hell are you doing here?' he asked when he looked up and saw him. 'You're supposed to be keeping our friend Alexander Knight alive.'

Jameson took a seat without being asked. 'I need to speak to you about something.'

'If it's not about your current assignment I'm not interested,' Finch warned him before sighing as he calmed down. 'Look, Ruben – there's been a murder over in Ponsonby. Some professional woman in her mid-thirties killed in her own home. Apparently it doesn't look good. Bishop wants me to go take a look, so if it's not urgent...'

'A stranger attack?' he asked, his interest piqued.

'I don't know yet,' Finch told him. 'Could be.'

'I'll come with you,' he said, inviting himself. 'Take a look.'

'You need to get back to Knight,' Finch ordered. 'If anything happens to him, I won't be able to save your neck.'

'It's covered,' he pleaded. 'Night shift said they'd cover till I got there.'

Finch stood looking at him with his hands on his hips for a few seconds before making his decision. 'Forget it,' he insisted. 'I need you to get straight back to Knight. Understand?'

'What?' Jameson asked, incredulous. 'Come on, Finch. You need me on this.'

'I need you to keep Knight alive,' he reminded him. 'Look. If I need to run anything past you, I will. But that's it, Ruben.'

'Fine,' Jameson gave in. 'But don't ask me to close my eyes.'

'What's that supposed to mean?' Finch asked.

'You'll see,' Jameson answered before turning on his heels and striding out of the office.

O'Doherty stood in the steaming hot shower in his new hotel room scrubbing himself hard with soap and a brush – removing any possible forensic evidence that could link him to the woman he killed. Once he was satisfied, he stepped out of the shower and went to the sink where a bottle of dark-brown-coloured hair dye waited for him. He tipped it over his head and rubbed it in thoroughly before washing his hands and checking the growing stubble on his face. Pleased with the overall results, he wrapped a towel around his waist and headed into the main room where he took a washbag from the safe before emptying the contents onto the bed – revealing several passports, driving licences and credit cards. He sifted through them until he found the one he wanted – a New Zealand passport bearing a photograph of himself with dark ungroomed hair, plenty of facial stubble and wearing spectacles. He put the other items back in the bag and returned it to the safe before opening the minibar directly underneath it, removing two small bottles of whisky and pouring both into a glass. He wiped the bottles clean of prints before tossing them in the bin and sitting on the bed with his drink, closing his eyes and taking a large mouthful. After swallowing he exhaled and seemed to relax as he searched for the remote and flicked the TV on before sitting back on the bed to watch for news if she'd been found yet.

40

London – 2009

A fourteen-year-old Jimmy Riley walked along the quiet backstreet in Kilburn, North London – his mother walking quietly by his side as the warm summer sun shone down on them, although neither was aware of the fine day. Jimmy should have been in school with little more to worry about than exams and girls, but he'd been sent home early after his mother had been summoned to school again for yet another lecture from the headmaster about his latest incident of bad behaviour – this time, fighting with two other boys.

'This has to stop, Jimmy,' Sarah suddenly told him, now her temper had cooled enough to allow her to speak calmly. 'You're lucky not to be suspended for a week or worse, expelled. Then what would we do?' Jimmy just shrugged. 'That attitude won't solve anything,' she warned him. 'Jesus, Jimmy. I don't know what's the matter with you these days. Ever since... ever since what happened, you've been all over the place. You can't use it as an excuse to throw your life away.'

'I'm not,' Jimmy argued – his voice shallow and sulky.

'Then why all the trouble at school?' she demanded. 'Fighting. Again.'

'They were saying stuff,' he grumbled.

'What were they saying?' she asked.

'Things about Abigail,' he told her.

'Things you should have ignored,' she chastised him. 'You've got to move on. You're young. I'm sorry, but that's just the way it is.'

'They said it was her own fault,' he explained. 'That she went with a lot of boys on the estate.'

'Christ,' she shook her head. 'There's a lot of mean-spirited fools out there, Jimmy. You've got to learn to ignore them.'

'Like dad?' he reminded her. 'He spends all of his time drunk these days.'

'That's not true,' she said, trying to defend her husband, although she knew that Jimmy's words were largely true. The agony of losing Abigail had sent him spiralling into a downward cycle of depression and alcoholism.

'Yes it is,' he argued.

'Your dad's got some problems, that's all,' she lied. 'He'll be all right in time.' Again Jimmy just shrugged. They walked in an uncomfortable silence for a while before he suddenly spoke again.

'I should have been there,' he quietly declared. 'I should have been with her. I could have stopped them.'

She was momentarily shocked into silence before finding her tongue. It was the first time he'd ever said anything like that. 'You couldn't have stopped them,' she assured him. 'You were only ten and there were two of them.'

'I can fight,' he defiantly insisted. 'I wouldn't have been afraid and I wouldn't have run away. I'd have stopped them.'

She stopped walking and looked into his eyes. It only seemed like yesterday when she'd have had to have stooped to do so, but now he was growing into a young man and was nearly as tall as she was. She knew the older he became, the more difficult his anger would be to control. 'I know you wouldn't have run away,' she told him. 'But it's not your fault you weren't there. None of it's your fault. Only those two evil bastards are to blame.'

A brief smile flickered across his lips. 'I've never heard you swear before,' he teased her.

'Well, I'm sorry about that,' she said. 'But when it comes to those two, the normal rules don't apply.' She turned and began walking again – Jimmy following suit.

'But they do, though, don't they,' Jimmy told her after few seconds.

'What do?' she asked, perplexed.

'The normal rules,' he explained. 'They do apply to them.'

'What do you mean?' she questioned.

'The rules,' he repeated. 'The rules that say they can only go to prison for a few years, then they'll be out and free to do whatever they like. Like nothing ever happened. Like Abigail never existed.'

Sarah swallowed the pain of the truth of his words. 'There's nothing we can do about that,' she managed to say, walking a little quicker without realising it. As if she could outrun her grief.

'What if there was something we could do?' he asked, with a seriousness in his voice that made her stop and spin towards him.

'But there isn't,' she reminded him. 'We can't even appeal against their sentence. The judge gave them as long as he could.'

'I'm not talking about the courts,' he replied, spitting out his words as if the mere mention of them caused a bad taste in his mouth. 'Or the police or anyone else who betrayed us. I'm talking about getting justice ourselves.'

'What the hell are you talking about, Jimmy?' she demanded.

'Finding them and...,' he stalled.

'And what?' she pressed.

'Killing them.'

'Oh Jesus, Jimmy,' she told him – stretching out and holding him by the shoulders. 'You shouldn't be thinking such things, let alone saying them,' she whispered. 'It's dangerous talk.'

'It's what they deserve,' he insisted – his eyes burning with hatred.

'You have to stop thinking this way,' she warned him. 'Besides – they're locked in prison.'

'When they get out,' he continued. 'We wait until they get out.'

'They won't be coming back here,' she explained. 'God, you're so naïve. They probably won't even be coming back to London.'

'I'll find them,' he promised. 'Wherever they go. I'll find them.'

'Forget it,' she snapped at him. 'Get those thoughts out of your head before they destroy you.'

'I can't,' he told her through gritted teeth. 'I just can't. Not until they pay for what they did to Abigail.'

'You'll never find them,' she insisted. 'It'll be impossible.'

'I don't believe that,' he argued. 'I'll never stop looking and one day I'll find them and I'll make them pay.'

'Okay, Jimmy,' she sighed, reminding herself he was just a fourteen-year-old boy whose anger would hopefully fade as he matured. 'Then let's just hope that day never comes.'

'It will,' he told her with a troubling coldness. 'I just know it will.'

41

New Zealand – Present Time

Jenny Jameson was sitting in the playground at school alone – reading a textbook, when she was approached by two girls the same age as herself. She knew the girls – Shelley Atherton and Kate Edwards. She also knew that Shelley's dad was a cop in Auckland.

'Hey,' Shelley interrupted her, making her look up from the book.

'Hey,' Jenny replied simply.

'What you doing?' Shelley asked.

'Just some revision,' she told her, a bit suspicious. 'I have a test.'

'You moved here from London, eh?' Shelley pried.

'My dad moved us,' she explained.

'Must be boring for you here after London?' Kate joined in.

Jenny just shrugged, wary of committing to an answer.

'I've seen you around a lot,' Shelley said, pleasantly enough. 'Always seem to be on your own.'

'I don't mind being alone,' Jenny said, dismissing it.

'You got a boyfriend yet?' Shelley smiled.

'No,' she laughed. 'I don't have a boyfriend.'

'How come?' Shelley asked. 'You're really pretty.'

'I don't think so,' she blushed.

'Yeah, you are,' Shelly insisted.

She just shrugged again.

'Maybe you could hang around with us,' Shelly suggested. 'My boyfriend's friends are always looking to meet new girls. We could introduce you.'

'Maybe,' she said without sounding keen.

Shelly glanced at Kate before continuing. 'Your dad's a cop, eh?'

'Who told you that?' she asked, warily, having been told all her life to be careful who she spoke to about what her dad did.

'My dad's a cop too.' Shelly confirmed what she already knew. 'He says he knows your dad.'

'I heard your dad's a cop,' Jenny said, surprising her.

'Yeah,' Shelly said, her face growing serious. 'Knows all about your dad too.'

'What d'you mean, knows all about him?' she asked, suspicious again.

'Says your dad won't be a cop much longer,' Shelly snarled. 'Got some other cop killed back in London and now everyone thinks he's going to do the same thing here.'

'That's not true,' Jenny told her, fighting her rising anger. 'You don't know what you're talking about.'

'My dad says no one here wants to work with him,' Shelly continued. 'And how he mostly has to work on his own.'

'You're lying,' she snapped back, losing the battle with her own feelings.

'Said it's only a matter of time before Professional Standards catch up with him and chuck him out of the police.' Shelly smiled, happy with her taunts.

'You lying bitch,' Jenny shouted before launching herself at Shelly sending both of them tumbling to the ground where they wrestled with each other, exchanging blows and grabbing each other by the hair as more and more children appeared from nowhere, gathering around to watch and cheer. After little more than a minute a young female teacher in a tracksuit appeared, parting the crowd until she reached the combatants and separated them.

'Break it up,' the teacher demanded as the girls tried to break free of her to continue their melee. 'That's enough. I said break it up.' She finally managed to keep them apart and dragged them to their feet. 'What the hell do you think you're doing?'

'She started it,' Shelly said, getting her accusation in first. 'She just attacked me for no reason.'

'You lying bitch,' Jenny repeated her earlier insult and again tried to get free to attack the other girl, but the teacher managed to hold her firm.

'Right,' she told them. 'Both of you with me to the principal's office. You can explain yourselves to her.' She held them as far apart as her arms could stretch and marched them towards the school building to learn their fate.

O'Doherty – with his new dark hair colour, stubble, glasses and casual clothes – stepped from his hotel room and softly closed the door, immediately wiping the handle clean with a handkerchief and headed off along the corridor to the lifts. He loosely wrapped the end of the handkerchief around the end of this index finger and pressed to call the lift. A few seconds later it arrived, the doors opening to allow him to enter. He used the same covered finger to send the lift down to the ground floor, always keeping his head slightly bowed to avoid the ubiquitous CCTV he assumed was watching him. When the lift stopped with a soft bounce, he stepped out and walked across the hotel lobby with his small suitcase in one hand and the keycard to his room pinched in the handkerchief in the other. He dropped the key into a bin without breaking stride as he headed to the exit and out of the hotel, quickly disappearing into the steady flow of pedestrians in Auckland's central business district.

Jameson sat next to Jenny in headmistress Helen Lock's office, both looking very glum. The slightly awkward pleasantries over with, the headmistress got to the business of why they were there. 'Jenny,' she began, looking stern. 'Perhaps you'd like to start by telling us what this is all about.' Jenny just shrugged. 'I'd really like to hear your explanation.'

'Yeah,' Jameson added, sounding frustrated and angry. 'Me too.'

Lock gave him something of a disapproving look that made him turn away to peer out of the window. She turned her attention back to his daughter. 'Jenny. The other girl said you attacked her for no reason. Is that true?'

Jenny just shrugged in silence and looked at the floor.

'Jesus, Jenny,' he snapped at her. 'I had to sneak away from an important assignment to get here. You need to tell us what's going on.'

'Nothing's going on,' she grumpily insisted.

'Then why were you fighting with the other girl?' Lock tried to take back control.

'I don't know,' she lied.

'What you mean you don't know?' he asked, exasperated.

'I mean I don't know,' she repeated, angry now.

'Jenny. I don't have time for this,' he told her. 'I had to call in a lot of favours to get cover so I could be here.'

'Mr Jameson.' Lock tried to calm them down. 'If you could just...'

'I hit her because of what she was saying about you, okay?' Jenny suddenly interrupted with a confession. A long uncomfortable silence engulfed the room.

'What d'you mean, because of what she was saying about me?' he eventually asked.

'Her dad's a cop, all right?' she answered, as if it explained everything.

'So?' he asked, confused.

'So,' she explained, almost shouting, 'he says you're going to lose your job.'

'What?' he said, barely able to believe what he was hearing.

'That none of the other cops will work with you because you got another cop killed,' she angrily explained. 'That it's only a matter of time before you mess up again and they can sack you.'

'Jesus Christ,' he pleaded, sinking into his chair and closing his eyes as another silence descended over the room.

Lock cleared her throat to break the silence before speaking. 'The other girl's surname is Atherton. Do you know the father?'

'Yeah,' he sighed. 'I know him – seen him around. A uniformed constable working central Auckland. Can't remember ever speaking to him.'

'If work's affecting Jenny's home life, perhaps it would be a good idea to inform the school,' Lock suggested. 'So we can give her extra support.'

'Work's fine,' he lied. 'And confidential. Atherton's an arsehole and by the sound of it so's his daughter.'

'Mr Jameson,' Lock protested. 'I'm not sure that attitude's helpful in these circumstances.'

'Fine. I'm sorry,' he told her without a hint of sincerity in his voice before tapping his daughter on the leg and flicking a finger towards Lock. 'Jenny. Tell Mrs Lock you're sorry and it won't happen again.' She rolled her eyes. 'Just do it, Jenny,' he ordered.

She rolled her head to one side, but eventually looked at Lock. 'I'm sorry,' she said with even less sincerity than her father. 'It won't happen again.'

'We all good now?' Jameson asked, leaning forward to push himself out of his chair.

'No, Mr Jameson,' Lock stopped him, making him slump back. 'This is a serious breach of the school's agreed standards of behaviour. I have no choice but to suspend Jenny for the rest of the week.'

'What?' Jenny protested. 'But that's not fair.'

He held his hand up to silence her. 'And the other girl?'

'Same,' Lock assured him. 'Suspended for the rest of the week too. And I'll speak to her about provoking Jenny.'

'Fair enough,' he agreed, leaning forward again.

'But dad,' Jenny said, stopping him.

'Finished,' he cut her dead. 'It's finished. One week suspension, then you come back and you start again. Understand?' Again she rolled her eyes. 'Understand?' he asked more sternly.

'All right,' she agreed, sounding miserable and persecuted. 'I understand.'

'Good,' he nodded once. 'Then there's no need to waste any more of Mrs Lock's time.'

Dolby was in his small kitchen washing up after lunch with Millsie and Detective Constable Rameka, one of the night-duty detectives protecting him. Mills sat at the table while Rameka looked anxiously out the window eager for Jameson to arrive so he could finally go home.

'DS Jameson is very late today,' Dolby said without looking up from the sink. 'I hope everything is all right.'

'He'll be here,' Mills told him, sounding a little agitated. 'Just got something he had to take care of first.'

'Family problems?' Dolby casually asked, still gazing down.

'I'm not here to discuss the personal life of DS Jameson, Mr Knight,' she answered, the concern in her voice clear. 'I'm here to keep you alive.'

'Of course,' Dolby agreed meekly. 'I'm sorry.'

Rameka looked at him out the corner of his eye before glancing at Mills. It was enough to let her know what he would like to do to Dolby.

'If it's all right with you I have things I need to take care of outside,' Dolby told them, turning away from the sink, drying his hands.

'Sure,' Mills agreed. 'Go ahead.'

'Thank you,' he said before throwing the tea towel onto the counter.

'No need to thank me,' Mills told him – emotionless and cold. Dolby nodded and headed for the door.

'I'll go with you,' Rameka jumped in. 'I could do with the air.'

'Fine,' she sullenly agreed. 'Just don't go too far from the house.'

'No need to worry, DC Mills,' Dolby cheerfully reassured her. 'I'm sure I'll be safe enough with DC Rameka watching over me.'

'All the same,' she insisted, 'I'd appreciate it if you didn't go too far.'

'I got it covered, Millsie,' Rameka assured her. 'You just find out where Jameson is. I could do with some sleep, eh?'

'Don't worry about Jameson,' she replied. 'He'll be here.'

'He'd better be,' Rameka told her, looking serious. 'Or he'll owe me more than a couple of favours.'

'Just look after Dolby, eh, Billy,' she rebuked him. 'Let me worry about Ruben.'

Jameson and Jenny were driving home in the frosty silence of his car until finally he felt the time was right to say something. 'You all right?' he asked gently.

'No,' she snapped back at him, as if she'd been waiting for the chance since they'd got in the car. 'No, I'm not all right. Nothing will ever be right until we go home.'

'You mean home in London?' he asked, sighing inside.

'I don't belong here, Dad,' she told him, calmer now. 'We don't belong here. No one barely speaks to me at school and now I find out no one wants to work with you in the police here. Can't we just go home?'

'This is home now, Jenny,' he answered, like he had dozens of times before. 'We can make it work. There's nothing back in London for me anymore.'

'You mean because Mum's dead?' she asked, looking out of the window as they passed rows of weatherboarded houses with their neat front gardens and driveways.

'That and other things that happened,' he shrugged.

'Because your partner got killed?' she pressed.

'Yeah,' he admitted, drawing a breath. 'Because of that.'

'People blamed you for that?' she asked, sounding surprised.

'They tried to,' he told her. 'It went to a central board. I was cleared.'

'But they still made you move?' she questioned.

'It was the best thing for all,' he assured her.

'You never told me this before,' she wondered.

'Couldn't see the point,' he tried to dismiss it. 'I didn't want you to worry.'

'I miss Mum,' she said after a long silence.

'So do I,' he said sadly.

'Why did she have to die?' Jenny asked.

'Because she had untreatable cancer,' he reminded her.

'I know what killed her,' she replied. 'But I don't know why it had to be her.'

'No,' he sighed. 'Nor do I.'

There was another silence before Jenny spoke again. 'If you get fired from the police can we go home?'

'I'm not going to get fired from the police,' he answered, shaking his head and smiling slightly.

'That's not what Shelley said,' she argued.

'Yeah, well,' he said, 'Shelley sounds like a little bitch.'

'You shouldn't say that in front of me,' she smiled. 'Mum would never say that in front of me.'

'Yeah, well I'm not your mum,' he nodded. 'She was a better person than I'll ever be.' He paused for a couple of seconds before continuing. 'Look. If Shelley or anyone else picks on you again just use your brain. You want to teach them a lesson, that's fine. Just don't do it in the middle of the playground and don't get caught.'

'That's not very fatherly advice,' she chastised him.

'You might as well start learning about the real world,' he told her.

She looked out of the window in silence for a while – deep in thought. 'What you doing at work right now?' she suddenly asked. 'Rose said you're protecting someone.'

'Something like that,' he answered, hoping it would be enough to satisfy her interest.

'Why do they need protection?' she said.

'Because someone might want to hurt them,' he explained.

'Why would someone want to hurt them?' she pried.

He took a deep breath before replying, torn between being honest with her and wanting to protect her from the sickening truth. 'Because a long time ago they hurt someone – very badly.'

'You mean they killed them?' she persisted.

'Yes,' he told her bluntly, glancing at her to see her reaction.

'Who did they kill?' she asked.

'A young girl,' he answered. 'Not much older than you.'

'Did they do other things to her?' she said, digging deeper.

'You don't need to know that,' he warned her.

'You said I needed to start learning about the real world,' she reminded him of his own words. 'Tell me.'

'She was very badly injured,' he said after a while. 'Before she died. They did... things to her.'

'They?' she seized on it. 'Then there were more than one?'

'There was,' he admitted. 'But there's only one now. The other was killed in Canada. Shot.'

She squinted with concentration. 'So, you think whoever killed them is coming after the one you're protecting?'

He looked over at her. 'Clever girl. You'll make a good detective.'

'Maybe I will,' she teased before becoming serious again. 'Doesn't sound like he deserves protecting. You should leave him to pay for what he did.'

'I can't do that,' he told her.

She thought in silence for a while before speaking. 'If you

keep him alive, things will be better for you at work?' she asked, hopefully.

'Don't worry about my work,' he insisted. 'I'm working on something that could change everything.'

'I thought you were just supposed to be protecting this man,' she said, and shook her head, confused. 'Keeping him safe will change everything?'

'It's connected,' he explained. 'It's complicated. But it's something I need to do.' He looked at her again, before returning his eyes to the road. 'Everything will be fine,' he assured her. 'I promise you. Everything's going to work out fine. Now,' he said, changing the subject, 'You need to give me your phone.'

'What?' she said, sounding incredulous. 'Why?'

'Punishment,' he said, smiling. 'You lose your phone.'

'That's not fair,' she insisted.

'Just for a few days,' he told her, holding out his hand in expectation.

'But what if I go out at night?' she reasoned. 'You wouldn't want me out without being able to get hold of me.'

'Good point,' he agreed, giving her false hope. 'You're grounded as well.'

'What?' she protested. 'You're joking, right?'

'I've got to do something,' he explained. 'You just got suspended from school for fighting. There has to be some kind of punishment.'

'Dad,' she pleaded.

'Hand it over,' he insisted. 'Just a few days. You're getting off pretty lightly, young lady.' She rolled her eyes as she pulled the phone from her blazer pocket and slapped it into his waiting palm with a huff. 'Thanks,' he said with a smile. 'Your mum would be proud of me.'

42

O'Doherty walked in a crouch from the bush and settled in the treeline on the crest of a hill that overlooked Dolby's farm. He took a set of binoculars from his backpack and looked down on the buildings below, scanning the area until he found Dolby stacking chopped wood at the side of the house while a woman he assumed was a cop, stood close by – the holstered pistol attached to her belt clearly displayed. He made the snap decision that this was as good an opportunity as he was likely to get, with apparently only one cop on duty and decided to take Dolby out there and then.

He pulled a pistol from his backpack, attached the silencer and slapped a magazine in, pulling back the top lever to put a bullet in the chamber and cock the weapon ready for firing. He was just about to head down to the farm when he was disturbed by the sound of an engine that made him look up to see a car in the distance approaching the farm. He snatched up his binoculars and focused in on the car bouncing along the dirt road before it skidded to a stop outside the farmhouse. The detective he recognised from before stepped from the car and held a hand up towards the woman as he walked towards her as if he was apologising for something.

He was a good shot and knew he could hit Dolby from some distance and melt away before a cop on their own could follow him. But two cops more than doubled the risk to himself and he didn't want to take on two armed detectives. He was only here for Dolby. Killing cops was bad for business. He gave a knowing nod of his head before quickly dismantling the pistol, packing it away and disappearing back into the bush.

Jameson headed for Mills and Dolby outside the farm as she started walking towards him, he assumed so Dolby wouldn't be able to hear what she was about to say to him. He held his hands up in anticipation of her impending wrath. 'Sorry, Millsie,' he said as soon as she was within range. 'I got here as quick as I could.' He looked around as if he was searching for something. 'Where's Rameka?'

'He couldn't wait any longer,' she told him, hands on hips to let him know she was pissed off. 'He had to go. Jesus, Ruben. There's supposed to be two of us here at all times. What if something had happened?'

'Nothing's going to happen,' he said, trying to reassure her.

'Everything all right at home, detective?' Dolby shouted over to them. Jameson's eyes narrowed as he started to walk towards him.

'Let it go, Ruben,' Mills said, trying to stop him, but he ignored her, brushing her shoulder as he passed by, walking until he was close to Dolby.

'What did you say?' he snarled into Dolby's face.

Dolby looked around nervously, trying to avoid eye contact.

'I was just saying... I hope everything's okay at home. I know you have a teenage daughter and that can't be–'

'You know what?' he interrupted aggressively.

'Just...' Dolby stumbled. 'I heard someone mention... you had a daughter and...'

'You know fuck all about me,' Jameson warned him before pointing his index finger into Dolby's face. 'You ever mention my family again I'll fucking bury you.'

Dolby cleared his throat. 'I'm sorry,' he said. 'I didn't mean to intrude. Perhaps it's best if I make us some coffee.' He took a wide route around Jameson and headed off towards the house.

'Yeah,' Jameson called after him. 'You do that.' He waited for him to reach the house before walking back to Mills.

'Well, that's going to help,' she told him – her hands back on her hips. 'Jesus, Ruben. You're such a fuck-up.'

'What you talking about?' he said, sulking.

'Our assignment,' she reminded him. 'Keeping Knight alive. Threatening him's not going to help us keep him alive.'

'Jesus,' he complained, shaking his head and grimacing. 'Don't give me a hard time, Millsie.'

'Give you a hard time?' she repeated, sounding indignant. 'You're supposed to be here with me, Ruben. What if someone does turn up who's prepared to go through me to get to Knight? One against one isn't good odds.'

'Relax, Millsie,' he said, dismissing her fears. 'Nothing's going to happen to you.'

'Well, thanks for being so concerned,' she said sarcastically.

'Look,' he told her, spreading his arms wide. 'The hit in Canada was probably a one-off. The guy who got killed probably just pissed of the local gangsters – the fact he was who he was is just a coincidence. Criminals drift into the criminal world no matter where they end up. Dangerous place to be.'

'Knight hasn't,' she reminded him, making him look towards the farmhouse before replying.

'Listen,' he said. 'Even if there is a hitman out there somewhere, which I doubt, he's not going to risk taking on even one armed cop. Too dangerous. He'll wait. He's not going to risk having his head blown off by a cop just for another job. He just wants to take out the mark nice and clean and disappear.' He took a breath and once more looked at the farmhouse. 'Believe me, Millsie – if you're in any danger from anyone it's from Dolby.'

'What the hell you talking about, Ruben?' she asked in a tone that let him know she didn't believe a word he was saying.

He sighed and looked everywhere but at Mills. 'Nothing,' he said, waving

it away. 'Forget it.' She just stood shaking her head. 'I'm going to take a look around the farm,' he said to break the silence.

'I thought you said there was nothing to worry about?' she reminded him. 'Nobody out there?'

'There isn't,' he told her over his shoulder as he was already walking away. 'I just need some air and to clear my head.'

'You do that,' he heard her say as he headed towards the bush – her eyes burning into the back of his head and thoughts of what he'd like to do to Dolby smouldering in his mind.

43

Jameson arrived home and entered the kitchen where Rose was at her usual station cooking away. She glanced over her shoulder when she heard him. 'You're back then?' she greeted him.

'Yeah,' he said, stating the obvious. 'It would appear so.'

'Heard there was some trouble at school today,' she casually told him.

'Yeah,' he confirmed, taking his jacket off and hanging it on the back of a chair he then sat on.

'Want to talk about it?' she asked.

'No,' he answered bluntly, kicking his shoes off.

'You know,' she told him, stirring the pot, 'maybe it would be better for Jenny if you were home a little more.'

He tried to massage the tension out of his neck while stifling a yawn. 'Well – that ain't gonna happen any time soon,' he replied. 'I'm gonna go check on Jenny.' He wearily pushed himself out of the chair and headed off along the hallway. When he reached her he knocked on the closed bedroom door and waited to be invited in.

'What do you want?' Jenny's voice asked from the other side of the door.

He sighed and rested his head against the door. 'Jenny. It's me.'

'I know who it is,' she replied.

He waited for her to say more but was disappointed. 'Want to talk about it?' he eventually asked, but there was no reply. 'Jenny?' He waited again but heard only silence. 'Can I come in?'

'It's not locked,' she replied a few seconds later.

He lifted his head from the door before taking a deep breath, opening it and stepping inside to find her sitting with her back to him as she sat at her desk pretending to study.

'Aren't you supposed to be protecting that murderer?' she asked without turning to look at him.

'Night shift's taken over,' he told her. 'I don't have to go back till morning.'

'I don't know why you didn't just stay there,' she complained. 'He's more important to you than I am.'

'Want to talk about what happened at school today?' he asked, refusing to take the bait.

'No,' she insisted, finally spinning to face him. 'Want to talk about the man you're protecting?'

'No,' he shook his head. 'Not really.'

Neither of them spoke for a while as he walked deeper into her room and sat on the bed facing her. 'At school today,' he said. 'I know you were only trying to stick up for me. Thanks.'

'You're *glad* I did it?' she asked quietly.

'Kind of.' He shrugged. 'Maybe not the way you did it, but the fact you did is pretty cool.' She just stared at the floor. 'Tough, though – times like this. It's when I miss your mum most.' She shrugged, but didn't say anything. 'I just want to... just want to speak to her, you know? Talk stuff through. Talk about you. She was so proud of you.'

'Sometimes,' she suddenly responded. 'Sometimes I can't remember what she looks like. I have to... I have to look at her picture.'

'You're young,' he dismissed it. 'Even younger when it happened. She knows you love her and she loves you.'

She got up from her desk, walked over to the bed and sat next to him. He put an arm around her and listened to her crying softly. 'I really miss her, Dad,' she said, weeping.

'I know,' he told her, choking back his own tears. 'I miss her too.'

'I remember... I remember she used to make me feel safe,' she said, reminiscing.

'I'll keep you safe,' he vowed, pulling her closer. 'I'll never let anything happen to you.'

'You promise?' she looked for reassurance, no longer a teenager, but a child again.

'I promise, Jenny,' he swore. 'I promise.'

44

O'Doherty sat inside his motorhome parked close to Piha beach with the net curtains drawn, his dishevelled hair and lengthening whiskers making him look increasingly like any other traveller chilling out as he toured New Zealand. The photographs he'd taken from the farm, as well as those of Dolby and the policeman, were spread out across the table. He looked at the photos of the farm, trying to find a way to get close enough, shoot Dolby and escape cleanly even with the cops there, but couldn't find anything obvious. He tossed the photos to one side in frustration and swapped them for a close-up of Dolby which he studied for a while before also tossing it away disinterestedly. He sat staring into space for a few seconds before picking up a close-up of Jameson, studying it for a long while, trying to get a feel for the man who stood between him and his target.

There was certainly something about the cop he recognised – a look he'd seen before in the faces of dangerous men he'd dealt with in the past. A determination not to let anything get in the way of what they want. It didn't bode well. He gave a resigned sigh and tossed the photograph back amongst the others.

～

Jameson sat in his car parked on the farm calling Sergeant Jack Neil on his mobile. 'Ruben,' Neil answered. 'And to what do I owe the pleasure?'

'You back at HQ?' he asked, dispensing with any niceties.

'Sure,' Neil replied. 'Why?'

'I need you to do something for me,' he told him.

'Go on,' Neil said, a little suspicious.

'I need you to log onto the PNC and look something up for me,' Jameson explained.

'And what would that be?' Neil asked.

'I need the details of everyone reported missing in the Greater Auckland area over the last four years,' he answered, knowing what reaction he was likely to get.

'What?' Neil laughed. 'You're joking, right? There'll be bloody hundreds, if not thousands. Could take days. Weeks.'

'No,' he shook his head. 'I'm not interested in the everyday crap – just young, slightly built women – lone travellers, particularly ones from countries that have less of a traditional link to New Zealand – Eastern Europe, South America – that sort of thing.'

'Okay.' Neil sighed. 'But it'll still take time.'

'Fine,' he agreed. 'Just get back to me when you have the results.'

'No problem,' Neil assured him. 'You need anything else?'

'Yeah,' he quickly answered. 'I'm already looking into a couple of missing person reports – two women who both disappeared within the last couple of years. I need you to find the informants for me.'

'You got their names?' Neil asked.

'First one's Anna Sarfas,' he began, knowing Neil would be ready with a pen and paper. 'From Latvia. Reported missing by her friend – Evelina Gulbis – also Latvian. Second one is Sofia Martinez – Columbian. Reported missing by Daniella Perez – another Columbian. You get all that?'

'You sure they didn't just jump ship somewhere?' Neil asked. 'Didn't fancy returning to the homeland.'

'I know what it looks like,' he told him. 'But can you find them?'

'Sure.' Neil sighed. 'Unusual names like that should make it easy – if they're still in New Zealand. If they're not...'

'Just do what you can,' he encouraged him.

'Will do,' Neil agreed.

'Thanks,' he said before hanging up. He was about to put the phone away but found himself looking for Lisa's number in his contacts. But once he had her number, he couldn't make his finger press the button. After a few seconds he sighed and stuffed the phone back in his pocket before climbing out of the car and heading towards the house when Mills came out to meet him.

'Everything okay?' she asked, sounding concerned.

'Yeah,' he told her, not wanting to talk about his conversation with Neil. 'Fine. How's our friend?'

'Why don't you go see for yourself?' she answered. 'He's inside. I'm going to check around outside. If you need me...' She patted the mobile phone attached to her waist belt and headed off into the field. He watched her for a couple of seconds before reluctantly heading towards the farmhouse. He entered the kitchen where he found Dolby preparing some food. Dolby looked at him briefly.

'I take it all is well?' he asked.

'Yeah,' Jameson replied, his voice thick with contempt. 'Fine.'

'And your daughter?' Dolby tried to be civil. 'She's well?'

'I already told you,' he warned him. 'Don't talk about my daughter. Understand?'

'If that's what you want,' Dolby said, concentrating on cooking.

'It is,' he snapped back.

They both stood in an awkward silence for a long while until Dolby broke it. 'Any sign of the mysterious assassin?' he asked slightly sarcastically.

'No,' he replied bluntly, not wanting to engage in conversation with him about anything.

'Maybe you and DC Mills should leave me to it or turn a blind eye, if the hitman ever turns up,' Dolby suggested. 'Let him kill me. Isn't that what everyone really wants? Maybe I even want it myself. Maybe it's what I deserve.' Jameson ignored him. 'You know what surprises me about you the most?'

'No,' he answered, disinterestedly. 'What?'

'That you've managed to resist the temptation to interview me about the crime I'm supposed to have committed,' Dolby explained. 'Every other cop I've ever met always ends up interviewing me about it. But not you.'

'I don't need to interview you,' he said, looking at him in disgust. 'I've read the case file.'

'Then you'll know that the British police never found any trace of my semen in or on the victim,' Dolby explained.

'No,' he admitted, 'but they did find the other man's semen as well as traces of spermicide – most probably from a prophylactic. Means he was dumb. You were smart. Makes you the cold and calculating one. Makes you a very dangerous animal. More dangerous than Anderson ever was. Before someone shot him through the head and put him out of his misery, that is.'

'I never touched the girl,' Dolby said quietly. 'The

spermicide came from her having sex with her boyfriend some time earlier. I'm sure of it. But no one would listen. No one wanted to hear it.'

'Fucking bullshit,' he told him calmly but threateningly. 'You just don't have the decency to admit your guilt. I read all about the boyfriend in the file. He was interviewed and denied ever having sex with her. For all anyone knew she was still a virgin.'

'Of course he did,' Dolby argued. 'She was only fourteen. If he admitted to having sex with her he would have been guilty of having sex with an underage girl and the police would have had no choice but to prosecute. Neither he nor his parents were ever going to allow that to happen.'

He thought about what Dolby had said for a couple of seconds before dismissing the possibility. 'It would be better for all if you just admitted your guilt.'

'I remember it like it was yesterday,' Dolby said, ignoring him as he appeared to be almost going into some sort of trance. 'So vivid still – after all this time. She was so scared. I... I suppose she must have sensed what was going to happen. She tried to get away, but Paul hit her – hit her hard. When she was on the floor he started tearing at her clothes – ripping them. I... I didn't know what to do, so I just stood there. I just stood there and watched as he... as he took the knife and... God – there was so much blood.' He paused to steady himself. 'Then he started... then he started to rape her and she was... she was crying – begging me to help her. I tried to pull him off, but he pushed me away – threatened me with the knife.

'When it was over, he turned to me and said it was my turn now. Told me what... what I should do to her. But I refused.' He swallowed hard, his skin ashen. 'I just wanted to run – to run away and keep running. To get away from that place, but Paul started going crazy – threatening me with the knife again and saying he was going to kill her if I didn't rape her, but I couldn't. I just couldn't. Eventually he gave up trying to make me. Then he went back to Abigail. That's when he started... started to stab her, but it was more than that. He was out of control. Like he was... like he was someone else. Something else. Not human anymore.' He grabbed hold of the kitchen counter, as if he needed it to stop himself from collapsing.

'I've read the case file,' Jameson snarled unsympathetically. 'I've seen the photographs of the victim and the crime scene. She wasn't just killed. She was butchered. Her breasts were cut off while she was probably still alive. You expect me to believe Anderson could have done that on his own? He would have needed help. *You* would have had to help him.'

'I don't care what you or anyone else believes,' he told him, finally making eye contact. 'Not anymore. All I know is that I see her face during every waking second and every sleeping moment of my life. I can't get through a single minute without remembering. Have you any idea what that's like?'

Some flicker of doubt about Dolby's guilt briefly appeared across Jameson's face while at the same time memories of shooting Sarwar jumped into his mind. 'More than you think,' he answered almost unwittingly.

'Really?' Dolby seized on it. 'In what way?'

'Never mind,' he snapped at him. 'Forget it.' He looked around the kitchen which suddenly felt claustrophobic and oppressive. 'I'm going to check up on DC Mills,' he said as an excuse to leave and headed for the door. He felt Dolby's eyes watching him every step of the way.

45

London – 2014

Harvey entered the generic-looking coffee shop in Kilburn High Road and scanned the customers until he spotted Sarah sitting alone, hidden away at a table in the far corner. He caught her eye as he waited in the short queue before getting himself a black coffee and heading over to where she sat, slipping his cup and saucer onto the table.

'Hello, Sarah,' he said.

'Hello, Fraser,' she said.

'I'm sorry. Can I get you another drink?'

'No, no,' she insisted. 'I'm fine.'

He took a seat opposite her. 'So. What can I do for you?'

'Jimmy,' she told him, shaking her head.

'Jimmy,' Harvey repeated, leaning back in his chair. 'So, what is it this time?'

'More trouble,' she explained. 'Getting worse too.'

'I've had people keeping an eye on him as best I can,' he told her. 'He's been dragged away from more than one fight and taken home instead of the station – I can tell you that.'

'It's a miracle he hasn't been convicted of anything serious,' she continued. 'But I fear it's only a matter of time before he is.'

'I'll continue to make sure the local police are aware of his situation,' Harvey promised. 'But I don't see that there's much else I can do.'

'He's obsessed with Abigail's murder,' she said, ignoring him. 'He spends most of his time researching the case. When he's not drinking and getting into trouble, he's on the internet looking for anything he can about it – searching for anything that might help him find them when they eventually get out – any clue as to where the police might put them.'

'He's wasting his time,' he told her. 'They won't be released for a couple years yet. No one would have thought about what to do with them yet and even when they do – there'll be nothing about it on the internet or anywhere else about where they'll be relocated.'

'Relocated.' She sighed. 'It'll be nice for them to have new lives. No one ever offered to *relocate* us.'

'I can look into it, if you want,' he suggested.

'No,' she said, dismissing it. 'It's too late now. Besides, running away won't make things better. Won't change Jimmy.'

'I'm sorry,' was all he could think of to say.

'He still has nightmares, you know,' she revealed. 'I never told you about it before.'

'No,' he agreed. 'About not being able to save Abigail?'

'Sometimes,' she answered. 'But mostly about being taken. Taken to some cold, dark place by those... monsters. Taken and killed like Abigail was.'

'I see,' he replied, before taking a sip of his coffee. 'That must be hard – on both of you?'

'Maybe it's because they were so close,' she said, ignoring his question – lost in her own memories. 'There was more than four years between them, but they loved each other.' She suddenly looked up at him. 'I never asked – do you have any children?'

He cleared his throat before answering. 'No. It never happened for us. For my wife and I.'

'Oh,' she said sadly. 'I'm sorry for that.'

'Don't be,' he smiled weakly. 'It's fine.'

'Anyway,' she continued. 'As I was saying, they were close – Jimmy and Abigail. She looked after him all the time. More like a second mother than a sister. Tell me, Fraser. What would you do if someone killed your mother like Abigail was killed?'

'I don't know,' he admitted. 'Try to move on and live my life.'

'I don't believe you,' she said accusingly, causing a silence to descend on them. After an uncomfortable few seconds, she spoke again – quietly. 'They took his sister, his father. The people he loved most in the world. And they took everything from me too. All I have left is that boy, but if things don't change, I'll lose him too. I'm sure I will. Then I'll have nothing – unless you *help* me. You're the only one who can help.'

'If you're asking what I think you're asking, then you're wasting your time,' he insisted. 'I don't know what's going to happen to them and even if I did, I wouldn't tell you or anyone else. Prison isn't a great place for a cop. And besides, my wife is... she's ill. Motor neurone disease. Amyotrophic lateral sclerosis, the doctors tell us. She needs me. I'm all she has. If I knew where they were and something happened to them, I would come under immediate suspicion. Apart from going to prison, I would lose everything. And I'm a cop. Not a vigilante. And Jimmy's no killer, I can tell you that. Tough kid. Confused. Angry, but he's no killer. What he's talking about, it's just fantasy.'

'Fantasy or not,' she told him. 'I truly believe I'll never have my son back unless this thing is finished. Once and for all.'

'Sarah,' he pleaded. 'Forget this. Get your priest to talk to him – anything, but forget this.'

'I've tried,' she explained. 'He won't. I swear I'm going to lose him if you don't help me end this. Jimmy will never stop – unless I can take it out of his hands.'

'What the hell are you talking about, Sarah?' he asked, increasingly exasperated.

'You were right when you said we'd never get away with it,' she reminded him. 'If we went after *them* ourselves. But it wouldn't be Jimmy. I could never let that happen. It would be... someone else. I... I know people. People who could help.'

'Who do you know?' he asked disbelievingly. 'How could you know someone?'

'I can't tell you that,' she whispered. 'It's better you don't know.'

'Sarah, I don't know what you're thinking about, but forget it. Help Jimmy as best you can, but forget all this talk of finding them,' he warned her.

'With or without your help, Jimmy will never stop looking,' she told him. 'But without you, he'll never find them and this will never end and that will destroy him – eventually. The only thing that will save him is if this... thing can be brought to an end.'

'I'm not interested in revenge,' he explained. 'I did my job and put them away.'

'Revenge is for Jimmy,' she reminded him. 'Your motivation is different.'

'My motivation?' he asked, leaning back into his seat.

'To stop them doing it again,' she answered.

'I don't know if they'd do it again,' he replied unconvincingly. 'No one does.'

'Yes, you do,' she insisted. 'I can see it in your face, just like every other time you've been asked.'

'Even if it's true,' he argued, 'they'll be constantly monitored. They won't get the chance.'

'But you're afraid they'll find a way, aren't you?' she asked. 'Aren't you?'

'It's out of my hands now,' he answered. 'There's nothing I can do – other than trying to keep Jimmy out of trouble.'

'Then we're done,' she told him. 'I won't bother you again. Needless to say, this conversation never took place.'

'Of course,' he agreed. 'I'm sorry I couldn't have done more, but it's just not possible.'

'Goodbye, Fraser,' she said, getting to her feet. 'I hope your wife recovers.'

For a split second he thought about telling her that his wife would never recover – her illness was a death sentence – but he decided not to. 'Take care, Sarah,' was all he said instead, before watching her head to the exit and walk away as he wondered if it would be the last time he ever saw her.

46

New Zealand – Present Time

Dolby crouched on his bathroom floor, his body so tense every sinew and muscle strained to breaking point – every vein and artery bulged as if they were going to burst. He bit down on his own hands, as if he needed to feel intense pain to try and control his convulsions as he struggled to breathe. Periodically he clamped a hand over his own mouth to stifle any noise escaping – fighting back the tears as his entire body twisted and jolted uncontrollably. After a while, slowly, he began to relax more and more – the convulsions become mere twitches until they stopped altogether. He lay on the floor a while longer, recovering his breath, regaining control of his muscles until he was able to stagger to his feet. He stood in front of the bathroom mirror checking his appearance before washing his face with cold water and smoothing out his hair. He took one last steadying breath and headed for the door.

He walked the short distance along the hallway and entered

the kitchen where Jameson and Mills watched him closely as he gingerly took a seat. They looked at each other and then back to Dolby.

'You okay?' Mills asked. 'You don't look too good.'

'I'll be fine,' he managed to tell her. 'Must have eaten something that disagreed with me.'

'You sure you'll be all right?' she checked. Dolby just nodded. 'Okay,' she shrugged. 'I need to check outside. Won't be long.' She glanced at Jameson before leaving them alone. There was an awkward silence until Jameson spoke first.

'Sure you're okay?' he asked, sounding less hostile that usual. 'You look a bit pale.'

'I'm... I'm already feeling much better,' Dolby insisted. 'Thank you.'

'Don't thank me.' He recovered his colder, hardened attitude.

'I'll need to go into town tomorrow,' Dolby told him, changing the subject. 'I need some supplies.'

'No,' he said. 'No trip to town. We'll have the supplies brought in.' His mobile rang before Dolby could argue. He checked the caller ID before answering and saw it was Sergeant Neil.

'Jack,' he greeted him.

'Can you speak?' Neil asked. 'I got that information you wanted.'

'Give me a minute,' he told him, looking at Dolby out the corner of his eye.

'Sure,' Neil agreed as Jameson headed out of the kitchen leaving his jacket hanging on the back of a chair. He missed Dolby's eyes turning into narrow slits of concentration as he walked from the farmhouse, talking into the phone as soon as he decided he was clear from Dolby's earshot.

'What you got?' he hurriedly asked.

'I searched Missing Persons using the criteria you gave me,'

Neil explained. 'Found about a dozen that fit. Want me to email them to you?'

'Yeah.' His mind was already swirling with the possibilities of what it could mean. 'Fine. And the informants – for the two I told you about?'

'No joy with the Martinez informant – Daniella Perez,' Neil disappointed him. 'She went back to Columbia a couple of years ago. I've sent a request for information to the local police, but don't hold your breath.'

'And Anna Sarfas?' he quickly moved on, desperate to give his secret investigation something solid to pursue. A real lead – a real person to speak to instead of just old, closed reports.

'You got lucky.' Neil made his heart miss a beat. 'The informant – Evelina Gulbis, applied for and was given New Zealand residency a few months after Sarfas went missing. She still lives in Auckland – works in the Hilton down in the Viaduct. I have her home address and contact details if you want them.'

'Yeah,' he replied, relief and excitement running through him in equal measure. 'Sure. Send them to me will you?'

'No worries,' Neil assured him. 'You want me to call her?'

'No,' he answered quickly. 'No. I'd rather see her in person. Thanks, Jack.'

'Any time,' Neil replied.

He hung up and headed back inside. As soon as he entered the kitchen he saw his jacket hanging on the back of the chair and remembered in a panic that he'd left his wallet in the inside pocket, such had been his eagerness to speak to Neil. Dolby seemed oblivious to him as he just stood staring out of the window. Jameson hurriedly pulled his wallet from the jacket and opened it, the first thing he saw being a headshot photograph of Jenny he always kept inside.

Dolby suddenly spun around, catching him off guard as he stood looking through his wallet. Dolby smiled slightly. 'My crime wasn't theft, Sergeant Jameson,' he reminded him. 'If only it had been.' He turned his back on him again and returned to looking out of the window.

Jameson carefully checked through the contents of his wallet – including his driving licence – before carefully closing it and slipping it back in his jacket – a little disappointed he hadn't found something missing. It would have given him just the excuse he needed to drag Dolby to the nearest police station and get himself reassigned. But it wasn't to be. Not this time.

O'Doherty was in his motorhome drinking a coffee and watching the news as he cleaned and checked the pistol and ammo. Suddenly an article came on the news about the woman he'd killed. He watched intently, breathing a sigh of relief that there didn't appear to be any CCTV footage of him yet, even though his appearance since had changed significantly.

Once the news item was over, he lifted a phone battery and attached it to the mobile phone sitting on the table next to him. He dialled a number from memory and waited for an answer. After a few rings the tentative voice of a man spoke into his ear.

'Hello.'

'It's Declan here,' O'Doherty replied. 'Just wanted you to know I'm having a great time over here. Any chance I could have a quick word with Uncle Francis?'

There was a few seconds' silence before the man answered. 'Sure. Wait there. I'll get him for you.'

He heard the phone being rested on something solid as he pictured the man in his mind running through the rain in a Belfast street until he reached Eamon Rafferty's front door and pounded on it.

He imagined Rafferty opening it without speaking – the man

telling him there's a call for him. He saw Rafferty nodding as he grabbed his raincoat from the coat stand, pulling it over his head before stepping outside – walking briskly along the street – entering the man's house as if it were his own – striding down the hallway – snatching up the phone and speaking into it. The sudden sound of Rafferty's real voice made him jump.

'Hello,' Rafferty greeted him confidently.

'Is this phone secure?' he asked, skipping any pleasantries.

'It is,' Rafferty answered briskly.

O'Doherty went through his normal checks anyway. 'It's never been used by a person of interest before?'

'I said it was secure,' Rafferty reassured. 'Where are you?'

There was a tense pause before O'Doherty answered. 'South.'

'And the job?' Rafferty enquired, a little pensively.

'Still waiting to be done,' he told him.

'Problem?' Rafferty asked.

'He has... company,' he explained.

'I understand,' Rafferty replied after a couple of seconds. 'Can you get round it?'

'Eventually,' he assured him. 'Just a matter of waiting for the right moment. It'll come.'

'You sure?' Rafferty checked.

'I'm sure,' he asserted.

'Good.' Rafferty sighed.

'There's something else,' he told him before Rafferty could end the call.

'Go on,' Rafferty said, the concern clear in his voice.

'There's been some... necessary collateral damage,' he explained.

'One of his *friends*?' Rafferty asked. O'Doherty knew he meant one of his police guards.

'No,' he told him. 'An innocent. A woman.'

There was another silence before Rafferty spoke. 'How?'

'Wrong place – wrong time,' he answered matter-of-factly.

'It happens,' Rafferty said.

'I need to know if it's been in the news – at home?' he told him.

'I haven't seen anything,' Rafferty answered. 'You're clear. Once you get north, you'll be safe.'

'Good,' he replied.

'Anything else?' Rafferty asked him.

It took him a while to find the right words. 'I've been thinking,' he eventually spoke. 'This'll be my last job. No more after this.'

'Okay,' Rafferty replied without arguing. 'If that's what you want.'

'It is,' he confirmed. 'I'll be in touch when it's done.' He hung up without saying another word and immediately removed the battery from the phone before sitting in silence – images of his past running through his conscience as he considered his future. Just this one last job and home to run his pub and restaurant. No more false passports or cleaning up anonymous hotel rooms around the world. No more knocking on the doors of old contacts and seeing the fear in their eyes. No more *collateral damage* to deal with. No more being the last thing his *marks* saw before leaving this world. He could leave the work behind, but he knew the ghosts of his trade would never leave him. Their faces would always be there – waiting for him every time he fell asleep.

47

New Zealand – 2017

Sergeant Hodges stepped from his marked police four-by-four and surveyed the small farmhouse in front of him and the land surrounding it. His intelligent, piercing green eyes wandered over the neglected building and fields as he remembered the young family who'd bought it as a *lifestyle plot* some years ago, before they abandoned it and fled back to the comforts of metropolitan Auckland. He stretched the stiffness out of his ageing back and legs, the legacy of too many years of playing rugby for the police and forced his tall, broad body towards the house. Like most police officers in New Zealand, he wasn't routinely armed, but after reading about Dolby's crime, he'd brought along one of his own shotguns from home, although he decided to leave it in the truck until he'd had a chance to take the measure of the man he was about to meet. A man who the British press had called a monster – even though he'd only been sixteen at the time of the killing. As he neared the front of the rundown building, Dolby stepped from inside onto the porch carrying a broom in one hand and a bucket in the other. He froze when he saw Hodges – his eyes narrowing with suspicion.

'Can I help you?' he asked politely, but coldly.

'Sergeant Hodges,' the big, uniformed cop told him as he climbed the small staircase and onto the porch. 'From Pukekohe police.'

'Ah, yes,' Dolby seemed to relax. 'The detectives who've been... looking after me said I should expect a visit from the local police.'

'The Serious Crimes Unit,' Hodges said, as he nodded while studying the man in front of him – every word he said and move he made – already feeling slightly unbalanced by Dolby's clean-cut, businesslike appearance and pleasant voice. 'They'll still visit you from time to time, as will someone from the British police, but mostly it'll be myself and the inspector keeping an eye on you. Making sure everything's okay.'

'Keeping an eye on me?' Dolby asked with a wry smile.

Hodges took a couple of steps closer, puffing himself up to his full size, but could see no sign of Dolby being intimidated. 'I'm fully aware of the crime you were convicted of, Mr Knight,' Hodges told him. 'So yes. I'll be keeping a very close eye on you. I didn't ask for you to be relocated here and I probably couldn't have prevented it, but be in no doubt, this is my town. I know everyone and everything that goes on around here. You're not in London anymore. You so much as step on a crack on the pavement and I'll be all over you. Clear?'

'Clear,' he agreed almost cheerfully.

'I don't like the idea of having someone like you around here,' Hodges continued, 'but the powers that be in Auckland tell me the situation is under control. That your assessments say you're low-risk.'

'Someone like me?' Dolby asked, seizing on Hodges' words. 'And what is it you think I am?'

'Someone who murdered and raped a fourteen-year-old girl,' Hodges told him bluntly. 'You try anything like that around here and the locals will lynch you and I'm not sure I'd try to stop them.'

'You've got the wrong man,' Dolby replied. 'I was in the wrong place at the wrong time. But I'm not complaining. I should never have put myself in that position. I'll accept whatever punishment I'm given. I just want to start again. Stay away from the past.'

'Good,' Hodges said. 'Best keep it that way,' he warned him as he looked around the dilapidated farm. 'Looks like you got a lot to do, Mr Knight. I hope you know what you're doing.'

'I studied farming and agriculture on the inside,' Dolby answered. 'Shouldn't take me too long to get this place sorted.'

'Farming, eh?' Hodges nodded his reluctant approval. 'I reckon the blokes in Auckland could have found you somewhere better than this place.'

'No,' Dolby quickly replied. 'I wanted somewhere like this. Somewhere I could really make my own. Something I could build with my own hands.'

Once again Hodges found himself a little unbalanced by Dolby's attitude and words. He certainly wasn't the unpleasant, snarling predator he'd half-expected. 'Well, I'd better let you get on,' he told him, looking around. 'Looks like you've got plenty to get on with.'

'Yes,' Dolby agreed, surveying his land with apparent joy. 'Yes, I do.'

'Just remember what I said,' Hodges reminded him. 'Don't

step out of line. I judge a man by his actions. Not his words, Mr Knight.'

'You'll get no trouble from me,' Dolby assured him. 'No trouble at all.'

48

New Zealand – Present Time

J ameson walked through the bowels of the Hilton Hotel in Auckland's Viaduct Harbour before entering the large working kitchen filled with chefs and other staff, all too busy to notice his presence. He stopped a passing kitchen hand and showed him his police ID. 'Excuse me,' he told the slightly startled-looking young man. 'I'm looking for Evelina Gulbis?'

'Over there,' the kitchen hand pointed with his chin, his hands busy with a pile of plates. 'The blonde.'

He looked in the direction the man was pointing and saw an attractive woman in her early twenties wearing a kitchen uniform – busily preparing a pile of vegetables.

'Thanks,' he told him before walking away across the kitchen until he was next to the woman. 'Evelina?' he said, making her look up. 'Police,' he told her, raising his voice above the din of their surroundings as he flashed his ID again. 'We need to speak.'

'About what?' she asked in her Eastern European accent, looking concerned.

'Anna Sarfas,' he explained. 'I have questions that I believe only you can answer.'

She looked around to make sure no one was paying them much interest before replying. 'Follow me,' she told him, throwing her knife down and walking away. He did as he was told until she led him to a small office set off to one side of the main kitchen. Once they were inside she closed the door to keep the noise out as well as people.

'So?' she immediately asked. 'What is it you want to know?'

'You reported Anna missing, right?' he checked.

'Yes,' she confirmed. 'But that was over two years ago now.' Her eyes narrowed for a second. 'Have you found something?'

'No,' he answered. 'She's still officially missing.'

'I see,' she said, looking at the floor in disappointment.

'Did you know Anna before coming to New Zealand?' he continued.

'No,' she answered. 'I met her while travelling around the South Island. She was Latvian too and travelling alone, so we hooked up. I liked her. She was fun.'

'Did you travel back to the Auckland area together?' he asked.

'No,' she explained. 'We both had pre-purchased travel tickets, so I had to go back first, but we planned to meet on a certain day, only she never turned up. I checked around with some of the people we'd made friends with while travelling, but no one had seen her for a few days. One of our friends said he'd been with her in some town, I can't remember the name of it, and that she was going to try and hitch a ride to Auckland to meet up with me. But, like I said, she never turned up.'

'Pukekohe?' he more told her than asked. 'The name of the town was Pukekohe?'

'Yes.' She nodded her head. 'Pukekohe.'

'Did she have a boyfriend?' he checked.

'No,' she replied, shaking her head. 'If she did, I would have known.'

'Was someone bothering her?' he asked, moving on. 'Did she ever mention anything like that?'

'No,' she insisted. 'She was happy. Un... unworried. Having the time of her life. We both were. Then she just... disappeared.'

'A lot of people think she's maybe still here,' he told her. 'Living under a different name – as an illegal immigrant.'

'I know they do, but they're wrong,' she shrugged. 'They're all wrong. Something happened to her. The police said they'd investigate it, but after a couple of weeks they stopped looking. I tried to get them to keep looking, but they wouldn't. As far as they were concerned, she was just another illegal immigrant.'

He thought for a few seconds before continuing. 'The report makes no mention of her family coming over to find out what was going on,' he questioned. 'If they really believed something had happened to her, surely they would have come to New Zealand – to try and find her? But if they knew she didn't want to be found – was alive and well...'

'I went back to Latvia,' she told him. 'I met her family. They were destroyed by her disappearance, but they are not wealthy people. They spent the last of what they had sending Anna here before she returned to Latvia to study to be a doctor. They had no money to come here. There was nothing they could do.'

'The Latvian government?' he asked.

'There is no embassy in New Zealand,' she laughed. 'Just a consulate. They tried to get them to intervene, but we are a small country trying to make its way in the world. Our government doesn't want trouble.'

'Evelina,' he said, taking a breath – looking hard into her

eyes. 'I'm trying to do the right thing here. The right thing for Anna. You swear to me you're telling the truth?'

'I swear to you,' she answered without hesitation. 'I swear to you – I'm telling the truth. Something happened to her. Something...' She couldn't finish what she was saying as her emotions got the better of her.

He gave her a moment before speaking. 'I believe you,' he assured her. 'I believe something did happen to her.'

'You think someone took her, don't you?' she asked, wiping the tears from her eyes. 'You think someone took her and...'

'I don't know anything for sure,' he admitted. 'But I intend to find out.' He took a business card from his pocket and handed it to her. 'If you think of anything else, you contact me straight away – on this number. Okay?'

'Okay.' She nodded. 'Find her, please,' she suddenly pleaded with him. 'Even if it's just...'

'I'll do everything I can,' he told her. 'I promise. In the meantime, keep this between the two of us. Anyone else comes around asking you questions about Anna, you let me know.'

'Of course.' She nodded again. 'But no one will. No one here cares about her.'

'I do,' he quickly reminded her. 'And I'll find out what happened to her,' he said as he thought of Dolby living on his farm. 'I always do.'

Jameson arrived home late. The house was mostly in darkness and everyone had gone to bed. He tossed his keys and everyday items on the kitchen table and headed off along the corridor to Jenny's room before quietly opening the door a few inches and peeping inside. He smiled as he watched her sleeping peacefully for a few seconds before closing the door softly and heading through the silent house to his office. He turned the small lamp on but left all the other lights off, took a bottle of whisky from the drawer and poured himself a large glass which he placed on the desk before turning on his computer and searching for the email from Sergeant Neil. He found it amongst dozens of other mostly junk mail, opened up the attachment and started searching through the Missing Persons' reports.

'Too old,' he complained about the first before moving to the next report. 'Too big,' he said, dismissing it with a shake of his head as he moved to the next, his body tensing as he saw the photograph of a pretty teenage girl. The file was marked – *Suspected Illegal Immigrant. No further police action required. Information forwarded to the Immigration Service.*

He read the information on the front page, nodding his head with interest before saving it and moving to the next.

'Too local,' he denounced before deleting it and calling up the next only to be greeted with the picture of a woman in her fifties. 'Jesus, Jack,' he moaned. 'I said young.' Again he deleted the file and pulled up the next. 'Too old – again. Too big. Too local.' He deleted file after file until another made him tense with interest as he was confronted with a photograph of a pretty young woman. It was also marked – *Suspected Illegal Immigrant. No further police action required. Information forwarded to the Immigration Service.*

He found himself nodding slowly before being sure to save the file in the same folder with the other. He skipped through the remaining files but found nothing to interest him further. He leaned back in his chair and took another sip of his drink as he stared at the ceiling, deep in thought. After a few seconds his eyes began to feel heavy. He fought against his closing eyes, but it was no good as he soon slipped into a fitful sleep.

Suddenly he was back in London, stuck in a world where everything moved in slow motion. His back was pressed against the wall as his friend Clarkie, dressed like a postman, stood waiting for the council-flat door to open. When it finally opened, he heard the bang of a gun echoing in a warped, elongated sound as Clarkie began to fall slowly to the ground. He struggled to push himself from the wall, as if he was trapped in a fast-setting glue and started to fire his pistol repeatedly – the bullets ripping through Sarwar as he stumbled backwards into the wall.

Suddenly the phone rang and woke him with a fright. He spilt a little of his drink on his chest. 'Fuck,' he said as he grabbed his mobile and answered it sharply. 'Hello.'

'It's me,' Finch greeted him.

'Harry?' he replied, rubbing his face. 'What's up?'

'You need to be at Central Headquarters first thing in the morning,' Finch told him, sounding serious.

'You want to tell me why?' he asked.

'Professional Standards want to see you about your latest incident,' Finch explained.

'The armed robbery?' he guessed.

'Yes,' Finch confirmed bluntly.

He sighed before answering. 'I'll be there.'

'Don't be late,' Finch warned him.

He heard the line go dead before standing and looking down at his phone. 'Shit,' he said before he found himself searching through his contacts to find Lisa's number. His finger hovered over the call button, but he couldn't bring himself to press it. Eventually he tossed it onto the desk where it lay next to the computer screen that still displayed the pictures of the two missing young women. 'Christ,' he whispered. 'What the hell am I doing?'

49

Jameson walked the short distance along a corridor at Auckland Central Police HQ carrying the Missing Persons' reports in a folder. He stopped outside a door, straightened his tie, knocked twice and waited for an answer. Within a couple of seconds, he heard the voice of Inspector Mark Warren from the other side.

'Come in,' Warren ordered.

He opened the door and stepped inside to find the slim, gaunt-faced Warren looking very much like the wily, determined man he knew him to be. Detective Senior Sergeant Bob Easton sat next to him – the very opposite of Warren – overweight with a reddening complexion, wearing spectacles. Jameson got the impression Easton didn't really want to be there, whereas the confrontation to come was everything to Warren.

'Take a seat, Jameson,' Warren told him. He sat in the only chair on the opposite side of the desk without speaking. 'You know why you're here?'

'No,' he answered casually. 'Why don't you tell me?'

'Just an informal talk.' Easton tried to lighten the already tense atmosphere. 'You're not being interviewed at this stage.'

'At this stage,' he repeated in a way that made it sound like he believed formal proceedings were eventually inevitable. 'So, what d'you want to talk about?'

'The little stunt you pulled outside the bookies in Glen Innes last week,' Warren said, taking over again. 'Pretty fucking risky, don't you think?'

'Would have been riskier to do nothing,' he argued. 'They were a cowboy crew. Something's always likely to go wrong with cowboys.'

'Then why didn't you get the proper authorisation?' Warren demanded. 'Have a proper firearms unit take them down?'

'There wasn't time,' he explained.

'Bullshit,' Warren dismissed his excuse. 'There's always time.'

'Not with this one,' he insisted. 'The source was sure the robbery was imminent. I had less than an hour to be in place.'

'Exactly our point,' Warren told him. 'You had an hour to do things officially. More than enough time.'

'To report back to the DI and wait for him to find the commander?' he smiled. 'To do the risk assessments they'd ask for? Scramble a firearms unit and brief them? No chance. I don't know what world you're living in, but I live in the real one. I acted as I thought best – the result being we took out a dangerous armed robbery team before anyone who matters got hurt. I sleep fine at night. What about you?'

'I don't believe you, frankly.' Warren ignored his question. 'Even if the information did come from a registered source, I doubt you only received it an hour before the robbery. I think you're just using that as a convenient excuse for not going through the proper channels.'

'Then you'd be wrong,' Jameson told him.

'Surely the informant knew they were planning the robbery days in advance?' Easton stepped in.

'These jokers don't plan,' he reminded them. 'Probably only decided to pull the robbery a couple hours at most before they tried it. They ran out of meth and woke up to the fact they needed cash to buy more and hatched this sorry excuse of a plan. We were lucky my source overheard them talking about it.'

'Come on, Jameson.' Warren threw up his arms. 'You expect us to believe that?'

'I don't give a fuck what you believe,' he told them with a wry smile.

'Your actions were bloody reckless and dangerous, Jameson.' Warren raised his voice, failing to control his anger. 'You could have got someone killed. Or should I say someone else.'

'All right,' Jameson shook his head. 'This has gone way beyond a friendly chat. Feels like an interview to me, in which case I want an association member here and a brief.'

'Fair enough,' Warren agreed, smiling like a serpent. 'No more questions. For now. But we will be needing the name of the informant who supposedly provided the information, along with the contact sheets, information sheets and anything else they provided in relation to the attempted armed robbery.'

'Forget it,' he told him. 'I'm not giving you anything. I protect my sources. You want the information you'll have to apply to the Registrar of Informants and even then I'll do everything I can to stop you.' There was a long silence as they all eye-balled each other. 'We finished? Good.' He eventually brought the stand-off to an end before quickly getting to his feet, spinning towards the exit and storming from the room leaving the door open behind him.

He strode down a long corridor and across the open-plan office until he reached Finch's office. The door was already open with Finch inside working at his desk. Jameson entered without knocking and flopped into a chair.

'Everything all right?' Finch asked, slowly looking up.

'Fucking Professional Standards,' he answered.

'Ah,' Finch acknowledged, sinking into his chair.

'Tried to interview me without a rep being present or a brief,' he complained.

'Nothing surprises me with Warren,' Finch just shrugged. 'What was his angle?'

'They're going after the informant,' he explained, anxiously running his fingers through his hair.

'And you can trust this informant?' Finch asked tentatively.

'Yeah,' he reassured him. 'Even if they ever get permission to speak to him, he's solid. It's covered.'

Finch raised his eyebrows with a knowing look. 'Well, I hope it didn't cost you too much?'

Jameson just shrugged, knowing fine well what Finch meant. Most detectives working the street would have a *go-to informant* they could use when the source of information was questioned. A reasonable cash payment usually ensured they'd be reliable if Professional Standards started digging deeper.

'Something else?' Finch asked, Jameson's silence tipping him off.

It was as if Jameson hadn't heard him before suddenly asking a question of his own. 'Remember the missing women I was telling you about?'

'Jesus Christ, Ruben,' Finch replied, sounding decidedly not best pleased. 'I remember telling you to drop it.'

'Just hear me out a minute,' he appealed.

'I must be as mad as you are,' Finch said, shaking his head.

'I found something, Harry,' he told him conspiratorially. 'Something I can't ignore.'

'What, Ruben?' Finch asked, keeping his voice quiet, but sounding sceptical. 'What have you found?'

'Two more missing girls,' he explained, making Finch roll his eyes. 'Both went missing from the Greater Auckland area within the last three years. Both young and slightly built and both from countries with no traditional ties to New Zealand – both travelling alone when they went missing.'

'So, two more illegal immigrants then?' Finch tried to pour cold water on his theory.

'Which is exactly what everyone else thinks,' he argued. 'Their Missing Person Reports were even forwarded to Immigration. No one's looking for these girls, Harry.'

'Except Immigration,' Finch said, with an air of relief, spreading his arms open as if it was the obvious end of the matter.

'Look,' Jameson told him, becoming increasingly frustrated. 'If someone was looking to prey on young women, then these missing girls are perfect. The fact they're from countries like Latvia is important to him. Not just because he knows we'll assume they're illegals, but because their disappearance won't attract any media attention either here or back in their own countries. Imagine an English girl going missing over here or an American. Jesus, Harry. It would be all over the news – here and abroad. His victim selection is careful and deliberate. With these girls there's nothing. It's like they've just been... forgotten.'

'Listen.' Finch struck a more conciliatory tone. 'You make an interesting argument. But you're forgetting one thing. No bodies, Ruben. If there'd been a serial killer operating in the Auckland area for the last four years, we'd have found bodies by now. But we haven't. Nothing. There's no serial killer out there. And even if there was, it couldn't be Dolby. No way.'

'But if he's somehow found a way,' he wouldn't let it go. 'A way to dispose of the bodies–'

'Jesus,' Finch interrupted him, losing his patience. 'You really don't like this guy, do you? Look. There's no way the Brits would have released him before he'd completed an evaluation programme. They say he's no longer a risk and that's good enough for me and should be good enough for you.' He took a breath. 'Ruben. This is beginning to look like some sort of personal witch-hunt. You can't afford any more shit to fall your way. Let it go.'

'And part of that programme was Dolby admitting his guilt,' Jameson reminded him.

'So?' Finch asked.

'So that's exactly what he did,' he explained. 'Only now he's denying it again. Blaming everything on Anderson. He just told them what they wanted to hear so he could get out. Sure, he puts on a show about being remorseful, but I'm not buying it.'

'You're making too much of it,' Finch insisted. 'Lots of people admit things to get an early release then change their tune. Wouldn't you?'

'The original investigating team were convinced Dolby used a prophylactic when he raped the victim,' he tried to persuade him. 'If they're right it makes him as cold as he is calculating. Maybe he's carried on where he left off over here. But now he only selects victims he knows no one will search too hard for. He's learnt from the mistakes he made when he was young.'

'Or he really is innocent,' Finch argued, beginning to sound bored with their conversation.

'Yes,' he admitted it was possible, his frustration growing. 'But surely there's enough here to warrant further investigation?'

There was a few seconds' silence before Finch answered with a sigh. 'Fine,' he relented. 'But do it quietly and whatever you do, Ruben, don't let it compromise your primary task. Keeping Knight alive.'

50

London – 2019

Sarah and Jimmy sat together in the small kitchen of their family home – Sarah staring absentmindedly out of the window while Jimmy read the sports pages of a Sunday newspaper, when a loud knock at the door made them both jump.

'Jesus Christ,' Jimmy complained angrily. 'It's Sunday morning. You expecting anyone?'

'No,' she answered. 'You'd better go see who it is.'

'Fine,' he said with a sigh, before slowly getting up and making his way to the front door. When he pulled it open, he was met by a slim, undistinguished white man in his forties, hiding from the cold rain inside his dark raincoat. 'You want something?' Jimmy abrasively asked – still annoyed at having his Sunday morning disturbed.

The man offered him his hand with a smile. 'Geoff Jackson,'

he cheerfully introduced himself. 'Crime editor for *The World*. Britain's biggest selling newspaper.'

'That rag,' Jimmy snarled. 'Best you disappear.'

'You have a right to say what you think about Abigail's killers being given new lives somewhere,' Jackson spoke quickly. 'They've been out almost three years now. Tell the country how you feel about this injustice.'

'Fuck off,' Jimmy told him before slamming the door shut – Jackson's voice calling after him from the other side.

'You'll be well paid,' Jackson promised. 'I wouldn't expect you to tell me your story for nothing. This could be big.'

Jimmy ignored his pleas and returned to the kitchen where his mother waited anxiously. 'Who was that?' she asked.

'Fucking journalist,' he cursed.

'Watch your language,' she warned him – her motherly instinct to correct her errant child superseding her curiosity and concern before she returned to the caller. 'Another one? It's been a while since the last one. I thought they might leave us alone now.'

'They'll never leave us alone,' Jimmy told her.

'What did he want?' she asked.

'Same as they all want,' he snarled. 'Said he wanted to know what we thought about those animals being given new lives.'

'Maybe we should tell him,' she suggested. 'Then maybe they'd leave us alone.'

'No,' he said. 'If we talk to one, more will come. People wanting to make TV shows about it. People wanting to write books about it. God knows who else.'

'Jesus,' Sarah pleaded. 'Will this never end?'

'There's only one way this will ever end,' he told her. 'Putting those two bastards six feet under.'

'I don't see how that'll help,' she argued. 'If they were ever killed there would be a media circus all over again. We'll be mobbed by the media. It'll only make things worse.'

'No,' Jimmy told her, conspiratorially. 'No, it won't.'

'How can it not?' she asked.

'Because the media will never know,' he explained. 'The police will never tell anyone. They wouldn't even bury them. They'd be cremated under their new names. No fuss. No fanfare. Just a record in a death register somewhere to make it legal. It would be the only way.'

'You don't know that,' she reminded him.

'It's the only thing they could do,' he insisted. 'Think about it. If you don't believe me speak to that cop Harvey. He'll tell you.'

'I haven't spoken to him in years,' she told him. 'Not since he came here to tell us they'd been released and even if you're right, we'll never be free of those vultures bothering us.'

'Yes,' he agreed, 'but we'll know the truth. They can ask their questions about what do we think about them being free to live their lives and we can act indignant and give them lines about our outrage to fill their rags with, but we'll know – it's all false, because we'll know their ashes would have been dumped somewhere they'll never be found.'

Sarah slumped in her chair. 'This is all just fantasy, Jimmy. There's no way we'll ever find out where they are.'

'You never know for sure,' he said, refusing to give up hope. 'Some journalist or someone may track them down one day and tell the world where they are.'

'And even if that was to happen,' she told him. 'What then? You're no killer, Jimmy.'

'For them I would be,' he insisted. 'I've waited too many years to miss the chance if it ever came along. Too many years of thinking of those animals waiting to be freed so they can live new lives, while Abigail and Dad are just gone. No one gave them a second chance, did they? I can't spend the rest of my life thinking about them living lives as free men. I just can't do it. It'll kill me.'

'And if you somehow did find them?' she asked. 'And found enough hatred inside you to actually do it. Then what? Spend the rest of your life in prison?'

'I'd do it smart enough,' he told her. 'No one would be able to prove it was me.'

'Bullshit,' she insisted. 'I've seen enough of the police over the last fourteen years to know they'll prove it eventually.'

'We'll see,' he dismissed her concerns.

'Jesus, Jimmy,' she said, closing her eyes and laying her hands flat on the table. 'None of this is ever going to happen. You're never going to find them and you'll never get a chance to *avenge* your sister. You've got to move on to save yourself.'

'I can't do that,' he told her quietly. 'I just can't.'

'Then I pray you never find out where they are,' she whispered.

'I'll find them,' he promised. 'Somehow. I just know I will.'

51

New Zealand – Present Time

Jameson's car bounced along the dirt track before sliding to a halt in a cloud of dust outside Dolby's farm. As he climbed out, Rameka and another detective from the night shift were already walking towards their parked car.

'Hey, Jameson,' Rameka called out as he opened the car door. 'Maybe you could be on time once in a while, eh? Getting sick of covering your arse. Know what I'm saying?'

'You don't like it talk to Finch,' he called out to them as he walked without ever looking in their direction to make sure they knew he didn't care what they thought before lowering his voice to a whisper. 'Arseholes.'

Rameka flipped him a finger, but he never saw it as he kept walking. He heard the car doors being slammed shut followed by the sound of the engine starting up as Mills came from the house and walked towards him looking pissed off.

'Jesus, Ruben,' she greeted him.

'What?' he asked, as if he hadn't done anything wrong.

'You need to sort your shit out and stop being late,' she told him. 'That's what. Rameka's getting well pissed off.' She thrust her hands onto her hips to make sure he knew she was serious. 'He makes a bad enemy, Ruben.'

'Fuck Rameka,' he said, dismissing her concerns as he looked over his shoulder at the detectives' car pulling away and bumping along the dirt road. He watched it for a few seconds before turning his back and looking up at the treeline of the hill directly in front of him – his attention drawn to what he thought was a slight sign of movement. He squinted into the sunlight that was shining directly in his eyes, using his hand to shield the worst of the rays. 'Can you see that?' he asked Mills. 'Up by the trees?'

'I can't see anything,' Mills replied without interest. 'The light's playing tricks on your eyes.'

'Could be,' he admitted, although he was sure he'd seen something. 'All the same – think I'll check it out.'

'You think you've seen something you should call it in,' Mills told him, taking him more seriously. 'Get someone else to check it out. Our job is to stay close to Knight.'

'I need a closer look first,' he insisted and started to walk off in the direction of what he thought he'd seen – real or imagined.

'This feels like a bad idea,' Mills called after him, but her warning fell on deaf ears as he kept walking towards the treeline. Mills turned away and stomped back towards the house in frustration leaving him on his own to chase shadows.

After a few minutes he reached the treeline and began to follow it, occasionally peering into the bush trying to find out whatever it was he saw – if anything. All he could hear was the eerie sound of the leaves blowing in the light breeze, which spooked him enough to make him draw his gun before continuing – crouching slightly as he made his way further along the edge of the bush, still looking into the dark and the menacing mass of trees and tangled bushes, searching for any signs of life.

~

O'Doherty watched him from his concealed position in the bush, looking down the sights of his silenced pistol that was trained on the detective who was no more than ten metres away as he, too, listened to the haunting sound of the trees in the breeze. As he watched him moving around on the outskirts of the bush, it was increasingly clear he was searching for something as he continually squinted and peered ever more intently into the dark forest, until he finally began to push his way past the branches and into the forest.

O'Doherty pointed the pistol's sights at the detective's chest as he struggled ever closer through the thick bush. Just a few more steps closer and he'd have no choice but to squeeze the trigger and take him out. If the cop hadn't already drawn his gun there was a chance he could have taken him out alive, but with his gun in hand, it was a risk he couldn't take. Once he'd killed one cop it made no difference taking out the other. A cop-killer was a cop-killer whether it was one or two. And then he'd have a clear run on the *mark*. After his *business* was concluded he'd drive his camper van south to Wellington, avoiding Auckland Airport which he knew would be covered, before catching a flight to Australia several days later and on to Ireland from there. Just a few more steps and his hand would be forced.

The sudden sound of a mobile phone ringing loud and shrill in the quiet bush almost startled him enough to make him accidentally pull the trigger. Once he'd recovered, he buried himself deeper into the undergrowth.

~

'Fuck's sake,' Jameson cursed as he struggled to unclip the chirping, intrusive phone from his trouser belt. When it was finally free, he checked the caller ID. It was Mills. 'Millsie,' he answered it, sounding slightly rattled.

'What the hell's going on?' she demanded, clearly concerned. 'Where the fuck are you?'

'I told you,' he reminded her before straightening and taking one last look around before continuing. 'I thought I saw something.'

'You all right?' she asked, picking up on the anxious tone of his voice. 'You find anything?'

'No,' he said, taking what seemed like his first breath in a long while. 'Nothing. I must have imagined it. I'll head back.'

'You do that,' she told him, trying to sound calm, but the tension in her voice betrayed her.

He puffed out his cheeks with relief as he holstered his pistol and started heading out of the bush, but just as he broke into clear ground, he almost bumped into an old Maori man, his face covered with traditional tribal tattoos, who seemed to appear from nowhere. It startled him enough to make him reach for his gun, before managing to stop himself. The old man looked him up and down suspiciously before staring at the gun on his belt, although he didn't say anything.

Jameson pulled his police ID from his belt and held it out towards the old man. 'Relax,' he told him. 'I'm a police officer.'

'Who says I'm not relaxed?' the man smiled. 'Your ID says you're a detective. What's a detective doing out here – in the bush? Not much to detect out here.'

Jameson looked around, irritated at having to explain himself. 'There was a break-in at the farm,' he lied. 'I'm just checking things out.'

The old man pointed with his chin down the hill towards Dolby's farm. 'That farm?' he asked.

'Yeah,' he answered, as he also looked down at the house. 'That farm.'

The old man just nodded, but his eyes betrayed that he didn't believe a word Jameson was saying. 'You should be careful if you're looking for things in the bush,' he suddenly warned him, looking into the trees. 'Bad spirits. Never used to be, but they're here now – all around us.' He stood nodding his head for a while before turning back to Jameson. 'I think maybe it's time I wasn't here,' he told him. 'Good luck with your detecting.' Without saying another word, he headed across the hill leaving Jameson feeling even more spooked. He watched him walking away for a while before turning and heading quickly back towards the farm.

O'Doherty waited for the detective and the old man to be a safe distance away before he stood and leaned with his back against a tree. He peeled the black ski mask from his head – the cool air hitting the sweat on his face and refreshing him from the stifling confines of the material. He took a few deep, silent breaths to compose himself before taking the small rucksack from his back and stuffing the mask inside. He took the silencer off the pistol, unloaded it and put it all inside the bag which he slung over his back, before quickly and quietly disappearing deeper into the bush, his green camouflage clothing making him almost invisible.

As Jameson neared the farmhouse, he saw Mills waiting for him on the porch looking annoyed but also concerned.

'Everything all right?' she asked.

'Yeah,' he replied, still sounding a little shaken. 'Light must have been playing tricks.'

'You sure?' she checked. 'You look like shit.'

'Thanks,' he said sarcastically.

Mills looked past him to where he'd just come from. 'Who was that you were talking to?' she asked. 'Up on the hill.'

'No one,' he answered. 'Just some old guy talking bullshit about spirits and shit.'

'What?' Mills asked, surprised by his answer before brushing it away and getting back to business. 'Maybe we should still get the bush searched? A dog unit maybe?'

'A dog unit?' he scoffed. 'Do me a favour. Damn things will just run off chasing possums. No. If there was something out there, I would have found it.' He looked back to the bush before turning back to Mills. 'Relax, Millsie,' he told her. 'You worry too much.'

He walked past her into the house without seeing Mills roll her eyes and shake her head before forcing herself to look away from the trees on the hill and follow him inside.

52

F inch stood in his office talking to a detective from his team when Inspector Warren wandered in, clearing his throat. Once the detective realised who was standing behind him, he took the hint and headed for the door.

'I'll come back later,' he told Finch, nodding once to Warren as he left. Warren took a seat without being invited.

'Something I can help you with?' Finch asked him.

'Heard you picked up a new murder investigation,' Warren said, sounding annoyingly smug.

'Then you heard right,' Finch answered, biting his tongue.

'Anything interesting?' Warren pried.

'Not really,' he lied, in the hope of getting rid of him as quickly as possible.

'Shame,' Warren shrugged, before smiling unpleasantly. 'So, how's Jameson?' he said, changing the subject. 'Haven't seen him around much lately.'

'Really?' Finch asked, feigning confusion. 'I thought you just had him in for an interview?'

'An informal talk,' Warren corrected him. 'Not an interview.'

'So, you have seen him then?' He enjoyed the look on

Warren's face as he realised his slip-up. 'But other than that, no, he hasn't been around much.'

'Any reason why?' Warren continued to dig.

'He's on a special assignment,' Finch told him. 'Need-to-know basis only.'

'Sounds important?' Warren said, jealously.

'It is,' he confirmed.

'Hardly the sort of officer I'd choose for an important assignment,' Warren argued.

Finch sat in his chair before locking eyes with him. 'But I'm not you – am I?'

'I appreciate your loyalty towards one of your officers,' Warren replied after filling his lungs, sounding annoyed and frustrated, 'but I think you'll find it misplaced with Jameson. The man's trouble. We both know it. If what happened back in the UK didn't finish him then his latest stunt will.'

'Ruben's a good cop,' Finch told him. 'We're lucky to have him.'

'I disagree,' Warren snapped back. 'He's dangerous and reckless. Policing has changed, Finch. There's no place for cowboys like Jameson anymore. They're... obsolete. Jameson's a dinosaur – overdue for extinction.' He stood and walked towards the door – stopping and turning when he reached it. 'Be careful, Finch. The likes of Jameson have a nasty habit of dragging others down with them. Trust me. I know.' With that he strode from the office before Finch could reply. Almost as soon as he left Jones appeared in the doorway.

'What you got, Jonesie?' he immediately asked.

'We've checked the hotel CCTV for the suspect, boss,' Jones explained.

'And?' Finch impatiently hurried him.

'It's weird, boss.' Jones shook his head. 'We've found footage of him arriving, but we can't find any of him leaving. Nothing.'

'Could he have sneaked out a side door?' he asked.

'They're all covered by CCTV,' Jones said, ruling it out. 'We checked them. Nothing.'

'He arrives but doesn't leave,' Finch said as he got to his feet and began to stroll around his office. 'Yet he's not there.'

'I don't know, boss,' Jones admitted.

Finch shook his head slightly with confusion. 'Then he got out some other way,' he concluded. 'Something we haven't thought of yet.' He moved quickly back to his desk and jumped into his seat ready to get back to the reports strewn across it. 'Okay. Keep on it, Jonesie and close the door behind you, will you?' Jones nodded once before leaving, closing the door behind him as he was told.

He picked up the first of many reports but immediately dropped it as he snatched the phone off his desk and looked up Jameson's number and pressed to call. 'Christ,' he moaned as he listened to the ringtone and waited for him to answer, trying to work out what Jameson had done to deserve his protection.

'Harry,' Jameson eventually answered.

'Just thought you should know I've just had a visit from your friend Inspector Warren,' he told him.

'Oh yeah,' Jameson said, immediately sounding wary. 'And what did that fucking snake want?'

'Your head,' he warned him. 'On a plate.'

'Fuck Warren,' Jameson dismissed it. 'He can't touch me.'

'Warren's dangerous, Ruben,' he tried to convince him. 'You sure this informant is covered?'

'It's covered,' Jameson reassured him. 'Trust me.'

He pushed himself deep into his chair, his brow furrowed with concern. 'If you say so.'

'I do,' Jameson insisted before changing the subject. 'What's happening with the investigation? Any closer to finding our man?'

'He's an interesting man, our man,' he thought out loud.

'Go on,' Jameson encouraged him.

'We have CCTV of him arriving at his latest hotel,' he explained, 'but nothing of him leaving, despite all exits being covered with cameras. He seems to have made himself invisible to CCTV.' There was a few seconds of silence while he allowed Jameson time to develop his own train of thought.

'Then... then we have to consider the possibility he changed his appearance, as well as his identity,' Jameson finally told him.

'Which would be very unusual,' he sighed. 'And something that he turned around in quick time. Something he was already prepared for.'

'Which fits with him being connected to organised crime,' Jameson concluded. 'It's what I thought before and I'm not hearing anything to make me change my mind.'

'Or the intelligence services?' Finch suggested as an alternative. 'The victim got in his way of something, so he removed her?'

'No,' Jameson dismissed it. 'If it was intelligence services they would have pulled him away by now. Trust me, I know. They wouldn't leave him running around Auckland. Would have probably got rid of the body too.'

'Organised crime then,' he said, settling on the only realistic possibility.

'That would be my guess,' Jameson agreed. 'An Aussie brought over for a specific job.'

'And Kimberly Hutchinson?' he asked.

'As we suspected.' Jameson shrugged. 'Collateral damage. Wrong place – wrong time. She discovered something that meant she had to die.'

'And yet even after his... mistake, he doesn't panic and run, he stays in town,' Finch spelt it out. 'Why?'

'Because he still intends to carry out whatever job he's been brought over or sent over to do,' Jameson answered. 'He's a professional. Doesn't want his reputation damaged by leaving the job unfinished.'

Finch took a deep breath. 'So question is – what job is he here to do?' he asked before saying what he was sure they both believed. 'Are you thinking what I'm thinking?'

'We have to consider the possibility,' Jameson said with a sigh. 'Dolby could be his target. The hit in Canada was the work of someone who knew exactly what they were doing and now we have a professional killer somewhere in Auckland. If he's still here, which I'm sure he is.'

'This is all I need,' Finch moaned, sinking deeper into his chair. 'Stick close to Dolby while I try to get extra cover for his protection,' he ordered. 'Maybe even some snipers and spotters in the bush around the farm, but it'll take time. The commander won't be so easily convinced.'

'If you think you can get it,' Jameson said.

'I can try,' he replied before quickly moving on. 'Listen – I want you and Millsie to start covering the night shift.'

'Seriously?' Jameson complained, sounding extremely unhappy. 'I have to be around this animal all night?'

'Dolby's most vulnerable at night,' Finch explained. 'I'll feel better knowing you and Millsie have it covered.'

There was a long silence before he answered. 'Fine,' he reluctantly agreed. 'But you owe me.'

'Just keep Dolby alive, Ruben,' Finch told him. 'For everyone's sake. I'll let you know when I've arranged the extra cover.'

'I'll be waiting,' Jameson answered.

Finch hung up without speaking again and lifted a photograph of Kimberly Hutchinson from his desk. 'Wrong place at the wrong time,' he bemoaned. 'But I'll find him,' he promised her at a whisper as he thought of Dolby hiding on his farm. 'Like a moth being drawn to the flame.'

O'Doherty stood outside his motorhome looking like any other camper, dressed in shorts and a T-shirt as he cooked some food on a small barbeque while sipping a beer. He knew the best place to hide was often in plain sight. If he'd stayed locked in his motorhome, people might have become suspicious or at least intrigued. Much better to be the chameleon and blend into his surroundings.

He looked up from his cooking and noticed a nice-looking young woman sitting outside one of the other motorhomes looking over with a flirtatious smile on her lips before turning away to join in the laughter of the small group she was part of. But within a few seconds she was looking back towards him. This time he returned her smile before reminding himself of why he was there and looking away, images of Kimberly flashing in his mind – of making love to her mixing with memories of holding her in a death-lock as the life ebbed away from her. Yet for some reason he couldn't resist looking back and smiling again – just like any other man on a touring holiday would if a pretty woman paid them attention. She smiled back at him, then after a few seconds she got to her feet and started heading towards him.

Jameson and Mills sat at the kitchen table in the farmhouse, while Dolby finished making a pot of coffee by the stove – the pleasant smell of the freshly ground beans in stark contrast to the frosty atmosphere permeating through the room. Dolby turned from the stove, pot in hand, towards the detectives, holding the coffee in front of him.

'Anyone for a refill?' he asked cheerily.

'Yeah,' Jameson told him, trying to make the night shift posting as bearable as possible. 'Why not? Gonna be here all night anyway.'

'I'm beginning to get the feeling someone somewhere doesn't like you,' Dolby said as he filled Jameson's cup, who smiled sarcastically as Dolby turned his attention towards Mills. 'Detective Mills?'

'No thanks,' she said, shaking her head before turning towards Jameson. 'D'you mind if I get my head down for a couple of hours?' she asked. 'A couple of hours' sleep and I'll be all good for the rest of the night.'

'Fine,' he agreed after pausing for thought, looking uncomfortable. 'Go ahead. I'll give you a shout in a while.'

'Thanks,' she said, getting to her feet. 'I owe you one.' She headed off to the spare bedroom leaving Jameson alone with Dolby who slowly took a seat. Both men seemed to be waiting for Mills to close the bedroom door before speaking. As soon as she did, Dolby spoke first.

'Well,' Dolby began tentatively. 'Here we are.'

'Here we are,' Jameson replied without much interest.

'Our old lives in London half a world and a lifetime away,' Dolby continued.

'I suppose,' Jameson reluctantly responded.

'Makes you wonder how we ended here,' Dolby persisted. 'A nothing town in the middle of New Zealand, of all places.'

'Well,' Jameson leant closer to him. 'You're here because you murdered a fourteen-year-old girl.'

Dolby stiffened for a second before replying. 'That was the crime I was convicted of,' he admitted.

'But one you still deny,' Jameson reminded him.

'It doesn't matter anymore.' Dolby shrugged. 'But yes. That's why I'm here now. I had no choice. But you?'

'It's none of your business,' Jameson warned him.

'Just it seems a strange move for a detective,' Dolby said, ignoring him. 'Leaving the *famous* New Scotland Yard to ply your trade here in New Zealand.'

'Listen,' Jameson snarled. 'I know what you did to her. You think I'm suddenly going to treat you like you're some *normal* person. I know what you are.'

'I know you're aware of the case,' Dolby reminded him. 'You told me you'd read the files.'

'No,' Jameson said, surprising him. 'I didn't just read the files. I was on the case. The original investigation.'

'You didn't tell me that before,' Dolby complained, sounding concerned.

'I don't have to tell you anything,' Jameson told him. 'Unless I want you to know.'

'And now you want me to know?' Dolby asked.

There was silence for a few seconds before Jameson decided to explain. 'I was pretty much new to the CID. Just moved over to plain-clothes, working on the crime squad in Kilburn. Street stuff mostly – chasing drug dealers, muggers, that sort of shit. After Abigail's body was found the murder team knew it was going to be a major investigation. They needed extra bodies, so I volunteered. I was only on the outskirts of the investigation – not a major player, but I knew what had happened to her. A lot more than if I hadn't been on the investigation and I knew that whoever killed her had to be some kind of monster or completely insane.'

'Do I look like either of those to you?' Dolby asked.

'Insane? No,' Jameson answered. 'As for being a monster – it's not always easy to tell.'

'But your detective instinct,' Dolby persisted. 'What does that tell you?'

'Well,' Jameson told him. 'I'll promise you this. Before this is all over, one way or the other, you'll find out exactly what I think.'

There was a long silence before Dolby broke it. 'So... who is it?' he asked cautiously.

'Who is it what?' Jameson asked, keeping things civil if not friendly.

'Who is it keeps giving you the jobs no one wants?' he clarified.

'Let's just say I've pissed a few people off lately,' Jameson answered with a weary sigh.

'Such as?' Dolby pushed his luck.

'It's not something I can discuss with you,' Jameson told him flatly.

'Fair enough,' Dolby nodded before getting up from the table and walking the short distance to a cupboard from where he took a bottle of Scotch and two glasses before returning to the table and sitting. 'I've been keeping this for a special occasion.'

'This is a special occasion?' Jameson asked.

'As special as it gets for me.' Dolby smiled. 'I'd hate to die tomorrow without sharing this with someone.'

'You won't die tomorrow,' Jameson reassured him without compassion or even sounding interested.

'Sure of that are you?' Dolby asked. Jameson looked him in the eyes but didn't answer. 'Thought so,' he said as he poured a generous measure into a glass and pushed it towards him before pouring himself a decent measure and lifting his glass into the air. 'Cheers.'

Jameson reluctantly took the glass and raised it from the table, although not as high as Dolby's. He had no intention of chinking glasses with him. He managed to say 'Cheers,' before they both took a long sip from their glasses and settled into a silence before Dolby eventually broke the peace.

'Do you resent being punished for whatever it is you're supposed to have done?' Dolby asked.

'Who says I've done anything?' Jameson argued.

'I spent a long time in prison, detective,' Dolby reminded him. 'I've seen that look on your face a thousand times – the look of injustice. After a while even the guilty convince themselves they're innocent or that it wasn't their fault.'

'Like you, you mean?' he asked, a little cruelly.

Dolby took a few seconds to compose his answer. 'I'm different from you,' he began. 'I know I didn't commit the crime, but still I don't resent my punishment. I deserve it.'

'If you didn't do it, how can you not resent being punished for it?' Jameson asked.

'It's complicated.' Dolby sighed. 'And we both know my rather sad, pathetic story. Whereas I know nothing about you.'

'That's the way it's supposed to be,' he reminded him. 'That's the way I like it.'

'If you're worried about me telling anyone I can assure you I don't know anyone to tell and the night is so young,' Dolby tried to encourage him to talk.

'All the same,' Jameson said, 'I'd rather not.'

'I understand,' he said in an empathetic tone. 'Talking about our mistakes can lead to dark places. Takes a lot of courage to open those doors.'

There was another silence before Jameson suddenly started speaking quickly, as if he just wanted to get the words out before his mind stopped him. 'It's alleged I made a mistake that got a colleague shot,' he confessed, still unsure of why he was telling Dolby his blackest secret.

'Did they die?' Dolby immediately asked.

He took a deep breath before answering. 'Yes.'

'I see,' Dolby said sympathetically. 'I hope you don't mind, but I heard your colleagues talking about it – not Detective Mills, but the others. Just the odd word – here and there. They seem to think it was your fault.'

'Nothing I can do about that,' he shrugged. 'It's nothing to do with them anyway. It happened back in London.'

'Where both our... misfortunes took place,' Dolby reminded him. 'Was it? Was it your fault?'

'Why you so interested?' Jameson clamped up. 'It's got nothing to do with you.' He took a sip from his glass, his eyes fixed on Dolby.

'My life is in your hands,' Dolby argued. 'Surely I deserve to know if you're a man who can be trusted?'

'Don't worry about me,' he glared at him. 'Worry about yourself.'

'Sorry,' Dolby smiled slightly. 'I didn't mean to intrude. I just thought it might help if you talked about it. In prison I was never able to talk honestly about what happened. My lawyer made it clear that if I continued to claim I was innocent I'd probably never get out. Having something like that inside you for so long can burn you up. If you're innocent, better to just accept the injustice and move on. If you're guilty, better to make peace with it and yourself. If you don't – it'll destroy you.'

'I've nothing to make peace with,' Jameson insisted.

'If you say so,' Dolby said before taking a drink.

There was a long, uncomfortable silence before Jameson spoke again. 'The detective who got shot was a friend of mine,' he confessed. 'His name was Jim Clark.'

'I'm sorry,' Dolby told him – his voice laced with sadness.

'Yeah,' he replied before draining his glass. 'Me too.'

O'Doherty sat in bed looking a little uncomfortable, while the pretty young woman propped herself up next to him looking happy and relaxed. Their clothes were strewn around the inside of his motorhome.

'You okay?' she asked. 'You look a little tense.'

'Yeah,' he lied. 'Sure. I'm fine.'

'You were certainly fine a few minutes ago.' She smiled suggestively at him. He managed to smile back, but looked nervous and self-conscious. 'Would you like me to go?'

'I never said that,' he answered.

'No. You didn't,' she agreed. 'But some men like to keep this sort of thing brief. I'm okay with that. I can leave if you'd like.'

'No,' he said, reaching out to touch her. 'I want you to stay. It's just I've been on my own a long time. Longer than I can remember. I guess I'm just not used to company.'

'If you're sure?' she checked.

'Sure I'm sure,' he told her and smiled.

'Well,' she said, stretching her hands out to hold his face. 'In that case.' She slid on top of him and started kissing his neck before moving up to meet his lips as they pressed into each other – all thoughts of Dolby lost in the embrace, but as much as he tried, he couldn't prevent the pressure of her mouth on his and the warmth of her breath from reminding him of Kimberly. He wondered if he could ever be with another woman again and not think of her.

'Do you blame yourself at all – for what happened?' Dolby asked as they sat in his dimly lit kitchen – a glass tumbler on the table in front of each of them – the bottle of Scotch in the middle.

'I could have done better,' Jameson answered, taking a sip of whisky to wash the bad taste of confession from his mouth.

'How?' Dolby asked the obvious question, but it was enough to make Jameson tense again.

'Why you so interested in me?' he asked, full of suspicion. 'Why d'you want to know about me so much? Always asking questions.'

'I'm sorry,' Dolby said. 'It's just been a long time since I talked to anyone... I mean properly talked. If it makes you feel uncomfortable... if I make you feel afraid–'

'I'm not afraid of you,' he quickly interrupted.

'No,' Dolby corrected himself. 'No, of course you're not. That's not what I meant.'

'Then what did you mean?' Jameson demanded.

'Sometimes it's easier to talk to a stranger than it is someone you know,' Dolby explained. 'I'm hardly likely to judge you, whereas perhaps others would.'

He considered the man in front of him for a while. The man he knew had been convicted of the most terrible crime. But he was indeed also a man who couldn't judge him or even tell another soul whatever he told him. To do so would risk exposure and end his life living in peace on his farm once the immediate threat of the stalking assassin was over.

'We were coming to the end of a long and difficult operation,' Jameson found himself explaining. 'There was real and credible information a terrorist cell was planning attacks on London. I was on the Anti-Terrorist Unit at the time.' He took a sip of his whisky. 'We were covering an address the main target had a connection to, but the rest of the team had headed off elsewhere chasing a tip-off. But then the target got the drop on all of us and turned up at the address Jim and I were covering.' He took a breath. 'I... I persuaded Jim we could take him out on our own – before there was a chance of losing him again. We tried an old trick to get the door open, but before we could do anything the target swung it open and shot Jim – in the head. He died instantly.'

'And the man who shot him?' Dolby asked.

'Dead,' he told him coldly. 'Shot and killed.'

'You?' Dolby cautiously probed.

'Yes,' he answered, still showing no emotion.

'So.' Dolby nodded knowingly. 'You've killed then?'

'I was just doing my duty,' he argued. 'It's different.'

'You mean different from what I did?' Dolby asked.

'Yes,' he told him sharply. 'You're damn right it's different from what you did. You raped and murdered a young girl.'

'Or at least that's what I'm... accused of,' Dolby protested.

'We've already discussed this,' he reminded him. 'You were tried and convicted.'

'And that's good enough for you?' Dolby questioned. 'Despite there being no DNA evidence against me.'

'You said you've learned to accept your punishment,' he replied, using Dolby's own words against him as he fought his rising anger and resentment towards him. 'So why don't you learn to accept your guilt too?'

'Guilt. Punishment,' Dolby repeated. 'They're just words. You don't strike me as being a naïve man, detective. Courtroom decisions aren't the real world. Am I guilty? Yes. I am, but not of rape and murder.' He closed his eyes as if he was transporting himself back to the time of the crime for a few seconds before opening them in a startled flash, staring almost blankly at Jameson.

'What I am guilty of is not stopping him,' he admitted. 'I should have, but I was a coward. I was afraid of him – so I did nothing and for that I accept any punishment I'm given – even death. Christ, it would almost be a relief. Every day and every night is just more torture – her face – what he did to her – the trial – prison. A nightmare that never ends. One in which no one will listen to you.' He rubbed his temples as if fighting against a developing headache. 'The public had their monsters – nice and simple and they wanted us caged or killed. Once her boyfriend denied having sex with her, I was dead and buried. As far as everyone was concerned, Anderson and I were the same.'

'And now he's dead and you're still here,' Jameson told him without any trace of sympathy. 'Free to build a new life for yourself – with at least two governments prepared to lie for you.'

'Really?' Dolby asked. 'You think I'm here to build a new life for myself? You think I'm planning on meeting someone – settling down and having a family? You know that can never happen for me. I don't want it to happen. My entire family life would have to be based on lies. What sort of person would stay with me if they knew the truth?' There was a moment's silence in which Dolby replenished their glasses before speaking again. 'That's the thing I miss most, you know.'

'What is?' he asked, despite himself.

'Being loved.' Dolby surprised him with his answer. 'The hope of ever being loved. You can never know how lonely and desolate that can feel until it happens to you. What do you have – a daughter? A wife?'

'No wife,' he answered sharply. 'Not anymore.'

'Divorced?' Dolby pried.

'No,' he answered and took another sip. 'Dead.'

'I'm sorry,' Dolby said, momentarily looking down at the table to avert Jameson's glare. 'But you have your daughter and others who love you,' he went on. 'Me? There's no one. After I was convicted, I lost everyone – even my own mother and father – my brothers and sister. I was little more than a child – abandoned to myself and a young offenders institution. I'd never thought about love until it was utterly taken from me, but Anderson – he talked about it all the time. He was obsessed with it. Who he thought was loved. Wasn't loved. He coveted love – yet also seemed to despise it.'

'I don't understand,' Jameson shook his head – intrigued.

'After the... murder,' Dolby explained, 'before we were caught, he spoke to me about Abigail. I tried to stop him – to run away, but he wouldn't allow it. He told me that what made killing her so necessary – so special, was that he knew she was loved – by her friends and family – that taking her from them, in the way he did, made him powerful – as if he was taking their lives as well as hers. He said it made him feel like... like a god. The fact she was so much to so many is what made him choose her.' He slumped in his chair, as if reliving what Anderson had said so many years ago had exhausted him.

'If you were so different what made you become friends in the first place?' Jameson asked, feeling more in control now he was the one asking the questions.

'I suppose because in the beginning I felt sorry for him,' Dolby told him, smiling very slightly, as if he was recalling a memory that was both happy and sad. 'Because of the things in his life and things he didn't have in his life. Things that later made him what he was. His father was a drunk who beat him before finally abandoning him when he was about seven. His mother barely ever showed him affection or anything like love.' He shook his head as he described Anderson's pitiful childhood. 'When we were younger the other children would isolate and ridicule him. He took a bad beating more than once. Eventually his mother succumbed to the inevitable and handed him over to social services saying she couldn't cope with him anymore. They placed him with a foster family, but the man of the house soon began to abuse him and that was when I think he changed forever – the final abuse of those he was supposed to trust that pushed him over the edge. You can't really blame him for hating those he knew were loved, when he'd had so little.'

'I've heard this story before – more times than I can remember,' Jameson said, cynically dismissing the excuses. 'Children abused like you wouldn't believe. Their trust betrayed by the people who were supposed to be looking after them. But they didn't grow up to be rapists and murderers. If you're looking for me to somehow understand him – forgive him – then you're wasting your time.'

'I don't expect you to understand or forgive him,' Dolby replied. 'Once circumstance had made him what he was, it would have been kinder to put him down – like a dog with rabies.' He leaned on the table, moving a bit closer to him. 'But I'm no better than he was, because I let it happen. I was loved. My parents taught me right from wrong, but still I didn't stop him. I had every advantage he never had. Yet still I was involved in the rape and murder of a young girl. I was there and I did nothing.' He closed his eyes and rubbed at his temples. 'I'd give anything to get these images out of my head. Even for just an hour. A minute.' He opened his eyes and sighed deeply before raising his glass. 'Well, here's to our mistakes and our punishments. May we take them to our graves.'

After a few seconds he reluctantly raised his glass. 'To Clarkie.'

'To your friend,' Dolby nodded in agreement with a pleasant smile, taking a sip from his glass – his eyes never leaving Jameson. 'And your daughter. May God watch over her.'

'She doesn't need God,' Jameson told him, beginning to feel the slowing effects of the alcohol. 'She has me to watch over her.'

'Of course,' Dolby smiled pleasantly. 'And for now, so do I.'

53

O'Doherty woke up in his motorhome with a start, instantly sitting upright and looking down at the woman sleeping in his bed next to him. He cursed under his breath before silently slipping from the bed and tiptoeing to the safe hidden in the wardrobe. He typed in the code and opened the door revealing, amongst other things, the pistol and silencer. He quickly assembled the weapon, silently cocked it and headed back towards the bed just as the young woman began to stir. He froze as she sat up, sleepily stretching and yawning, smiling when she saw him, unaware of the gun he was holding behind his back.

'Hi,' she said sleepily.

'Hi,' he managed to reply, but his face was rigid with tension and fear.

'Shit.' She laughed. 'I don't even know your name. I asked, but you didn't say.'

'James,' he answered nervously. 'It's James. Friends call me Jim.'

'Yeah.' She nodded. 'Jim. You look like a Jim. You got

anything to eat around here. I don't know about you, but I'm starving.'

'Listen,' he said, trying to sound as casual as possible. 'Last night – did I say anything?'

'You said a lot of things,' she smiled.

'No,' he stumbled. 'I mean... I mean... did I say anything, you know... anything...?'

'Are you married or something?' she asked, looking quizzical.

'No,' he assured her. 'No. I'm not married.'

'I mean it's okay if you are,' she told him. 'I mean I'd understand.'

'I'm not married,' he insisted.

'Okay,' she shrugged, her smile returning.

She slid from the bed still naked and walked to him, draping her arms around the back of his neck. He wrapped his free arm around her waist as the other gripped the pistol behind his back. She pressed her lips against his and kept them there for what seemed an eternity before eventually pulling away.

'Now,' she told him. 'I need to freshen up, then you can take me to breakfast.' She quickly kissed him again before disappearing into the bathroom.

He exhaled deeply, trying to slow his heart rate before looking at the pistol he now held in front of him. He looked from the gun to the bathroom, knowing he needed to make a decision there and then. After a couple of seconds, he quickly dismantled it and put it back in the safe. As he was still crouched on the floor the young woman stuck her head from the bathroom and saw him.

'You okay?' she asked.

'Yeah,' he lied. 'I'm fine. I was just looking for something.' He checked the safe was locked before turning back to her. 'Listen – I have to go out. I need something from the shops.'

'Good luck with that.' She smiled. 'Not many of them around here.'

'I'll take my bike,' he explained. 'I won't be long. Make yourself at home. I'll see you later.'

'Okay,' she shrugged and ducked back into the bathroom.

He waited a second before grabbing his rucksack and quickly opening the safe again and taking the gun and binoculars from inside before hurriedly packing them in the bag. He dressed fast in the same clothes from the night before and headed outside to his motorbike. He kick-started it to life before putting his blacked-out helmet on and speeding away.

Jameson appeared from the spare bedroom at the farm looking a bit rough and dishevelled. Mills was already in the kitchen alone drinking a coffee while keeping watch through the window. She looked over her shoulder at him as he wandered into the room.

'You want some coffee?' she asked, looking him up and down. 'You look like you need it.'

'Yeah. Sure,' he told her, rubbing his unshaven face and yawning as he sat heavily at the table where the whisky glasses from the night before were still, placing his mobile phone next to them. Mills poured him a coffee from the jar and put it on the table in front of him.

'Anything happening?' he asked, still sounding half-asleep.

'Nah,' she answered without much interest as she turned back to look out of the window. 'All quiet.'

'Just remember what I told you,' he reminded her. 'There's a better than good chance there's a hired hitter out there just waiting for his opportunity.'

'Then why are we still here?' she complained. 'Tactical Support should be all over it.'

'Finch is working on it,' he assured her. 'Won't be long now.'

'I bloody hope so,' she told him. 'Beginning to give me the creeps being stuck out here.' She stood in silence for a few seconds before changing the subject. 'I heard you two chatting away last night,' she confessed, keeping her voice down, as if she was saying something clandestine.

'Hardly chatting,' he argued, tensing with defensiveness.

'Okay,' she let it go, still looking out of the window. 'Talking then.' After a few seconds of him not taking the bait she pressed him for more. 'What about?'

'His conviction, mostly,' he told her disinterestedly, hoping she'd drop it.

'And what did he have to say about that?' she disappointed him.

'The usual,' was all he replied, trying to make it sound as uninteresting as possible.

'Which is?' she persisted.

'That he didn't do it,' he surrendered, knowing she wouldn't give in.

She turned slowly from the window. 'Do I detect a softening in your attitude?'

'He can be very convincing,' he admitted. 'I'll give him that.'

'You believe him?' she asked bluntly.

'I didn't say that,' he corrected her just as his mobile started ringing and ended the conversation. He checked the display, but there was no name – just a number he didn't recognise. Curiosity enticed him into answering it. 'Hello.'

'I was trying to reach Ruben Jameson,' the slightly nervous-sounding voice of a man replied.

'You've reached him,' he told him cautiously.

'My name is Adrian Howell,' the caller told him. 'We met at the Pukekohe Town Hall a few days ago.'

'Yeah, sure,' he said, closing his eyes and rubbing his forehead as he recalled their meeting. 'I remember.'

'You asked me to get a survey map from our central records for you,' Howell reminded him.

'Yeah,' Jameson told him, thinking about his conversation with Dolby the night before and how perhaps Finch was right about allowing his feelings towards him affect his judgement. 'Listen, thing is I'm not sure I–'

'Of course, they were quite difficult to get this quickly and I can only hold on to them for a day or so before they have to be returned,' Howell interrupted. 'Perhaps you could come and take a look at it sometime this morning. I'd really appreciate it – so I can return the plans as soon as possible.'

'Okay,' he eventually agreed with a sigh as he rubbed his temples. 'Okay, fine. I'll be there soon.'

'Great,' Howell told him cheerily. 'I look forward to it.'

He stared at his phone after the line went dead – thinking what to do.

'Be where soon?' Mills broke his train of thought.

'I've got to go into town,' he answered, getting to his feet.

'Auckland?' she asked, sounding surprised.

'No,' he corrected her. 'Pukekohe town centre.'

'Pukekohe?' she said. 'What the hell for?'

'To look at a map,' he explained, unsatisfactorily.

'What?' Mills asked, increasingly frustrated.

'I asked some council clerk to get me a copy of the old survey map of the farm,' he expanded, speaking as quietly as he could.

'This farm?' she checked, hands on hips, looking at him with deep suspicion.

'Yeah,' he confirmed as he gathered his phone and his jacket.

'Why?' she demanded.

'Just something I need to take a look at,' he said, trying to dismiss it. 'Don't worry about it.'

'You're going after our shift, right?' she asked. 'You're going to wait for the day cover to get here before taking off?'

'I can't,' he told her. 'I promised I'd get home in time to see Jenny before she heads to the library. If I wait till our shifts are over before going into town, I'll miss her.'

'The library?' she picked up on it, taking her hands off her hips and folding them across her chest. 'Why not school?'

'Uh?' he replied, distracted as he gathered his belongings. 'Oh, she's been suspended. Just for the week.'

'What for?' she pried.

'Just teenager stuff,' he assured her. 'And if I miss her there'll probably be more. I'll only be a few minutes. It'll take me no time to get into town and back. You'll be fine.'

'You just told me there's probably a professional hitman out there,' she reminded him. 'And now you're telling me I'll be fine.'

'Just keep Dolby indoors,' he advised her. 'But make sure you're visible in case the farm's being watched. Keep your badge where it can be seen.'

'You want me to give him an easy target?' she asked, looking confused.

'Listen,' he said. 'He sees a cop around he's not going to risk showing himself. He's not going to go through a cop to get to Dolby. He's a professional. He knows he can't afford to have an entire police force after his head.' He looked towards Dolby's bedroom door before lowering his voice to a whisper. 'He puts a bullet through Dolby's head – how hard d'you think we'll be looking for him? He shoots a cop...' He spread his hands to make the point before lifting his cup, taking a gulp of coffee and heading for the door. 'I won't be long,' he promised before striding across the small kitchen and through the door.

'Well this is great,' Mills said to herself sarcastically as she looked around the room shaking her head. 'Just bloody great.'

O'Doherty was virtually invisible as he lay in the treeline of a hill looking down on the farm through his binoculars when he saw the male detective from his previous close encounter coming from the front door and heading to his unmarked car. He watched him closely as the detective drove away at speed, kicking up a dust storm behind his car. He lowered the binoculars and nodded slowly to himself before turning on his heels and heading back into the bush as quietly and quickly as a forest animal.

Jameson entered the office in the Pukekohe council building, making Howell look up from his desk. 'Mr Jameson,' he said, greeting him with a smile, getting to his feet.

'Morning,' he replied, sounding like a man in a hurry. 'You said you had the survey map.'

'Yes,' Howell confirmed, a little flustered by Jameson's bluntness. 'Yes. I have it.'

'I'm a little pushed for time, so...' he hurried him.

'Of course,' Howell agreed. 'Of course.' He began to search amongst a collection of tubes on the side desk until he seized and lifted the one he was looking for. 'Here it is. Let's take a look,' he said, pulling the map from the long tube and unrolling it on the main table in the office – smoothing it out and using a mix of items close to hand to weigh the corners down.

'How old is this map?' Jameson asked as he casually looked

over it – his tiredness and conversation with Dolby the night before somewhat dampening his interest.

Howell scanned the map and pointed at the label. 'Er, ten years now. If anything's been changed on the farm since then this map will show it. They started to look at the map together, but Jameson was anxious to get back to Mills and hand over to the day shift team so he could get back to Jenny, regretting he'd ever started his own personal investigation, reprimanding himself for not having listened to Finch. 'As you can see – little has changed – a few alterations to the farmhouse and outbuildings, but very minor. Essentially it's the same farm.'

He played along, glancing at his watch – until something caught his eye making him suddenly tense. Slowly and deliberately he pointed at a circular shape on the map of the farm. 'What's that?' he asked tentatively, suddenly afraid that he might actually be right about Dolby.

'Um...' Howell pondered, leaning in for a closer look. 'Possibly a storage facility. A grain silo.'

'Underground?' he asked, feeling almost sick with nervous excitement.

Howell looked again. 'Yes,' he answered, sounding a little surprised. 'How did you know?'

'The other map,' he rushed him, a dreadful sense of urgency surging through his mind and body. 'The recent map. I need to see it.'

Howell turned to the wall where dozens of maps in tubes were pigeonholed. 'It's here somewhere, but I'm sure nothing has changed.'

'There was no underground storage on the current map,' Jameson told him, moving to the other maps in their holes, trying to find it himself.

'I'm happy to check, but I'm sure there will be,' Howell assured him, as he cast his more experienced eye over the other maps until he eventually pulled one from its hole. 'Ah! Here it is,' he declared and headed back to the table with his prize, shadowed every inch by Jameson. Howell unrolled it – holding it in place with his outstretched hands while they looked at it together.

'It's not there,' Jameson excitedly declared, stabbing the new map with his finger where the silo should be, only now it had been replaced by a new symbol. 'It's not there,' he repeated, trying to understand what it could mean, if anything at all.

'No,' Howell agreed. 'It's... it's been changed.'

'What does it mean?' he demanded, with an ever-increasing sense of fear, tapping the new symbol repeatedly with his finger. 'What does this picture mean?'

'It's the symbol for a copse,' Howell answered, standing straight. 'A small forest of trees or thicket.'

Jameson also straightened as he closed his eyes to better help him visualise the farm. 'Jesus Christ,' he whispered, opening his eyes. 'Jesus Christ. Millsie. I have to go,' he insisted and walked fast from the office without explaining himself.

'Is there anything else I can help you with? Mr Jameson?' Howell called after him. 'Mr Jameson.'

But he just kept walking, cursing under his breath. 'Fuck. Millsie.' He pulled his phone from his belt as he virtually ran along the corridor and called Mills' number – holding it to his ear, muttering impatiently as he waited for her to answer. 'Come on, Millsie. Answer your damn phone. Answer your damn phone.'

Mills sat in the kitchen looking out of the window with her mobile phone and pistol on the table within easy reach. Suddenly her phone started ringing and vibrating – making her jump. She smiled at her own skittishness before leaning forwards to pick it up. She never heard Dolby walk up behind her, standing motionless, his face expressionless as he looked down on her. Just as she was about to pick up the phone, he quickly raised his hand holding a small leather cosh and brought it down hard on to the back of her head, knocking her unconscious to the floor – her phone still ringing. He stood over her as he picked up her phone and checked the caller ID, smiling when he saw it was Jameson before pressing the decline icon and slipping the phone into his pocket. He took the gun from the table and slipped it into his waistband before quickly turning and heading towards the door.

O'Doherty rode his motorbike along the dirt road towards the farm, when suddenly he saw a car in the distance heading towards him. He quickly pulled off the track and tucked himself away in a small clearing in the bush to wait for the car to pass by. A few seconds later the car sped past, but he was able to see that it was Dolby alone inside. For a while he was confused and couldn't understand how Dolby was suddenly allowed to leave the farm without his close protection, but soon his experience of dealing with rapidly changing fluid situations kicked in and he stopped trying to work out what was happening and pulled out from his hiding place to follow the car at a safe distance. He reminded himself that the best thing he could do was let things play out for a while – make sure it wasn't a police trap and then put two 9mm rounds in Dolby's chest and two in his head the first chance he had.

Dolby arrived at the main road intersection at the end of the dirt road and turned right – heading towards Auckland. A short time later O'Doherty also arrived at the junction, waiting a few seconds, using the dust cloud as cover before pulling out and heading after Dolby, staying back as far as he could while still just about being able to see the car in the distance ahead. Minutes later, as he and Dolby headed towards Auckland, Jameson approached from the other direction, driving fast, reaching the dirt road after the dust had settled, leaving him no clue of the recent departure of the other vehicles.

He bumped around inside the car as he drove too fast for the dirt road – driving one-handed, the other holding his mobile phone, cursing as Mills still didn't answer. 'Fuck,' he shouted in the confines of the car. 'Fuck.' He gave up and stuffed the phone into his pocket. A few seconds later he skidded to a stop outside the farmhouse and immediately looked at the spot where Dolby's car was usually parked. 'Shit,' he shouted loudly as he realised Dolby was gone. As soon as the car came to a standstill, he leapt from it and started running towards the house without bothering to turn the engine off or close the door, shouting as he ran. 'Millsie. Millsie,' he called out, but there was no sign of life.

He reached the house and burst into the kitchen to find Mills lying on the floor – the back of her head matted in blood. He crouched next to her and tried to gently rouse her. 'Millsie. Millsie,' he said softly until she finally started coming around and managed to speak quietly. 'Someone jumped me,' she explained, still sounding confused. 'Came up behind me. I never heard them coming.'

'Just take it easy, Millsie,' he told her. 'I'll call an ambulance.'

'Dolby?' she asked, trying to get to her feet. 'Where's Dolby?'

'It was Dolby who jumped you,' he answered as he stopped her from attempting to stand. 'It was Dolby.'

'Dolby?' she asked, sounding weak, like she was about to pass out again. 'Why?'

'It's a long story,' he told her, shaking his head. 'Just try not to move.' He stood and sprinted around the room, grabbing a tea towel, rug and cushion before going back to her side – covering her in the rug before wrapping the towel around her wounded head and resting it on the cushion. He cradled her face in his hand as he pulled his phone free with the other and called Finch who answered almost immediately.

'Ruben,' Finch greeted him, sounding slightly guarded.

'Harry,' he replied, speaking with increasing urgency. 'Listen. There's a problem at the farm. Millsie's been hurt.' He took a breath. 'Dolby's missing.'

'What?' Finch demanded, his guardedness turning to deep concern. 'Jesus Christ. Has he been hit?'

'I don't think so,' he answered, calm but alert and wired. 'I think it was Dolby who jumped her.'

'What?' Finch said again. 'Why the hell would Dolby jump Millsie?'

'I think I'm right, Harry,' he told him as he stood and walked towards the window as he talked. 'About Dolby. I think I'm right.' He looked out of the window and in the distance saw the copse from the survey map where the silo used to be, his heart racing at the thought of what he might be about to discover.

'What the hell you talking about?' Finch asked in confusion.

'The missing women,' he explained, sounding detached and almost emotionless as he stared out at the copse. 'He took them. I know he did.' He sighed as he nodded his head slowly. 'I know where they are, Harry.'

'How?' Finch asked. 'How d'you know?'

'Get an ambulance and backup to the farm for Millsie,' he said, ignoring the question. 'I have to check something out. I'll call you back.' He hung up before Finch could argue, slowly walking towards the door and heading outside.

He walked tentatively towards the copse – afraid of what he might find, until he found himself standing just in front of the trees, looking at the thick, thorny bushes that had grown around them – nature's perfect design to keep unwanted prying strangers away. He stepped into the copse and started pulling at the bushes, slowly at first but then increasingly frantically as he fought his way into the trees, ignoring the cuts on his hands, arms and face, breathing more and more heavily as the sweat began to cover his skin in a thin sheen until he literally tripped over something hidden under the weeds. He cursed as he pushed himself up on his knees, padding the weeds on the ground until he found what looked like a giant lid – about one metre in diameter. He ripped the weeds and roots away to reveal the entrance to something underground. He gripped the handle on the lid and twisted it, surprised at how easily it turned – as if it had been used recently – despite the surrounding vegetation. He took a steadying breath to brace himself as to what he might find before heaving the lid upwards – struggling a little against its weight.

As soon as it was open the stale, putrid smell of decaying flesh rushed him and made him recoil – forcing him to cover his mouth and nose with his hand as he reared back away from the stench. 'Fuck,' he said, gagging, before forcing himself forward, fully lifting the lid and letting it fall open. Again, he recoiled at the smell before peering over the top into the darkness. He pulled a mini Maglite torch from his belt and shone it down the small shaft. He saw a ladder leading into the darkness. 'Shit,' he said, looking to the sky before steeling himself for what he had to do.

He sat on the edge of the opening and hung his legs over the edge until his feet found the top rung of the ladder. Gingerly, he began to climb down, the torch clamped in his teeth – grimacing against the smell as he battled not to retch. He turned his head from side to side as he descended, trying to see danger before it would be too late, until finally, he reached the bottom where he took the torch in his hand and immediately drew his pistol with the other. He swept the light from his torch around the old bunker, bit by bit, illuminating a scene of complete horror, that made him gag and turn away. It took him a few seconds before he was able to compose himself and turn his eyes back to the three almost mummified corpses hanging chained to the wall, each more decomposed than the other – all showing signs of extreme mutilation. Instruments of torture lay on a table in the middle of the room that was covered with old, dark bloodstains. More tools hung from the walls next to the bodies – curved knives, hacksaws, long metal nails, hammers amongst other things that were beyond his imagination as to how Dolby had used them to torture his victims. He suddenly doubled over, trying not to vomit, retching dryly for a few seconds before he managed to recover enough to continue his search – his torchlight falling on a pile of clothes and backpacks in a corner of the bunker. He walked cautiously towards them, his pistol and torch constantly sweeping the bunker for danger until he reached the items and began to search through them. He immediately began to find personal items; passports, bank cards amongst other things, the light from his torch illuminating the names of the owners.

'Jesus Christ,' he pleaded as he read the names and looked at the photographs of the beautiful young women. He'd found Anna Sarfas and Sofia Martinez along with another he'd known nothing about – Leena Halliste. Her passport said she was Estonian. He took a moment to consider how his enquiries could have missed her. Perhaps she hadn't ever been reported as missing.

He placed the items back into the packs and returned the light to the wall where the women now hung in chains. 'Jesus Christ,' he said again as the realisation that he'd been right truly dawned on him. Dolby was indeed a serial killer who simply couldn't stop – one who'd learnt through age and experience, honing his twisted, sick skills to the point where he could kidnap, kill and torture right under the noses of his watchers.

His mind wandered to how long Dolby had kept them alive for – how long he'd tortured them for before finally releasing them from their misery and horror, when his previous thought made him freeze with terror. *Dolby was indeed a serial killer who simply couldn't stop.* 'Shit,' he said as he bolted upright and scrambled for the wallet in his back pocket, pulling it free and opening it. The first thing he saw was a picture of Jenny, right next to his driving licence bearing his home address.

The memory of his jacket hanging on the back of a chair in Dolby's kitchen when he'd gone outside to talk to Jack Neil suddenly thundered through his mind. He imagined Dolby moving fast and silently across the room, searching through his jacket until he found the wallet before opening it and seeing the photograph of Jenny. He imagined Dolby running his fingers over the picture before pulling out the driving licence and checking the address. Within seconds he returns the wallet and goes back to the window.

'No,' he screamed into the darkness of the silo, the word reverberating from wall to wall at the horror of his realisation.

54

London – Several Days Ago

Harvey sat in a wheelchair in the pleasant garden of the hospice wrapped in blankets that hid the morphine pump that automatically supplied and regulated the flow of the drug into his body to control the excruciating pain he would otherwise be feeling. A thin transparent tube clipped to the columella of his nose where it split in two, fed oxygen to both nostrils. But his breathing was still painfully laboured and the frequent coughing bouts cut through the morphine and made him wince with pain. Yet, despite his worsening condition, he remained as vigilant and aware of his surroundings as ever – his eyes soon focusing on two men in suits being led towards him by a female nurse he'd come to know over the last few weeks. When they reached him, the nurse spoke first.

'These men are from the police, Fraser,' she said, introducing them. 'They say they need to speak with you, but I really don't think you're well enough to talk.'

'It's all right, Tanya,' he told her, weakly raising a hand to stop her protests. 'I know who they are and what they want. It's fine.'

'Fine,' she agreed before looking towards a nearby bench. 'I'll just be over there. If you want to be left alone just look over and I'll come to the rescue, okay?'

'Thank you,' he nodded as he watched her hesitate for a second before walking out of earshot to the old bench.

'DS Fraser Harvey?' the taller, slimmer detective asked.

'We both know you know who I am,' he said smiling. 'Let's get on with it.'

The two detectives glanced at each other with knowing looks before turning their attentions back to Harvey. 'I'm DI Knowles and this is DS Atherton,' the taller one explained. 'We're from Professional Ethics and Standards. We'd like to ask you a few questions about Paul Anderson.'

Harvey looked around to make sure they weren't being overheard before replying. 'Didn't you get the brief?' he asked in a wheezy voice. 'You're not supposed to use that name anymore.'

'Doesn't matter too much anymore,' Knowles told him.

'Oh?' Harvey asked, looking away from them into the distance. 'Why's that?'

'Because he was found shot to death in some backwater in Canada a couple of days ago,' Atherton joined in. 'Two in the head and two in the chest. All from close range.'

'A professional hit then,' Harvey more stated than asked.

'Very professional,' Knowles confirmed. 'The shooter came from nowhere and disappeared without trace. No witnesses. No forensics, other than the bullets, which the Canadian Police have already confirmed appear to have come from an untraceable, unregistered firearm. Someone knew what they were doing.'

'Apparently,' Harvey shrugged. 'Well, thanks for letting me

know. Can't tell you I'll be shedding too many tears over Paul Anderson.'

'It's not that simple,' Atherton told him.

'Really?' Harvey asked. 'How so?'

'Because if this was someone looking for payback for what he did to Abigail Riley,' Atherton explained, 'the question is how did they find him hidden in the arsehole of Canada?'

'Abigail Riley was fifteen years ago,' Harvey reminded them. 'Payback? After all this time? I don't think so.'

'What about her family?' Knowles asked. 'It won't matter to them how long ago it was.'

'They don't have the means or the capacity to hit someone like this,' Harvey said, dismissing it.

'What about the brother?' Atherton asked. 'He's got previous for violence.'

'Jimmy's a little wild,' Harvey explained. 'But he's neither capable of carrying out nor organising something like this. You're barking up the wrong tree, detectives.'

'Maybe he found a way?' Atherton continued.

'Spoken to him yet, have you?' Harvey changed tack. 'Spoken to Abigail's mother?'

'No,' Knowles admitted. 'Thought we'd better speak to you first.'

'You going to tell them Anderson is dead?' Harvey asked.

The two detectives looked at each other before Knowles answered. 'If we end up having to bring them in for questioning, then I suppose we'll have to tell them.'

'They have a right to know,' he insisted.

'If we think they're involved in Anderson's murder,' Atherton told him, 'they'll know soon enough.'

'And if not?' Harvey asked.

'If not, it's possible they won't be told,' Knowles answered. 'Nobody wants to open up old wounds. He'll be cremated under his new name – his ashes scattered at the side of some road somewhere. The death certificate will say Peter Delph.'

'Fair enough,' Harvey nodded.

'Thing is,' Atherton got back into it. 'Not many people knew where to find him. And you are one of those people.'

'Shouldn't you caution me or something?' Harvey smiled. 'Interview me at a police station?'

'We both know that's not possible,' Knowles answered. 'And we both know you've got nothing to lose by telling us the truth. You're never making it out of this place and I hear you lost your wife a few years back. I'm sorry. But truth is, you don't even have anyone to leave your pension to. Better to die with a clear conscience.'

'My conscience is just fine,' he told them. 'Last time I saw Anderson, I could tell it was only a matter of time before he fell back into criminal ways. He probably just pissed off the local heavies and got himself taken out. He had it coming.'

'Maybe,' Knowles admitted, 'but we still have to speak with everyone who knew where he was.'

'You speaking with the CPS who knew?' Harvey questioned. 'People at the Home Office and Foreign Office? The information could have come from anyone – if indeed that's what happened, which I doubt.'

'We'll be speaking to everyone,' Atherton told him. 'Including your partner at the time of Abigail's murder.'

'Connie.' Harvey tensed – making him cough violently for a few seconds.

'You all right?' Knowles asked, sympathetically.

'No,' he answered as he recovered his breath. 'I'm dying.' No one said anything for a few seconds before Harvey managed to continue. 'Connie never knew where they were sent. I never told her and she never asked.'

'All the same,' Atherton insisted. 'We'll need to speak to her.'

'You'll be wasting your time,' Harvey tried to dissuade them.

'Maybe,' Atherton shrugged. 'But the thing that interests me about you is that you volunteered to help relocate them. You even carried out follow-up visits on Anderson although not Dolby, for some reason.'

'New Zealand is too far away,' Harvey replied.

'But why did you want to help them at all?' Atherton asked – his eyes narrowed with suspicion. 'You worked hard to put these animals behind bars. It must have hurt when they got out after only, what, twelve years?'

'Eleven years,' he corrected him. 'It was eleven years.'

'So why were you so keen to help them set up their safe new lives?' Atherton demanded.

'I don't know.' Harvey shrugged. 'I suppose I thought it might give me some sort of closure. A case like that can haunt you for the rest of your life. I thought seeing it through might prevent that.'

'And did it?' Knowles asked.

'No,' Harvey answered. 'It didn't.'

'I don't know.' Atherton shook his head. 'That doesn't quite wash with me.'

'Really?' Harvey asked, sounding disinterested.

'Really,' Atherton repeated. 'See, I think you volunteered so you would know exactly where they were. So that when the day came, a day like this, when you had nothing left to lose, you could give the information to someone who could use it to have Anderson hit. Maybe you already knew you were sick when you volunteered. Maybe you knew exactly what was going to happen.'

'Well,' Harvey smiled, taking a deep breath through his nose. 'I guess we'll never know. Will we?'

'Maybe not,' Atherton agreed. 'But you don't strike me as the sort of man who'd want revenge. She wasn't your daughter.

You'd dealt with plenty other murder cases and never went looking for revenge. So, if not revenge – what? Did Anderson know something that got him killed? Did he have some dirt on you or something? Was he threatening you?'

'No,' he shook his head. 'For the sake of argument, let me just tell you this. People who kill in the way Abigail was killed, aren't your everyday killers, detectives. They're wired wrong. Wrong beyond our imagination.'

'What's your point?' Atherton hurried him.

'Dolby. Anderson. Maybe both,' Harvey explained. 'They were only one-time killers because they were young, careless, which meant we caught them before they could do it again.'

'You can't say that for sure,' Atherton argued.

'Worked many murder cases, have you?' Harvey silenced him. 'No. Didn't think so. Well let me tell you, gentlemen. People like them are a mercifully rare breed. Doesn't matter where we put them or how much we monitor them, they'll find a way. They'll find a way to do it again. Believe me – it's all they live for.'

'So that's why you volunteered to be part of the relocation team?' Knowles said. 'To stop them doing it again?'

'I've said enough,' Harvey told them. 'I'm tired.'

'Of course,' Knowles agreed. 'We'll try not to bother you again.'

'Appreciated,' Harvey told them before stopping them as they prepared to leave. 'Just one thing,' he said. 'Dolby?'

'Under protection in New Zealand is all we know,' Knowles answered. 'I understand he's refused to go into full protective custody. They're having to keep him safe where he is. All information is being closely guarded.'

'A farm,' he told them. 'He'll be on his farm. Where he believes he can control things, but none of us can control everything.'

'Do you know something I need to know?' Atherton asked.

'Is the same person who took care of Anderson going after Dolby?'

'All my life I played by the rules,' he explained. 'But you don't stop someone like Dolby by sticking to the rules. He's the rarest of animals. He didn't kill because of some screwed-up childhood or mental illness. He was loved. Had a good family and he was smart. Too damn smart. He killed Abigail because he just wanted to. He thought it was his right.'

'Then you never believed Anderson was guilty?' Knowles asked.

'Oh, he was guilty,' Harvey corrected him. 'He went along with it and probably even enjoyed it, but I always thought it was Dolby who instigated it. Probably only took Anderson along so he would have someone to blame. Only I could never prove it. So, I was happy to send them both down. But they got out, didn't they? Maybe this time none of us should worry about the rules. Then I can go to my grave knowing that he's in his and that there won't be any more Abigail Rileys.'

'So, you do know something?' Atherton insisted.

'Even if I did,' he answered. 'It's too late now.'

'But if you thought Dolby was the main offender,' Knowles said, 'why did you go to see Anderson, but never Dolby? I mean the real reason.'

Harvey filled his damaged lungs as best he could, drawing in the oxygen through the thin plastic tubes. 'The truth?' he repeated. 'Because I was afraid of him. I didn't want to be anywhere near him. Not in an environment he controlled. It was unnerving enough being close to him in a place I could control. But out in New Zealand – on a farm he'd had time to make his own. The thought of it terrified me. Fear, Inspector, can be the greatest of all motivators. I didn't want to die a frightened man.'

'You're involved in this,' Atherton accused him. 'You're in it up to your neck.'

'I'm just an ex-cop waiting to die,' Harvey told him, managing a wry smile. 'Take my advice. Don't try too hard to find whoever it is maybe looking for Dolby. No more questions. I need to rest.'

'Sure,' Knowles agreed.

'But he knows exactly what's going on,' Atherton argued.

'He's told us all we need to know,' Knowles said – his eyes never leaving Harvey's.

'What?' Atherton barked.

'Let's go,' Knowles ordered, jutting his chin towards the car park. 'Thanks for your time,' he told Harvey. 'Good luck.'

'Take care, Inspector,' Harvey wheezed. 'And try to leave the Rileys alone. They've been through enough.'

55

New Zealand – Present Day

'No. Jenny. Jesus Christ, Jenny,' Jameson screamed as more memories of Dolby flashed in his mind. The conversation the night before when he'd told him the reason Anderson had picked the victim was because she was loved – because killing someone who was loved made him feel like a god. Only now he knew Dolby had been talking about himself and not Anderson. 'Jesus Christ. No. Please no,' he pleaded one last time before shaking off the shock and forcing himself to act. He stuffed the wallet back in his pocket and ran to the ladder, climbing too fast, his feet slipping on several of the rungs until he reached the entrance to the bunker and scrambled out – getting to his feet and fighting his way through the branches and thorns.

He ran across the field, blood from cuts mixing with his sweat as he tugged his mobile free and searched for Jenny's number and pressed the call icon. If he was lucky, Dolby wouldn't have reached his home yet and there could still be time to warn Jenny – tell her to get out of the house and run to the nearest police station. His blood turned to ice when her mobile went to answerphone as he imagined Dolby already inside his house, snatching the mobile from his daughter before he remembered with both relief and anguish how he'd confiscated her phone as punishment for being suspended from school and locked it in his desk. 'Damn it,' he said in frustration before considering using one of the numerous other ways of contacting her through social media but he knew that she did everything through her precious phone. Without it, she was virtually uncontactable. Quickly, he tried the last thing he could think of and called his home number, but after several rings it went to the answering service. He reassured himself that it didn't mean Dolby was already there as Jenny never answered the home phone anyway and even viewed it with a degree of suspicion. 'Shit,' he cursed the situation as he jogged towards the farmhouse and burst into the kitchen where Mills was still on the floor, although she looked to have recovered slightly. 'Millsie,' he said quietly but urgently as he crouched next to her. 'You okay?'

'Got a hell of a headache.' She tried to smile. 'Feel like an idiot.'

'You couldn't have seen it coming,' he said, comforting her.

'You did,' she reminded him.

'Maybe,' he said, dismissing it, desperate to move on. 'Millsie, listen. I think he's going after Jenny.'

'What?' she asked sounding confused. 'Why? Wait. He doesn't know where you live.'

'I fucked up, remember?' he reminded her. 'I left my jacket with my wallet in alone in the kitchen with him a couple of days ago. I know he looked in it. It had my driving licence in it. He knows my address.'

'Why go after Jenny?' She shook her head. 'It doesn't make sense to go after her.'

'Not now, Millsie,' he answered. 'I've got to go.'

'Call for backup before you go,' she told him. 'Patrols can be at your house in minutes.'

'I can't risk that,' he insisted. 'He has too much of a start on me. He could already be at my house. If he hears police approaching, he'll kill her without hesitating. I know he will. No. He knew I'd work it out. He wants me to come to him – wants me to see what he's going to do to her. Could be Jenny's only chance if I play along. It'll buy me time until I can work out some way to get the drop on him.'

'My gun and phone were on the table,' she warned him.

He glanced at the table, but there was nothing there. 'He took them.'

'So now he's armed,' she whispered. 'Be careful, Ruben.'

'I will,' he promised her without meaning it. 'I've got to go.'

'I know,' she told him.

'Help will be here soon,' he assured her. 'Just hold on.'

'Go,' she insisted.

He gave her a nod before springing to his feet and running from the farm.

Dolby walked along the small driveway heading towards Jameson's house – looking calm and collected – dressed in his smart clothes. As he drew ever nearer to the house he allowed his mind to take him back to when he and Anderson led Abigail to the bunker in North London – his face twisted and contorted as he raped her while Anderson cowered in the background crying. When he was finished, he demanded Anderson did the same or he'd cut him. Reluctantly, Anderson began to do as he was told, while he stood behind him smiling – the knife still in his hand.

When it was all over, they both knelt next to the body as he rested one hand on Anderson's shoulder – the other holding the knife. Both were covered in blood and Anderson was still sobbing. At first he comforted him, but then he changed – his snarling face only inches from Anderson's. He could still remember the words he used as if it were only yesterday. 'If you ever betray me – I'll kill you. Do you understand, Paul? I'll kill you. I swear I will.'

He knocked on the front door and stepped back to wait for an answer as his mind drifted back to more happy memories. A lone female hitchhiker walking along a deserted road thumbing for a lift. His car slowing and drawing level with the hitcher – his delight at seeing she was pretty and petite – her accent betraying that she was probably from Eastern Europe. He wasn't interested in local girls or ones from Britain or Australia that would attract too much attention. Later, shortly before torturing her to death, he discovered her name was Anna. He wound the passenger window down. She leaned in through the window.

'Hi,' she'd said with a smile.

'Where you heading?' he'd asked.

'Auckland,' she'd told him.

'It's your lucky day,' he remembered telling her, although it was the unluckiest day of her soon-to-end life. 'Jump in.'

'Great.' She'd beamed as she jumped into the car, totally unaware of the monster she'd just met.

He stepped forward and again knocked on the door once more. A few seconds later Jenny opened it.

'Hi,' she said a little nervously, looking him up and down.

He pulled his jacket to one side so she could see the police badge and gun attached to his belt. 'Hi. Jenny, right?' he asked with a smile. She just nodded. 'DS Granger. I'm a friend of your dad's. He's... he's supposed to meet me here this morning.'

'My dad's not home yet,' she told him, relaxing a little as she eyed the badge, opening the door wider.

'I guess I'm a bit early,' he explained casually. 'Maybe I could wait inside.' She didn't immediately reply. 'Or I could just wait in my car,' he added quickly, turning slightly as if he was going to walk away.

'No,' Jenny suddenly stopped him. 'You can wait inside. Dad won't be long.' She stood aside and opened the door wide to let him in.

'No.' Dolby smiled as he entered the house. 'I don't think he'll be very long at all.'

Jameson drove his unmarked car far too fast through increasingly heavy traffic – cursing at the other drivers for getting in his way – narrowly avoiding colliding with several cars as the light attached to the roof swirled and the siren screamed. He felt his mobile vibrating on his belt and managed to tug it free – struggling to steer with one hand as he glanced at the caller ID. It was Finch. 'Shit,' he complained, wondering what he should do before tossing the phone onto the passenger seat and returning to concentrating on the road ahead of him – the instinct to protect his daughter driving him on – the fear flooding his body with adrenaline. If Dolby wanted some sort of ritual face-off, then he'd give him what he wanted, but he already knew it wasn't going to end with him leading Dolby away in handcuffs. Only one of them was going to walk away. For Jenny's sake, it had to be him.

Jenny and Dolby stood in the front room of the house looking a little awkward.

'Do you want to sit down?' she asked, more for something to say than anything.

'I'm fine,' he told her as he began to pace around the room.

'Can I get you something to drink?' she asked, trying to be polite.

'No,' he answered without looking at her. 'I'm good.'

There was an uncomfortable couple of seconds before she tried to engage him in conversation. 'So, how long have you known my dad?'

'Oh, a little while now,' he replied, looking at the everyday items lying around the room with apparent interest.

'You work with him a lot?' she asked as she watched him brush his hand across a small statue of a dolphin.

'All the time,' he answered with a smile.

'You sound English,' she told him.

'That's because I am,' he replied, heading towards the window. 'Just like your dad.' He calmly reached for the curtains and pulled them closed.

'What the hell are you doing?' Jenny asked, looking and sounding concerned and confused.

'Just for security,' he reassured her, looking back over his shoulder.

'Security for what?' she demanded.

'You know, I'm a little surprised you're at home,' he told her. 'I thought for sure your dad would have called you. Did he call you, Jenny?'

'I... I don't have my phone,' she nervously explained.

'Oh?' he replied.

'I got into trouble at school,' she told him, sounding increasingly unsure. 'My dad took it away.'

'Really?' he chuckled unpleasantly. 'You see, Jenny – some things are just meant to be.'

'I think maybe you should wait outside,' she told him, feeling increasingly uncomfortable as she headed towards the door, but he suddenly moved across the room with frightening speed and grabbed her around the throat with one hand, squeezing hard as he pushed the gun into her face before she could react or even call out.

'Keep quiet and do exactly as I say or I'll kill you,' he hissed into her face. 'Understand?'

She nodded, her eyes wide with terror. 'Who are you?' she just about managed to ask through her strangulated throat – her words barely audible, but he was close enough to hear them.

'Don't you know?' He smiled and laughed softly. 'I'm the man your dad's been working so hard to keep alive.' As soon as she realised who he was she tried to pull away, but he just tightened his grip to the point where she could barely breathe and pulled her even closer. 'Shush, shush,' he said, mock-comforting her. 'Daddy will be along very soon. Very soon. But why don't we give him a call? Just to make sure. I think he'd like that very much.'

Jameson was still driving hard through the traffic when his mobile rang again. He grabbed it from the seat and checked the caller ID, expecting it to be Finch, but it was Mills' phone. He immediately knew who it had to be. He answered it cautiously. 'Dolby.'

'Detective Jameson.' Dolby sniggered slightly. 'You have a very nice house. Very... tasteful. Oh and I have someone here who'd like to say hello, but she's a little tied up right now.'

'You touch her I'll fucking kill you,' he said.

'Tut, tut, tut, detective,' Dolby said tauntingly. 'You really shouldn't be so... rude. What if your pretty little daughter was to hear? And she is oh so pretty. I'm going to enjoy spending some time alone with her.'

'I swear, Dolby,' he snarled through gritted teeth. 'I'll...

'Shut up and listen,' Dolby demanded. 'So you worked out I'd come pay your pretty little daughter a visit. Then I'm assuming you also worked out not to tell anyone. That I want you to come alone. More than three would be too much of a crowd – don't you think?'

'I'm alone,' Jameson told him. 'No one else knows.'

'Good,' Dolby said. 'Because if I so much as hear a siren I'll cut her pretty little throat, but not before I've... done things to her. Understand?'

'I understand,' he managed to reply, struggling to keep himself together.

'Good,' he said again.

Jameson took a deep breath. 'Listen. Michael,' he tried a different tactic. 'Why don't you just let her go? It's over for you. I found the others, Michael. I found the silo.'

'Of course you did,' Dolby replied pleasantly – his old charming self again. 'Eventually I knew someone would. I'm glad it was you.' There was a moment of silence. 'I... I respect you. Not like all those other fools, with their fumbling questions and false pleasantries. You've always been honest and open with me. I... I appreciate that.'

'Then let her go,' he encouraged him, sensing hope.

'I can't do that,' Dolby insisted, sounding almost sad. 'I wish I could, but I can't.'

'It'd go better for you if you let her go,' he said, trying to persuade him, shouting above the car's screaming engine as he drove even faster through the Auckland traffic.

'You understand so much and so little.' Dolby sighed before

letting out a small laugh. 'Getting caught is inevitable. I've always known that. Ever since the first time, I understood that. But it was worth it. It was all worth it. The years locked in prison were all worth it because I had my memories. Memories like you wouldn't believe. I felt like a god. Eleven years of my life to feel like that. It was a small price to pay.' Jameson heard him release a long, slow breath. 'And that was only one life. One loved life. But now I have so many to dream about. Enough for a lifetime. It doesn't matter what dark hole they lock me in – they can't take away my memories. They can't take away the wonder of what I've done. Of what I have become.'

'Don't do this, Michael,' he pleaded as he felt whatever humanity Dolby had slipping away forever.

'Come alone and maybe I'll let her live,' Dolby demanded – his voice cold and mechanical again. 'Maybe.' He hung up before Jameson could reply.

He suddenly felt dazed and confused by the awful reality of what was happening – so much so he didn't see a junction approaching and drove straight into it without giving way, colliding heavily with one car that then knocked him into the opposite lane and into another car, sending him spinning to the side of the road – his car a broken, steaming mess. There was a complete stillness and silence for a few seconds until he slowly managed to open his door. A few seconds later he used all his will to throw his legs out and onto the tarmac before unsteadily hauling himself from the car. He staggered from the wreckage, shaking his head clear as he started to walk away before one of the drivers from one of the other cars in the accident tried to stop him.

'You all right?' the man asked.

'I'm fine,' he lied, wiping the blood from a deep cut on his brow from his eyes as he walked unsteadily – pain from other injuries beginning to register.

'You can't just walk away, mate,' the man argued. 'We need to report this to the police.'

He pushed him aside and pulled back his jacket so everyone could see his police ID and his pistol. 'I am the police,' he told the man. 'Get out of my way.'

The man backed away and let him past as he half staggered, half jogged off along the street holding his injured left arm and blinking the blood from his eyes. Despite the pain, he pulled his jacket off as it was beginning to overheat him while also obstructing his ability to draw his pistol quickly if he had to and he was sure he would. He tossed his jacket onto the ground and continued to half run unsteadily along the road towards his home, his daughter and his final face-to-face confrontation with Dolby.

Dolby crouched next to Jenny who still lay bound and gagged on the sofa. He holstered the pistol and swapped it for a small but deadly-looking lock knife – the type used by fishermen to fillet their catch. He held it close to Jenny's face while he stroked her hair and spoke softly into her ear.

'No time to wait for your daddy,' he told her. 'I think we'd better start without him. Don't you?' She started wriggling and bucking, trying to scream through the tape plastered over her mouth, but he grabbed her hard around the throat and pinned her to the sofa. 'Uh-uh. The more you struggle the more this will hurt.' He took a breath to compose himself. 'Tell me, Jenny – does your father love you? Are you loved, Jenny?' Through her tears she managed to nod her head slowly. Dolby closed his eyes and smiled with relief – speaking softly and intently. 'Good. Good,' he whispered. 'It's very important to me that you're loved.'

She again tried to push him away, but it only made him angry. 'I told you not to fight me, Jenny,' he warned her as he started to tear at her shirt – his eyes wide and reddened with rage and lust. 'You're only making it worse for yourself.'

She ignored his warnings and continued to struggle frantically, trying to call out, but he kept her pinned to the sofa as he fumbled to undo his trousers before the calm voice of a man he didn't recognise froze him.

'Michael Dolby,' the soft Irish voice said.

Dolby's eyes darted from side to side before he slowly turned his head towards the door – confusion spreading across his face as he saw a man he'd never seen before in his life standing in the doorway with a silenced pistol in his hand down by his side.

'I have a message for you from James Riley,' O'Doherty told him.

Dolby's eyes fired wide open with realisation at who the man must be and why he was there. He knew there would be no point asking for mercy, just as Abigail and the others had wasted their time when they'd begged him for the same. He only had one chance of surviving. A split second later he made a desperate attempt to draw the holstered pistol, but it was hopeless. O'Doherty was too fast and efficient.

His pistol puffed quietly twice, sending two 9mm bullets thudding into Dolby's chest. He dropped his own pistol and fell to the ground on his back from his crouched position – his shaking hands slowly rising to his chest as the blood poured out. He coughed blood as his lungs began to fill with fluid. As the life drained from him, he managed to raise his head a little and look at the man who'd just given him a death sentence, wheezing as he tried to speak but the holes in his lungs made it impossible.

O'Doherty slowly crossed the room and pointed his gun at the stricken Dolby before turning towards Jenny. 'You should look away now,' he told her, giving her a second to bury her face in a cushion. He levelled the pistol at Dolby's face who lifted his hands in front of him in a vain effort to shield himself from death as the gun puffed once – the bullet taking one of his fingers off on its way into his forehead. His head and arms fell heavily to the floor – his entire body going rigid before twitching uncontrollably until another puff from O'Doherty's weapon put a bullet through his brain, entering through his right eye.

O'Doherty pulled a flick knife from his jacket pocket, released the blade and used it to cut the tape from Jenny's wrists while her head was still buried in the cushion. She realised her hands were free and used them to rip the masking tape from her mouth and look at the man who'd saved her, scrambling away from him, still terrified and in shock – the sight of Dolby's body taking the last of her breath away. After a few seconds of puffing and panting, her eyes never leaving O'Doherty, she managed to speak.

'Who are you?' she asked him in a faltering voice.

He just looked at her, saying nothing, expressionless, before turning and heading to the doorway, taking the silencer off his pistol as he walked and tucking the gun into the back of his waistband. When he had a chance, he'd clean it of prints, dismantle it and toss it into the Pacific Ocean on his way to Wellington.

Jameson stumbled a little from side to side as he ran the last few metres along the street where he lived, suffering the effects of shock from his injuries, until he reached his driveway. He stopped, warily looking the house over where he believed Dolby waited inside with his daughter, ready to spring whatever trap he'd prepared. Slowly, he reached for his holstered pistol. As his hand rested on the gun the front door suddenly opened and a man he'd never seen before stepped out before immediately freezing when he saw him standing bloodied and battered at the end of the drive. He smiled slightly while Jameson frowned in confusion, tensing as he heard the sound of sirens approaching in the background. The man appeared to have heard the sirens, too, as the smile slipped from his face and his eyes narrowed.

In that moment he knew who the man was and what it meant. Without waiting another heartbeat, he reached for the pistol in his holster as the man went for something concealed behind his back. They both drew their weapons together and took aim at each other. A matter of seconds felt like an eternity as the air was filled with the sound of several shots – rapid and close together – until everything suddenly went silent as the man stopped firing. Jameson also ceased fire but remained in a crouched shooting position, his pistol pointing at the man's chest.

The man stood dead still – the gun grasped in his hand as he looked down at his chest and the growing patch of crimson spreading on his shirt over his heart. He clutched at the wound with his hand, but it was no good as the blood kept coming. He dropped to his knees, the pistol falling from his hand as he looked up at Jameson and smiled slightly before toppling forward face first on the ground just as Jenny appeared in the front doorway. She looked at O'Doherty dead on the floor before running past him and into the arms of her father as he remained crouched on the ground, pistol still in his hand as they held each other tighter than they ever had before.

It was a long time before either of them spoke. 'The man who came to the house?' he asked in an urgent whisper as he remembered Dolby still hadn't been accounted for.

'Inside,' she told him through her tears. 'He's dead.'

'It's okay, Jenny,' he reassured her, holding her even tighter. 'Everything's going to be okay.'

Jenny looked over her shoulder at O'Doherty's body. 'Do you know him?' she asked.

'Shh, shh,' he said, comforting her, shaking his head. 'No. I don't know him, but I think I know who he was.'

'What d'you mean?' she asked, turning away from O'Doherty. 'I don't understand.'

'Shh,' he said, trying to quieten her again. 'It doesn't matter now. It's over now. It's done.'

He looked behind him as the sound of sirens engulfed them to see Finch amongst other detectives and uniformed officers walking towards them until Finch put his arms out to stop them when he saw O'Doherty's body on the ground. Jameson gave him a single nod that was enough to let him know that whatever had happened was over now. He returned all his attention back to what was most precious to him in the world although he couldn't help but think of Dolby as a million questions raced through his mind. Had Dolby planned this to happen the moment he discovered he had a daughter – patiently chipping away at his instinct to never to turn his back on him even for a second, or had he simply taken the opportunity once he'd made the mistake of leaving Dolby alone with his jacket and wallet? Truth was the only thing he was really sure of was that he prayed he would never meet anyone like him ever again. But if he did – he knew what he would do.

56

Jimmy Riley and his uncle Eamon sat in his small, over-furnished living room, back in Belfast, sipping from mugs of tea. They'd shared small talk until Rafferty felt comfortable enough to get down to more sensitive business.

'Sorry to have to drag you all the way over here, Jimmy,' he said. 'But this wasn't something that could be discussed over the phone.'

'I understand,' Jimmy assured him.

Rafferty sighed long and deeply before continuing. 'The job our mutual friend took on has been completed. The contract has been fulfilled.'

Jimmy suddenly looked very pale before taking a deep breath to right himself.

'You all right, son?' Rafferty asked.

'Yeah,' he answered. 'Just didn't expect it to feel like this.'

'And how does it feel?' Rafferty gently asked.

'I... I just feel sick,' he told him. 'Like I'm dreaming.'

'Not an easy thing to be involved in,' Rafferty explained. 'Even if it's done on your behalf and not by yourself.'

Jimmy just nodded his head slowly.

'Take my advice, Jimmy,' Rafferty went on. 'Go home and forget this thing ever happened. Put it behind you and never speak of it again. You can still have a life. No need to tell your mother any of what's happened.'

Again he nodded slowly before remembering something. 'What about the money?' he asked. 'I still owe half.'

'No further payment will be necessary,' Rafferty told him.

'I... I don't understand,' Jimmy replied.

'I'm afraid our friend won't be coming back,' Rafferty informed him. 'Ever. Something happened. We won't be seeing him again. No one will.'

'What... what happened?' Jimmy innocently pried.

'You don't need to know,' Rafferty insisted – his expression telling Jimmy to drop it. 'Just keep your money and go home.'

He nodded, placed his mug on the table and stood to leave. 'Thanks,' he told his uncle. 'Thanks for everything.'

'Don't thank me, son,' Rafferty told him with an ice-cold look. 'Just go home and like I said – forget any of this ever happened.'

Jimmy walked along an anonymous corridor in University College Hospital, London, until he reached the department signed *Oncology*. He paused outside before entering where he was immediately stopped by a male nurse.

'Can I help you?' the nurse asked.

'I'm here to see Detective Sergeant Harvey,' he replied.

'DS Harvey?' The nurse raised his eyebrows, apparently surprised by Harvey's previous life as a detective. 'You mean Fraser Harvey?'

'Yeah,' he nodded. 'Sorry.'

The nurse looked him up and down. 'It's not visiting hours, you know.'

'I know,' he acknowledged, 'but... I think he'd really like to see me.'

The nurse thought for a second before agreeing. 'Okay, but be quick,' he insisted. 'He can't talk for long. Down the end. Ward three. Bed number four.'

'Thank you,' he told him before walking slowly through the unit until he reached the ward and entered. He scanned the patients until he saw Harvey lying in the bed with an oxygen mask on, looking thin and pale. He crossed the room and sat close to him. His eyes flickered open and then widened as he recognised him. He unsteadily removed the mask and spoke in a very quiet voice. 'Jimmy Riley,' he whispered. 'How did you find me?'

'Social media,' Jimmy shrugged.

Harvey managed a faint smile as he nodded slowly.

'Just thought you'd want to know,' Jimmy told him. 'It's over. Both of them.'

Harvey's eyes narrowed. 'I don't know what you're talking about,' he said, without trying to sound too convincing.

'I think you do,' Jimmy whispered.

'Worked it out, did you?' Harvey smiled as he wheezed.

'I always thought it was you,' Jimmy told him, leaning in close so only Harvey could hear. 'Once I found out about your cancer – I was sure.' He leaned away and spoke normally. 'How long do you have?'

'Days,' Harvey answered with a resigned expression. 'Maybe a week or two.'

'Nothing to lose, eh?' Jimmy asked.

'Something like that,' he answered weakly as his body seemed to shrink.

'You don't have to worry about anything,' Jimmy promised

him. 'No one will ever know.' Harvey managed to nod his head. 'By the way,' Jimmy told him. 'You were right about Dolby.'

'I know,' Harvey whispered as his head sank deeper into the pillow and his eyes closed, his entire body relaxing. Jimmy reached out and patted him on the back of his hand before standing and walking towards the rest of his life.

THE END

ACKNOWLEDGEMENTS

I would like to my agent, Leslie Gardner at Artellus, for all her hard work on my behalf since we started working together and for believing in me and my writing. She really inspired me to get back on the horse and start creating again.

Thanks, Leslie.

A NOTE FROM THE PUBLISHER

Thank you for reading this book. If you enjoyed it please do consider leaving a review on Amazon to help others find it too.

We hate typos. All of our books have been rigorously edited and proofread, but sometimes mistakes do slip through. If you have spotted a typo, please do let us know and we can get it amended within hours.

info@bloodhoundbooks.com

Printed in the USA
CPSIA information can be obtained
at www.ICGtesting.com
LVHW042253150124
768989LV00038B/739

9 781914 614422